THE BRIGHTER SIDE OF THE APOCALYPSE

Phillip H. Voss

Cover Design: Levierre
99designs.com.au/profiles/levierre

Producer/Manager: Melissa Hadley
www.techmotivated.me

ISBN: 978-1-7329507-0-2

DEDICATION

For Mom and Melissa,
I couldn't have done this without the two of you.

ACKNOWLEDGMENTS

Many thanks are due to the people who have given me all kinds of support since the day I decided to follow my dream and started writing.

First and foremost, my family: Lucina, Lauren, Lydia, Mary, Shelly, Jessie, Ashton, Rick, Renee, Selle, Maaike, TED and Hans, Mascha and Chris, Erik, and Alana. I appreciate you standing by me and encouraging me throughout my process—even when I've been an impatient pain in the ass. Thank you all from the depths of my heart.

I also have a ton of appreciation for my friends who took the time to read my sloppy drafts and shared their thoughts on them. Patricia, Bryan, Keri, Shabba and of course my "Friday With The Fellas" writing class: Mr. Blue, Cool Breeze, Snake Doc, Rasool, Black, Banga, Shak, and Dewan. All of your feedback has made me much better than I was when I started out.

And a very special thank you to my #1 ally in Nerdom, and the coolest chick I've ever met in my life: Lis. You think you only do a little, but that little makes a world of difference to me. My gratitude to you could fill every inch of the TARDIS, and so much more.

Last, but certainly not least, I thank each and every one of you who decided to give my story a chance. Your satisfaction is the measure of my success. I'll always do my best to write novels that you'll enjoy from start to finish, and your feedback is always welcome by me.

PROLOGUE

Subject 1 holds the gaze of the only chimpanzee left alive in the lab with him. Locked in a cage and enclosed in a large glass box, the young primate has pain in its eyes. Tormenting pain stemming from famishment.

For days Subject 1 has literally felt the ape's anguish, along with his own ravenous need to fill a bottomless pit in his gut. The hunger is nothing to Subject 1, though. It doesn't begin to compare to the never-ending soreness in his heart. A demand for revenge dominates his thoughts and emotions day in and day out.

The lab walls are a heavenly shade of white. Ironic, considering the hell that went on there. Subject 1 and the chimp witnessed unnatural things done to the other subjects and other primates. When the other subjects finally expired, all of their organs were removed to be examined then they were off to the incinerator. Subject 1 had been anticipating his own death and destruction from the moment he was secured to a chair resembling a stainless steel chaise lounge with armrests expanding away from his body. It should have come soon after a Stryker saw was used to cut off the top of his cranium, but that was just the beginning.

A blast of air hisses and the pressure sealed door opens. A woman with blue-green eyes hustles into the lab, followed by two men taking casual strides. The woman is inside of a bright yellow biohazard suit, with the image of a double helix and the word GEN-ASCEND printed on her right sleeve. The men are encased in a type of black armor that looks like it was patterned after the comic book hero Iron Man. The words MACE TEAM 1 printed in white letters on their left chest plates. Name, rank and a set of numbers on the right.

Rage flares in Subject 1 upon sight of the men. At the same time, the chimpanzee's fingers grip the titanium bars on its cage door and begins shaking it violently. The chimp presses its face against the bars, trying to force its mouth between two of them as it bites the air between itself and the people in the lab. The box that the ape is enclosed in is soundproof, due to its thickness, but

Subject 1 can hear the erratic shrills blasting from the ape's throat.

"Can we please get this done quickly, Sergeant Granger?" Dr. Gianacola impatiently says, extending her arm towards Subject 1 and twirling her index finger in a circular motion.

"I can't promise quick, ma'am," Michael Granger responds through a speaker located within the front of his faceplate. "But I can promise it is getting done right. Your safety and the security of this facility is my priority, no matter how long it takes. I gotta follow-"

"Standard protocol," Dr. Gianacola interrupts, rolling her eyes. "Yes, I know. I've heard it from Lieutenant Granger a hundred times already."

"And you know, if you couldn't change Trent's mind, there's no way you're changing mine. This is gonna take as long as it takes."

"Fine," Dr. Gianacola says, then turns and heads towards a bank of computers. "But please keep in mind that time is of the essence."

Michael nods to the soldier covering him by pointing a weapon that looks like a rocket launcher at Subject 1. Knowing that McKinnley would squeeze the trigger if Subject 1 even twitched the wrong way, Michael begins to examine the carbon nano-tube mesh fiber restraints that bind Subject 1's wrists, arms, legs, feet, torso, neck, and head to a chair. After determining that all points are well secure, he examines the titanium covering Subject 1's mouth. The oval piece of metal is bonded to Subject 1's skin by a strong epoxy, but for an added layer of security, screws were driven into the bones of his face and jaw. Once satisfied, Michael takes a moment to study the exposed portion of brain on top of Subject 1's head.

"Well?" Dr. Gianacola asks, slipping a thumb drive into a port on one of the computers.

"Okay. Lover boy's all yours." Granger shifts his gaze down to Subject 1's eyes and tilts his head as he studies the prisoner's expression. Then he says, "What, too soon?"

"Enough!" Dr. Gianacola barks. "I don't have much time before Doctor De Reske and the rest of our team arrives. We're on a tight schedule to get the mutation under control before we can fine-tune the virus."

"Lab's yours, doc. We'll be outside if you need us."

Dr. Gianacola scans the information on the monitors in front of her, then she gets up and approaches Subject 1.

"I didn't bring you here," Dr. Gianacola says, low enough for only him to hear while appearing to observe the opening in Subject 1's skull. "And I'm sorry about everything that's happened to you... and her."

Subject 1 coldly stares into Dr. Gianacola's blue-green eyes through the clear plastic of her suit.

"I can't change what happened, but I can give you something you want." Dr. Gianacola's eyes roam over the restraints keeping Subject 1 in the chair, then she glances at the keypad on the wall where a combination can be entered to release the locks on the chair. "If you think you can make it out of here, I'll let you go. Just one condition. I'll need you to take me with you."

CHAPTER ONE

It hit Amy like a rogue wave, a sense of foreboding that makes her spine tingle. She freezes in place and her temperature rockets under her translucent poncho. The lumpy pillowcase full of scavenged supplies swings from her hand like the pendulum on a doomsday clock. If danger is as close as she feels it might be, then time won't be on her side for long.

The only sound she hears is something like faint static. Rustling, coming from the cornfield behind the farmhouse.

The moment she realizes what is bothering her, Amy gasps into the paint speckled respirator covering her nose and mouth. The swishing that she heard when the breeze blew over the cornfield earlier was more gentle, almost rhythmic. Now she hears something more steady and unyielding, like an oncoming freight train.

Amy presses her back against the wall and cranes her neck to look out the kitchen window. She raises the goggles shielding her hazel eyes and frantically scours the wall of corn. None of the stalks are swaying, as they would be if the wind were caressing them. She tries to decipher what she is hearing and her mind defaults to the image of cornstalks being mowed down by a swarm of chompers rushing towards the house.

"Fuck that!" Amy says, completely giving in to her impulse to run straight to the truck. "I'm out."

She sprints down the hallway, hurdles over an overturned end table in the ransacked living room, and opens the front door. One step onto the porch and she is forced to stop dead in her tracks. The Chevy Silverado is there waiting for her, door open and engine running, just like she left it. However, there is now a full grown coyote standing on the hood of the pickup.

The coyote lifts its head and sniffs the air, looking in Amy's direction with squinted eyes.

Amy lets go of the pillowcase and props her shotgun up against the door jamb. She raises the rifle hanging from her body by a leather sling and takes aim at the animal. A flash of movement causes her to dart her eyes at the cabin of the truck. She grit her teeth when she sees two more coyotes nosing around in the back of the cab, but quickly re-focuses on the one standing on the hood.

The coyote has her scent and is baring its flesh-ripping teeth as it growls. Fortunately for Amy, the carnivorous animal is infected with the Puissance virus, and it can't see her well. Still, it postures to attack the prey whose scent brought it to the farmhouse.

The sun beaming down from a clear blue sky is Amy's ally as long as it keeps shining bright. Chompers have only a few weaknesses, one of which is an aversion to sunlight. Not that it stopped them from trying to chase down a meal during the day.

The other coyotes are alerted to Amy's presence as well. The Apache blood storming through her vessels doesn't allow her to get flustered. Everything her brother taught her about shooting comes automatically as she settles the crosshairs of the rifle's scope on the grayish-brown patch of fur between the coyote's eyes. She exhales slowly, following her target as it hunches down to pounce, and she squeezes the trigger.

Amy sees a burst of blood over fur as her shot cracks across the mute landscape. The coyote yelps from the bullet tearing into its right eye and destroying half of its small cranium before the animal is pitched off the hood of the truck.

The other coyotes howl, vexed by the loud gunshot but not discouraged enough to run away. Amy pulls back the bolt on the rifle, ejecting the spent shell onto the porch, then she pushes it forward again to chamber a new round. The coyotes swiftly slink out of the truck and Amy takes a step back into the house as they sniff the air to lock in on her scent.

With the short distance between her and the coyotes, she might be able to kill one before the other's teeth are upon her. But even as good as she is with the rifle, she won't be able to pull off two head-shots on such small targets in time. Reluctantly, Amy grabs her shotgun and slams the front door shut. Seconds later there is a loud thud, immediately followed by snarls and frantic scratching. She locks the door, as if the coyotes might figure out how to paw the knob enough to open it, then she hustles over to the only piece of furniture that wasn't knocked over by previous looters.

The ornate wooden feet of the hutch scrapes the floor, moaning like a whale in agony as Amy moves it over to the stairway. When the hutch is in place, she tips it over face-up, shattering the glass doors and breaking some of the commemorative Elvis Presley plates inside. The overturned piece of furniture creates a small obstacle to climb over, not the barricade that she would've preferred but it was the best she could do with the little time that she had. Two coyotes at the front door are trouble enough. Not knowing what is heading her way through the cornfield adds to the dilemma. Regardless, she has to defend herself, and the second floor is the best place to do it. The windows are a safe place to snipe chompers—human or animal—and if any of them get inside of the house, then the narrow stairway makes a good kill box.

***

Ten minutes ago, Amy's instinct had advised her to move on to the next farm. But hunger and pessimism warned that she could be passing up a safe place to loot, only to walk right into a death trap.

The evidence of this farm being operational before the State of Emergency was declared was a pile of blackened horse and cattle carcasses behind a white wooden fence. Those dark pyramids of death were the trademark of the military's presence. The beasts of burden were shot in the head, bulldozed together, then sprayed with a napalm-like fluid and set ablaze. All standard protocol.

The military's protocol was not flexed in the slightest. Not even for any man, woman or child merely suspected of being infected by the Puissance virus. Amy had the misfortune of witnessing this firsthand when she saw her mother and a dozen neighbors disposed of like they were tainted cattle. Six weeks has passed since that day, but the god-awful odor of charring flesh still remained with her.

After taking a deep breath to calm her nerves, Amy had kissed the set of dog tags wrapped around her wrist by a ball chain. Then she ran the back of her hand across her forehead, wiping sweat from her reddish-brown skin. She covered her eyes with a pair of goggles and secured a paint-speckled half face air purifying respirator to protect her nose and mouth.

With the mask on, Amy was assaulted by the foulness of her own breath. She inhaled through her mouth, yearning to come across at least a half-empty tube of toothpaste when she searched the house. There were other toiletries she was in desperate need of, but none of which are necessary for her immediate survival. Food, water, and bullets were the essentials at the moment.

As much as Amy hated the mere thought of it, she knew she had to clear the barn and the silo before she checked the house. She pulled the hood of her poncho over her jet black hair then eased her foot off the brake, allowing the Chevy to roll forward.

The closer she got to the barn, the tighter the knot felt in her stomach. No one in their right mind purposely took on the chompers head-on anymore, except for the militia. Most of them were borderline psychos, but they had the numbers and firepower. Amy, on the other hand, was a lone, 18-year-old girl packing a 30-30 rifle and a 12-gauge pump-action shotgun. As much as the odds were stacked against her, she was proud of herself for holding her own for so long.

Amy had abruptly stopped the pickup about ten feet from the barn and snatched the 12-gauge from off the back seat. Her pulse pounded but she felt a touch of relief when the barn doors don't swing open.

"Yeah, right," Amy said to herself, stepping out of the pickup with her finger poised on the trigger. "Been there, done that, and I fucked shit up! Now come get some!"

The lack of an attack hadn't lulled her into a false sense of security. Chompers infected more than 24 hours weren't smart, but they were extremely aggressive and focused on one thing: eating flesh. As for those still in the first stage of infection, they were as cunning as can be until the last bit of their humanity eroded away. But aggression and cunning weren't the most dangerous thing about the chompers. The Puissance virus was given its name by the CDC because it virtually super-charges its host, making them remarkably stronger, faster, and able to survive most mortal wounds. Chompers are hard to kill but not indestructible. Massive brain trauma, courtesy of a large caliber bullet or a shotgun blast was the preferable method of snuffing one out.

The heat of high noon was amplified under Amy's poncho, and breathing inside of the respirator added discomfort. She stopped complaining to herself and pressed her back against the closed door of the barn. Using her foot, she pushed open the door that was already ajar. It swung open with a rusty moan as Amy backed away, ready to blow the head off anything with a hostile response. She exhaled when nothing happened, then she opened both doors to let in a heavier volume of sunlight. Keeping her line of sight parallel with the length of the shotgun barrel, she swept from corner to corner of the barn's musky interior until she was satisfied that there weren't any chompers laying in wait. Backing out of the barn, she set her sights on the silo, finding its doors padlocked.

That was when a warm gust of breeze rustled leaves and swayed stalks of corn behind the house.

"Creee-Pee!" Amy had said, glancing at the cornfield.

***

Amy curses at herself for not taking that creepy feeling as a sign to move on when she was looking at the cornfield. But she doesn't waste a lot of time on self-admonishment.

One of the flimsy shelves in the pushed over hutch gives off a woody squawk from the slightest pressure under Amy's foot. She tiptoes her way up along the edge, trying to gauge the degree of difficulty a chomper will face getting in and out of the big box. The shelves will break easily, and the rest of the plates should shatter, creating some slipperiness that should significantly slow down a chomper. If it came to it, she would need all the time that she could get.

Amy hurries up the stairs, listening to the coyotes still clawing the front door. The window in the bathroom looked like a good place to cover the backyard, so she heads to the end of the hallway. Upon entering the bathroom, Amy sights something through the small window that incites more fear: a swarm of human chompers in the backyard. Some of them brandishing objects that they use as bludgeoning weapons, including hammers, shovels, pieces of lumber, even a car jack.

Chompers are unmistakable. Wild hair, dirty skin, and grimy clothes were as much a dead giveaway as the brownish, dried blood staining their faces down to their necks. A chomper's appearance is only rivaled by the painful look of hunger in its eyes. Another characteristic of a chomper is their unbelievable stench. Not the fetidness of decay expected of the living dead. This odor was far more disgusting. Chompers digested whatever they ate and also passed waste, but they don't use toilets. They go whenever they have to, in whatever clothes they are wearing—if they're wearing clothes at all.

There are more chompers in this pack than Amy is used to seeing in a rural area. A few of them are already at the barn, investigating it with a sense of urgency. More are bursting forth from the cornfield.

Amy removes a box of rifle bullets from her pocket, regretting every bullet she fired over the past few weeks that didn't hit their mark. As she places the box on top of a clothes hamper, she notices that one of the coyotes has left the front door to sniff some of the new arrivals. Neither of them attack each other. For some unknown reason, chompers don't eat their own. Amy wished they did. There are already at least a dozen of them that she can see, and more coming. Most of the chompers looked like they were once the transient workers who provided cheap labor to the farmers in this area. Some looked like the farmers, themselves, and their families. Others looked like the normal, everyday people you would meet in any small town, U.S.A., including a Deputy Sheriff.

Amy lays the shotgun on the top of the toilet tank to keep from feeling encumbered while she aims and shoots. With less than twenty bullets left for the rifle, she can't afford any misses. She doesn't know if she has enough ammunition to hold them all off, but she's determined to kill as many chompers as she can—saving the last bullet for herself if it comes to it.

As soon as Amy raises the window all of the chompers look up in her direction. She eases the rifle barrel outside and fixes her sight on a large Mexican man. The chomper has massive lacerations all over his face and body, clearly caused by the long length of razor wire snagged on his flesh and clothing. Amy tries to focus on his forehead as he snarls at her, but she can't ignore the gash in his belly with a bit of lacerated small intestine bubbling out of it.

Amy takes the shot. A hole pops in the man's forehead amd a pinkish-red spray spewed from behind his head. She works the bolt on the rifle, sending the spent shell tumbling through the air before it clinks across the tile floor. She chambers a new round and blows a John Deere cap off of another chomper's head, along with a quarter of his skull. Then she focuses on the shirtless chubby man standing next to him. By the time she put a hole in the rotund man's head, the collective of chompers are rushing to the back of the house. She leans further out the window, adjusting her aim to kill the ones closest to the house first. Using her fourth bullet, she drops one of the transients then stops an old woman from smashing one of the kitchen windows with a tire iron.

Amy pulls back the bolt and, as the fifth empty cartridge hits the floor, she plucks a new bullet from the box on the hamper. Her 30-30 rifle only holds 6 bullets in its clip, and she has used them all. From this moment on, she will have to load the rifle manually. It's a little slower but still do-able. She is more concerned about running out of ammo. For the rifle, there are thirteen bullets left from the box of twenty. As for the shotgun, it is loaded with five double-0 buck shells, plus seven more in her pocket. Every one of her twenty-five remaining shells has to count.

The chompers close to the window are Amy's priority. She splatters a teenage girl's brain matter onto the face of a man beating on the back door of the house with a 2X4. Then she takes a shot at one of the transients planning to do the same thing with a claw hammer. She reloads and selects another target, but before she takes the shot she is startled by the sound of shattering glass echoing throughout the house.

Amy's heart pounds in her chest as she stuffs the box of bullets into her pocket. She lowers the goggles back over her eyes, grabs the shotgun, and takes off. Before she reaches the end of the hallway, she hears a rapid clicking and clacking sound that is getting closer to her. Instinctively, she raises the shotgun just as a coyote's snout comes into view.

The coyote pounces before it reaches the top step. Amy braces the butt of the gun on her shoulder and waits a nerve-racking two seconds for the coyote to be in optimal range before she squeezes the trigger.

The shotgun booms. Amy feels the kickback on her shoulder, and the coyote's head is torn from its body. Blood, bone, and fur splash the walls and floor. Amy's face and body are also generously sprinkled with bits of furry gore, making her thankful for the goggles, respirator, and poncho.

Amy races to the top of the stairs and sees a little boy chomper crawling over the back of a transient, both trying to get in through a broken window in the living room at the same time. She momentarily turns her attention from them, switching back to the rifle to deal with a gaunt-faced chomper wearing a uniform, making his way through the hutch.

The chomper slipping on the glass in the hutch bears a shocking resemblance to a sheriff from Socorro, New Mexico that Amy knows all too well. It stuns her for a moment, but she quickly realizes that there is no way it could be Wayne Mathis. The sheriff extends his arms, reaching for Amy even though he is still a distance away. Amy notices the color of his fingers. They are all deathly black, as if frostbitten. It is an odd thing that she hadn't seen on a chomper before, but at the moment it doesn't matter much to her.

"Here piggy, piggy, piggy!" Amy sings out.

The chomper snaps his jaws at her, the clicking of his teeth echoes off the walls. Amy smirks and squeezes the trigger, sending a bullet plowing all the way through the sheriff's brain.

More glass shatters over the thumping of chompers beating on the back door and walls. Amy reloads, keeping her eyes on the two chompers climbing through the window. She takes aim at the transient and fires. The shot pops open his scalp like the lid on a Jack-in-the-box and sends part of his cranium flipping through the air.

She reloads, giving the little boy chomper enough time to crawl into the hutch. Before he could get out she shoots, and he falls back into it like it was his coffin.

The house is infiltrated by a loud crack from wood splitting, followed by the reverberating pounding of footsteps on the hardwood floor. Amy knows she is in major trouble. The chompers in the backyard finally broke down the back door. Manually reloading will take too long to kill them one-by-one. She isn't sure if she even has enough bullets for all of them. The plan was to kill as many of them as possible and fall back to the bathroom if it looked like they were going to overwhelm her. Then she would decide if to risk jumping out the window or just ending it there.

A rabble of chompers trampling each other storms into the living room from the back of the house. Amy takes aim at the bald chomper leading the pack. Just as she squeezes the trigger she hears three loud pops, like the report of high caliber rounds being fired right outside of the house. The sudden distraction causes Amy's shot to go off course. Instead of putting a hole in bald chomper's skull, the slug carves a trench into the side of his head and plunges into the neck of another chomper wearing overalls.

Amy swears to god as she quickly reloads. Bald chomper climbs into the hutch, with most of the other chompers bunched up on the landing, fighting for position. Amy takes aim at his head again but sees another chomper—whose bottom lip looks like it was bitten off—attempt to climb over the banister. She sprays one-lip chomper's brain matter out the back of his head before he can circumvent her obstacle, then she reloads again and tries to get a bead on bald chomper. Glass crinkles, cracks and scrapes the wood under his feet as he tries to catch his balance inside of the hutch.

In her peripheral vision, she glimpses a goth kid chomper staggering across the porch as if he was knocked backwards by something. He comes to a stop in front of the broken window, then turns his head and locks eyes with Amy. His dry, cracked lips quiver and a tongue with a yucky white coat creeps out to lick them.

The loud pop of the high caliber weapon thunders again, and the forehead of the goth chomper violently explodes. He falls face first into the open window and what's left of his brain pops out of his skull.

Amy tries not to think about who is doing the shooting outside. The last thing she wants to see is the militia or the military. But at the moment she doesn't have time to dwell on it. She'd be too dead to care if she doesn't kill the chompers that are only an overturned hutch away from overwhelming her, plus how many else are still coming in through the back of the house.

The bald chomper climbs out of the hutch and starts up the stairs. Amy takes her shot, hitting her target perfectly. Bald chomper falls backwards, knocking overalls-chomper over the banister. She reloads and gets off another shot that takes out a high school jock chomper with a douchey soul patch. She then let the rifle drop to her side as she reaches for the shotgun. She hopes to kill at least three more chompers before retreating back to the bathroom, starting with the chomper raising a hatchet high as he rushes up the stairs to bury the blade in her skull.

Amy blows the hatchet-chomper's head off and racks the shotgun as the others stumble over him. She aims at the next in line and beheads him, too. Then a loud boom draws her eyes to the front door as it flies off its hinges.

CHAPTER TWO

A young man wearing dark sunglasses storms into the house brandishing two black Desert Eagle handguns. Strapped to each of his thighs are scabbards containing bladed weapons with H-shaped handles. Amy recognizes the knives immediately: katars. She had seen them in movies before but never thought she would actually see one, much less two of them, in real life.

The gun in the man's right-hand thunders and the head of the chomper closest to him explodes like a balloon chock-full of chili con carne and tuna. A split second later the gun in his left fires. The slug strikes the only chomper still focused on Amy above the ankle of his left leg, snapping his bones like carrot sticks. The chomper topples over, leaving his foot and dirty sneaker behind on the step as he falls backwards towards the hutch.

All of the chompers on the first floor rush towards the gunman, snapping their jaws like mad dogs. A loud string of gunfire is unleashed and the wall nearest to the stairs mottled with blood and clumps of brain matter.

Both Desert Eagles fall silent. Bluish smoke wafts around the gunman as he synchronously twirls his guns backwards and forwards with his trigger fingers like a victorious gunfighter showboating after a high noon showdown. He crosses his arms and simultaneously slips them into their respective slots on his double-sided shoulder holster.

Amy watches in fascination as the man's hands fall to his side and his fingers curl around the cross bars on the handles of his katars. Gleaming, nine inch, double-edged blades are revealed as he pulls them out of their sheaths. Displaying no sign of urgency, he ignores the remaining chompers in the kitchen coming towards him. Instead, he waits for the chomper who landed in the hutch to sit up. Then, with a snap of his arm like he's throwing a jab, he thrusts one of his blades dead center into the chomper's face and pushes it through the back of his head.

The man withdraws his blade and rushes headlong at the chompers bearing down on him. Moving like a martial arts master, he exhibits impressive speed, grace, and accuracy as he dances through the swarm. Amy smiles at the beauty of his weapons' design. They function as an extension of his arm, making his strikes infinitely deadly as the blades virtually supersede his hands. And the legs of the H-shaped handles, which stretch halfway up his forearm, prove to be highly effective in blocking attacks.

The man decapitates the last chomper, then flicks the excess blood from his weapons and slides them back into their sheaths. Amy isn't easily impressed by anyone, but the stranger excites her in a way that no man ever has before. She likes how his worn leather cowboy boots match his seasoned gunslinger persona. His sweat-soaked, blood speckled white T-shirt clings to his lean muscles, displaying his athletic build. And the addition of a double-sided shoulder holster boasting big black guns enhance the attractiveness of his physique. Plus, his unkempt curly brown hair and the stubble on his face gave him the rugged look that she likes in a man. She takes note that the only piece of jewelry that he's wearing is a gold ring on the trigger finger of his right hand.

Amy wishes to see the man's eyes, but they are shielded by the extremely dark lenses of his wrap-around sunglasses. The fact that his shades are so dark is the catalyst to snap her back into survivor mode.

Regardless of how appealing the stranger is, she can't trust him. For all she knows, he could be one of the militiamen. What she fears worse than that is the possibility that has is infected by the virus but not fully turned chomper yet. A sense of danger churns her stomach. Without hesitation she raises the shotgun, aiming at his chest.

The man reacts to Amy's hostile action in a flash, drawing both of his handguns from their holsters and training them on her as well. Then in a tight-lipped way of speaking, like a bad ventriloquist, he says, "Miss, you sure got a funny way of sayin' thank you."

"Thank you for what?" Amy replies. "I had everything under control."

"If you say so."

"My twelve-gauge and the double-O buck in it says so!"

The gunman cracks a smile, barely revealing the whiteness of his teeth. "Okay, I see your twelve gauge with double-O buck, and I raise you two forty-five cal. magnums with pre-fragged rounds."

"Okay, Kung Fu cowboy, I'll call. Bet you don't even got any bullets left."

"Right back at ya'."

"Nah, I'm good," Amy says, flexing her trigger finger. "Try me."

"Tell ya' what," the man says, slowly removing his index fingers from inside the trigger guards of his guns. He makes sure Amy sees that he's standing down and he returns the Eagles to their holsters. "Let's start this over. My name is Eli. Elias Kincade, really, but everybody calls me Eli. I'm running low on water. So I got off the freeway to look for some when I heard your gunshots, and I figured I lend a hand. That's all there is to it."

"Uh-huh," Amy responds sarcastically. "So, what's with the dark shades,

Eli?"

Eli smiles. "What, it's a sin to wear sunglasses?"

"No, but it makes me suspicious as hell. And I couldn't help but notice how you controlled the kick of those 'forty-five-cal. magnums' single handed like they were BB guns."

"Oh, you think I'm infected?" Eli chuckles, seemingly relieved.

"Don't expect you to tell me if you are."

"I'm not," Eli says, sliding his sunglasses up to the top of his head.

Amy gets chills from Eli's icy blue eyes. They are so light and clear, they're almost spooky.

"I'm not infected," Eli says, staring directly at Amy's goggles. "If I was, I'd blow my own head off before I let myself turn into a...."

"Chomper?"

"That what y'all call 'em down here? For the past few weeks, I've heard everything from 'zombies' to 'ghoulies.'"

Amy shrugs her shoulders. "It won't matter what you call them when you finally turn into one. Anyway, there's no bottled water here, and the stuff coming out of the faucets in this area is brown, so I don't advise drinking it."

Eli glances at the pillowcase on the floor. "That yours?"

"Yes, it is! And there's nothing in it for you!"

"Relax," Eli says, scooping up the pillowcase. "My mother taught me to never let a lady carry something when I got two good arms hanging from my shoulders."

"Don't!" Amy puts pressure on the shotgun's trigger but hesitates on squeezing it enough to drop the hammer before Eli walks out the door.

Annoyed with herself, Amy releases a grunt and hurries after Eli as fast as she can maneuver over the slippery steps and the bloody bodies. She keeps her eyes on him as he walks down the porch steps and lays the pillowcase in the back of the Silverado. His sunglasses are still on top of his head, and he doesn't seem to have a problem seeing what he is doing.

Amy also notices a black Ford Bronco parked about thirty yards from the Silverado. The older model SUV is on oversize tires and has strips of metal welded over the windows and windshield.

There are well over a dozen more chomper bodies scattered around the front of the house, plus the carcass of the third coyote. A few have bullet holes in their skulls, but most have long, slender head wounds like the ones Eli put in the chompers that he killed in the house with his blades. Amy admits to herself that it was a stroke of luck for Eli to come along when he did. She didn't have enough bullets to kill so many chompers, and there is no guarantee that she would have made it to the Silverado alive if she had jumped out of the bathroom window.

"You should be more careful," Eli says, leaning against the back of the Silverado. "The chompers are leaving the cities and roaming around in larger packs now. I guess their food source has dried up and they're migrating in search of more."

"I'll keep that in mind," Amy responds, lowering the shotgun as she stares at his captivating eyes. "Why do you talk like that?"

"Like what?"

"Like your jaw's wired shut. That supposed to be sexy or something?"

"Only if you think it is," Eli says and smiles a tight-lipped smile. "You heading somewhere in particular or you just out here scavenging?"

"What's it to you?"

"Nothing, really. Just wanted to know if you want to ride with me. I mean, I'm heading toward Florida and my truck is safer than yours. Plus, I've got lots of firepower. Surviving could be easier if we had each other's back, and to tell the truth, I wouldn't mind the company."

"I'm doin' alright on my own," Amy says. "And I wouldn't make good company. Trust me!"

Eli chuckles. "Alright, suit yourself. Is there anything I can help you with?"

Amy thinks about Eli's mention of firepower. She looks over at the Bronco and sees the barrel of a shotgun resting in a clamp mounted to the dashboard. Chances of him having 30-30 rounds for the rifle are slim, but he might have 12-gauge shells. The problem is that she doesn't have much to barter with. The only thing that he might want in trade is out of the question, regardless of how attractive she finds him.

Eli follows Amy's line of sight, and says, "So, you are low on ammo, huh?"

"Yeah, I still got some, but I can use more 12-gauge shells. Thing is, I really don't have much to trade for 'em."

Eli smiles again. "That's not a problem. I got plenty of ammo, and I'm not gonna miss a box of shells. I'll give 'em to you if you do something for me first."

"Yeeeah," Amy says skeptically. "And what would that be?"

"I gotta know if you're as cute as you are badass, so I want to see your face. Oh, and a smile would be nice, too."

"You can't be serious?!"

"I am serious. That's my offer, take it or leave it?"

Amy keeps an eye on Eli as he turns and walks over to his truck. She finds herself indecisive about what to do. There is no reason to trust him. Then again, he hasn't given her a reason not to. As long as she has her gun she has a fighting chance if he tries anything slick. Still unsure of what her intuition is telling her, she follows behind him.

Eli removes his katars and lays them on the roof of his Bronco, then he lowers the tailgate and takes a seat. Amy keeps a safe distance from him as she scans the interior of the truck. The top of the dashboard is littered with empty protein bar wrappers. Most of the items in the Bronco's cargo space is covered by dropcloth or blankets, but she makes out a few cardboard boxes with a grocery store logo printed on them and a few large, canvas duffle bags.

Amy considers how long Eli's food and ammo could last her if she had a justifiable reason to claim his stockpile as her own.

Eli slides a duffel bag from the cargo space onto the tailgate and retrieves a box for Amy to see. "Twelve-gauge shells. All yours when I see your face."

"My face, and that's all!" Amy says, firmly.

"Don't forget the smile, too."

"Fine!"

Keeping the shotgun in her right hand, Amy uses her left to remove her goggles and pull the respirator down from her nose and mouth. Then she pushes the hood off of her head, revealing her jet black hair pulled back into a ponytail and skin like cinnamon glistening from a sheen of sweat.

Eli's lips part and he releases the sigh of a man snared by a siren's spell. He remains frozen as he takes in the superb combination of genes gifted to Amy by her ancestors. The Native American features of her father are most dominant, accented by hazel eyes and high cheekbones contributed from her mother's European bloodline. Not even the indignant scowl on her face can take away from her captivating appeal.

"Wow," Eli says, regaining his composure. "It figures, I'd wait until the fuckin' Apocalypse to run into the most beautiful woman I've ever seen in all my life."

Amy grits her teeth and delivers the second part of their deal, hoping Eli isn't able to discern that the true source of her smile is the compliment he gave her.

"Alright," Amy says, forcing a stern voice, "you owe me some shells!"

"That I do." Eli tosses the box to Amy.

She catches it with her free hand and slips it into her pocket.

"Here," Eil says, offering a milk jug half filled with water. "You got some blood around your neck. You might want to wash it off."

Amy stares at the liquid in the jug and considers the possibility of Eli's backwash spit mixed with it, or possibly something else that would render her incapacitated if she drank from it. Then she looks at her reflection in one of the Bronco's back windows. There is a decent amount of chomper blood on her neck, just as Eli says, and having it on her skin creeps her out.

Amy tilts her head back and pours the water out on her neck. She even runs some over her face to get whatever blood that might have gotten between the goggles and respirator. When the bottle is empty, she checks the window again to make sure all of the red blotches are gone. Then something else catches her eyes.

On the far end of the cargo space, peeking out from under a sheet of white dropcloth, Amy spots the bottom corner of a case of bottled water. Judging the shape under the cloth, Amy wagers that Eli has at least three cases hidden.

Immediately, she drops the empty jug and aims her shotgun at Eli. "Hands up!"

"You gotta be kidding me?" Eli says, complying with Amy's demand.

"No, I'm not! You said you got off the freeway to look for water, but it looks like you already got plenty in the back of your truck."

Eli darts his eyes at the cases of water. "Yeah, I got some, but no sense waiting 'til I run out to get more."

"No, you said you were running low. That's a big difference! Now, where are your keys!?"

Eli slowly lowers his right hand and taps the front pocket of his jeans.

"Good. Now, carefully take out your Eagles one and a time and lay 'em on top the truck next to your katars."

"You know what my knives are?" Eli asks, genuinely impressed.

"Duh!" Amy snaps. "Now do as I said. After that, I want you to walk away."

"Yeeeah," Eli says, arching one eyebrow, "I got a problem with that."

"Live with it, 'cause a shit load of double-O buck up your ass is gonna be an even bigger problem if you want it."

"Leave my ass out of this," Eli says, then aggressively slaps his hand on his chest. "But if you're going to shoot, then go for it!"

Amy's conscience ebbs in protest. She knows that she doesn't have a problem pulling the trigger on a human as easily as she can with a chomper, especially when her life is in danger. But Eli's lie doesn't necessarily translate into a threat. She doubts he would've respected her personal space as much as he had if he was infected, but she can't fight the feeling that he has an ulterior motive.

If she squeezes the trigger right at this moment, the sole reason would be to gain his truck and supplies. That would make her the lowest of thieves. But she'd be a lowly thief with plenty of weapons, ammo and a formidable truck to keep her going until she finds a place she feels safe.

"Eli," Amy says in a regretful tone, "I don't want you to die today. So please do as I say. Leave your guns and your keys and just walk away, man?"

"So sweet of you," Eli responds, then fearlessly takes another step towards Amy. "But I'm not going to die today."

"Stop!"

Eli chuckles and takes two more steps.

Eli's next step brings him too close for comfort and the next thing Amy knows, her shoulder is absorbing the violent recoil of the shotgun.

A cluster of holes explode on Eli's chest with splashes of blood. The impact of the 12 pellets—each approximately the size of a .32 caliber bullet—knocks Eli off his feet and sends him flying backwards. He sails through the air, then hits the ground hard and briefly skids over the gravel before coming to a stop.

Amy sighs as she watches a sea of red growing on the front of Eli's white shirt. Her breath catches in her throat when his hand rises up and comes down on his wounds. Guilt consumes her as she watches the rise and fall of his chest slow down. His breathing becomes more shallow, leading to the moment the last breath leaves his lungs.

Amy tries to convince herself that she did what she had to do. That might have been easier if she could just walk away from Eli's lifeless body. But she needs the keys to his truck, and the stubborn fool died with them in the pocket of his jeans.

Shuffling her feet, she approaches Eli's body. She keeps her gaze on his irises. They might as well be mirrors reflecting the blue sky above. She considers it a shame that the world is what it has become. Her life before the pandemic was far from a bed of roses, but she would've liked to have gotten to know a guy like Eli. Even eventually acting on her attraction to him. But he lied about the water, and there was no telling what else he might've lied about.

"Why'd you make me do this to you, man?" Amy says, aiming the shotgun to decapitate Eli. "This isn't what I wanted, but that doesn't matter now. I don't expect you to forgive me when I see you on the other side, but I hope you'll let me make it up to you when I do."

Amy squeezes the trigger.

The shotgun booms, hurling a bevy of slugs at Eli's skull. In the blink of an eye, there is an explosion of gravel and a crater blown into the driveway—exactly where Eli's head should've been at the moment of impact. But there is no Eli on the ground. Not his head. Not his body. No evidence that he just died there, except for the blood that came from the exit wounds in his back.

Stunned and confused, Amy can't make sense of what she just saw. Even the best magician needed some kind of diversion to execute a disappearing act like that. And as far as she knew, not even the greatest of them all managed to pull that kind of trick off after they were dead.

A shadow appears on the ground, almost blending with the one cast by Amy. She spins around, racking the gun as she does, only to feel it be yanked away from her grip.

Her heart thunders. Her brain feels like it is shortcircuiting as neurons scramble to assemble a logical explanation of why Eli is standing on his own two feet. He smiles at her as he flings the shotgun in the direction of the burned cattle carcasses. There is no mistake about the blast that she thought she had put him down with. The wound over his heart is still fresh and oozing crimson.

"Naughty girl," Eli says, mockingly rubbing both his index fingers together.

"I got your naughty girl," Amy responds, raising her rifle faster than ever before.

Amy is fast, but Eli is faster. He grabs the muzzle of the rifle as it spits out a shot. The slug might as well had missed him by a mile. He yanks the rifle towards him, and Amy goes along for the ride because of the sling around her shoulder.

Moving on instinct and adrenaline, Amy dips to her right and slips her shoulder out the sling. Flowing with the momentum, she pivots on the ball of her foot to break off in a sprint but loses her footing on the loose gravel.

Unable to stop herself from falling, Amy braces for impact with the ground. Her right-hand hits first, absorbing most of the shock.

Keeping her wits, she goes to scamper away but is thwarted by Eli's grip on her hips. She screamed as he flips her over so that she is face-up. Jagged edges of gravel dig into her back as he settles his body on top of hers. She uses all her strength to keep her legs locked together, but he easily pries them apart with his knee and settles in between them.

Horrific thoughts rush through Amy's mind, and she tries her best to scratch his eyes out. Eli rocks his head back, dodging her clawing fingers, then he swiftly catches her slender wrists and forces her arms over her head.

Amy continues to resist as Eli clamps both of her wrists within one of his hands and pins them to the ground. She writhes in the gravel and futilely tries to buck him off. Nothing she does has any effect. She is at his mercy.

Fear rushes throughout her body as she anticipates what is going to happen next. She feels hotter than ever, and it takes her a moment to realize that the remarkable heat is radiating from Eli's body. Anyone with a fever so hot would be dead. But Eli doesn't seem to have a problem disagreeing with things that should end his life.

Amy prays for a miracle, anything to stop the nightmare she anticipates is moments away from happening. Even a heart attack would be welcomed. She'd rather be dead than be raped by a chomper in the making, and then eaten by him after.

"Get off me!" Amy screams, wriggling her body, even though she knows that she isn't going anywhere.

"Wish I could," Eli responds and licks his lips, "But you forced me into a corner, here. Besides, you said you wanted to make it up to me. This'll do."

Amy shakes her head vigorously. "No! Please don't do this to me, please don't. I'm sorry."

"Shhh, I promise it won't hurt much," Eli says and flashes a big smile, exposing the devilish rictus that he had been hiding by restricting the movements of his lips.

Amy gasps at the sharp set of fangs in Eli's mouth. Electricity runs the length of her spine like fingers gliding the span of a piano keyboard.

Eli lowers his face down to Amy's. She turns her head, expecting him to try forcing a kiss on her. Instead, he smells her neck, appearing elated as he closes his eyes inhales deeply. Then his lips softly touch down on her skin and she feels the incredible heat of his mouth. She whips her head back and forth to get him off, but he clutches her forehead with his free hand and holds her in place. Unreal scenarios played in Amy's head as Eli's tongue drags up and down on her skin.

A yip leaps from Amy's throat when Eli's fangs sink into her skin. She thinks to herself, "This can't be happening." But she knows that it is for real when she feels the suction of Eli's mouth tugging at her skin. He greedily sucks in as much blood as he can force out of her blood vessel and gulps it down loud enough for her to hear.

Amy screams, even though there is no one to hear it and come to her rescue. She summons all her strength to break her wrists free from Eli's hand. No matter how hard she tries, his grip remains as powerful as a steel clamp and she ends up tiring herself out. A whirly feeling begins to envelop her like quicksand as she lays victim to Eli's assault.

Amy feels Eli suckling blood from her like a starving baby taking milk from its mother. The brightness of the day becomes more dazzling than ever. She starts to feel like she is floating on a cloud. Tiny bright dots appear to pop up in her eyesight and waft listlessly in front of her. Time passes. She can't tell the difference between one minute and ten. Her last drop of strength dwindles like a flame at the end of a match, and she lays helpless.

Amy receives shade from the sun when Eli raises up and stares down at her with a candied-apple shade of red coating his lips. She finds it strange that his expression seems that of genuine concern as darkness encroaches the outer rim of her vision. The darkness thickens, and within a few beats of her heart, everything goes black.

CHAPTER THREE

Coldness feels like piranha teeth nipping at Amy's skin.

She dreams of running into the open arms of a young Native American man dressed in a Marine uniform. Even on days when she was at her worst, one of Aaron's hugs would melt the world away and she would feel like they were floating together on a cloud. In this dream, though, his embrace is tight and uncomfortable, making her feel like his arms are the bodies of boa constrictors. Regardless, she doesn't want to let Aaron go, not ever again.

Aaron starts to feel heavier in her arms, and she struggles to hold him up. She looks up to ask him what's wrong and is stricken with horror when she sees his boyish face marred and bloody. There is something heavy in her hand. She looks down and finds that she is holding a Glock 17 handgun. Spent of all energy and unable to hold Aaron up any longer, Amy is pulled down to the dusty desert ground by his dead weight, and they continue to free fall down a dark abyss.

Amy's eyes spring open, only to immediately snap back shut as she turns her head away from the direct blast of sunlight. She goes to raise her hand to use as a shield. Both arms moved at the same time and are yanked to a sudden stop after moving only a few inches. Confused and groggy, she forces her eyes open again and battles the morass of light.

Her pupils fight to acclimate, and images of her reality become clear. She is tied to the passenger seat of a vehicle by rope the width of a clothesline. There is also duct tape wrapped around her wrists and ankles. She snaps her head to the left and sees a young man wearing dark sunglasses and a black cowboy hat steering an SUV down a rural road.

Amy doesn't recognize him for a moment, but everything comes back her in a flash. Her muscles twitch as she recalls the struggle to fight Eli off. Her sore neck reminds her of the creepy sensation from his tongue caressing the puncture wounds that his burning hot mouth sucked the blood out of. Rage and humiliation entwine as she wonders what else Eli did to her after she passed out. She still has on her black "Rick and Morty" T-shirt and her blue jeans. Her poncho and hiking boots, however, were removed. She doesn't feel violated, but that's no guarantee nothing happened. Not knowing for sure is almost as bad as living through the horror.

Amy's mind races. Eli could have fulfilled his sickest desires with her back at the farm and left her for dead, but he kept her alive for a reason. She dreads finding out what that reason is before an opportunity to escape presents itself.

Her eyes drift around the cabin of Eli's Bronco. The shotgun clamped to the dashboard is the number one thing on her wish list, but it is impossible to reach. She turns her head and gets a glimpse of the back seat. There she finds her own shotgun, rifle, the pillowcase with her scavenged supplies and the backpack that she had in the Silverado. Eli's katars, an open box of protein bars, and an AK-47 with a folding stock are on the back seat as well. Amy eyes the weapons. So close, but they mean nothing as long as she is wrapped up like a fly in a web, waiting for the spider to develop an appetite.

"Told you I wasn't gonna die today," Eli says, still looking straight forward.

Amy glares at her captor while the air conditioner bellows a steady, frosty breeze over her. She begs any deity within earshot to grant her another go at Eli with the 12-gauge in exchange for her undying devotion. She also can't help but wonder how Eli can look so normal after receiving a chest full of double-O buck. PCP might've explained why he still lingers among the living. The flaw in that scenario, though, is he should've bled out already. It only leaves one logical conclusion: He must really be a chomper. That causes Amy to imagine legions of submicroscopic parasites flowing through her bloodstream and slowly devouring her brain tissue, steadily turning her into a chomper, too.

"Not talking to me, huh?" Eli continues. "I get it. Things didn't go exactly as I hoped it would back at that farm, either. But, you shot me, I drank you, let's call it blood under the bridge and move forward? Whadaya say?"

Amy's icy glare says all that needs to be said.

Eli scoops up a protein bar from on top of the dashboard and peels the wrapper halfway down. Then he holds it in front of Amy's mouth for her to take a bite. The chocolate coating the bar is slightly melted. Amy is tempted to sink her teeth into the gooey treat. But after what Eli has done to her, she refuses to mollify her craving—at least until after she kills him.

"You haven't been eating well." Eli gently taps Amy's bottom lip with the bar, leaving behind a dab of chocolate. "I had to take more blood from you than I wanted to, but you still shouldn't have passed out like that. You don't taste anemic, but I can tell you're not getting enough iron in your diet."

Amy fixes her mouth to curse at him but holds her tongue. Instead, she turns and looks forward, allowing her anger seethe as she thinks about the fangs that she just saw again in his mouth. Even with his casual talk about taking her blood, she refuses to play along with his vampire fantasy.

Eli shrugs then chomps off half of the protein bar. "Okay, you don't have to eat, and you don't have to talk to me," he says with his lips smacking as he chews, "but it would be nice to at least know your name. Unless you'd rather me just call you Mrs. Gouyen."

Amy is surprised that Eli correctly pronounced her last name as Goy-yen, instead of Goo-yen.

"Sure we can keep it formal," Eli continues, "but where's the fun in that? Aaron probably had cute pet na-"

"Don't you ever say his name again, you fuckin' psycho!" Amy screams with rage. "I swear I'll kill you if you do! You hear me?"

"Hey, sorry if I pushed a sensitive button. I didn't mean no harm, honestly."

Amy continues to glare, and one question crosses her mind. She looks down and sees her dog tags pushed up higher on her forearm by Eli before he duct tapped her wrist.

"Yeah, I read 'em," Eli says. "A Marine, huh? Is he still in the service or did he-"

"When I said I didn't want you saying his name, I meant I didn't even want you talking about him, asshole!"

Eli releases a sigh of frustration, then finishes off the protein bar. "I knew it was going to be tough getting you to cut me some slack, but damn."

Amy clams up again. With her emotions running wild, she revealed a wound that has yet to heal. Forcing the image of Aaron's bloody body out of her head, she buries the pain that she feels, determined to deny Eli any perverted pleasure that he might get out of it. The one thing she wants to focus on is getting loose. Then she can work on getting even.

"Look," Eli says, "I'll cut to the chase. I like you. You're tough, smart; you've got the mean streak of a wounded rattlesnake, but you still make me laugh."

"So, why don't you untie me so I can give you something that's gonna crack you up," Amy says and flashes a false smile.

Eli laughs. "See what I mean. I really would like to let you go, Mrs. Gouyen, but there's rules I gotta follow. You know what I am and I can't let you go. Our best option is for you to agree to stay with me for a while. I'm on my way to meet a friend who we'll hook up with in about a day or two. She's working on a vaccine for the virus, and my money's on her finding it. You'll be safe with us. I promise I'll protect you, and I'll make sure that you get the vaccine when we have it."

Amy scoffs. "The blood-freak with the vampire fetish who's got me all tied up in his truck like he's a fuckin' serial killer is going to protect me?! Yeah, and all I gotta do is bleed for you, right?!"

"I know it sucks, but the answer is yes. I lost my companion about a week ago, and eventually, I'll need to feed again. I'll only do it when I absolutely have to, and I won't take more of your blood than I need. When things settle down, you can go free if you decide that's what you wanna do. I'll give you enough food and ammo to last you at least a couple months, and since you like my truck so much, I'll let you have it, too. But I'd be happier if you stay with me."

"Yeah, I bet you would! And I'm supposed to be dumb enough to believe you're just gonna let me go after you did whatever sick, perverted things you already did after I passed out."

Eli removes his sunglasses and stares directly into Amy's eyes. "Hey, the only thing I did after you passed out was took off your bloody poncho and boots. After that, I tied you to the seat so we could talk without you trying to kill me again. Believe me, I was a perfect gentleman."

Sensing sincerity, Amy wants to believe that Eli is telling the truth, but she can't afford to be deluded by blind hope. She hadn't forgotten the look of pleasure on his face when he sniffed her before kissing her neck, then biting it. But, given her circumstances, she decides the best thing to do is to keep Eli talking.

"Alright, you didn't touch me like that," Amy says, "but what's with you and drinking blood?"

"If I go too long without it, the hunger gets unbearable and I get weaker."

"Eli, stop the bullshit, man! You're not a vampire. In case you didn't notice, we're out in the blazing sun. If you were, shouldn't you be smoking or on fire? Or at least be all sparkily since you're obviously on *Team Edward*?"

Eli grits his teeth. "I resent that."

Amy grins, satisfied that she pushed one of Eli's buttons.

"But I'm glad you brought that up," Eli continues. "Just about everything you know about vampires is what our leaders want you to know. Some are lies. Some exaggerations. All of it is to cover the truth and keep our existence a secret. The thing about the sun being deadly to us is one of the exaggerations. We can survive in the sun. We get hotter than we did when we were human, but we don't burst into flames. And ultraviolet rays are also hard on our eyes, but we manage just fine."

"So you're a vampire, but you can't prove it since you don't really fry in the sun. I guess crucifixes and holy water don't burn your skin either?"

"Nope. They make for good stories in books and movies, but it's all bullshit."

"Okay, tell you what. Let me drive a wooden stake through your heart and let's see if that kills you?"

Eli raises the front of his shirt, exposing his torso, and says, "What, this wasn't good enough?"

Amy's jaw drops when she sees the shiny circles of scar tissue on Eli's chest that match the scatter pattern of her shotgun blast. Unless she has been asleep for months, there is no way he should have healed so fast. Eli also has a narrow scar, about 2 inches long, on the left side of his chest that looks old and almost faded. From the looks of it, his heart was once pierced by something like a sword, and the shotgun pellets that she put within close proximity to the stab wound had no more effect on his vital organ than the blade did.

"I hope you're proud of yourself," Eli says, pointing to his left pectoral muscle. "You done shot my nipple off."

Unable to help it, Amy laughs at Eli's reference to his mutilated nub.

"Believe me now?"

Amy shakes her head. "Everything I know about you says you're on your way to being a full-fledged chomper. You can't be a vampire. That's just crazy. I know a world full of zombies is crazy, too. But I can understand them. Vampires...."

"You know I'm not a chomper. I only drank your blood. I didn't eat you, and I'm not trying to eat you. And seeing as how it's been almost two hours since I bit you. Why aren't you showing any of the initial symptoms?"

Amy realizes that Eli makes a good point. If he was infected, he would be a little less human by now, and probably gnawing the marrow from one of her bones like any good chomper would.. If the clock on his dashboard is right, since being bitten by him, she should at least be feverish by now. Other than being fatigued, hungry and frustrated, she feels just fine.

Before a mutated super-virus started turning humans into chompers, Amy didn't believe in zombies.. Now they were a fact of life. As for vampires, she could no longer be skeptical about them. Reluctantly, she accepts what she has been denying. That means there is a living, breathing, fang-mouthed, blood-sucking vampire sitting in the seat right next to her.

"Yeah, I know," Eli says, recognizing the moment Amy accepts the truth. "That's pretty much how I felt when I found out what vampires were. And it's pretty much how I felt when I ran across my first chomper, too. I'm tellin' ya, if frickin' werewolves start coming out the woodwork I'm just going to call it a day and off myself."

"So you can die?" Amy grumbles.

Eli breaks into laughter but doesn't answer the question. "Think about my offer. I'm gonna get off the road for a little while. If my map is right, there's a river or stream about five miles from here. I figure it's a good place to avoid a military patrol. I'll make you a hot meal, and we'll talk more after you wash up and take care of the lady business you got going on down there."

Amy's rage spikes. "You lying bastard!" she snaps, lunging at Eli, even though she can't pull away from the seat.

"Whoa, you got me all wrong. I didn't have to take off your pants to know that you're... well, you know. I can smell your blood. I did lie to you back at the farmhouse when I told you I was looking for water. Truth is, my gut told me to go down the road I was on. While driving I picked up on the scent of your blood, and that's what I was really following when I heard your gunshots."

"Is that the truth?"

"I swear on my mother's grave it is. I wouldn't take advantage of you. I wouldn't do that to anybody."

"All right," Amy says. "I believe you."

"Good," Eli responds and stops the Bronco in the middle of the road. He then reaches to the back seat and grabs one of his katars. "I want you to trust me, and I figure I should start by trusting you." With that, he guides the blade to surgically sever the rope binding her to the seat, then he splits the duct tape around her wrists and ankles before returning the katar next to its twin on the back seat.

Amy relishes the feeling of being liberated once again. Part of her wants to open the door and take off through the woods, but she rejects that notion. She even dismisses the idea of snatching the shotgun and testing how Eli's immortality will hold up after she blows his brains out. At the moment she doesn't want to kill him as badly as she did before. She still doesn't trust him, but he's an honest-to-God vampire, endowed with supernatural powers that provide an edge to compete against chompers, the militia, and the military.

"If we're going to do this," Amy says, rolling strips of duct tape into a sticky ball with the palm of her hand, "I want you to answer a few questions for me first."

"Shoot."

"All right, you said our best option is for me to stay with you until you trust me to keep my mouth shut. But the truth is, I really don't have any other options, do I?"

Eli clenches his jaw and a soft rumble reverberates in his throat. "No. If I let you go I'd be breaking a rule, and it could lead to a big mess that you don't want to be a part of when someone comes to clean it up. Believe me, I know. I'm one of the cleaners. Look, I'm sorry I got you into this the way that I did, but we're in this together now. Otherwise, there's only one way to guarantee that you don't expose us."

With the confirmation of what she suspected and more, Amy nods her head. "Okay, next question. Obviously, you can heal quick or, like, regenerate. Does that mean the Puissance virus doesn't affect vampires?"

Eli shakes his head. "The same virus that turns humans into chompers is lethal to vampires. That's why eliminating chompers and finding a vaccine is so important to us. If chompers took over everywhere, then there'll be little to no humans left for us to feed on. We'd be as good as dead."

"Wow," Amy says. "I'll give it to you, you are honest."

"I always try to be. If I can't tell you the truth about something, then I just won't tell you anything. If that happens, you have to trust that I have my reasons. Are you cool with that, Mrs. Gouyen?" Eli asks, offering his hand for Amy to shake.

"It's Amy," she says, taking his hand. "And yeah, as long as you don't bullshit me, we're cool."

"You have no idea how happy that makes me, Amy. Now, I want to take advantage of what daylight we have left. So whadaya say we get to that place I was telling you about?"

Amy nods her head and settles in the seat. She keeps her eyes on Eli, still working on accepting the fact that she is in the company of a vampire. Though not thrilled with herself for lowering her guard once again, she does believe that Eli doesn't want to hurt her. And if she is his only blood supply, then he will do everything in his power to protect her. She also thinks about what he said about his friend who is working on a vaccine for the virus. If that's true, then crossing paths with Eli might be the best thing to ever happen to her. But if she's wrong, then it will turn out to be a lethal case of fool me once, shame on you; fool me twice, I might as well be dead.

The number of pros quickly stack up against the cons. One pro, in particular, put a stranglehold on Amy's mind. She has done quite well surviving on her own up until now, but Eli could provide her with a way to do it exponentially better. It comes with a down-side, but she is confident that she can get used to drinking blood. There is still a lot of angles to cover, and Amy doesn't make a decision in haste. But deep down inside, she already knows what her heart desires. What she needs to figure out is how to get it.

CHAPTER FOUR

For the first time since the night her life took a nosedive, Amy feels like she can breathe again. After losing the person that she loved the most in the world, as well as her freedom, she lived every minute of life on the edge of a razor. It wasn't until she was bathing in the stream that she realized she wasn't waiting for an attack or another reason to unleash her furry. She was as close to feeling at peace as possible, and she felt safe. It was because of Eli. When Aaron was around, she knew in her heart that he would never allow anything to happen to her. And as crazy as it is, she senses the same thing with a vampire that's been in her life for only a matter of hours.

Holding the towel in front of her body, Amy peeps around the tree she has been drying off behind. She sees Eli's bare back as he crouches in front of the fire that he made. She appreciates him keeping his word to respect her privacy. But a part of her is a little disappointed that she didn't catch him sneaking a peek. Regardless of the deception and violence that was exchanged between them, she can't deny feeling the same attraction to him that she felt after he kicked down the farmhouse door and set his guns blazing.

Amy retreats back behind the tree and begins rummaging through her backpack. She is thankful that Eli took all of her possessions out of her stolen Silverado, including a picture of her and Aaron, instead of leaving them at the farmhouse. She selects a clean pair of black panties, a blue pair of shorts and a sleeveless black T-shirt. As much as she would like to wash the smelly clothes that she took off, Eli doesn't want to stay where they are for too long. He promised that she will be able to take care of that when they get where they're going, and if necessary, there is still some of his former companion's clothes in the Bronco.

Amy makes use of one of the tampons she scavenged from the farmhouse and quickly gets dressed. She wonders about Eli's ex-companion. What kind of woman was she? What exactly was their relationship? He speaks like he cared about her. However, he doesn't seem too heartbroken about losing her or having to be the one to kill her before she turned into a chomper.

After coating her underarms with deodorant, Amy slips on a pair of socks and then her hiking boots. Dressed and feeling refreshed, she drapes the wet towel over her shoulders and carries her backpack in her hand as she walks back over towards Eli.

Keeping her steps as light as a stalking cat, she sets herself on an experiment to see how close can she sneak up on a vampire—if it can even be done. She gets close enough to Eli to make out on the scars on the upper left side of his back. The exit wounds from the shotgun pellets are almost completely vanished. The light, vertical 2-inch scar that corresponds with the one on the front of his body, however, doesn't appear to be under the effect of his vampiric healing.

"You smell really good," Eli says, without turning around.

Amy shakes her head. "I bet you say that to all the girls."

"Only if it's true." Eli turns to face her. "And in your case it absolutely is."

Amy catches herself smiling when she sees her reflection in Eli's sunglasses.

"You were walking lightly," Eli says. "Light enough for me to suspect that you were trying to creep up on me."

"I was. Actually, I wanted to see if I could."

"Not even when I'm sleeping. Vampires are always aware of everything around them."

"You sleep? Funny, I didn't notice a coffin in the back of your truck."

"Coffins are for dead people. Vampires are not dead, and no self-respecting vampire would even take a crap in one, much less voluntarily lay in the damn thing." Eli lifts the lid off the pot on the fire and stirs its contents. "I heated up some pouched beef stew that I had, but I shoulda asked if you were a vegetarian or whatever."

Amy takes in the heady aroma, and her stomach churns in anticipation of what is sure to be the best meal that she's had in forever. "Whatever," she responds, "meaning whatever's in the pot is good enough for me."

"Ha! My kind of girl."

Amy lays the backpack on top of the Bronco and takes a seat on the tailgate. "I guess we should finish putting our cards on the table, huh?"

Eli replaces the lid on the pot, and says, "It's going to be a while before this is done so we can talk now if you want to."

"All right." Amy rubs her neck where a gruesome hickey is darkening, and she puts on a polite smile. "I think we both agree that you need me and I can use your help. I'm willing to let you feed on me, but I have one condition."

Eli sighs, and says, "You want me to make you a vampire."

"Is it that obvious?"

"This isn't my first time down this road."

"I don't just want to be a vampire. I need to be. You can give me all the food and ammo in the world, but eventually, they're gonna run out. I can take care of myself, but I'll be able to do it a lot better if I was like you."

"Amy, it's not as simple as that. Right now you can be my fountain. But to make you my legare I would first need permission to turn you. That's a law that I must follow. If I turn you without permission, and you survive it, then one or both of us will be killed if my reason for doing it isn't accepted."

Eli explains that all vampires and the humans who know about them are required to follow the laws set by a tribunal of three elder vampires called The Synodus. The head of the Synodus is Pelagius, the oldest vampire still walking the Earth. His title is Imperator, and he maintains order over Calavius and Titus, his Proconsul and fellow Synodus members. Pelagius also has the power to make decisions without input from his Proconsul, though he rarely does it.

Amy also learns that the laws of The Synodus are enforced by a select group of vampires called regulare. Regulares are feared by the guilty because of their reputation as the harbingers of death, and they are obligated to show no mercy.

Eli makes a fist with his right hand, his knuckles facing Amy for her to see the gold signet ring on his finger. She makes out three stars arranged in a triangle on the upper half of the shield, and below them are two crossed swords. There is writing engraved on the blade of each sword. The inscription is small and a bit worn down, but Amy can make out the word PROTEGERE carved into one sword and REGULARE on the other. Eli then explains that the words on the swords mean Protect and Regulate, and he reveals that he, himself, is a regulare.

Amy sighs and says, "Fine. I understand that you enforce vampire law, so you can't break it. But you can get permission to make me a vampire, right? I can wait until then."

Eli remains silent for a moment, then he says, "Even if that happens, there's at least a twenty-five percent chance you won't survive the transformation from human to vampire."

Amy shrugs. "I'm willing to risk it."

"There are other things you have to consider. When you become a vampire, you're gonna have to make so me sacrifices.. Like, everyone you love now will eventually die-"

"They're already dead!"

Eli sighs again and gives Amy a pitiful look. "You'll also never be able to have children. Whatever makes us vampires also restricts us from procreating. That affects some vampires over time, females especially."

"That's not going to bother me. I wasn't planning on having kids, anyway."

"All right, let's say you can deal with that. Can you accept that I might have to kill you because there's a good chance that things will go wrong and I'll have to."

Struggling to control her frustration, Amy asks, "What can go wrong?"

Eli's voice takes on an even grimmer tone. "The most concerning, and potentially dangerous thing for a vampire is the unquenchable thirst for blood and the lust for power that we have to live with every day of our immortality. If you can't handle it, you'll become a rogue vampire, and you'll want to drink the blood of other, stronger vampires. And if you turn rogue, it will be up to me to make a harsh example of you."

"I'm not afraid of death, Eli," Amy says when Eli pauses to gauge if she is taking him seriously. "I don't want to die, but I'm not afraid to. If you're worried that I won't be able to control myself if you turn me, then don't be. I think I can handle the cravings. And if I don't, then screw it, kill me. I'm willing to take that risk."

Eli shakes his head. "It's a risk that doesn't bode well for you. Even though the power that we pass on to a human with our blood isn't as strong in them as it was in us, the bloodline that I belong to isn't as diminished as it is in most other vampires."

"What do you mean?"

"Think of it like a new generation whenever a vampire is made, and every new generation doesn't inherit the full power of its predecessor. So, say a tenth generation vampire is nowhere as strong as a fifth generation vampire. That being said, your problem is that I'm like a third generation vampire. That means I have dangerous blood, and it'll be harder for you to deal with if I turn you."

"Eli, it doesn't matter how dangerous your blood is, I won't let it beat me! Look, I lost my dad in an accident before I even learned how to walk. I lost my mother to alcohol long before soldiers killed her and burned her body. I lost..., everything worth living for in this world but I'm still here. Sometimes I don't know why I bother, but I keep fighting every day, and I survive. I don't know what's in your blood, but you seem to be doing just fine. So what makes you think I can't handle it, especially if it's going to be weaker?"

Eli lowers his head and shakes it. "There is way more to it than that. And I'm not saying that you can't handle what's inside of me, but you're hot blooded. That should disqualify you from the start because it indicates a lack of self-control."

Amy gets up from the tailgate and crouches down in front of Eli. She raises his glasses, looks into his eyes, then she takes his hand and says, "Please give me a chance to prove myself, Eli. I admit that I need to work on my temper, but ever since the night...."

Eli follows Amy's eyes as they drift down to the dog tags on her wrist. "Tell me about Aaron," he says.

"He was my brother," Amy responds, her voice cracking with pain. "He's the only person who ever really loved me, and I loved him more than anyone in the world."

"Did the chompers get him?"

Amy shakes her head. "No. He got back from Afghanistan a few months before the outbreak, and he was murdered by a gang of drug traffickers."

"Was he a dealer or a trafficker, too?"

"No. He had a job at a hardware store, but he sold guns on the side to help make ends meet. The bastards who killed him set him up to rob him for some Glocks that he was moving."

Eli squeezes Amy's hand. "I'm sorry about your brother. I asked because trust and honesty between a magister and his legare are important at this stage, on both sides. You told me the truth. That's a good start for us."

"Wait." Amy explodes with excitement, "Does that mean you'll do it?!"

Eli nods his head, and Amy wraps her arms around him and hugs him as hard as she can. Again she feels the remarkable heat of his body. It's much hotter than anyone she has ever touched who was suffering from a bad fever. If she had to guess, she would estimate his body temperature to be at least 105 degrees.

"Don't celebrate just yet," Eli says. "You have to spend time as my fountain first. And I can't ask The Synodus for permission to turn you until I think you're ready. It might take a month, a year, a decade; however long depends on how well you learn everything that I teach you. And you need to listen to me when I tell you something."

Amy can't see spending ten years as Eli's fountain, waiting for him to make her a vampire, but she still says, "I can do that."

"I'm serious, especially about the listening part. I lost Natasha, my last fountain because she didn't listen when I told her to stay in the truck. An infected rat hiding in a storm drain bit her while I was siphoning gas from an abandoned car. She had been with me for eight years, but after she was infected, I had no choice."

Amy nods her head, receiving his message loud and clear. Even with his warning stapled to her brain, she is still rejoicing at the new development. She didn't think that Eli would give in so easily. Her pessimistic side wonders if he is just blowing smoke up her ass, but she is willing to trust that he will keep his word.. She is hellbent on doing her part listening to everything that he says and learning all that he teaches her, all to lessen the time between her being a fountain and a legare. As for controlling the cravings that he mentioned, Amy is sure that she can prepare herself to handle the adverse effects of Eli's vampire blood. Regarding the trust part of their relationship, at least Eli says that it has to be earned on both sides. It's going to take time to trust him completely, and she is sure that the feeling is mutual.

"There's one more thing you should know," Eli says, only now returning Amy's embrace. "If I turn you, you and I are going to be linked together for life."

"Huh?"

"I mean as long as you and I are alive we'll always feel each other's presence, no matter how far apart we are. You'll feel the presence of another vampire if you make skin to skin contact, but as your magister, every cell in your body is going to feel like there's a magnetic force in it that is pulling you towards me.

That's the main reasons why the relationship between a magister and legare is so intimate. Oh, and you can forget about us ever playing hide and seek."

Amy takes a moment to consider what she has just been told. She likes Eli, but if she gets what she wants from him she'll have to accept that their relationship will essentially be till death do them part.

The embrace between them loosens and Amy glances at his torso. She is amazed at how the nub on his pec is starting to look like the nipple it once was. Using her index finger, she traces over the long, fine scar on his chest and asks, "What's up with this?"

Eli looks down at Amy's finger. "That happened the day I brought a gun to a sword fight."

"Shouldn't you have won that one? What, were you up against Zorro? I don't think Zorro was real, like Wyatt Earp and Doc Holiday, though. But if you got ganked by a dude with a sword, you probably would've had a tough time with Doc and Wyatt, anyway."

"Ha!" Eli scoffs. "Wyatt was all right with a six-gun, but even on my worst day as a human, he was no match for me. Now, Doc, he was a true gunslinger, but even he couldn't take me."

"So, you're trying to tell me you knew Wyatt Earp and Doc Holiday?"

Eli nods his head. "I played cards with Doc in Tombstone about a month before the famous gunfight. He was the kind of guy you couldn't help but like and have respect for. As for Wyatt, I bumped into him before I left town. He was kind of a prick but other than a staring contest, we didn't get into it."

"No way," Amy says, with her natural sarcasm. "Now that we're on it, just how old are you, anyway?"

Eli laughs. "I was born in eighteen-forty-nine, and I became a vampire in eighteen-sixty-eight."

Amy quickly does the math in her head as she settles on the ground and crosses her legs. Eli was 19 when he became a vampire, and altogether he's around a hundred and seventy years old.

Okay, that's it!" Amy says, eagerly. "You gotta tell me how you went from cowboy to vampire cowboy."

CHAPTER FIVE

In 1866, at the age of seventeen, Eli left his family's cattle ranch in the territory that eventually became the state of Wyoming. Burning with a rage that revenge didn't satisfy, he earned a reputation of a fearsome bounty hunter within two years. He was swift on the draw, outstandingly accurate, and blessed with a prodigious ability to track down anyone anywhere they were hiding.

Eli roved the lawless territories, accumulating a frightening body count with the two pistols he carried. One was his own, the other belonged to his murdered father. He obsessively hunted down the worst-of-the-worst criminals, gladly exercising the DEAD option of their WANTED posters. He had the fear and respect of men, the adoration of women, and he was content living his dangerous life with no promise of tomorrow. But Eli didn't start riding the wave of infamy that would have made him a legend in the old Wild West until he had a run-in with a band of Lakota warriors who refused to let him take one of their own. The few survivors of that bloody massacre described Eli as the most fearless, ferocious, black-hearted beast they had ever encountered, referring to him as Kin Wakansica Hoka: The Devil Badger. That name and Eli's exploits swept across the West like the shifting winds blowing in every direction, and he was sought out by those in need of a hired gun to do what the law couldn't, or in many cases, wouldn't.

As good as Eli was at what he did, he was not destined to leave his mark in history as the archetype for future Clint Eastwood movies. The course of his life changed on the night a woman approached him as he sat a the bar in a rowdy saloon and asked, "Are you the one they call The Devil Badger?"

It was a challenge for Eli to follow what she said because she spoke softly, with stiff lips and a German accent. He was also taken aback because she was dressed in a man's jacket, shirt, and trousers. However, the attire didn't take away from the feminine lure of her subduing hazel eyes, flawless fair skin and long red hair.

"Are you The Devil Badger?" the woman asked again.

"Yeah, that's me," Eli finally responded. "Somethin' I can do to you..., sorry, for you?"

"Mind your mouth, boy!" The burly blonde man standing behind the woman grunted in an accent similar to hers.

"Relax, Sig," the woman said, her tone calm but firm.

Eli slowly sucked his teeth as he sized up Sig. Standing at six-foot-five and built like he was carved from a mighty oak tree, Sig was easily the biggest man Eli had ever run across. Shooting him or sticking him with a knife just wouldn't do. The Devil Badger was eager to see if he could chop the big man down with his bare knuckles if Sig didn't take the woman's suggestion.

"My name is Lygia," the woman said, reclaiming Eli's attention by patting the top of his hand. "My companions and I are searching for someone we need to find as quickly as possible. We tracked him to a camp outside of Little Rock but lost him during the storm. Can you pick up on his whereabouts for us?"

"If he walks the Earth I can track him down," Eli said and gulped down the rest of his whiskey. "But what happens when you find him?"

"He dies," Lygia answered matter-of-factly. "Along with everyone with him."

Intrigued by her answer, Eli signaled the bartender to refresh his glass and bring one for Lygia—no hospitality shown towards Sig. "Tell me more..., Lygia."

Lygia explained that she and her companions were searching for the man who had killed some of their friends. She offered to pay Eli a ridiculous amount of money if he could pick up on the trail where it ran cold for them, plus a bonus if they found the killer within a few weeks. The money was three times the highest bounty that Eli ever collected, with the potential to be more. But his decision to help Lygia was driven by physical attraction and a desire to see if she had it in her to exact the revenge she wanted so badly.

What Eli didn't know at the time was that Lygia, Sig and the four other men traveling in her twelve-person entourage were regulares sent by The Synodus to find and execute a rogue vampire named Hadrianus. Unlike the rogues before him, Hadrianus' insurrection began before he gave in to the cravings and started drinking vampire blood. He wrote and secretly circulated a manifesto encouraging vampires around the world to rebel against The Synodus and stop living in the shadow of the inferior human race. By the time The Synodus caught wind of the manifesto, Hadrianus had amassed almost a hundred acolytes.

With acolytes being rounded up and regulares close to discovering his identity, Hadrianus was forced to prematurely attempt his overthrow. But the vampires loyal to Imperator Pelagius successfully defended the headquarters of The Synodus. Hadrianus and his most trusted vampire were the only rebels to escape, leaving his Acolytes behind to be slaughtered as he hightailed it in search of a place to hide and rebuild his army.

Eli only had a sketch of Hadrianus and the information Lygia gave him about the rogue's personality and tendencies. Eli relied on his instincts, and within a week he picked up on a trail that looked promising. During his time with Lygia and her companions, Eli found it strange that she and the men in her entourage all spoke with moving their lips as little as possible. They all also wore dark shaded spectacles over their eyes from dawn to dusk, and along with their guns, they each were armed with different kinds of bladed weapons.

Eli also found it interesting that Lygia was the leader of the group instead of the burly blonde Sig, who appeared to be her second in command. Lygia didn't answer many of the questions Eli was curious about, but she did promise to tell him everything he wanted to know, and more if he succeeded in finding the man they were looking for. That was fine with Eli since he was enamored with her and enjoying the amatory relationship that had ignited between them. Plus, he was confident that his quarry would not elude him.

Maintaining his reputation, within three weeks Eli proved his ability to find anyone, anywhere. Hadrianus had doubled-back east and made his way to Arkansas. There he found an old, abandoned French fort and turned the humans that he had recruited along the way into his vampire army.

Eli was itching to charge the fort with Lygia and her men, especially since they were outnumbered, but Lygia forbade him.

"You did good, Elias," Lygia said, sliding the blade of her katana into its scabbard, "but we'll take it from here."

"There's at least twenty men down there," Eli responded. "You're gonna need another gun, and I got two of 'em."

Lygia gently placed her hand on Eli's cheek. "Thank you for wanting to help, but this is a personal vendetta. What I really need is for you to stay back and protect the women."

Eli grit his teeth as he cut his eyes towards the six women traveling with Lygia and her men. Unknown to Eli at the time, they were fountains traveling with Lygia and her vampire comrades. Being told to stay behind and babysit made Eli indignant. He was only being paid to find Hadrianus, but he couldn't stay behind like he was one of the women when there was a fight to be had.

"Tell you what," Eli said and pulled Lygia's body to his. He then leaned in and kissed her with passion and a touch of aggression. Not knowing if he would ever see her again, he made sure to etch into his mind her taste, her smell, the caress of her tongue and the heat of her body. When he broke the kiss, he was pleased to see that Lygia was dumbstruck by his actions. He smiled, tipped his hat and said, "If you don't want me going down there with you, then my job's done. I'll be at the Boots Up Tavern playing cards, and I expect the rest of my payment if any of y'all live through this."

Eli turned away from Lygia and headed towards his horse without waiting for a response from her. When he mounted his stallion, he focused an intense gaze on Sig, cut his eyes to Lygia, then returned them to Sig. Understanding what Eli said without using words, Sig nodded his head and raised his own katana. Eli sucked his teeth and then rode off towards the last town that they had passed through.

After riding a couple of miles, Eli's conscience got the better of him. Lygia and her men didn't want his help but leaving them in a bad situation didn't sit right with him. And if Lygia died at the hands of the infamous Hadrianus because he turned his back on her, that would've bothered him for as long as he lived. Eli cussed himself for letting his pride sway him from doing what he knew he should have done all along, and he turned his horse around, heading back to the fort at full gallop.

As Eli approached the broken-open gates of the fort, he saw dismembered and decapitated bodies everywhere. The clamor of metal clanging from multiple sources rang out. Whoever was left alive remained engaged in an extraordinarily fast and fierce sword-fighting melee. Lygia and the other regulares had slaughtered most of Hadrianus' newly turned acolytes, losing only two of their own in the process. They had done well, so far, but they seemed to be having trouble finishing off Hadrianus and the rest.

From the anomalous speed in which everyone was moving, Eli knew that he was getting into something strange and unnatural. And even though the fact that most of the dead were armed with guns while those still standing wielded swords didn't fare well for Eli, turning back wasn't an option. He drew one of his revolvers as he entered the fort and took a shot at an acolyte, who was involved in a double team on a regulare. The bullet struck the acolyte's heart, but instead of dropping dead he turned and glared. Eli glanced at his gun in disbelief, and when he looked at the acolyte again he saw that his failed shot had created enough of a distraction for the outnumbered regulare to lob off the acolyte's head with his short sword.

Seeing the regulare now on the attack, Eli turned his attention to Lygia and Sig. They were having a hard time with Hadrianus, who had already slew one regulare and was fighting with resolution to kill at least two more. Since a bullet to the heart didn't work on the last person that he shot, Eli aimed at Hadrianus' head and squeezed the trigger. In the blink of an eye, Hadrianus dipped his head to the right as if he knew exactly when the bullet was going to impact his skull and moved out of the way. Believing that it had to be a freaky stroke of good luck, Eli decided to take another shot. He cocked his gun and suddenly felt something hit him hard on his right side. He barely had time to brace for the impact with the ground, and after a few dusty rolls he found himself looking up at the sky.

The Acolyte who tackled Eli off of his horse had instantly popped back on his feet and was bearing down on Eli with the tip of a saber aimed at his chest. With no time to think, Eli rolled to his left and shot from the hip as the blade that was about to skewer him plowed into the ground. The bullet slammed into the Acolyte's temple, and Eli saw a spray of gore blow out of the other side of his head. Lucky for Eli, and unknown to him at the time, that acolyte was made a vampire by another acolyte who was much weaker than Hadrianus. Had the acolyte been turned by Hadrianus himself, Eli's life would've ended right there.

Relieved to see his attacker fall, Eli turned back to Lygia's direction and saw Hadrianus whirling like a dust devil as he closed in on her. She backed up quickly, stumbling over a dead acolyte's legs as she narrowly avoided Hadrianus' whooshing Roman gladius.

Sig thought he had an opening and launched a death strike. For his misjudgment, Sig received three wicked gashes carved into his chest and a severed arm. Before Sig's arm hit the ground—his hand still clutching his katana—Hadrianus took his feet out from under him with a sweeping kick. Hadrianus then stepped on Sig's chest to keep him pinned to the ground as he continued parrying blows from Lygia's katana.

The three other regulares were occupied with Hadrianus' acolytes. That left Lygia alone against an opponent whom she appeared to be no match for. She was fighting for her life, and Eli knew that she wouldn't last long. He sprang to his feet, grabbed the saber that dead acolyte left stuck in the ground, and began making his way to Hadrianus as quickly and quietly as possible. Hadrianus' back was to Eli, affording Eli an opportunity to get the jump on him while he was occupied with Lygia. As he approached, Eli saw fear in Lygia's eyes as she blocked a series of sword strikes. It disturbed him when she glanced and slightly shook her head to signal that he shouldn't do what he was planning. But he continued on.

As Eli drew closer, he saw Hadrianus block a high strike from Lygia's katana then turn his gladius downward and drive the blade into Lygia's shoulder, sinking it deep into her torso as she screamed in pain. Lygia involuntarily let go of her katana and dropped to her knees, her face wincing in agony as Hadrianus twisted his blade inside of her.

Fearing that he was too late, Eli quickened his pace and leaped into the air with the saber held high above his head. He brought the blade down with all his might, intending to bury it in Hadrianus' skull.

Hadrianus twisted his body and leaned back as he withdrew his sword from Lygia. In a quick counter strike, he sent the blade plunging into Eli, running through him until the hilt slapped against Eli's skin.

Hadrianus held Eli suspended off the ground as he stared into his eyes, puzzled as to who he was and why he attacked him. As for Eli, he felt as if his chest was on fire and the blaze was spreading throughout his body with each painful thunder of his heart. He glanced at Lygia and saw her fighting through her pain as she struggled to reach for her katana. Hadrianus read the worry in Eli's eyes and flashed an evil smile, revealing a set of fangs that Eli thought belonged in the mouth of an animal.

Logically thinking that he wouldn't have long to live after receiving such a mortal wound, Eli knew that he had to do something fast if he was going to take Hadrianus with him. He rallied against the oncoming effects of shock and howled as he forced his right hand to raise the saber high as he possibly could.

Before the sword was raised halfway up, Hadrianus seized Eli's forearm and squeezed with enough force to crack the bones under his grip. The saber fell to the ground, and Eli hawked a bloody gob of spit and mucus into Hadrianus' eyes.

Lygia rose up, swinging her katana as she wailed like a banshee.

Hadrianus yanked his gladius out of Eli's chest.

Eli gripped the revolver in the holster on his left side and cocked it.

Hadrianus was quick enough with his sword to save his neck from the wrath carried through Lygia's blade, and he followed up with a kick to her gut.

As Lygia was launched across the sandy courtyard, Eli raised his gun high enough for the muzzle to be inches under Hadrianus' chin and he didn't waste a second squeezing the trigger. Hadrianus tried to rock his head back, but the bullet hit his jaw and popped out of his cranium.

Eli laughed as he and Hadrianus crashed to the ground. His gamble to shoot at close range, his aim in anticipation of Hadrianus' attempt to dodge another bullet, had paid off. Hadrianus was fast, but his fantastic speed wasn't much of a factor at almost point-blank range. Eli was in pain and felt like he was burning alive, but he was relishing the victory.

Sig got up and nodded at Eli with respect. Eli nodded back. Eli's demise appeared imminent, so neither men knew at the time that they had just laid the foundation of their brotherhood, instead of bidding each other farewell. Sig removed the katana from the fingers of his severed limb then hurried to help his friends finish off the acolytes.. Moments after that Lygia appeared, nursing her wounds.

Lygia looked at the blood staining Hadrianus' sword, now a combination of hers and Eli's. A warm smile grew on her face, and for the first time, Eli got a clear look at Lygia's teeth. Seeing that she had fangs like those in Hadrianus' mouth didn't surprise him, not after all that he had witnessed since riding into the fort.

"You can't leave me twice in one day," Lygia said, settling next to Eli.

"I shouldn't have left," Eli rasped and coughed up some blood. "I'm sorry. I wanted more time with you, but I don't know how much longer I got."

Lygia lifted Eli's head and laid it in her lap. Then she leaned in and kissed him. He tasted blood in her mouth, but he didn't care. Eli enjoyed the bliss until the pleasure was overruled by the torturous inferno growing within his body.

"You are strong, Elias," Lygia said, finally removing her mouth from his, "and you don't know how to stop fighting. That's good. Now I need you to fight death and beat it for me. Do that, and I promise we'll have all the time in the world together."

Eli wanted an eternity with Lygia, but he didn't know how to beat death.

The best he could do was hold on to the image of her face smiling down at him with bloody lips, and everything else that he liked about her. The pain grew intense. He felt like he was on fire on the inside, from his toes up to his brain. The torture made him feel like he should welcome death, but the part of him that was in love with Lygia refused to let go as he closed his eyes for the last time as a human.

CHAPTER SIX

Amy braces herself for impact as the Bronco's engine growls like an angry beast. The ram bar on the front of the SUV hits with a rapid series of thunks, sending bodies and body parts flying like bowling pins. One of the chompers' head rolls up the hood and bounces off the metal strips protecting the windshield. Amy was able to make out the snarling face on it before it went spinning into the night, a blonde girl with braces who looked like she was still going through puberty.

Amy remembers reading something about the human brain not dying instantly after it is separated from the body. There are at least ten to twelve seconds before it slips into unconsciousness. It's not the same for chompers. Their heads and bodies remain animated for some time after decapitation, but they will eventually die. Amy thinks about the blond girl who was just detached from her body. It's a shame for such a young life to be cut so short, but the girl was all but dead long before she kissed the ram bar of the Bronco. At least she won't have to live such a miserable existence for much longer.

"Sorry about that," Eli says and switches off the Bronco's headlights. "Now, you were about to tell me what you've learned so far about blood."

"Okay," Amy says, eager to show Eli that she has been paying attention to all that he has told her. "Obviously, a vampire needs to feed on blood. The longer they go without it, the weaker they get, and the slower they heal. Blood outside of a body more than a few minutes is useless to a vampire because there's an undetectable form of energy within blood cells that dissipates after it is drawn. That energy is absorbed by the altered energy of the vampire who consumes it. And as far as the altered energy in a vampire goes, it is dependent on the body's electrical system, particularly the, ah... Reticular Activating System in the brain."

Eli nods his head. "Continue."

"If a vampire goes an extremely long time without feeding on blood they, either voluntarily or involuntarily, go into a state of hibernation that mimics death."

"Very good," Eli says, approvingly. "Now remember, blood is blood. It's frowned upon to drink from an animal, but no one's going to blame you if you suck a rat dry in an emergency. But you must never drink the blood of another vampire. Never!"

Eli sternly warns Amy that she must follow this law of The Synodus without question. Even if she is starving to death, it will be better to go into hibernation because drinking another vampire's blood will get her killed if she is found out. Then Eli explains that if a vampire were to drink the blood of another, they could receive sustenance from just a little bit of it, but it can become addictive and lead to the most dangerous thing to the vampires' secret society, as well as the human race: A rogue vampire. And a vampire who ingests a large amount of a stronger vampire's blood will acquire the power and energy within that blood, as well as an increased lust for more blood and power. If they cannot resist the increased craving, it leads to loss of self-control which will inevitably foster a desire for total domination of both the vampire and human worlds. Once a vampire goes rogue, he or she becomes the top priority on a regulare's to-do list.

In centuries past, vampires who fed on other vampires went rogue and turned humans who were willing to serve them with blind loyalty into vampire subjects, and they subjugated ancient civilizations. Some of the captives were blessed with the privilege of becoming a vampire in exchange for them overseeing the bondage of the other humans, and the rogue vampire was worshipped as a god. The humans were regarded as livestock, used for labor and a steady supply of blood. This led to wars with the vampires who believed that they were better off if humans didn't know of their existence because the humans greatly outnumbered them and they always resisted captivity. The rogue vampires always eventually lost, but whole civilizations were wiped from the face of the planet in the aftermath. The ruins of some of those ancient civilizations still haven't been discovered yet. As for the ones that have been unearthed, archaeologists can only speculate about what led to their destruction, as well as the disappearance of all its people.

"A rogue vampire is more dangerous in this day and age," Eli says. "Exposure could lead to extinction since there are only a couple thousand vampires and billions of humans, especially since humans have the weapons and technology to eradicate every living thing on this planet, themselves included."

Amy recalls a radio broadcast she heard before the airwaves went silent. "A while ago I heard that because of the way different hot spots popped up during the first twenty-four hours of the pandemic, it was let loose on us intentionally by terrorists or something," she says. "You know anything more about that?"

Eli shakes his head. "During the first twenty-four, I was in Seattle tracking an acolyte leader. After that my orders were to round as many vampires and their fountains as I could and make sure they were in a safe place. Then I was ordered to go to Lygia and protect her. When we find her, we'll be able to find out everything that the CDC knows about the virus, including where it might've come from."

"Can't wait to meet your beautiful and brilliant magister," Amy says, with more sarcasm than she intended.

Eli's responds only with a smile and Amy wants to kick herself for being jealous of the relationship that Eli has with his maker. Lygia is more than the vampire whose blood gave Eli immortality and connected them for as long as both are alive. She also has an adopted human daughter, Kristin, whom Eli is like a father to.

Lygia is also the equivalent of vampire royalty since she is the biological daughter of the Imperator, Pelagius. She is one of the only two vampires made by the Imperator. One of his Proconsul, Calavius, is the other. And since Eli was turned from her blood, he is considerably more powerful than most other vampires. His strength is equal to the few vampires that are legares of Calavius, including the third member of The Synodus: Titus. Many of the older vampires harbor animosity towards Eli because of his place in the bloodline and the close relationship that he has with the Imperator and his daughter, but no one dares to openly speak out against him.

Amy stares into the darkness outside of the windshield and thinks about the day she will be able to see in the dark like Eli says he can. Actually, she wishes that she already had all of his powers. He's incredibly strong and fast, especially when he's had his fill of blood. His bones are almost as tough as steel, and all of his sense are heightened. He has a keen sense of hearing that is as acute as his ability to smell like a bloodhound. And his sense of touch parallels extra sensory perception since he has the ability to feel his surroundings by picking up the vibrations around him and practically visualize the scene.

"So," Amy says, "when are you going to snack on me again?"

"I'm going to try to hold out for a couple days... unless somebody shoots me again."

Amy giggles and slugs Eli in the arm, letting her knuckle rest against his bicep. She has made physical contact with him a few times since he pinned her to the ground and drank from her, but the heat radiating from his body still fascinates her.

Eli smiles from the interaction with Amy, but his expression suddenly changes. "Shhhit!" he hisses, shutting the engine off and letting the Bronco coasts off to the side of the road.

"What's up?" Amy asks.

"A chopper, heading this way."

Since military aircraft are the only ones in the sky, Amy knows that the chopper is probably a patrol. That's not good. She needs to avoid the military at all cost, and she isn't ready to tell Eli the reason why.

Eli hits the brake and reaches into the back of the Bronco for his AK-47. "Get out and get under the truck!"

Amy follows his order without question. If Eli wants to avoid the military, too, that's fine with her. She gets out of the Bronco and slams the door at the same time as Eli, then she hits the ground and rolls until she and Eli bump into each other. Because of the huge size of the tires on the Bronco, there is plenty of headroom underneath the truck. There is ample space, too, but she and Eli remain shoulder to shoulder as they listen. It takes a moment, but eventually, she hears the faint whoop-whoop-whoop of rotor bladed dicing the air.

"So, what are we doing down here?" Amy whispers, as if the crew on the chopper are endowed with super-hearing.

Eli lays the AK-47 over Amy's body and removes one of his Desert Eagles from its holster. "If they're equipped with a FLIR, they'll see the heat from my engine and swing over to check us out. Since my body temp's a little over a hundred degrees they'll think I'm infected, and I really would like to avoid that, if possible."

"Cool," Amy says, gripping the AK-47 like a war-hardened Marine. "I got your back.

"Thanks, but I can handle a few soldiers in a chopper. You just hold on to the A-K, just in case."

The words "just in case" makes Amy realize that she is out in the open—at night. The mosquito population has been sprayed to within an inch of extinction, but the chompers made from the people they transferred the infection to aren't. And night time is their prime time.

Amy looks to the left and surveys the landscape on her side. Her vision isn't great, but she thinks she sees a field beyond the trees and shrubs lining the roadside. She should be able to see chompers approaching long before that make it to the truck. She's more worried about the chompers a couple miles down the road who survived being mowed down by the Bronco. This situation is her best argument why Eli should go ahead and turn her into a vampire now and explain the rules later. But that's an argument that she doesn't expect to win against a regulare loyal to the all-powerful Synodus.

As time passes, Amy can't tell if the chopper is heading their way or flying circles around them. There are times when the sound of its spinning blades gets louder, only to fade without completely going away. She trusts that Eli is able to tell what the damn thing is doing, but he has been silent and still.

Finally, out of frustration, Amy says, "What the hell are they up to?"

"Seems like they're flying in a big circle," Eli responds. "I don't know if they're looking for something, or what. But at least they're miles away, for now."

"Think maybe they got a distress call from some of the militiamen? I know this is quite a ways from one of their strongholds, but the dumb bastards actually go out on chomper hunting safaris.”

"Could be,” Eli responds. "But we're stuck here until that chopper leaves and, well, you want the good news or the bad news first?”

"Bad.”

"We got chompers coming up on your side.”

"And the good news?!” Amy says as she turns to her right to search for a swarm.

"There's only three of them.”

"You sure they're chompers? I mean, only three of 'em? That's a pretty small pack.”

"Yeah, they're chompers. They stink like all hell. Maybe they got separated from their clique?”

"Whadda we do?”

Eli lays his Desert Eagle on his crotch, then he wiggles on the ground as he lifts his shirt up over his head. After he has the shirt off, he wraps it around the barrel of his gun, as he says to Amy, "Get on top of me.”

That was the last thing Amy expected Eli to say. Without questioning it, though, she lays the assault rifle on the ground, turns over onto her stomach and creeps like a crab until she is laying on top of Eli. It's a tighter fit under the Bronco now, but there is still space between her body and the undercarriage. Amy rests her head on Eli's chest and she looks in the direction that he told her the chompers would be coming from.

Eli extends his gun-hand, only but so much. He keeps a bend in his arm that doesn't allow the muzzle of the Desert Eagle to come close to poking out from under the Bronco. Amy recognizes that he wants to keep the muzzle flash as concealed as possible. It's the same reason he wrapped his shirt around the gun. The layers of cloth around the muzzle should dampen the flash and hot gasses that the gun is going to spit when it shoots.

Silently they watch and wait. Amy is anxious about what might happen next. She is also surprised to find herself physically reacting to laying on top of Eli's hot body. No sooner than she acknowledges her arousal, she feels a part of Eli grow and stiffen under her. For the life of her, she can't figure out why her body seems to have had a mind of its own lately. She remembers hearing that dangerous situations can intensify the attraction between two people. She figures that has to be the answer. Either that or her menstruation cycle is responsible for her steadily increasing lust.

"Are you squeamish?” Eli whispers.

Thinking that she is being set up for a joke about Eli's genitalia or a possible introduction to it, Amy cautiously whispers back, "No. Why?”

"There's something small, with eight legs, coming towards us. I'm pretty sure it's a scorpion.”

"Son. Of. A. Bitch!” Amy says through clenched teeth, as the heat in her privates subside. "What do we do?”

Eli snakes his hand across Amy's back, and he holds her in a comforting embrace. "If it crawls over us, stay still and be very quiet. It shouldn't attack if it doesn't feel threatened."

"Yeah, easy for you to say. What if it's infected with the virus like the mosquitoes were?"

Eli's stomach trembles, like he is trying hard to hold in a laugh. "It's not, I would've smelled it."

"You can smell the virus, too?"

"Viruses, cancers, all that good stuff. The Puissance virus has a really weird smell, too. It reminds me of baking soda, cheddar cheese, and chicken livers."

"You didn't you tell me this before?"

"You were asking so many questions, I didn't really get a chance to bring it up 'til now."

"Anything else you'd like to tell me?"

"Yeah," Eli says. "We should do that staying still and quiet thing now. The scorpion's crawling up my shoulder."

Amy seals her lips and takes the shallowest of breaths. She waits for what starts feeling like an eon, anticipating a prickly footfall traipsing over her skin. Not being a typical girly-girl, she isn't afraid of scorpions or spiders. But her rule concerning them is: she doesn't bother them, they don't bother her. Now one of the little bastards is breaking that rule, and it couldn't have picked a worse time.

As she waits for the creepy-crawly to breach her personal space, Amy tries to use the scarce light of the quarter moon to help her keep a watchful eye on the field. She begins to doubt that she will be able to see the chompers coming until they're dangerously close to the Bronco, but something does catch her eyes. At first, she thinks that her mind is playing tricks on her. The more she focuses on the object, the more she can distinguish what looks like a little black ball barely standing out against the darkness. The object is about the distance of two football field's away, which will put it in the middle of the field if she is seeing correctly.

Amy's brain puts two-and-two together, and the image that she is seeing suddenly makes sense. What she thought was a flat expanse of field is actually the top of a hill, and a chomper is now coming over it. The chomper's movement is slow, like its wandering, but soon its body slowly rises like a creature emerging from the Black Lagoon. She darts her eyes back up at Eli and almost gasps when she sees the pincers of the scorpion extended over the ridge of his chin. The arachnid languidly turns in a semicircle The arachnid languidly turns in a semicircle over Eli's lips, giving Amy a good view of its long, flat body. She quickly shifts her gaze to the field and now sees two chomper bodies, plus one more rising. She looks back up and strains her eyes to make out the wicked curve of the scorpion's tail, with the stinger hovering above right above its head.

The far-off sound of the chopper blades is now more steady than it was before. Amy considers closing her eyes, but she would rather keep them on the scorpion's outline. If it stings her, she would rather see it coming. That notion gets a second thought when she imagines the sight of the stinger flying towards her eye. Just the thought of the stinger's pointy tip piercing her cornea and injecting venom in her eye is enough to make her cringe. But she decides that if she is meant to lose an eye, then that's what will happen. Of course, Eli could save her from that fate if he just opens his mouth and eats the damn thing. Regardless, she refuses to stare at the back of her eyelids when there is a scorpion and chompers to keep sight of.

Amy checks on the chompers again, trying to discern what they are doing. Their movements remind her of the coyotes outside of the farmhouse, causing her to think they are searching for something that they know is there but can't see. At least not yet.

The scorpion finally stops dancing on Eli's face, and it begins to amble down towards his right cheek. Amy loses sight of it when it descends down Eli's neck until it reappears when it stops on his shoulder. At least she can keep an eye on the scorpion and the chompers at the same time, which is good because there is no doubt about it now, they know where she and Eli are, and they're coming.

She shifts her eyes back to Eli's gun-hand. He looks poised to fire, only waiting for the right time to hit the chompers with the angled line of fire that he is limited to. As the harrowing seconds proceed, the scorpion moves from Eli's shoulder and begins to traverse the curve of his bicep. With only a few more steps to go before the scorpion reaches the bend of Eli's elbow, it stops. The scorpion appears to be leery about something, and it cautiously turns towards Amy.

A roaring sound, like a jet engine, shakes up the night. Mere moments later, the ground quakes and the Bronco rocks as the thunder of a detonation seizes the night, along with a pillar of fire lighting up the sky.

The spooked arachnid leaps from Eli's arm to seek refuge deeper under the cover of the Bronco and Amy braces herself for a face full of scorpion. In a flash that she almost doesn't see, the hand that Eli had been reassuringly holding her shoulder with jerks and catches the scorpion in mid-flight. Amy hears a soft crunch inside of Eli's tightening fist, and she smiles when she sees the scorpion's mangled body drop to the ground when he opens his hand.

Another explosion rocks the night, and Eli says, "Cover up your ears."

Amy slaps her palms against her ears, and the Desert Eagle booms as Eli fires a bullet that tears through the shirt wrapped around its muzzle. Instantly the head of the chomper crossing the tree line snaps backwards. The cloth around the muzzle ignites as the dead chomper falls backwards, and Eli fires two more shots. Those bullets strike the knees of the chomper behind his fallen comrade, and he drops to the ground like he suddenly wants to pray. Eli fires another shot that hits the chomper dead-on, ending its miserable life. As the chomper falls over, Eli jostles his arm to slip more of the shirt down over his gun, and he allows it to burn as he waits for a shot. Amy looks down the length of Eli's arm, and she can see that he is waiting for the chomper to clear the tree in front of its path. Thinking in the frame of mind of a shooter, she bends her finger the instant that Eli fires two more rounds, ending this present chomper problem.

"You know," Eli says, vigorously rubbing his gun and shirt in the dirt to put out the fire, "I done lost two good shirts in the nine hours since meeting you."

Even though her ears are ringing, Amy hears Eli, and she laughs. "So sue me."

"Smart ass."

Amy giggles. "What the hell were those explosions?"

"Missiles," Eli responds, now using his smoking shirt to wipe scorpion guts from his hand. "They came in fast from the south. I don't know what kind, but they were really heavy duty. I think it's safe to say whoever's in the chopper found what they were looking for. They were circling an area for a while before half of hell fell on it."

"The last time the radio worked, a report said that they were planning to bomb chompers gathered in large numbers. Maybe they got intel on a big swarm and decided to pound 'em?"

"Could be, but with millions of chompers running around, that's a lot of bombing."

"What's the chopper doing?" Amy asks.

"Right now they're just hovering. Hopefully, they've completed their mission and will be going away soon."

"Oh god, don't tell me we got more chompers coming."

"Nah, we're good for now. I'd just rather they go away so we can get back on the road. But it's not like I'm complaining. This feels... nice."

Amy smiles, but she doesn't respond with words. Now that the danger is gone and Eli's pass has reminded her about the position that they're in, her body is starting to misbehave again. And as Eli said it does feel "nice". In a way, she is thankful there isn't enough room for them to kiss with her laying on top of him. If Eli were to move in to kiss her right now, she doesn't think she would deny him her lips. But anything more than that just wouldn't happen. She would be too mortified to have sex while she's on her period, and having sex underneath the Bronco multiplies that notion.

For now, Amy is content with letting go of her standoffish nature and enjoying the moment. As she listens to the chopper blades, waiting for the aircraft to go away, she closes her eyes and fantasizes about what her life is going to be like with Eli, as a human and as a vampire.

CHAPTER SEVEN

"Mmmm," Amy moans as she awakens. She nudges the brim of Eli's cowboy hat up from her face to see where they are and ends growling as she pulls the hat back down.

"What's that about?" Eli asks and slams the hood of the Bronco shut.

"The stupid sun! I frickin' hate bright light in my eyes when I wake up."

Eli laughs as he wipes oil and grime from his hands with a dingy rag, damp with gasoline. "Spoken like a true vampire. Open the glove box. There's an extra pair of shades that you can use."

Amy opens the compartment and takes a quick mental inventory of the items inside. There are wraparound sunglasses, just like the one Eli is wearing. Also some papers in a plastic folder, most likely the Bronco's registration, insurance, and other pertinent information. Eli's satellite phone, which he hasn't been able to acquire a signal on for weeks gone by. Rounding out the items are a ruggedized flashlight, a bottle of rubbing alcohol, a small black leather case, a black semiautomatic handgun, and two fully loaded magazines.

Amy disregards the glasses and reaches for the gun. "This is pretty."

"Nine millimeter Beretta. Sixteen in the clip, plus one in the chamber. I had given it to Natasha, but she never liked guns. It's yours if you want it?"

"Seriously?"

"Yeah. It never hurts to have one more, right?"

"Fuckin' A!" Amy says, admiring her new chomper-killer. She glances over to the glove box to see if the spare magazines are for the Beretta, and she becomes curious about the black leather case. "What's this?"

"Go ahead and open it."

Amy unzips the case and her eyes zoom in on the long, gleaming needle on something that looks like a syringe. Instead of a plunger on the top of the syringe, there is a hose that runs to a transparent sphere that is the size of a fist, which has two other hoses coming out from the opposite side. One of those two hoses leads to a rubber bulb, like ones that pump up the cuff when the doctor takes your blood pressure, and the other hose is left open-ended. Amy can't figure out what the contraption is, but it makes her think of a heroin user's science experiment gone bad.

"It's a siphon," Eli explains. "It's not necessary to bite a fountain everytime we feed. Some fountains are into it, but we'd rather not have a bunch of people walking around with fang holes in their necks."

"Like these?" Amy says, turning her head for Eli to see his handy work."

"Yeah..., again, sorry about that."

"Don't sweat it. Ahh, since we have this out, do you need me for breakfast?"

"No, I don't need to feed right now. I got a taste for a cup of coffee, though. Want some?"

"Coffee? God, yes!" Amy gets out of the truck and slips the Beretta into her waistband. Then she stares at the back of what she guesses is a garage because of the stacks of old tires, drums of dirty oil, and rusted vehicle parts strewn about the yard. "Where are we?"

"Not far from Waco. I drove all night until the engine started overheating."

"The radiator?"

"Nah, that looks okay. I think the thermostat is getting a little wonky on me. I thought I got lucky when I found this 'Last Chance' gas station-slash-garage but somebody already made off with all the stock and tools. So I cleaned out the thermostat as good as I could, and we're just going to have to take it easy until I find a replacement for it."

Amy takes a seat on top of a weather-beaten picnic table and continues to look around. She has no idea what time it is, but she feels like it's still early morning. That brings back memories of walking to school with Aaron. Every day they would stop at a small mom-and-pop grocery store where Aaron would buy her a Charms sour apple Blow Pop, her favorite. Amy never got a chance to properly grieve for Aaron after he was murdered, and she still regrets not being able to go to his funeral.

To fight the pain welling up inside, Amy imagines what this apocalypse would be like if Aaron hadn't died. She pictures them flipping coins to see who gets to shoot chompers from a sniper's perch set up on the roof of their house. Aaron's marksmanship was exceptional before he joined the Marines because of the things their father taught him while hunting. Since a head-on collision with a tractor-trailer took their father away from them before Amy could form memories of him, Aaron passed the knowledge on to her, as well as what learned during his enlistment.

On the same day that Aaron was killed, he and Amy had been shooting cans with the M-16 that he kept at the house. For the first time, she didn't miss a single can with the assault rifle at maximum range, and Aaron had mussed her hair while proudly smiling at her. Nine hours later she found his bullet-riddled body inside of his pickup. Rather than focusing on that image, she fondly recalls his laughter that day and his proud smile.

"What's on your mind?" Eli asks, holding out a cup for her to take.

Not wanting to share those private thoughts, at least not yet, Amy takes the cup and sips some coffee. She savors a taste that she hasn't had in about a month, then she looks at Eli and says, "I had a dream about you last night."

"Yeah?" Eli takes a seat next to her and scoots up close. "Tell me about it."

Amy smiles. "I dreamt you and some guy who was supposed to be Billy the Kid got into one of those high-noon shootouts."

"I take it I won?"

"Well, you let him shoot you in the chest a few times and just stood there smiling your ass off. Billy looked at his smoking gun and was like, 'what the hell?' and that's when you plugged him right between the eyes."

"Sounds 'bout right," Eli says, with a big smile. "So what brought on that little dream?"

Amy shrugs. "Probably because I was thinking about you being a regulare before I fell asleep. It occurred to me that you must've loved it when the movie *Young Guns* came out. You know, Regulatoooors!"

Eli laughs. "Yeah, I did get a kick out of that."

"Since you played cards with Doc Holiday and bumped into Wyatt Erp, I suppose you met the real Billy the Kid, too?"

"Nah. I was still in Mexico when the Kid was making a name for himself."

"Mexico? What were you doing down there?"

After defeating Hadrianus, Lygia took Eli to The Civitas—a mansion in Michigan with subterranean levels that served as headquarters for The Synodus. There they had to stand before The Imperator, Pelagius, and his Proconsul. Lygia had to take responsibility for Eli and explain why he became a vampire without permission from The Synodus. When his part in Hadrianus' downfall was revealed, with emphasis on Lygia's blood already being on the blade that pierced Eli's heart, Lygia was exonerated of her crime and Eli was accepted as a vampire.. Lygia, Sig and the other regulares were honored for their triumph. Eli also received veneration, and with the passionate case that Lygia made on his behalf, he was granted permission to begin training to become a regulare.

For five years after that, Lygia and Sig put Eli through an intense training program to build his martial arts skills. He also trained with bladed weapons, becoming most proficient with the katar. During that time, Pelagius took an interest in Eli and personally taught him everything that he needed to know about being a vampire and a regulare. Eli put his heart and soul into becoming a regulare, and it wasn't long before he was as good as the best of them, even the ones who had been around for hundreds or thousands of years.

After Eli was officially in the regulare's ranks, Pelagius gave Lygia an assignment to continue an ongoing quest to compile vampire history and search for the origin of vampires. Eli's was assigned to protect her and her team. For nine years they traveled throughout America, interviewing the Elders of Native American tribes as they searched for vampire lore, artifacts, records, anything that could lead them to the whereabouts or remains of the first vampire.

Following information Lygia received from Maya glyphs about a vampire who saved the life of a chief around 900 A.D., she moved the search down to Mexico. They explored the jungle in the Yucatán for years until they found a lost temple containing a wealth of information on the vampire that the Maya tribe called Fire Skin. Then Eli and Lygia moved on to other places around the world. Together they searched for ancient vampires and artifacts until the 1950's when Lygia turned her attention to science and Eli went back to work full time for The Synodus. Right around the same time, whispers of Hadrianus' beliefs began circulating again, spawning modern-day acolytes.

Amy thinks about all the places that Eli and Lygia explored over the course of decades. Before The Puissance virus, she had never been outside of New Mexico, and she can imagine how great it must have been to explore South America, the Caribbean Islands, Europe, Asia, as well as Africa and Australia.

"What's the coolest thing you and Lygia found when you were exploring?" Amy asks.

"Well," Eli responds, rubbing the stubble on his jaw, "when we were in Australia we discovered a series of rock paintings deep in a cave in a place called Bullita. The first painting was of a diamond-shaped thing in the sky that looked like it was glowing, and it had a snake coming out of the center of it. The next picture showed the snake being swallowed by a figure shaped like a man. The one after that showed the man with fangs hovering in the sky as a bunch of other figures on the ground worshipped him. The Synodus sent a team to remove the paintings and bring them back to The Civitas, where their scholars studied it and compared it to a scroll found hundreds of years ago in Saudi Arabia that has a similar fanged creature on it. They couldn't say conclusively what the diamond and the snake are; if they're just symbolism or a record of something that really happened. But they did agree that the Saudi scroll corroborates their belief that the man in the painting is The Primus..., the first vampire. The only problem is that no one has ever been able to decipher the writing on the scroll, so there's still unanswered questions. Regardless, the scientist working for The Synodus carbon dated the paint on the rock and determined that it is the oldest record that we have of The Primus."

"So you brought back the oldest record of a vampire, huh? You musta got some serious brownie points for that one?"

"I got a good pat on the back, but the thing that really gave The Synodus stiffies was when I found the ancient vampire who turned Pelagius."

"You actually found the magister of The Imperitor?"

"Yeah. The last name that he went by was Anaximenes. He was one of the few survivors from the island of Crete after a series of massive tidal waves all but wiped out the Minoans around sixteen-hundred B.C.. From what I understand, he had been around for thousands of years before that, so he's pretty frickin' old."

"Man, I would love to have a conversation with that dude."

Eli chuckles. "So would everybody else. We don't know why, but he buried himself and went into a deep hibernation shortly after he turned Pelagius and taught him how to live as a vampire. I don't know what he looked like way back then, but when I found him, he looked like a mummy..., with a skull that's a little smaller than the average human's."

"Is he still alive?"

"There's faint electrical activity in his brain, and of course, you know...?"

"As long as there's blood and electrical activity in the brain," Amy answers, "a vampire will live."

"That's my girl. Anyway, The Synodus calls Anaximenes and the other ancient ones like him senexes. They hope that he will awaken one day, or at least give some sign that he wants to wake up. We know that there are other senexes buried out there somewhere, but it's forbidden to disturb them since they chose to sleep instead of live among us."

Amy nods her head, then an interesting question strikes her. "Eli, how did you find him, Anaximenes?"

Eli shrugs. "I've always been good at finding people and things, especially when I have information to work with. Lygia thinks I have some sort of ESP, but there's nothing really special about it."

Amy takes in all that Eli has told her. He had lived the most interesting life, before and after he became a vampire, and she finds all of his exploits completely fascinating. She can't help but feel fortunate that this special vampire will be the one who makes her into one of them. If not for chompers ruining the world, she could be off on awesome adventures with Eli. Instead, they are on their way to find his old-old flame, hoping that she will be the savior of both, human and vampire kind.

"Can I ask you something about you and Lygia?" Amy asks.

"Yeah, I don't mind."

"Are you still in love with her?"

Eli shakes his head. "I will always love Lygia, but I'm not in love with her anymore. I'll always be connected to her since she's my magister. And since Kristin is-"

Amy's hand finds the handle of her new gun, but she doesn't remove it from her waistband just yet. As much as she wants to hear Eli finish what he was saying, something serious must have blipped on his vampire radar because he has closed his eyes and has his head cocked to one side as if he's concentrating on listening to something.

"You hear something?" Amy asks.

Eli nods. "Engines. Small ones. Four of 'em. Maybe motorcycles or-"

"ATVs?"

Eli nods again. "Could be both."

"Militiamen?"

"Unless chompers have learned to ride, that'd be my best guess. And if they're militia, things are going to get hairy."

CHAPTER EIGHT

Amy cusses under her breath. ATVs are one of the vehicles commonly used by militiamen. They ride them when they're out on patrols or escorting supply trucks. Between militiamen, soldiers, and chompers, she harbors the most disdain for the militia. During the first days of the outbreak when news reports warned of crazed people infected by a new virus, the militiamen helped the police fill in the gaps that they couldn't protect—mostly communities that were in the lower tax brackets. At that time they were thought of as heroes, but Amy's pre-existing opinion of them led her to believe that they were just crazy gun-nuts abusing an authority that they didn't really have. She didn't like them then, and after the mosquitoes exploded The Puissance virus upon the population, she found reasons to regard them as scum, lower than any mindless chomper.

No more than two weeks have gone by since she was checking out a farm near Amarillo, Texas. Hidden at the edge of a field of pecan trees, Amy watched the farmhouse through binoculars and discovered that the family was still there. While debating if she could sneak up to the house to swipe some food she heard motorcycle and truck engines approaching. Not wanting to blow her cover, she decided to stay where she was until the visitors left. The things that she ended up witnessing a group of militiamen do made her shed tears of sorrow and anger. The Emergency Broadcasts eventually warned women who were still outside of the safe zones of what could happen to them, but by that time it was too late for the woman and her daughters. And Amy has been living with guilt for not helping them, regardless of being outgunned and low on bullets.

"They're still a ways off," Eli says, looking at the tracks curving around the garage that were left by the Bronco. "Chances are they'll spot those and want to check it out."

Amy considers their options, and it's not long before she begins to hear the drone of the vehicles in the distance. "I hate the militiamen. And to tell you the truth, if we get into it with them I'm gonna shoot to kill."

"Why else would you shoot?"

Amy follows Eli to the back of the Bronco and together they efficiently gear up for a fight. She releases the clip on the Beretta and checks to see if it is fully loaded. After finding the magazine stacked with rounds, she slaps it back into the handle of the gun then she pulls the slide back far enough to see a chambered round all ready to go. She makes sure that the safety is off and Eli passes her the two extra clips for her 9-mm, then he shoves extras for his Desert Eagles into his pocket. It occurs to Amy that, unless the militiamen are circus performers, there can't be more than two of them on one bike. As good as Eli is, he only needs eight shots maximum to deal with two people on four bikes. And since she's no slouch with a firearm, either, she knows that she doesn't need all the bullets that she is packing. It makes her feel like she's wearing a prom dress to the pool hall.

"You know you'll be safer in the truck," Eli says, slipping his katars into the scabbards strapped to his thighs. "If things get hot, I can take care of it by myself."

"Aw c'mon!" Amy replies. "I can handle a shootout. Trust me, I got your back!"

"Have you ever been in a shootout? This isn't the movies. All of the bullets don't miraculously miss the heroes."

Amy bites her tongue, then says, "I know I can do this. Give me a chance to prove myself."

Eli brandishes an admiring smile. "Have I told you that I really like you?"

"Between meeting you yesterday, me shooting you, you biting me, helicopters, scorpions and bombs blowing shit up at night, it never came up."

Eli grins. "Maybe I should take off my shirt now before I lose this one, too?"

Amy checks out Eli's vintage Lynyrd Skynyrd T-shirt. An old man joke forms in her mind, but before it reaches her tongue, the sound of the bike engines suddenly stop.

Eli's brow furrows.

The silence is like concrete filling a grave, and Amy gets a bad feeling.

Less than a minute goes by, and with urgency, Eli says, "Get in the truck!"

"But-"

"Do as I say! Now!"

Amy's anger in response to Eli yelling at her is only quelled by her promise to listen to him. Reluctantly, and grumbling under her breath, she stomps over to the driver's side of the Bronco. When she gets in she slams the door, which makes Eli cringe like he really wishes she didn't do that.

As Amy sulks in the driver's seat, Eli gives her a nod that conveys an apology. Then he withdraws both of his katars, instead of his guns, and he steps backwards away from the Bronco until his back is pressed against the wall of the garage. Amy erratically darts her eyes from one end of the garage to the other, finding nothing but sure Eli's body language indicates that trouble is going to come from around both corners.

In a loud and authoritative voice, Eli says, "Unless you want to die today, I suggest you show yourselves!"

Amy continues to glance at both corners with her adrenaline pumping. A few more second s go by and the muzzle of an automatic rifle appears on the right side of the garage, slowly growing into the body of an AR-15. Amy sticks her hand through the metal slats in the Bronco's window and trains the Beretta on the young girl with cornrows braided in her hair who emerges from around the corner.

The girl's brown skin is glistening with sweat. Her camouflage tank top doesn't have a prayer of concealing the swell of her ample breasts, and her denim cut-offs showcase her curvy hips and luscious thighs. Amy can't help but notice that even with the dark pair of Oakleys covering the girl's eyes and her stoic expression, she has the kind of face that catfishers steal to use for fake social media profiles.

"Alright, Hot Pants," Eli says. "I take it you're in charge?"

"Yeah," the girl answers. "I am."

"Lower your gun and call off your boys or this is going to the shortest day of your lives."

"Tough talk. Think you can back it up?"

Eli grins, fully exposing his fangs for her to see. "Yup."

The girl gasps, then she smiles big. Amy finds it strange that instead of being freaked out at the sight of Eli's canines, the girl lowers her weapon and nods approvingly.

"It's all thirty degrees, man," the girl says, lowering her weapon.

"Thirty degrees?" Eli asks, still with both katars poised to strike.

"Yeah, you know. Thirty degrees, a nice, cool temp for us vampires."

"No way," Amy whispers.

"Yeah way, sweetie," the girl says turning towards Amy, then winks at her.

Amy scowls to show that she is not amused. Inside, she feels mostly shocked by the girl's claim to be a vampire, even though she doesn't have the iconic fangs. A moment of discomfort washes over Amy when the girl's brow furrows as she stares like she is trying to force herself to put two and two together.

Eli keeps up his poker face and reminds the girl, "Your boys. They're gettin' antsy, and I'm running out of patience."

The girl nods her head, then she sticks two fingers between her lips and whistles three rapid tweets. Amy cuts her eyes over to the left side of the garage and sees a tall teenage boy with mirror lens sunglasses step around the corner. At the same time, two other boys rise up from the position they were laying in on the garage roof. One boy is short and stocky, the other a shirtless Latino with tribal tattoos on his chest and arms. The sunglasses that they are both wearing is enough of a clue for Amy to figure that they are vampires, too.

Amy keeps her eyes on the boys as they walk down to the edge of the roof and pause, holding M-16s across their bodies as they look down at Eli.

"It's alright, dudes," the girl says. "He's one of us."

The boys look more relieved now that they have the all clear from their leader. They nod their heads and smile at Eli like they just recognized a long lost friend. Amy takes note that they are fangless, as well.

"You can put your... knives away now," the girl says to Eli. "We welcome all vampires into the brotherhood. We're all Sons and Daughters of God."

"Tell me who your magister is!" Eli snaps.

The girl appears nervous about Eli's disposition. She falters for a moment, but says, "Preacher. You know him?"

Eli returns his katars to their scabbards. "Yeah, Antonio and I go back like the slides on my forty-fives. I'll need you to take me to him."

"No problem."

The boys on the roof jump off and land comfortably on both feet, each on one side of Eli. Amy eases back the hammer on her Beretta, but Eli motions his hand in a downward motion, signaling her to stand down. She does as she is told, even though she doesn't trust any of the young vampires. And the boys start making her feel even more uneasy when they appear to leer at her behind the cover of their shades. She decides to keep the muzzle of the Beretta pressed against the door so she can raise it and shoot in a hurry if she has to.

The Latino boy turns to the girl, and says, "Lark, you know this fool from somewhere?"

"No," Lark responds. "But I'm looking forward to gettin' to know him."

The wiry kid looks at Eli with burning contempt written all over his face. "Maybe we should see if he's as tough as he thinks he is before you start gettin' all friendly."

"Easy, little puppy," Eli warns. "Trust me, you ain't ready to get into it with a big dog."

"Stay cool, Stretch," Lark says, holding her hand up. "He's right. You don't want to do that. He's a regulare."

"You better believe it," Eli says, brandishing his ring and waving it in an almost taunting way.

"Just like a fuckin' cop," Stretch grumbles. "I fuckin' hate cops!"

Eli shrugs, showing that he couldn't care any less about Stretch's comment as all the boys take their places behind Lark.

Stretch, living up to his name, towers over his female commander as he glowers with jealousy. The stocky boy who was on the roof is about the girl's height, and his gaze is fixed on Amy. He all but drools out the sides of his mouth, and the bulge in the front of his pants hasn't escaped her attention or her ire. As for Lark, if she weren't female, she would most likely be pitching a tent like the stocky boy. She has been staring at Eli like she wants to tear his clothes off and do the nasty with him right then and there.

"So, 'big dog,' who exactly are you?" Stretch asks Eli.

Eli smirks and doesn't answer.

"Elias Kincade," Lark says and wets her lips. "The Devil Badger. I should've known when I saw your knives."

"How do you know my name?" Eli asks.

"Preacher. He talks about you a lot."

"Yeah, and what does he say?"

"Well, besides all the cool things you've done," Lark says, beaming with admiration, "he said that if anything ever happened to him, I was to try to find you. You can be trusted, and you'll always do the right thing. And one day when The Imperator steps down and his daughter, Lygia, takes his place, you'll be first choice for her Proconsul. You and her in The Synodus will be a good thing for all of us."

"Antonio has always been a dreamer," Eli says, shaking his head. "I assume he turned all of you?"

"Me, Stretch, and Bear here," she says pointing at the stocky boy, "plus most of the other vamps at the compound." Lark then ticks her head towards the Latino boy. "Cruz over here joined us a couple weeks ago."

Eli looks at the boy, and says, "Cruz. I take it you're Lilly Rucerato's legare. Where is she?"

Cruz looks surprised that Eli knows who he is, then his expression turns somber. "Dead. Her fountain was infected, and Lilly fed from her before she became a full chomper. I had her cremated before I left Lufkin."

"And you just ended up in Waco?"

"No. Lil told me that if Sig and Kelly didn't show up within twenty-four hours, I was to get with some of the other vamps and stick with them until we got orders about what to do. So I hooked up with some and, long-story-short, we ended up here."

Eli grits his teeth. "So Sig and Kelly never showed?"

Cruz shakes his head. "Nah, they left long before shit went crazy. Sig said something about wanting to disappear to spend some alone time together and they just never came back. We tried calling for weeks but only got voice mail until all cell service went dead."

Eli sighs and returns his attention to Lark. "How many of you at the compound are Preach's legares, and how many humans do you have there?"

"Ten legares, but we got a total of seventeen vamps in all. As for humans, there are sixty-one, including eighteen militia P.O.Ws. Oh, and we also got one fucked up chomper that you just gotta see."

"Hey, Devil Badger," Cruz says. "Is that your fountain? She's cute. And she smells yummy, too!"

Eli growls, bares his teeth, and postures like the alpha male of a pack warning a potential challenger. Then he says to Lark, "Take me to your compound. I want to see my old friend, Preacher, again."

"Thirty degrees," Lark responds and starts walking towards the Bronco.

"Uh-uh," Eli says, walking over to the back of the Bronco to shut the window and the tailgate. "It's a nice enough day. You guys can hoof-it to your bikes."

Lark and her crew bitch and moan about the walk in the hot morning sun, but nobody challenges Eli about it. Amy goes to move over to the driver's seat, but Eli walks over to the passenger side and opens the door.

"You do know how to drive a stick, right?" Eli asks as he climbs into the seat.

"Yeah, I can drive stick."

Eli chuckles, and says, "That's my girl. Let's go. We're going to follow them to their bikes, then on to the compound."

Amy nods and starts the Bronco as Lark, Stretch, Bear, and Cruz start walking. She puts the truck in gear, eases up on the clutch and lets it roll slowly as she follows the vampires to their bikes.

Bothered by the unknown, Amy hopes that Eli knows what he's doing. She doesn't like the idea of going to a compound full of vampires, especially if they are going to be like Lark and her boys. But she has begun to trust Eli. And considering Lark's reaction when she realized that Eli wasn't just any old regulare, Amy wants to believe that the other vampires will show the same respect since the reputation of The Devil Badger seems to proceed him.

CHAPTER NINE

"Ho-lee crap!" Amy says, steering the Bronco around the bend of a dusty hill. "That place looks like a fortress."

"Yeah," Eli responds, "that's exactly what I was thinking."

While steering her ATV down the hillside, Lark turns her head and jabs her finger in the direction of what looks like a compound protected by high walls, still a distance away down on the valley floor.

"Duh!" Amy says. "Like we didn't figure that out by now."

Lark turns back around and throttles the ATV, causing the front wheels to raise up, and she recklessly continues down the hill.

With the compound within sight, the rising anxiety gives Amy the sensation of spiders skittering over her skin. Eli said that he is eager to see his old friend, Preacher, again but his demeanor indicates anything other than a happy reunion. There is also a shadow of sorrow cast over Eli, and Amy figures that it's because the regulare in him can't allow friendship to overcome duty, especially when it comes to disposing of a rogue vampire. The fact that Preacher has made so many legares without permission from The Synodus is all Eli needs to suspect his friend has turned rogue. That doesn't fare well for Preacher, but Amy doesn't know if Lark and his other legares will share his fate.

Because of Eli's temperament, Amy k new that he wasn't in the mood to answer a lot of questions, but there was one that burned on her tongue that she couldn't hold back. Now she knows that vampires don't automatically grow fangs. When turned, they remain with the same teeth they had as humans, but if their eye teeth are knocked out, they will regenerate new and improved fangs. The majority of vampires in the modern world don't have fangs. It's forbidden by the Synodus as a precaution to keep the vampires' existence concealed. And since siphons are available for vampires to feed from their fountains, there is no need for fangs. However, every regulare earns the right to have fangs by the time they complete their training.

Now even closer to the compound, Amy realizes that she has seen it before. The huge painting of Old Glory on one side of the entrance and the Texas Lone Star flag on the other triggers the memory of numerous news reports. The infamous compound has Amy in awe as she considers how much bigger its concrete walls look in real life as opposed to on a TV screen. The front wall looks like it probably stretches out about the distance of four city blocks, the ones along the side twice as long. The ATF had a hell of a time figuring out what to do when the militiamen inside refused to acknowledge the warrant to search for illegal weapons and explosives. That tense standoff was almost four years ago, but the details of the story remain in Amy's head.

Approaching the gates of the compound, Lark makes the OK symbol with her fingers. One of the guards standing on a walkway along the front wall nods and gestures a signal to someone inside. Shortly afterwards, the big, metal double doors begin to swing open and Amy gains a view of the some of the structures within. She remembers an aerial shot on the news that showed about fifteen buildings that resemble ranch-style houses, plus several others that look like cabins.

Amy glances up at a bleached longhorn skull as she follows the ATVs through the entryway. Then her eyes dart over the people that she sees, including children who are playing as they would on any normal day in the world that once was. She takes note that a lot of the adults are wearing sunglasses, making it impossible to tell who's a vampire and who's not. She glances at Eli for any last minute instruction and she notices how tense the muscles in his jaw are.

"Just stay in the truck when we stop," Eli says, glaring straight ahead. "And don't worry, we'll be fine. Trust me."

Amy nods and continues to follow Lark's lead down a long path between the buildings, taking them straight into the gut of the compound. Every face she sees is loaded with curiosity, and Amy feels the tension increase when she glances at the rearview mirror and sees that the convoy is being followed on foot.

They come to the wide-open square at the center of the compound, with a flagpole in the middle of it. The ATVs veer off towards one of the L-shaped buildings, one with a big white dove painted above the door. Eli raises his hand, and Amy stops in the middle of the road as the young vampires park their bikes.

The door to the building opens. A man dressed in a simple white shirt and tan Dockers saunters out, slipping on a pair of sunglasses as he enters the sunlight.. He smiles at Lark and the vampires flanking her, then glances at the Bronco. Amy can't see his eyes, but she imagines them becoming as big as baseballs when he recognizes whose SUV is feet away from his doorway because his mouth drops open in a moment of cartoonish shock.

Eli opens the Bronco's door and hops out, then slowly unsheaths one of his katars as he calmly walks to the front of the vehicle.

Amy puts her hand on the shotgun mounted to the dashboard.

"Elias, my friend," the man says, hurrying towards Eli with his arms open wide to offer an embrace. "I know what this looks like, but let me explain."

That's all Amy needs to confirm her suspicion that the person approaching Eli is no other than Antonio, the vampire called Preacher.

The moment Preacher is within reach, Eli thrusts his left arm forward and clamps his fingers to Preacher's neck. Eli lifts him off the ground and slings him around, slamming Preacher's back against the Bronco. Some of the inhabitants of the compound raise their weapons to shooting positions as they quickly but cautiously hurry towards Eli and Preacher.

Eli's polished katar blade sends a beam of light dancing on Amy's face. The sharp edge pushes into the skin on Preacher's cheek, with just enough pressure to nick his skin.

Amy recalls how light Eli's blade felt in her hand when he let her examine one the night before. She learned that regulares don't use ordinary bladed weapons. They are made from a special magnesium alloy that's stronger than titanium, but lighter, and sharp to death. She doesn't know Preacher, but she feels bad for him being on the wrong side of Eli's weapon.

Instead of panicking, Preacher calmly signals for his people to stand down. All souls comply, but the crowd continues to approach the Bronco with concern in their eyes.

"Explain this to me, Preacher!" Eli growls. "Because this place reminds me of Hadrianus' fort. These vampires remind me of a flock of acolytes. And you can guess what you remind me of right now."

"No," Preacher rasps, "Eli, I haven't gone rogue. That's my word as a Son of God, a vampire loyal to the Imperator, and a loyal brother to you."

"C'mon, let him go!" demands a portly man, easing the hammer back on a .357 magnum. "Or else!"

"Richie, no!" Preacher shouts as loud as he can with the amount of pressure on his throat, "Elias is only doing his duty. He is a high ranking regulare, and he is the authority here. All of you must respect him, no matter what happens to me! We all knew the probability of this day coming."

Amy watches as the news of a regulare in the compound incites a flurry of shocked glances and murmurs among all those gathering around the Bronco.

"Richie one of your legares?" Eli asks.

"No, he's human," Preacher responds.

"Good, 'cause there's nothing funny 'bout a morbidly obese immortal."

"He's a good man, Elias. All of the humans and vampires here are good people. They wouldn't be here if they weren't."

"Preacher," Stretch grumbles as he glares at Eli. "Just so you know, if he takes you out I'm dropping him myself."

Preacher shakes his head. "Vengeance is mine saith the Lord. I gave you all the tools you need to control your temper, and I know that you won't disappoint me."

Stretch stops bristling, even though the anger remains burning in his eyes, and takes on a submissive posture.

"Puppies still in training, huh?" Eli says. "Who are they? And why did you make so many of them?"

Preacher explains that Lark and her friends ran a program mentoring younger children after school at his old church. The rest of his legares were his parishioners before the outbreak. They all sought refuge at the church when things went from bad to worse. Bad being chomper attacks. Worse being militiamen running wild. After weeks of no contact with Sig—the regulare responsible for the vampires throughout central Texas—Preacher felt he had no choice.

A squad of militiamen constantly harassed the people in Preacher's town, demanding payment form the residents in exchange for protection without much of a choice attached. After taking everything of value, demanding most of the food supply, and almost completely draining the town of whatever resources it had left, there was only one more thing that the militiamen wanted. Everyone who put up a resistance was murdered on the day when the militia came to claim all of the young women that they fancied.

"I should've done something to stop them," Preacher says, his voice cracking, "but I followed the rule and didn't reveal what I was. I felt like I deserved to die for not protecting my people, good people. I had never felt so low, Elias. I wished I was dead for failing them. I couldn't undo the damage that was already done, so I decided to give these people a fighting chance, even if it meant sacrificing my own life. I sent word with Barney Blackwell to The Synodus about what I did."

"Wait," Eli says, "you're tellin' me that Bushy-browss Barney was here, too?"

"Yes. He volunteered to make the trip up to Michigan. I sent one of our humans with him. They should've arrived and reported already. I accept whatever judgment they bestow upon me. I just asked that my legares be spared. They have all already pledged loyalty to the Imperator and his Proconsul. We've just been waiting for their response."

"You know, Preacher," Eli bares his fangs, "I don't take kindly to people lying to me. Especially the people who know better than to do it."

"He's not lying!" Lark pipes in. "The militia took my sister, and we never would've got her back if Preacher didn't help us. Between them and the chompers, we'd all be dead by now."

"Stay out of this!" Eli snaps at Lark, then turns his attention back to Preacher.

"Elias, look at these people," Preacher says, gazing over his flock. "They're not soldiers. They're mothers, fathers, sons, daughters, brothers, sisters..., neighbors. They would help a stranger in need, just as selflessly as they helped each other every day of their lives. I've watched them, listened to them, I've taken their confessions for over ten years. I know them better than they probably know themselves. They're not the kind of people that make Acolytes. I see it. And I know you, you see it, too.

Eli glances over the faces gazing at him, then he sucks his teeth and says, "I was told that you made X-amount of legares. Where did Cruz and the others come from?"

Preacher looks confused by Eli's question, but he answers, "One of the teams out searching for supplies ran across Kwesi, Gregory Three Feathers, and the young vampires traveling with them. A patrol team also found Bushy-brows Barney making his way to Austin, and they brought him here. That's all there is to it."

Eli removes his knife from Preacher's neck and lowers him back down to the ground. "I thought of you as I got closer to this part of Texas, but I had no idea where you would be by now. And I definitely had no idea you had gone and committed suicide. You were supposed to walk the Earth until your savior comes back or this planet dies, whichever comes first. Remember?"

Preacher smiles. "The day has just begun, my dearest friend. Either of those things can still happen. Just as you can still make a judgment call and take my head."

Eli shakes his head and slips his katar back into its scabbard. "As long as you sent word to The Synodus, this isn't my problem. I'm just glad my sat-phone's dead. If they decide that this whole incident needs an undo, I don't want to be the one they send to handle it."

"Funny, if I had to die at the hands of a regulare, I'd rather it be you," Preacher says, then he turns and assures the crowd that everything is all right, that Eli is a friend who can be trusted, and everybody should go on with their day as normal.

All of Preacher's people seem to breathe a sigh of relief at the same time. And just when Amy is about to do some exhaling of her own, she hears a booming voice imitating Yosemite Sam yell out, "Elias Kincade, you ole, low-down, dirty, whoremongering, mustang-ridin', Bronco-drivin', two gun slingin', crazy-ass knives wieldin', cheap whiskey guzzlin', Karate fightin', cowboy hat and boots wearin', yella belly varmint! I got a bone to pick witchu!"

CHAPTER TEN

Amy turns and sees a large dark skin man with the sun glinting off his sweaty bald head approaching from a path on the left side of the compound. His dark sunglasses make his angry face even more intimidating than his stout physique. His stiff posture, muscular arms, and big-balled fists fill Amy with adrenaline.

Eli grimaces, and yells back, "Whoa, looks like a dick done grown arms and legs and started talkin' shit. Ain't that a bitch?"

"Guess you the bitch, then," the man says, instantly breaking into a sprint, "'Cause you 'bout to get dick whipped!"

The man covers the distance between himself and Eli in a couple of seconds, moving at a speed twice as fast as an Olympic Sprinter. He slams into Eli and wraps him up in a bear hug. It happened fast. Amy expected Eli to react before contact was made, but he just stood there and allowed himself to fall into the clutch of a vampire much bigger than he is. She snatches the shotgun from the clamp and shoves open the door, planning to send the vampire's bald head sailing across the compound like a punted football.

By the time Amy's feet hit the ground she hears Eli laughing. When she looks again she sees that the man is cracking up, too. He drops Eli to the ground and they slap their right hands together before engaging in a manly half-hug.

"What the hell you doing here, Kwesi?" Eli says, breaking their embrace.

"Surviving," Kwesi responds. "Me and Three Feathers were kickin' chomper ass down in Austin when we hooked up with these two fine, little puppies. But we had to get outta Dodge when the soldier boys locked-down the city to set up a safe zone. We were passing through Waco when some of Preacher's people found us and brought us here."

"Whose puppies you traveling with?"

Kwesi shrugs. "Some hot-shot who called himself Ricochet. I take it you know him?"

"Yeah, he runs around San Antonio. Sig told me he's always good for guns and ammo if I'm in town and I need 'em. I know his legares, too. Sisters. Kaylee and Becca, right?"

"Yeah, that's them. Ricochet got chomper blood in his eye. That's how we found out there's no coming back from that."

Eli shakes his head, then asks, "I take it you didn't hear from Sig before you left San Antonio?"

Kwesi tells Eli practically the same story that Curz told him about Sig and Kelly going off to have some quality time and dropping off the face of the Earth. The extent of Eli's concern clearly shows on his face. No one seems to know what happened to the viking-turned-vampire and his bride, Kelly. Eli states that he wanted to go looking for Sig and Kelly, but he was tracking an acolyte who has been preaching Hadrianus' beliefs and the rogue vampires that were with him. At the dawn of the outbreak, Sig's magister, a vampire named Trajanius, was sent looking for him. Since then Eli lost contact with The Synodus, so he doesn't know what became of them.

"First chance I get I'm going looking for Sig," Eli says. "But right now I'm carrying out orders straight from the Imperator, hand-delivered by Tijeri. I'm to find Lygia and protect her at all cost until she finds a cure or vaccine for the virus."

"If there's one person I'd put my money on to find a way to stop the virus, it's Lygia," Kwesi says. "She still operating under the name Rosa?"

Eli nods his head. "Yep. Dr. Rosa Contaldi, head researcher at Genevolution."

Kwesi nods his head then turns his attention to Amy, focusing on the bruise and two small scabs on her neck. "Where's Natasha?"

Eli lowers his head, conveying that his last fountain is no longer among the living. "Amy's with me now," he says, with a stern expression as he eyes the shotgun in her hands. "She was supposed to stay in the truck."

Kwesi laughs and slaps Eli on the back. "I see you still got a thing for the cute fiery type," he says, then he looks at Amy again, takes a long whiff of the air and licks his lips. "She smells... very ni-i-ice."

Eli growls, exposing his fangs in an alpha mien as he steps between Amy and Kwesi. Kwesi appears to contritely back off. Eli settle s down, then he properly introduces her, specifying to all vampires present that she is his potential legare, not just a fountain.. The expressions on Kwesi and Preacher's faces tell Amy how surprised they are to discover that Eli is even considering taking on a legare, and it makes her feel special.

An uncomfortable feeling overcomes Amy. She darts her eyes around and discovers that one person is focused on her more intensely than all others. Lark is staring with a big smile on her face. Amy's heart begins to race when Lark nods her head, and she mouths the words, "I know you."

Amy pretends to be oblivious to Lark's insinuation, but on the inside, she's scared to death that Lark might expose the secret that she has been keeping.

Eli turns the conversation back to Preacher, and says, "Your half-dressed legare here tells me you're keeping, 'one fucked up chomper,' at this compound?"

Preacher nods his head. "Yeah, and you might want to take a look at it."

Eli agrees wholeheartedly that he wants to see what's so special about this chomper. Amy is eager to see what exactly makes this chomper more fucked up than the others, as well. Reading Eli's body language, she sees that he wants her to stay by his side, something that she had planned on doing anyway. At any other time, she would be offended by anyone telegraphing possession over her, but she knows that Eli has to be behaving that way for a reason. For all she knows, the scent of her menstrual blood must be like hot apple pie to all these vampires, and he wants to make sure that everybody understands that she's hands-off. Whether she wants to admit it or not, she likes how everyone knowing that she is his feels.. But the most important thing right now is that Eli doesn't think Preacher has gone rogue.

Stretch strolls back to his ATV mumbling something under his breath. Cruz and Bear follow behind him as Preacher leads Eli, Amy, Lark, and Kwesi down one of the paths slicing between the buildings. Kwesi does most of the talking, vividly painting a picture of how crazy Austin became as the number of chompers multiplied.

They near a shack at the corner of the compound where dozens of food and beverage delivery trucks are parked along the walls, as well as a couple of gas tankers. Amy hears what she initially thinks are lawn mowers, but without a blade of grass in sight, she quickly realizes that she is listening to generators running. Preacher points to the shack and fishes a ring of keys out of his pocket. If Amy didn't already know that there was a chomper somewhere inside of the shack, she would have sensed danger lurking there by the guard posted out front and the absence of children playing anywhere close it, as they are everywhere else.

"This is one of the places the militia hid their full-auto weapons and illegal ammunition before the big raid," Preacher says, and releases an unbelievable stench when he opens the door. "The chomper was already in the well when we took over. One of the prisoners said that he used to be one of them and after he turned they decided to keep him as a pet."

Preacher turns on the light, revealing a circular pit in the middle of the floor. Amy glances at a slab of wood propped up against the wall. The size of the wood looks like it would fit perfectly the missing floorboards around the pit.

As Amy gets close to the edge of the pit, she sees that its walls are made of cement. She hears the rattle of a chain, then the gravely howl of a famished chomper rises from the hole and Amy sees a shadow grow on the wall. She takes three more steps and makes out the top of a head covered in long, matted hair. Finally close to the edge, she gasps when she sees the face and body of the trapped chomper, secured to a large stack of rusty weight lifting plates by a thick chain around its ankle.

The shirtless chomper surpasses all of Amy's expectations. The first thing that she can't help but notice about him are his short, dolphin-like arms. Though skinny, they look normal from his shoulders down to his elbows. But where forearms should be, there are short, shriveled, floppy limbs with hands as tiny as a newborn baby's. As freakish as the arms are, their creepiness is exemplified by the deathly black color of the miniature hands. They remind Amy of the sheriff chomper that she killed yesterday, whose fingers looked frostbitten. Frostbite would seem like a good diagnosis for the chomper's condition, considering his nose and ears are also the black of dead tissue. But the pit doesn't appear to be refrigerated, and the weather hasn't been near cold enough to freeze anything, not even at night.

The chomper's limbs and the spots of black contrasting his pale complexion are disturbing, but it doesn't compare to the thing that probably has the vampires concerned the most; as well as Amy now that she's seen it. As the chomper wails and chomps at the air, one long tooth stands out prominently in its mouth: a fang. One as long as Eli's.

"Ain't that a bitch!" Eli whispers as he squats at the edge of the pit.

"I asked what happened to him," Preacher says, squatting next to Eli. "The prisoner said that they gave him a good beating when they realized he was turning into a chomper, and they cut his arms off before they chained him up and threw him in the pit. They were surprised when they saw that his limbs looked like they were going to grow back, and they had no idea how to explain the fang that replaced one of the teeth they knocked out."

"There is no explanation for that. At least none that makes sense."

"I had the same thought. That's why I didn't kill him. He hasn't eaten anything in three months, and I want to see how long he'll last."

"Good call."

"Ahm," Amy says, as she taps Eli's shoulder. "I don't know if this is important, but yesterday I killed a chomper whose fingers were as black as this one's hands. Does that mean anything to you?"

Eli nods his head. "That happens to us, too, if we go too long without feeding. Just like a human body starts restricting blood from the limbs to help keep its core warm when it's cold, ours restricts blood flow to conserve energy, especially in the brain. It's an involuntary response. If it's happening in this chomper and it happened in the one you killed, well, I don't believe in coincidence. They're too much like us, even though they're too different to be us."

"If they're so much like us, I wonder how come they have a harder time seeing in the sun than we do?" asks Lark.

"Probably the virus," Kwesi says. "It's supposed to screw up the brain. Maybe all they can focus on is the brightness and the pain, just like you probably did the first time you went out in the daytime as a vampire. Until Preacher taught you how to focus, you were practically blind, right?"

Lark nods her head. "So, you think maybe the virus started in one of us?"

"Doubt it," Eli says. "It's not like any of us are carriers. Every vampire I know of who got infected died within hours. This right here, I can't explain it."

"And I thought seeing a black Iron Man fighting chompers down in Austin was weird," Kwesi says, covering his nose.

Amy and Eli both look at Kwesi confused.

"Seriously," Kwesi says, "I saw somebody in a suit of armor killin' chompers. It looked just like Iron Man, but he was all black."

"If you say so," Eli replies.

"It's true. I saw him with my own two eyes."

"Eli smiles and shakes his head.

"Okay, can we get out of here," Kwesi says. "The stink from this thing is turning my stomach. I left Three Feathers back at the place we set up as a garage when I heard your truck riding through the compound, and he's going to be happy to see you. Besides, you're looking kinda light in the skin, buddy. And Amy looks like she can use a break from feeding you. There's a thick, cajun fountain here who I'm sure won't mind donating some of her gumbo to a dumbo."

Eli stands up and looks into Amy's eyes as he responds to Kwesi. "I guess it won't hurt to get in a little extra boost."

Amy feels an abnormal kind of jealousy. Less than an hour has passed since Eli turned down feeding on her. Now he's planning to go off and get an "extra boost" from some strange woman. The thought of him sinking his teeth into another woman and licking her neck every time he swallows her blood makes Amy's own blood begin to boil.

"Hey, Amy," Lark says, putting an arm around her shoulder. "When was the last time you had a nice, cold Pepsi?"

"Thanks, but I'm good," Amy responds, declining the offer for a drink that she really would rather have.

"Go ahead," Eli says to Amy. "I'll catch up to you as soon as I'm done."

"Don't worry," Preacher assures Amy. "You're among friends here."

"Yeah," Kwesi joins in. "And there isn't much of a chomper problem out here, either. I've been here a couple weeks and probably only seen, like, ten of 'em. Plus stinky down there."

Eli looks at Preacher for confirmation of that.

"I don't know why," Preacher says, "but shortly after we took over the chompers hardly ever show up. The few that do, we usually take care of with crossbows and save on the ammo."

"This place is isolated, but that's still a little strange, ain't it?"

"Yeah, but I never question a blessing," Preacher says, then pats Eli on the shoulder. "I have some things to check on. You and Amy think of this place like home for as long as you're here. I'll meet up with you all later."

"I appreciate the hospitality, Preach," Eli says, then takes Amy's hand and squeezes it. "Go with Hot Pants. I won't be long. I promise."

A teasing chorus of "Awww" rises over the cries of the hungry chomper and Eli shakes his head as he lowers it, appearing to accept the mocking from the peanut gallery that he brought on himself. Then he leads Amy outside and, after another squeeze of the hand, he reassures her that he will rejoin her soon.

As Amy watches Eli walk away, her emotions use her body like an amusement park. She hadn't realized just how much she doesn't want to be separated from him until now, and can't believe that she actually feels this way for him. Not this soon. She pushes the emotions back down into whatever hole they crawled out of, and even though she's not keen on being in the company of Lark, she reluctantly starts walking with her as Eli and Kwesi go in search of cajun blood.

CHAPTER ELEVEN

"If you're hungry, we can go back in the kitchen and I'll whip you up some eggs," Lark says, walking with Amy towards the canteen.

"Eggs?" Amy asks, surprised such a thing still exists.

"Yeah. And I'm talking the real deal, straight out a cloaca—eggs. Not the powered crap in the militia stockpile. We got chickens and a few goats, too. The milk sucks, but you get used to it. Oh, and don't worry about the animals being infected. We take precautions to make sure that don't happen."

"I'll just take the soda for now."

"Thirty degrees," Lark says, then stares at Amy. "Man, that Eli must have way more self-control than I can imagine, or the two of you are banging each other's brains out on the regular."

Amy's brow furrows. "Whatever."

Lark inhales deeply. "You don't know, do you?"

"What, that you vamps can smell I'm on my period? Duh!"

"No, sweetheart. I'm talking about the heavy pheromones you're putting out. Your natural sent, alone, is off the charts. Mix in your estrogen, adrenaline, and the scent of your blood..., pshhh! One good sniff of you is better than hard-on in a bottle. Hell, I'm not into girls, but right now I just want to kiss you and never stop. So I can imagine how much more intense it is for Eli inside that truck with you."

Lark's revelation has Amy too stunned to respond. She figured that Eli probably had a tough time dealing with the scent of her blood, but she had no idea that her body was secreting other things that might be driving him crazy.

"Eli puts out a heavy dose of pheromones, too," Lark continues. "Plus, he's got a ton of testosterone. Can't blame a girl for needing to change her undies after being around him."

Annoyed, Amy grumbles, "Sounds like you need to go take care of some soggy panties."

Lark laughs. "Actually, I do. And I will. But we should talk first. You know by now that I recognize you, don't you?"

Amy's heart becomes a jackhammer. "I seriously doubt that."

"No. It took me a minute to realize why you looked so familiar, then it hit me. You shot up a house full of drug dealers over in New Mexico, like, a couple months before everything went crazy in the world."

"Look, bitch!" Amy snaps, glancing back to make sure Eli and Kwesi didn't double back and are following them. "That wasn't me. I never shot anybody in my life."

"That's a lie. I saw you on TV. I definitely remember those eyes, especially now they're burning with rage. That's how they were when you attacked that sheriff in the courtroom. Oh, and don't forget what I am. I can hear your heart beating even faster than it does when you look at Eli."

Lark's words are like a spotlight that causes sweat to gush from Amy's pores.

"Look, I'm not out to get you, " Lark says, holding open the door to the mass hall. "I'm actually on your side. From the look on your face, obviously, Eli doesn't know about you. I didn't say anything in front of everybody because I didn't want to put you out there like that, just in case. And I'll keep your secret. All I want is for you to tell me all about how you shot-up everything moving in that house and walked out without a scratch."

"Listen, even if that was me, why would I tell you something like that?"

"Because I'm probably your biggest fan and I want to know what happened. They said you never spoke a word after you were arrested, so I want to be the first person you tell your story too. Besides, I got a feeling we're going to be good friends."

Feeling as if her hands are tied behind her back, Amy walks into the mess hall and takes a seat at the closest table. She watches Lark prance over to an older woman wiping down a counter separating the dining area from the kitchen and ask her to retrieve two bottles of sodas from the fridge.

Lark turns around and smiles. Feeling the Beretta tucked in her waistband gives Amy serious thought to using it to solve her nosy vampire problem.

Lark returns with two ice-cold bottles of Pepsi. Amy lets out a long sigh when she finally decides to play the vampire's game. If Lark betrays her, there will be hell to pay. Amy will make sure of that. For now, she takes the bottle from Lark and twists the cap. Hearing the crisp schwip of gas suddenly escaping the bottle is almost as good as feeling the cold, carbonated beverage bubbling on her tongue. She keeps a gulp in her mouth for a full minute before she swallows it down, along with her pride.

Lark listens attentively as Amy talks in the lowest voice she can muster without being mute. She starts her story with the bad feeling that she got when Aaron was late returning home from a meeting he had set up to sell three Glock 17s. Amy didn't like the guys that Aaron was doing the deal with, but Aaron assured her that nothing would happen since he knew them from high school.

But the bad feeling persisted, and she took off to the location she knew the deal was supposed to take place.

The moment she saw Aaron's pickup parked under the bridge, she knew that something was wrong. When she got close enough to see broken glass on the ground, she prayed that she was wrong about what she expected to find. She wasn't.

Aaron's body was slumped across the bloody front seats. There was one empty shell from a 9mm on the floorboard, but no gun anywhere in sight. Aaron had managed to get off one shot before a shogun blast destroyed his face. And from the holes torn through the back of his shirt, Amy knew that somebody made sure he was dead by shooting him a second time. She couldn't stand seeing Aaron like that, and she couldn't stop crying.

Tears were still in Amy's eyes when took Aaron's M-16 out of the hidden compartment in his closet. She made sure the cops had taken her anonymous call seriously and were on their way to find Aaron's body. She wasn't going to allow them to arrest his killers, though. Her rage was in full control by then. Aaron was the most important person in her life, and somebody was going to pay for doing that to him.

After stealing her mother's car, she drove straight to the house of the meth trafficker that she knew Aaron was meeting. She didn't step on the brake until she was on the front lawn, causing the Honda Accord to skid, regaining traction just in time to keep the front end from slamming into the house.

Amy hopped out of the Honda with the M-16 in her hand. Not caring about the people in the neighborhood witnessing the start of her rampage, she went right up to the front door and started to kick it.

"Who the hell done gone and lost their fuckin' mind?!" A man's voice yelled from inside the house.

"Got something good for you, if you got something good for me, baby," Amy responded sweetly, readying the M-16.

The doorknob turned and when it cracked open Amy kicked it the rest of the way. The scrawny, scruffy-looking young man who answered the door was stuck in shock at the sight of Amy. She was the last thing that he saw before she double-tapped his skull at point-blank range.

Amy could hear the rumbles and bumbles of a mad scramble when she charged into a living room full of marijuana smoke. She squeezed off a round, piercing the heart of a man who had just snapped shut an old, sawed-off double barrel shotgun and was about to point it at her.

She turned to chase whoever had run into the next room and saw two muzzle flashes blink like Christmas lights. Bullets whizzed past her head, but there was no fear in her as she stood like a statue and fired back three shots. The shooter had too much of his body exposed from behind an overturned table as he fired a pristine looking Glock-17 at her. She saw two of her bullets strike flesh, one hitting his shoulder, the other ripping through his throat.

Amy's next target was a man whose arm was all she could see of him as he pointed another Glock from around the corner in the kitchen. A bullet flew past her face so close, she felt the wind from it. She cut her eyes to the right and saw a man firing a Sig Sauer semiautomatic at her from the top of the stairs. Instantly she moved, but instead of running for cover, she scooted for a better angle and unleashed a volley of rounds that hit the gunman as his bullets punched through the floor by her feet.

Any inkling of doubt Amy had that she might've been wrong about who killed Aaron was completely gone. It was too much of a coincidence for these guys to want Glock-17s from Aaron and now they suddenly have at least 2 of them. There was also the fact that one of them had a shotgun and another had a Sig Sauer 9mm., just like Aaron's. Even if all the people that she killed so far wasn't there when Aaron died, she knew that they still had something to do with it. No gang does dirt like that without being down together, and Amy knew that there was one more from this gang to get. He was the leader, the one who had set up the meeting with Aaron.

Holding the M-16 at the ready, she took off for the kitchen intending to blow away anything she saw, except for a child if one happened to be in the deplorable dwelling. The arm was no longer sticking out from around the corner, and she made it all the way to the kitchen without sight or sound of her target. As sirens wailed in the distance, she looked at the back door and saw that it was open. She made up her mind to go outside and see if she could track which direction the coward went. As soon as she turned towards the door, a flash of light through the window snagged her attention. Glass shattered. Bullets came flying at her. But her mind remained focus on executing her shot. Three bullets plunked into the refrigerator door next to her, and she fired one shot that brought an exclamation of pain from outside the house.

Amy ran outside as fast as she could, straight to the man that she had come to seek retribution from. The red buzz cut, pierced eyebrow, and a tattoo of a dollar sign under his left eye; he was the one. She stared at his face in the dim light coming from the kitchen, watching him cough up blood.

"You killed my heart tonight," Amy said, coldly. "For what, some stupid guns? You knew my brother. You knew that if you robbed him, he wouldn't have let you get away with it. You planned on killing him all along, didn't you?"

"Blow me, bitch!" the wounded man groaned.

"Nah," Amy responded and shoved the M-16's muzzle deep into the man's mouth, "you blow this!"

Amy squeezed the trigger and pumped eight bullets through the back of his neck. Then she emptied the rest from the M-16's magazine directly into the face of her victim. Aaron didn't have a face anymore, and neither would he.

Amy got what she came for. When the M-16's firing pin dropped into an empty chamber she heard the sound of keys jingling behind her. She turned just in time to see Sheriff Wade Mathis' face just before he tackled her..

"Daaamn!" Lark says. "Girl, you frickin' crazy."

"Aaron would've done the same for me," Amy says. "Besides, I got lucky. They couldn't shoot for shit, to begin with, and they were high as hell by the time I got there. It didn't matter then, but later on I figure it helped me from catching a bullet."

"Still, that took some balls. Big ones!"

"I guess. Now, you promised you won't tell Eli about this. I'm going to do it myself. And after this, I think I better do it sooner than later."

"Thirty degrees. I swear on my life I won't mention one word of that to anybody. But, I don't see what you're worried about. If anybody's gonna understand, it's gotta be Eli."

"Why do you say that?"

"Because..., wait, you mean you don't know what happened to him before he left home and became a vampire?"

Amy shakes her head. That was one of those things that Eli glossed over.

Lark looks genuinely surprised, and without waiting to be asked, she begins telling the story. "Elias' dad was a militia lieutenant during the Black Hawk War. After Black Hawk surrendered, Elias' Dad moved his family to Wyoming to start a cattle ranch. That's where Elias was born. He grew up working the ranch, and since there wasn't really much law back then, he and his family defended their own. They were so fierce with their guns, Elias' dad was made Marshall of the town. Elias ended up helping his dad out when he didn't have to be at the ranch working. He even used to go with his dad when they needed a posse to bring in bad guys, dead or alive."

"Wait," Amy says. "How do you know this?"

"Preacher told me in case I needed to convince Elias that he was my magister. Now, do you want to hear it or not?"

Amy nods her head.

"All right," Lark continues. "So Elias' dad was a kickass Marshall. And when Eli was seventeen, he ended up becoming his dad's kickass deputy. All good, right? Wrong. One day Elias is on his way to give his girlfriend, the blacksmith's daughter, some of her favorite licorice. While Eli was hanging out with her, he hear shots in the town. So he ran to the place where the shooting was coming from, and he found his dad dead. Some bandits his dad had a beef with ambushed him and shot him in the back. Bad move.

"That night Elias tracked them down, all by himself, and aired out all seven of them with two guns, one his and one his father's. After his father's funeral, Elias laid down his badge and left home. From that day he put fear in the hearts of any man whose face was on a WANTED poster, plus anybody else stupid enough to get in his way. He probably would've been a legend like Wyatt Earp if he didn't become a vampire."

Amy smiles as she remembers what Eli had told her about Wyatt Earp.

"So you see," Lark says, "both of y'all went on a killin' spree after somebody you loved was murdered. That's like fate, ain't it?"

"I guess," Amy responds. "Thanks for the story. It's good to know."

"Thirty degrees. Now let me ask you a question. You think Elias is really going to turn you?"

"Yeah, when he thinks I'm ready."

Lark shakes her head. "From what I understand, his blood is strong because he's so close in line to The Imperator. He's not going to make you his legare if he doesn't think you can handle it."

"And what makes you think I can't?!"

"I'm not saying you can't. But let me tell you, Preacher's blood ain't even half the strength of Elias', and you wouldn't believe how it makes me feel."

Curiously, Amy asks, "How does it make you feel?"

"You know how people say they feel alive? Well, vamp blood takes that to a whole new level. Ever since Preacher turned me, I've felt more alive than I've ever felt in my life! And at the same time, I feel like there's something powerful alive in me. It's the spirit of God in our bloodlines."

Amy holds back a laugh, and says, "I take it you're talking about that Sons and Daughters of God thing you mentioned earlier?"

Lark nods her head. "And it came to pass when men began to multiply on the face of the earth, and daughters were born unto them. That the sons of God saw the daughters of men that they were fair; and they took them wives of all which they chose. And the Lord said, My spirit shall not always strive with man, for that he is also flesh, yet his days shall be a hundred and twenty years. There were giants in the earth in those days; and also after that, when the sons of God came in unto the daughters of men, they bare children to them, the same became mighty men which were of old, men of renown. Genesis six verses one through four."

"So you're saying that vampire blood goes back to the children of the women who the sons of God slept with? Like a vampire was one of those offspring, and that's why they are basically the sons of God, too?"

"Yeah, basically," Lark replies. "Preacher can help you understand it better than I can. He's got references that tie into giants like Goliath and creatures like Leviathan and other things in the Bible that explains it all. There's even a verse in Genesis, chapter nine, that refers to life in the blood. And it just so happens that our lives are sustained because of blood. Coincidence? I don't think so, but you got the gist of it."

Not knowing if Lark is aware of the rock painting that Eli and Lygia found in Australia, or how any interpretation of it can contrast what she believes, Amy decides to keep that information to herself. The last thing she wants is to get into a debate about God with a vampire who thinks she shares blood with the same deity.

"Think about this," Lark says. "There's no guarantee that Elias is going to turn you. And if he does, you're in danger because of the strength of his blood.

But the best way to live through this chomper thing is to be a vampire. So, if you're not sure that Elias is going to turn you, I want you to know that Preacher will do it for you if I ask him to."

Amy laughs. "Yeah, right! I'm not in a hurry for Eli to chop off my head. Are you?"

"Of course not. But think about it, Preacher already took responsibility for us. The Synodus should be willing to give us a chance since, technically, we didn't break the rule. Preacher did. And he thinks there is a chance that he will survive this. If not, he's more than happy to sacrifice himself for us."

Amy shakes her head. "I don't-"

"Don't answer yet. Just think about it. Talk to Preacher. Better yet, if you trust Elias ask him what would happen."

"Why do you want me to be one of Preacher's legare's so bad? What are you getting out of it?"

Lark shrugs, and says, "I guess I just like you, especially after hearing that story you just told me. And I don't mean that in a girl-on-girl sort of way. Most of the chicks here don't get me, so I hang with the guys. As for my sister, well..., she hasn't really been the same since we rescued her. But I think you and me will be a steady thirty degrees."

"I'll have to think about it."

"I know. It's probably hard to even think about being away from a nice piece like Elias, but you gotta think about what's best for you. You can stay being his Fountain of Life, enjoy the sex, and hope he's going to turn you one day. Or stay here where it's safe and have the power to protect yourself. You have options. That's all I'm saying. Okay?"

Amy nods her head and finishes her soda. Initially, she dismisses Lark's offer. But the more she thinks about the bigger picture, the more she begins to sway. Her whole reason for staying with Eli after he kidnapped her was to get him to turn her into a vampire. With him, she is going to have to work for that. She'll have to serve time as his fountain, learn all of his lessons, and wait patiently until he decides that she is ready. Then would come the dangerous part. Eli's blood is a double-edged sword. It could make her practically invincible or doom her to death if she can't handle its power. Preacher's blood isn't as strong as Eli's, but she will still be a formidable adversary in a chomper attack. And the point of becoming a vampire is to survive the chomper apocalypse.

The plusses in Lark's column are adding up in Amy's head, but another part of her doesn't want to give up on Eli so easily. To her surprise, there's nothing sexual about that notion. And she can't escape feeling like she's betraying him by even considering accepting Preacher's blood over his. She has no idea what she's going to do. And all she knows is that she can't make a stupid decision.

Amy's thoughts are disrupted when she hears men's laughter. Eli's laughter, in particular, brings her out of her trance. She turns around just as Eli opens the door and smiles at her, with Kwesi hovering over his shoulder.

"You okay?" Eli asks.

Amy nods her head, and sarcastically says, "You had a nice meal?"

"Feels like I just had a V-8."

"Good for you," Amy says, with more emotion than she intended and immediately wishes the words never left her mouth.

"You going to tell her the good news or what?" Kwesi says, kneading the muscles on Eli's shoulders like a trainer getting his boxer loose for a fight.

Amy looks at Eli, anxiously awaiting his response.

"We're going to hang out here until tomorrow morning," Eli says. "Kwes is gonna do some work on my truck to make sure it gets us to Florida, and I want to study that chomper a little bit more."

"Awesome!" Lark says, then looks at Amy. "I was hoping I'd get a chance to show you around. This works out great!"

Eli looks at Lark, and jokingly says, "Wow, Hot Pants, you actually passed up a chance to say, 'thirty degrees'?"

Amy laughs along with the vampires, but her mind is weighing two different futures. Both in which she is a vampire, but leading completely different lives. The road to one of those lives is a fairly easy one. She can stay here and hang out with Lark in the virtually chomper-free fort and wait out the Apocalypse. Or she can go with Eli and face the unknown, with no promise that she will get what her heart desires and no guarantee that she will live to see the sunrise from day to day. The compound provides safety and numbers, then there is Eli with his guns and his Bronco. The choice should be obvious, but it's not. And as Eli smiles at her, Amy wonders if he would even care if she decided to part ways with him here and send him off alone to find his old flame, Lygia.

CHAPTER TWELVE

Amy's humming reverberates sweetly off the walls. There's hardly enough space for two people to breathe without bumping into each other in the small bathroom, and the color reminds her of the inside of an avocado, but it might as well be her slice of Heaven. She wasn't looking for another reason to take Lark up on her offer, but opportunities for a hot shower sweetens the pot. Showers like that are a luxury, mostly enjoyed by the rich and important people in the safe zones. If she stays in the compound, she would only be able to have one every so often, as long as the water reserves are good. That is a very tempting prospect.

She continues to hum as she slides on a pair of boy shorts that matches her tank top. The mirror above the sink is wet, but she can still see her reflection. She turns to the side and considers how much her curves have shrunken. Her body is not all of what it was before she went to jail, but she is satisfied with how she looks in the clothing that she will be sleeping in. Normally it wouldn't matter, but tonight is different.

It has been a long day. Amy is thankful to be spending the night in one of the select cottages on the grounds of the compound. The special cottages were once the personal quarters of the top-ranked militia leaders. Now, the new residents all live in the dorm-style buildings and the cottages are a place where spouses and lovers share private time, or someone can have alone time. It all runs on a rotating schedule. Since Amy and Eli are special guests, and everyone assumes they are lovers, Preacher insisted that they take the cottage because he wanted to make sure that they had a comfortable night.

Amy takes a deep breath and turns the doorknob. When she steps out of the bathroom she finds Eli sitting on a loveseat with his shirt off, bare feet resting on a small coffee table, and his hat pushed forward on his head to cover his face. It looks as if he hasn't moved a muscle since he sat down. He's even clutching the bottle of Jack Daniels the same way, and the whiskey inside doesn't look like it has gone down more than what Amy drank while he was showering before her.

She can't help but wonder what's going through his head. Something is bothering him that he doesn't want to talk about it. That annoys her, but she accepts that he must have his reasons. What she does know is that the regulare in Eli has been looking for anything that Preacher or someone else at the compound doesn't want him to see. And when he went back to the chomper shack he spent at least a half hour staring down into the dry well, looking as if he was trying to figure out how a square peg got into a round hole. By the time they came to the cottage to call it a night, Eli looked like a man damned to carry the weight of the world.

"What's that song you were humming?" Eli asks.

"Show Me How To Live," Amy responds, realizing that her subconscious had selected the tune.

"Ha! I thought that was Audioslave but wasn't sure."

"Whoa, you know Audioslave? I'm impressed, old man."

"Old man?" Eli slips his hat off his head as he turns towards Amy. Whatever he was about to say next gets stuck in his throat and his jaw goes slack when he sees her in what she's wearing.

Amy tries to hold back her smile as much as possible. Eli's reaction to her is so much more than she expected, but she still wants to play it cool.

"Ahh," Eli says, "You look incredible."

"Thanks," Amy says, plopping down on the cushion next to him. "Lark showed me all the stuff they've looted and stockpiled. She gave me this and a bunch of other stuff that's my style."

"You and Hot Pants really hitting it off, huh?"

Hanging out with Lark for most of the day turned out much better than Amy ever expected. The only tough part was meeting Lark's elder sister, Robin. Robin had tried to put on her best face when Lark introduced her, but Amy could see that she was still suffering from the abuse she endured at the hands of the militiamen. Seeing how compassionately Lark takes care of Robin, Amy lowered her walls enough to discover that she and Lark actually get along quite well. Not that she's not willing to say that they are now BFFs, but it is nice to have a new friend.

It was also nice getting to know Kwesi and Gregory Three Feathers. Amy found it funny how the two burliest guys at the compound were the most gentle. As big as he is, Kwesi is a fun-loving teddy bear. And Three Feathers, a barrel-chested Navaho tribesman with long, jet-black hair, spoke with the calm and wisdom of a sage. He seemed to see into Amy's soul, noticing the black spots that were like a cancer. But Three Feathers didn't probe about her buried pain. Instead, he commented on a wellspring of strength that he sensed inside of her and said that there is nothing she couldn't overcome. It could be equated to psychobabble, but his words lifted her spirits.

The only person in the compound who rubbed Amy the wrong way was

Cruz. He flirted with her every time they crossed paths, and he tried his best to get her to be alone with him. She ended up having to warn him that she was with Eli, and it would be in his best interest to back off.

From what Amy had seen throughout the day, life in the compound seems pretty good for vampires and humans. Under Preacher's leadership, the place runs like a responsible and caring community should. Humans get the first priority for food and water since the vampires don't need them as much, and the humans provide the vampires with the blood necessary for them to remain healthy, according to vampire standards.

The vampires had successfully wiped out the majority of the chompers from the surrounding towns. They also scavenged and stockpiled basic essential products that are used in everyday life and enough non-perishable food to last months. That food, coupled with the emergency rations in the militia's massive inventory, can sustain everyone in the compound for at least a year. That doesn't even take into consideration them finding more food or the crops that the humans are attempting to grow. There is even a grasshopper farm in one of the buildings that looks like it will yield a good source of protein as long as the insects keep breeding. Everyone does their part to keep the compound running, and it functions as a successful little community.

"Lark's cool. I like her." Amy beckons with her fingers as she says, "You gonna pass that bottle or you plan on babysitting it all night?"

Eli hesitates for a moment but hands it over when Amy starts to glare.

She takes a big swig and scrunches her face from the burning in her throat.

"What do you think about Preach's compound?" Eli asks.

"It's impressive," Amy responds, leaning against the lumpy cushion of the loveseat. "Everybody's so nice here. There's a kinda crazy cult vibe, but I think they're sincere."

"I agree."

Amy smiles. "Hey, I got a question for you. What's the story with you and Kwesi? Seems like y'all been best buds forever."

Eli chuckles. "Actually, since nineteen fifty-eight, but it seems like forever. I met him after I split up with Lygia. I had spent about a decade in Japan before I was called back to the U.S. I was fillin' up at a gas station in Alabama when Kwesi pulled in on a motorcycle. A couple a good ol boys started hassling him, and I decided to put in my two cents about it. We didn't even realize that we were both vampires until we were in the middle of kickin' the shit out of some redneck ass. Ever since then, we've been as thick as thieves."

"That's cool. How long has he been a vampire?"

"Since eighteen sixty-three. He used to be a Maninka warrior before he was captured and made a slave. That didn't sit too well with him, so when the time was right, he broke an overseer's neck and escaped the plantation. He was on the run for almost three weeks before the mob that wanted to lynch him started to close in, but a vampire named Horatio found Kwesi first and took him up

North."

"Wow, Kwesi was an African warrior and a slave. That's chilling."

Eli nods. "Unfortunately, he has to live forever with the whip scars on his back. I have a lot of respect for him. I couldn't begin to imagine going through some of the things that he had to and still enjoy life as much as he does."

Amy files Kwesi's story in her head, along with what she learned about Eli and Preacher. Ironically, Preacher's magister is an atheist named Sheridon. Sheridon used to frequently debate Preacher about the existence of God. One day when Preacher talked about the return of Christ, Sheridon bet him that if he could live for eternity, eventually Preacher would lose his faith because the Rapture will never happen. When Sheridon revealed that he was a vampire and offered the gift of immortality, Preacher decided to risk his own soul to be able to live long enough to see the return of the Son of God, and to do much more good than he would have been able to do with his average human lifespan.

After taking another brave swig from the bottle, Amy says, "Can I ask you something?"

"No reason to stop now," Eli replies, with a smile.

"Can you stop being a regulare for a moment and talk to me as the person who you are, not the job that you do?"

Eli sighs. "I can't make any promises, but I can try."

"I guess I'll have to take what I can get," Amy says, with her tongue loossening up from the whiskey. "Any idea when you're going to make me your legare?"

"Honestly," Eli responds, "I'd have to say no. You have a very strong will, which is good. But you're also impulsive and sometimes hardheaded. That's no bueno. If I were forced to make that decision today, I wouldn't turn you. The thing is, as long as I've been a vampire I've never met anyone that I wanted to pass my gift on to until now, so it's only a matter of time before I keep my promise to you. But there's one thing that really worries me the most."

"Yeah, I know, the possibility of me going rogue because I might not be able to handle the power of your crazy-ass blood."

Eli leans over enough for his shoulders to touch Amy's. "You want to stay here with Hot Pants and Preacher, don't you?"

Amy's heart booms, sending a shock wave of guilt throughout her body. "I was talking with Lark, and it's possible that I can still be counted as one of the vampires that Preacher took responsibility for. I know it's a risk, and The Synodus might still wipe us all out, but I've been thinking about it," Amy admits, and lowers her eyes before her whole being shrivels up into a tiny ball.

Eli lifts her chin so that she has no choice but to look at him unless she closes her eyes. "I told you that I wasn't going to force you to do anything. You don't have to stay with me if you don't want to. We both know that you'll be safer here and you'll have friends. It's not a hundred percent guaranteed that The Synodus will let Preacher's legaries live, but they should be alright. That's more appealing than being cooped up in an old Bronco with me-"

"It's not you, Eli!" Amy interjects before Eli says something that will make her feel worse than she already does. "Next to my brother, you're the coolest guy I ever met."

Eli smiles, and says, "Can I at least be the coolest vampire you've ever met?"

The comment makes Amy laugh, which helps unloose some of the knots in her stomach. She nods, acknowledging that he is the coolest vampire, then she takes a big swig of alcohol to multiply the tipsy feeling overcoming her.

Amy puts the bottle down on the coffee table and Eli takes her hand, interlacing his fingers with hers. He squeezes gently, and says, "Listen, I understand what's going through your head right now. Tomorrow we can say goodbye and you can let either Hot Pants or Preacher turn you. Their blood is much safer than mine. The regulare in me can look the other way on this if that's what you really want to do, but only if you keep yourself from going rogue. And it's not like we'll never see each other again. I feel like we already have something special. And no matter what happens to the world, you and I are going to finish what we started."

Amy fights to keep the water welling up in her eyes from spilling out. She had no idea how beneficial talking it out with Eli was going to be. His words went directly to her heart and mingled with the feelings that she has been feeling for him. Her mind is made up now, and there isn't one fiber of her being that harbors a shred of doubt about what she wants more than anything.

"I wanted to be a vampire because it's my best chance to stay alive," Amy says. "And Lark's offer was tempting, but something kept nagging me. I thought it was guilt at first, but I realize that it was more than that. As bad as I want to be a vampire, it's more important to me to be a vampire that you're proud of. I only want you to be my magister, and I want to be connected to you for as long as we live. The honor of being your legare is worth waiting for until you think I'm ready. And if the craving gets to me and I go rogue, it's only right that you take me out. Nobody else but you."

For the second time in one night, Eli is left looking as if he has been left breathless, and Amy loves it. Her words might've stunned him, but Eli quickly recovers. With his eyes beaming he leans in closer to Amy. She doesn't resist as he gets close enough to initiate something that she has been fantasizing about. Their lips touch and their kiss quickly avalanches from a soft peck to hot, probing passion. The sharp tips of Eli's fangs graze her tongue whenever she slips it into his mouth, but it excites her even more, and she loses herself in the fervor, basking the heat of his skin that is burning as much as the fire between her legs.

Amy feels herself softly tipping over, and she doesn't fight it. The back of her head comes to a gentle rest against the arm of the loveseat, and she scoots her hips forward to lie more comfortably, while at the same time her legs allow Eli into the most intimate positioThe back of her head comes to a gentle rest against the arm of the loveseat. She scoots her hips forward to lay more comfortably, while at the same time her legs allow Eli into the most intimate position. She moans into his mouth when she feels the upper half of his rigid manhood pressing on her lower belly under the weight of his body. If not for the fresh tampon, she would be tugging at his pants to give herself to him completely. So Amy enjoys the kiss as it goes on, thankful that Eli doesn't try to take this moment between them further, even though an outstanding part of his body definitely wants him to.

Eli breaks the kiss and presses his forehead against hers. "I'm sorry," he says, "I shouldn't have done that."

"Why?" Amy asks. "I wanted you to."

"Yeah, but... alcohol doesn't affect me. You're drunk. I'm not. And I don't want to take advantage of you."

Amy giggles. "I'm a little drunk, but I know what I'm doing. I don't ever move this fast with a guy, but I don't regret kissing you. I needed that."

"I did, too," Eli says, raising up from the love seat, "but I think I better go now. Get some sleep. I'll be out in the truck if you need me for anything."

"Eli, when was the last time you slept in a bed?"

Eli shrugs. "Dunno, maybe a couple weeks."

Amy smiles at him, and says, "I don't want to have sex because..., you know. But I do want you to spend the night with me. If you want?"

Eli looks at Amy like she's insane, then he scoops her up from the loveseat, and says, "Even if that mattress were made of razor wire, I'd gladly lay in it with you."

Amy smiles and rests her head against his chest as he carries her over to the bedroom. At that moment she realizes that she is experiencing true happiness once again. She hasn't felt like this since Aaron died, and now she wishes that there was a way for her to never lose this feeling ever again.

CHAPTER THIRTEEN

Eli's sudden movement jerks Amy out of her sleep.

She covers her breasts with the sheet as she sits up on the bed and looks around. The cottage is still dark. She can't see Eli, but she hears the rustle of denim and the zippy sound made when skin and high-speed friction is added.

"What's going on?" Amy asks.

"An alarm," Eli says, buttoning his jeans.

Amy slips out of bed. "I don't hear anything."

"You wouldn't. It was whistled from out by the gates."

"Chompers?"

A rooster's crow blares across the compound from the window of the building the farm animals are kept in.

"Don't know, but I'm gonna find out."

"I'm coming with you." Amy bends down and sweeps her hand across the floor to find her top. "Just gimme a sec."

Her eyes begin to adjust to the darkness as she pulls her jeans up over the boy shorts that she slept in. Her vision is even better by the time she slides the barrel of the Beretta into her waistband and pushes her feet into her boots. She can now make out Eli quickly strapping one of his katars to his thigh, and she foregoes tieing her laces to get going as quickly as possible.

When she comes face-to-face with Eli he freezes for a moment, looking unsure if he should kiss her or not, but he does the right thing, and it makes her smile.

Memories of the night before flash through Amy's mind, making her warm and tingly. The moment Eli gently laid her on the mattress they were in a whirlpool of passion. Kissing was quickly entwined with hands eagerly exploring each other's bodies. Amy was the one who removed Eli's jeans, and she didn't resist when he lifted her tank top over her head. Her nipples harden as she recalls the sensation of his hot mouth. The pleasure was so intense, she almost gave in to her true desire. Besides wanting her first time with Eli to be menstruation free, she also felt the need to prove to him that she could maintain control, even though she wanted something really bad.

Eli opens the front door of the cottage. There is a soft glow in the sky from the sun beginning to crest over the horizon. Vampires and humans are also emerging from the surrounding buildings with weapons in hand. Amy finds it strange that none of them are moving with a real sense of urgency. She looks at Eli. He shrugs, stumped about the unfazed disposition of the others.

"Eli!" Kwesi calls out.

Amy turns around and sees him approaching with the equally imposing Gregory Three Feathers and the two female vampires who were traveling with them.

Amy genuinely smiles at Kwesi and Three Feathers but her cordial greeting is feigned towards Jodie and Becca. Both sisters are blonde, with bangs, and they seemed to have prioritized lip gloss as their must-have item for the apocalypse. They remind her of the drunk college girls whose boobs built the Girls Gone Wild empire, and Amy doesn't get along with that breed of skank. Plus, the way that both girls shamelessly fawned over Eli when Kwesi introduced them to him especially rubbed her the wrong way.

"What's going on?" Eli asks as they join the flow towards the front of the compound.

"That was the signal for somebody coming. If it were a military vehicle or something like that, the whistle would sound more like a siren. All we know right now is that something heading our way and it doesn't look threatening."

"Could be somebody from The Civitas," Three Feathers says optimistically. "It's been enough time for a run to Michigan and back."

Everybody within earshot turns in Eli's direction, eagerly awaiting a reaction from him. His face remains stoic, his feet keep pace, and he doesn't so much as twitch to offer a clue as to what he thinks about Three Feathers' suggestion.

"Don't put the cart before the horse," Kwesi says. "For all we know, somebody's coming to the militia for help. If we can help them, we will, and then send them on their way. If they want to make more of it, we can handle that, too."

"Sounds good," Becca says, sweeping a hand through her long hair in a flirty way.

"Yeah," Jodie chimes in. "At least we'll finally get some action around here."

Eli shakes his head. "Calm down, puppy. Right now your job is to look, listen, and learn. If you jump before anybody tells you to, you're going to learn a hard lesson from me in the worst way possible. Got it?"

If Jodie and Becca had tails, they would be tucked between their leg s as they nod their heads, acknowledging that they take Eli's words seriously. Slowly, they begin trickling to the rear of the group as they continue on.

A rapid patter of footsteps grabs Amy's attention. The smile on her face from Eli scolding Jodie and Becca gets a little brighter when she turns around and sees Lark hurrying to catch up them. Amy also experiences an undercurrent of sadness because she is going to have to let her new friend down with the news that she will be moving on with Eli instead of staying at the compound.

Lark greets everyone when she joins the group, but she doesn't ask the question that is burning in her eyes. Amy pretends to be oblivious as they close in on the mass gathering in the courtyard by the front gate.

Preacher is already there, standing on one of the parapets observing the road leading to the compound. He turns around, holds up a reassuring hand, and says, "It's all right. It's just one vehicle, and it doesn't look military or militia."

"What kind of vehicle?" Eli asks.

Preacher turns around again and stares for a moment, then he says, "Ahh, an SUV. I don't know what kind."

"A Cadilac Escalade," the young guard standing next to Preacher says. "That's what it looks like to me. It's got mirror tint on the side windows and dark black on the windshield."

Eli grits his teeth and says, "Fuck! Me!"

"What's wrong?" Amy asks.

"Members of The Synodus are driven in Escalades with mirror tinted side windows. That doesn't mean one or all of them are here, but that's what my gut's telling me."

The crowd murmurs about the possibility that either The Imperator or one of his Proconsul, or even all of three of them, have come to the compound. Amy understands their anxiety. She had only learned about The Synodus a couple days ago, and she feels like a guilty person about to stand in front of a judge who just found out that his wife is cheating on him with the man who killed his faithful old dog. She can only imagine how these vampires feel since their fate lay in the hand that governs the vampire world, and they are only moments away from finding out if that hand will remain open, welcoming to them, or snap shut and crush them to dust.

Eli turns Amy so that she is looking directly at him and a sense of dread grows in her when she realizes he seems to be agonizing about something.

"Stay by my side," Eli says. "Do what I do. And don't say anything unless you're spoken to. If something goes wrong, do exactly what I tell you to. You understand me?!"

Amy nods her head. "What's wrong, Eli?"

"A member of the Synodus personally showing up here can't be good. I gotta see who's here and find out what they want to do before I figure out our best move." Eli then looks at Kwesi and Three Feathers. He lets out a frustrated sigh, and says, "If this turns bad, what side are you coming down on?"

Kwesi shrugs. "If I have to stay out of your way, I will."

Gregory Three Feathers sighs and nods in agreement.

"What does that mean for us?" Lark asks.

Eli shakes his head. "It means, if Pelagius is here and he commands me to draw my blades, then you and everybody else here will have to run like hell or fight for your lives. And you better not hesitate to do either."

"But we can't beat you, and we can't all outrun you."

"I'm bound by my word to obey The Imperator, even if I don't want to do what he asks of me. Regardless, if it comes to it, I can't help you guys unless you try to help yourselves. I'll do everything in my power to keep this from going sideways, but you all knew that there was a possibility of this happening. If a Proconsul is here, we might have some wiggle room, but I honestly don't know how this thing is going to go down."

The growing sunlight illuminates the fear on Lark's face. In a glance, Amy sees that same expression on the faces all around her. When she turns to Eli she finds worry in the eyes of the legendary, cold-hearted regulare. Yesterday he could have slaughtered everyone in this compound without giving it a second thought. But after spending time with the vampires and the people here, he knows that they don't deserve the death that he is capable of delivering.

Kwesi and Three Feathers also look as if they are struggling between doing what they know is right and obeying the word of authority.

Amy realizes that she also has a choice to make. She likes Preacher, Lark, as well as all of the other vampires and people that she has met here at the compound. She doesn't expect Eli to tell her to help him kill any of them, but she doesn't know if she will be able to sit idly by if he tells her to do nothing while he massacres everyone. She felt like a coward when she didn't help the family being brutalized by the militia, and she can't bring herself to do that again. Her predicament is further complicated by the possibility of going up against Eli. That's the last thing that she wants to do.

Preacher jumps the forty feet from the top of the wall down to the ground and lands with a thud that probably would have shattered his bones if he was still human. He tries to calm everyone by telling them that Eli is only thinking of the extreme in this situation. None of them has done anything wrong, and as long as they be themselves, they will have nothing to worry about. Then he tells the vampires manning the gate to remove the heavy steel bar reinforcing it and let the vehicle in.

The tension within the compound is as thick as fog, and it only increases when the Escalade pulls into the compound and stops in the middle of the space that the parted crowd made for it.

Amy tries to see through the windshield's tint as the Escalade sits idling. She is unable to make out any shapes of whoever is inside of it. Each lumbering second strengthens Amy's notion that whoever is in the vehicle must be a first class asshole for making such a dramatic entrance.

Finally the front doors of the Escalade open. Two men in white button-up shirts with shoulder holsters cradling Sig Sauers step out. Both have stern, no-nonsense glares. Their Slavic facial features and stiff mannerisms remind Amy of KGB agents portrayed in '80's movies. The one on the driver's side is taller than the other, and he is holding a large, gleaming sickle in his right hand that is connected to a long chain wrapped around his wrist and forearm. The other vampire has a set of short swords, and he appears to be looking for the slightest excuse to use them. Amy doesn't know who they are but she does know one important thing about them: they are rergulares. The rings on their fingers say so.

The vampire with the sickle shuts his door and takes a few steps backwards. With the decorum of a well-mannered chauffeur, he opens the back door and bows to someone inside.

Amy catches sight of the silver tip on a skinny black cane as it appears under the bottom edge of the door and digs into the dirt. A polished wingtip shoe follows. Then the other shoe plants firmly on the ground and a tall man with silvery gray hairs on his temples emerge from the Cadilac. Immediately, Eli and all of the vampires make a fist with their right hands and places it over their hearts, then they lower their heads in veneration. Amy does the same, keeping one eye on Eli to make sure that she mimics his every move.

A beautiful Asian woman is assisted out of the Escalade by the driver next. She looks around at the walls and buildings within the compound. Her expression reeks of disgust as the vampire with the cane futilely tries to smooth out the wrinkles in his expensive suit.

A man with eyebrows like two woolly bears and a young woman with long blonde hair are next to exit the vehicle. The woman makes a beeline to some of the compound's residents. From the way she is received with open arms, Amy assumes she is one of them and the man with her is the vampire, Barney "Bushy-browss" Blackwell, who was sent by Preacher to give his
report to The Synodus.

Once the vampire with the cane is satisfied that he looks as pristine as possible, he glances around at the faces of the vampires surrounding him, then displays his whitened fangs while needlessly adjusting a gold shield-shaped pendant dangling from his neck by a chain. His expression slightly changes when his eyes run across Eli. Amy reads it as possible disdain. The vampire quickly regains his composure and continues to visually inspect what he can see of the compound.

One of the roosters continues the regiment of crows, which draws the attention of the important vampire. He finally smiles, then looks at Preacher and says, "Antonio Robles. I was concerned when I heard about this place. But I must say, apparently, you are doing quite well for yourself."

Preacher bows his head again, and says, "Thank you, Proconsul Calavius. Had I known you were coming today, I would have prepared a better reception for you."

"I think we can do without the fanfare, Antonio," Calavius says. "And I am no longer Proconsul. I am now The Imperator, at least until things get back to normal and I restore order within our society."

Amy glances at Eli and sees the shock on his face, as well as a spark of anger in his eyes.

Preacher opens his mouth to respond to what Calavius just said but is silenced by a wave of Calavius's hand as he starts walking directly toward Eli.

"Elias Kincade," Calavius says, "What are you doing here?"

"I just found this place yesterday," Eli says, sounding detached from his own being.

Calavius chuckles. "Why am I not surprised? Leave it to you to find anything, anywhere in the world. Can I assume that the presence of a high ranking regulare here and no corpses burning on a pyre means that there is nothing for me to be vexed about?"

"Preacher is doing a good thing here..., Imperator? What happened to Pelagius?"

Calavius sympathetically puts a hand on Eli's shoulder and somberly says, "I'm afraid I have some bad news, son."

Eli's eyes grow in anticipation as Calavius appears to struggle getting the words out of his mouth. Eli's face all but says, "Spit it out!" followed by a few choice expletives.

From what she observes, Amy feels strong about her speculation that Eli bears some level of resentment towards Calavius and he is only respecting the vampire leader's authority because of his sense of duty.

"It's The Civitas, Elias," Calavius finally says. "It was completely destroyed. Pelagius was inside at the time. He perished, along with every soul who was in and around the grounds at the time. Everything that we have worked so hard to build, all that we've collected on our species over the centuries has been lost... even the records of The Primus... and Pelagius' magister, Anaximenes."

"What?" Eli says, shaking his head in disbelief. "How is that possible?"

Calavius talks to Eli but his words are for everyone to know what happened. The Civitas was being used as a safe haven for all of the vampires in Michigan and the surrounding states, including their fountains and the families. After weeks of administering for the smooth function of The Civitas and making sure that everyone within its walls were safe and sustained, Calavius wanted a few days away to be alone with his wife and fountain, Kimiko. So they and his guards, Nicholi and Aleksi, took a trip out to Lake Huron to spend a couple days on his yacht.

On the way back, when they were a mere few miles away from The Civitas, they heard what they thought were jets. Seconds later there were loud explosions and pillars of fire reaching up to the sky. Calavius's estimated that the blast zone had to be at least a mile wide, and the crater left behind where The Civitas once stood was even deeper than the six stories of structures underneath it.

The vampire with the bushy eyebrows who found Calavius and brought him back to the compound nods in agreement about Calavius' assessment of the damage done to the once sprawling mansion that hid secrets within its walls and underneath its marble floors.

"That sounds like something I experienced a couple nights ago," Eli says, now grimacing in anger. "We heard a military chopper flying around, then something came in fast and pounded the hell out of the ground."

"We?" Calavius says, shifting his eyes over to Amy.

Amy notices Calavius' nostrils flare slightly, even though her eyes are more focused on the shield around his neck. The pendant looks exactly like the emblem on Eli's ring.

Calavius places two fingers under Amy's chin to lift her head, then he says, "And who are you?"

Amy overrides her impulse to look at Eli, and staring into Calavius' eyes by force, she attempts to bow before she says, "My name is Amy Gouyen, Imperator Calavius. It is an honor to meet you in person..., sir."

"You didn't necessarily answer my question, Amy Gouyen. I now know your name, but I still don't know who you are."

Not knowing what to tell Calavius, and without Eli so much as twitching a muscle to steer her in the right direction, Amy takes a breath and hopes that she doesn't make things more complicated than they already are. "I am Elias' fountain, Imperator Calavius. I'm still learning all the laws of The Synodus, so I hope I haven't done anything to offend you."

Calavius shifts his eyes over to Eli. Amy does the same, and she sees that he is still stoic, probably still dwelling on what he has just learned about The Civitas and the death of all the vampires there, including Pelagius. It would be nice to know from him if she has made a mistake by revealing too much to the defacto leader of the vampires, but all she can do is wait and see what is going to happen next.

"What happened to Natasha, Elias?" Calavius says.

"She got infected. I was lucky to find Amy. She has potential. I believe she will make a trustworthy vampire one day and a good candidate for regulare training."

Calavius turns his eyes to Amy again. He removes his fingers from under her chin and places the palm of his hand on top of her head, as if he is about to bless her. "If Elias believes that much in you, then you must be a special young lady. I won't give permission for you to become one of us today. But if that day ever comes, don't disappoint him, or me. Believe me, you will regret it if you do."

"I won't disappoint you or him, sir," Amy says, smothering the flames of anger from the rejection, but still taking Calavius' words seriously.

Calavius flashes a creepy smile, then he turns his attention back to Eli.

"Now, about Antonio and his unusual number of unsanctioned legares. What do you have to report?"

Holding back a grimace, Eli says, "Preacher hasn't gone rogue. He and his legares are all loyal. He made a judgment call when he turned them, and his intentions were good. They and the humans here all know the laws and respect them. And all they're doing is protecting their families and defending this place from chompers. Speaking of chompers, there's one here that you really should take a look at."

"A chomper?!" Calavius says, appalled. "Why on earth would I want to see one of those accursed things?!"

"A couple a reasons. For one, it grew a fang."

Calavius appears to be indifferent to this news. "And why haven't you killed the abomination yet?"

Eli shakes his head. "Because we can learn a lot from it. I knew that there were similarities between us, but I didn't know about the fangs until yesterday. If Lygia doesn't know this already, I'm sure she'll appreciate the information."

"Speaking of Lygia, why aren't you with her?"

"I'm getting back on the road in about ten minutes. I should meet up with her in a day or two."

"Good. When you find her, please pass on my condolences." Calavius places his hand on the medallion resting on his chest, and says, "She and I are brother and sister since we are Pelagius' only legares; equals in his bloodline. And her place as Imperator is hers if she wants it. The Synodus may be fractured, but it won't be long before we reestablish contact with Titus in Germany. So, if she's ready, please escort her back here so we can set things right."

Calavius turns away as if he is suddenly bored with the conversation.

"Imperator!" Eli says. "Was Sig at The Civitas when it was destroyed?"

"No. Sigodur has disappeared," Calavius responds, without turning back around. "We assume he has gone rogue. Trajanius was sent after him since he was the only person who could track him. Tajanius didn't make it back. So, for Sig to kill his magister, there is no question of what he has become. That matter will be resolved, though, once our forces are gathered and order is restored."

Calavius beckons Preacher to walk with him. "Nicholi and Aleksi are in need of fountains," he says as they move away. "The fountain you sent with Barney couldn't sustain all three of them, and as you know, I am the only one whom Kimiko nourishes...."

Calavius' entourage follows as they make their way into the compound, while most of the other vampires dispersed to spread the news that they have just learned.

Eli, Amy, and the vampires that they walked to the gate with hang back by the Escalade. Jodie and Becca look as if they aren't sure if they should go with the crowd or stay where they are. As for Lark, she looks relieved that she has been spared from one of Eli's katars teaching her what a blade of grass feels like when it is mowed down. Eli, Kwesi, and Three Feathers, on the other hand, communicate their thoughts with their eyes. Amy feels the same way that they apparently do. Her first impression of Calavius categorizes him as a pompous jerk, and she has a feeling that he will be wielding his power with an iron fist in no time. She is glad that she had already decided to leave with Eli this morning. After meeting Calavius she would've wanted out as soon as possible, and it might have been hard to convince Eli to take her back. It probably would've been hell earning back his trust after that.

Words aren't being spoken but Amy can see, primarily from the fury brewing in Eli's eyes, that something else is bothering him and Kwesi. She can only speculate as to what it is, but she won't know for sure until she and Eli are outside the gates and far enough from the compound to talk without risk of being overheard by the wrong vampire. Thinking about leaving makes her feel like she is going to miss Lark. She turns to her new friend and sees that Lark must have been having the same thought because Lark now has a sad look on her face. The time that they had spent together was short but Lark has grown on her since their first meeting, and now she hopes that their friendship will last. It would have been nice to say that their friendship will last as long as they are vampires, but Calavius just put the kibosh on that, and she is on the downside of the equation.

CHAPTER FOURTEEN

Amy squints as she and Lark make their way to the Bronco. The compound is now flooded with the natural light of the rising sun. Amy finds it ironic that this bright mo rning is probably the dawn of a dark day here. It's been less than twenty minutes since Calavius and his entourage had arrived, and their presence has tainted the community atmosphere that Amy had enjoyed discovering the day before.

"I really wish I could roll with you guys," Lark says.

"I know," Amy responds, then she lets out a sigh that says the things that she can't risk putting into words.

Lark nods her head and stays in character. "I really liked hanging out with you, Amy. It was nice having a girl friend again, even if it was just for one day."

"Yeah, I feel the same way." Amy puts her arm around Lark's shoulder and gives her a gentle squeeze. She hopes that Lark deciphers her gesture as saying, "Please be careful. I'm worried about you."

Worried is an understatement. Amy truly fears for Lark and the others. Eli won't verbally say much, but his urgency to get out of the compound speaks loud and clear.

"You got enough supplies to get you where you're going," Kwesi says, staring at the cargo space of the Bronco. "That thermostat we put in wasn't new, but it'll hold up. I'd feel better about this hunk of junk, though, if you had let me put a new head gasket on it."

"The gasket's fine," Eli says. "And this 'hunk of junk' hasn't let me down since I drove her off the lot. So respect her or kiss her grill while she's doing seventy."

"Seventy? I didn't think you can get this thing to do more than twenty, even if you were pushing it down a hill," Kwesi says and laughs as engages Eli in one of their bro hugs. "Still, keep an eye on that temp gauge."

"Gotcha."

"Hey," Kwesi says and fakes a sucker punch to Eli's gut. "Me and Feathers got this if things get rowdy."

"Listen to me. Do not underestimate Nicholi and Aleksi. Nicholi is deadly with that sickle and chain. As for Aleksi, once he gets goin' with those short swords, it's like tryin' to stop a tornado with a butterfly net. You gotta catch him before he ever makes a move, and that ain't gonna be easy if you ain't faster than he is. So no matter how rowdy it gets, I want you guys to stand down. And if I hear you talking like that again, I'll consider it treason and execute you on the spot myself. Got it?"

Kwesi nods his head. "Got it."

"All right, we better get going," Eli says, then he turns to Amy. "Ready?"

Amy holds up her backpack and Beretta. "Yep."

Kwesi laughs, and says, "Eli can find anybody, anywhere, but he has to be the luckiest bastard in the world to find you."

Amy smiles, and says, "I guess I should say thank you."

"Nothing says thank you like a nice hug from a pretty girl."

Amy looks to Eli to see if he is okay with that. Then she gives Kwesi a hug that lasts until Eli's growl says it is time to break it up.

Eli then looks at Lark, and says, "Well, Hot Pants, I guess I'll be seein' you."

Lark nods her head and hugs him. "Via con Dios, cowboy. Make sure you take care of my girl."

"Don't worry about Amy. She can hold her own, but I'll keep her safe. You just take care of yourself, and only do what I expect of you."

As if rehearsed, everyone says, "Thirty degrees," at the same time that the words come out of Lark's mouth. Then they all break out into laughter.

Amy and Eli get into the Bronco. After Eli turns the ignition, he says to Kwesi, "Tell Preach I said I'm sorry I couldn't say goodbye."

"Me, too," Amy says.

"Will do," Kwesi responds and raps his knuckles on the driver side door. "Take care, brother."

Eli nods and puts the Bronco in gear. He pulls away from the cottage and coasts down the path leading to the gate. Amy watches Kwesi and Lark in the side view mirror and hopes that they will be all right as long as Calavius is here at the compound. She also wishes that she was able to thank Preacher and say goodbye to him like she had originally planned to. But Preacher was preoccupied with Calavius and Eli wanted to get going as soon as possible. She could have made an effort to get Preacher's attention but thought it was best to stay out of Calavius' way. He makes her uncomfortable. And his bodyguards' cold gaze makes her feel like they suspect her of being an assassin.

The vampires manning the gate open it up as the Bronco approaches and Eli taps his horn twice to bid them farewell. Once outside of the walls, Eli steps on the accelerator and pulls away from the compound like he can't get away from it fast enough. Amy glances at the rearview mirror, but the bulk of her concern is for Eli. He hasn't been the same since Calavius broke the news about

The Civitas to him, and she wishes that she could do more to help him with whatever he is struggling with inside.

Amy reaches over and places her hand on top of the hand that Eli has resting on the gear shift. "I would ask if you're all right, but I hate when people ask me stupid questions like that."

Eli cracks the slightest of smiles.

"I know you're upset about what happened to Pelagius, as well as what you heard about your boy, Sig," Amy says with all sincerity. "I'm sorry."

Eli nods his appreciation of Amy's commiseration. "I was lookin' forward to you meeting Pelagius. He would've liked you, and you would've understood why I'm so loyal to him."

"Guess he was nothing like Calavius, huh?"

"Definitely not. Calavius always rubbed me the wrong way, and I hate myself for what I had to do back there before we left."

"What, take orders from an asshole?"

Eli scoffs. "No. I'm talking about leaving that bastard alive! It took everything I had for me not to take his head when he was in front of me but I can't without permission from Lygia first, or even from Titus since he is a member of The Synodus."

"Would Titus grant permission to kill his magister?"

"Titus is honorable. He shows no mercy to acolytes, rogues, or traitors. I would have his blessing if he were here."

Amy stares at Eli, noting the fury raging more intensely inside of him. She isn't surprised that he wants to go after Calavius. She has her own suspicions about the story that Calavius told about conveniently being away from The Civitas when it was pounded by missiles. But she seems to be reading something more from Eli, something that feels extremely personal.

"It's the way he said for me to bring Lygia to him 'if' she wants to take her father's place," Eli says as if he read Amy's mind. "Pelagius' wishes were clear, so there should be no 'ifs' about it. With Pelagius gone and Titus an ocean away, Calavius is pulling a power play. Pelagius warned that something like this might happen one day, and now it's up to Lygia and me to decide if we use the contingency plan."

"So what's the contingency plan?" Amy asks.

Eli shakes his head. "It's best you not know until you absolutely have to."

"Can you at least tell me if you think Calavius has gone rogue? And if he is, can you beat him?"

Amy's question stems from her concern about Eli taking on a vampire who is stronger than he is? It was a miracle achievement for Eli to defeat a rogue vampire when he was still a human, but that would've cost him his life is Lygia blood wasn't on the sword that pierced his heart. Amy believes in Eli, but she also fears what can happen if a war with a rogue vampire erupts in the near future. Suddenly, chompers have become more of pests than a problem, although, they cannot be forgotten.

Eli grits his teeth. "I don't know, but I'm looking forward to finding out. First things first, though. We're taking a detour."

"A detour?"

"Yeah. It was already on my mind, but now my gut is telling me to check on a safe house that Sig knows about. Rogue or not, I need to find him and get to the bottom of what's going on. Plus, I got a nagging feeling I better check on something important."

CHAPTER FIFTEEN

Abandoned cars and buildings are the headstones of humanity. The bones of dead are like litter underfoot of the things that don't know how to die. And through it all, Amy enjoys feeling like she and Eli are the last two people on Earth. But they aren't, and Eli has been pushing the Bronco's engine to get from Texas to where they are now in northern Louisiana.

"We're close," Eli says, slowing down to navigate around an overturned RV. "It's a long shot, but I hope Sig is there. Rouge or not, I can use his help. I might even end up kissing the big bastard when I see him."

"What, my lips aren't good enough?" Amy says and smirks.

"You bet they are! And I'm looking forward to kissing your other lips, too."

"You perv," Amy says, slugging Eli in the arm.

"Like you'd have me any other way."

Eli makes a sharp turn onto a private road that looks like it leads directly into the swamp. Amy wonders if their destination is going to be a wooden shack decorated with alligator skulls, resting on the banks of a murky bayou.

A few miles down the winding road, Amy spots two brick columns standing out against the vegetation up ahead of the next bend. One of the wrought iron gates between them is wide open, while the other hangs loosely by one hinge. Amy turns to Eli and sees the hostility growing on his face. As fast as the Bronco is already going, he applies more pressure on the accelerator and grits his teeth.

Amy picks up her 9mm and racks it. The gates look like they were rammed open. It's possible for a good size swarm of chompers to break through the gate like that. It's also possible that a freshly infected chomper could have done it with a vehicle. But there's no way of telling what happened, at least until they get there.

Eli rounds the small corner, and a pair of Chevy Suburbans come into sight. He keeps his foot on the gas until he is almost upon them, only hitting the brake just in time for the Bronco to skid to a stop before smacking into a bumper. He removes his hat and stares at the Suburbans blocking the driveway leading up to a plantation-style mansion. All four doors of both big SUV's are wide open, and Amy can make out bullet holes in the rear windows and windshields.

"Stay with me!" Eli says as he opens his door. "There are chompers in the house, and I want you by my side until they're all dead. Then we'll try to figure out what the fuck happened here!"

Amy doesn't take Eli's harsh tone personally. He has to be running on emotion and adrenaline. Feeling amped up, herself, she simply nods her head to let him know that she is with him. Then she pockets two extra magazines for her Beretta and gets out of the Bronco at the same time as he does.

Walking briskly with Eli around one of the bullet-riddled SUV's, Amy notices tattered clothing strewn around the huge front yard, along with an absurd amount human bones. Skulls, femurs, rib cages and more. All clean of flesh. Definitely chomper M.O., but this close to the swamp the ravaged bodies could also be the work of animals that were more than happy to come across a meal that they didn't have to work for. Maybe even chomper animals, for that matter?

Amy and Eli come around the Suburban and find two bulletproof vests with multiple rounds embedded in them. Most of the remains of the men who died wearing them had long been devoured. She glances at the debris of bones around the yard and the decomposing bodies closer to the steps in front of the house. She estimates the total body count to be at least thirty, but without a CSI team at her disposal, she has no way of telling if these people were fighting chompers or each other. And at the moment she has no way of telling why the bodies closer to the house aren't as marauded as the rest, but her hunch is that they must've been chompers when they were killed.

An unmistakable moan comes from the direction of the house. Eli's hands first settle on his katars, but he ends up sliding his Desert Eagles out of their holsters instead. Amy points her handgun at the open front doors of the mansion, wishing that she had ammo for her 30-30 rifle. She can handle the 9mm well enough, but there is nothing like old reliable when it comes to putting down chompers. It doesn't bother her too much, though. As long as she is with Eli, she knows that the chompers don't stand a chance of getting close enough for her to smell their stench.

The first chomper comes through the door, stopping at the upper landing of the steps to sniff the air and lock in on the new scent. The chomper, dressed in a filthy wife-beater and jeans with one leg split up the seam, barely gets a good whiff of Amy and Eli when another chomper in a sequined party dress comes running out of the house and plows into him.

Wife-beater chomper and the female who ran into him tumble over in a mass of flailing arms and legs. Party dress chomper lands on top of wife-beater chomper with her legs spread-eagle, giving a hideous up-skirt of her soiled, once-white panties. Neither of the chompers miss a beat after the hard fall. They scramble on their hands and knees, crawling over the bodies in front of the mansion, clumsily trying to get back to their feet as more chompers pour through the doors.

Amy and Eli wait patiently for the chompers to get closer before opening fire. She knows that Eli could hit his targets at a further distance that she can, but he wants to inflict maximum damage when he shoots. That's fine with her. She's only decent with the Beretta between forty to fifty yards, but once the distance starts getting less than that, she turns deadly.

Amy kisses Aaron's dog tags and puts a bead on wife-beater chomper, who is leading the pack by just a few steps. She keeps her breathing soft and steady, holding the chomper's head in her line of fire. When she has him in range, she squeezes the trigger. The Beretta pops a shot that snaps the chomper's head back and knocks him off his feet. Before the chomper hits the ground, she has her sights on a chomper wielding a rusty chain. She pops off another shot that knocks a chunk out of the side of his head as it spins him around. A chomper with dreadlocks, wearing a New Orleans Saints jersey, is selected as her next target.

Eli's Desert Eagles begin to roar. He fires nine shots that swiftly decimates the heads they hit, including the chomper in the party dress. Then he fires a shot at the last chomper, blowing apart the whole brain casing off of the Saints fan.

"That one was mine," Amy says.

"Sorry," Eli responds, revolving his guns as he crosses his arms to reholster them, "couldn't help myself."

It occurs to Amy that Eli's extravagant way of holstering his weapons might be a subconscious thing. Normally he's smirking when he does his cocky move, but this time his expression is grim and his eyes look as though his thoughts are miles away.

Eli turns his attention to the skeletal remains that are closest to them. Amy follows behind him as he moves towards the bones of the person who was once dressed in a pair of black leather pants and ended up with a bullet through the skull. Eli crouches next to the body and stares at the gold chain around its neck bones and the diamond-studded crucifix pendant laying askew on its partially shattered ribs.

"Sig?" Amy asks.

Eli shakes his head. "Matthew, one of the humans who guarded this safe house. Looks like he's been dead for weeks, months even, along with most of the bodies out here with gunshot wounds. Matt and the guys out by the SUVs were eaten by insects and animals. Not the work of chompers."

"So, what..., you think whatever might've gone down here happened before the outbreak?"

"I want to say yes," Eli says, then stands up and slowly looks around, "but

I didn't hear anything about a distress call from this safe house. The most disturbing thing is, I don't see the two vampires responsible for protecting this place, or any signs of the ones who would've been gathered here until they got orders about what to do."

"Maybe there's clues or a message inside the house?"

"Well, we're gonna find out. Plus, there's something I need to check on. But I don't want to leave my truck parked that far away."

They get back in the Bronco and drive around the SUVs, as well as the dead chompers and humans. Eli parks in front of the steps leading up to the mansion. When they get out Eli takes her hand and quickly leads her through the foyer and on into a grand greeting room.

The mansion reeks of a horrible odor concentrated within its walls, chomper stench overpowered by the putrid aroma of decay. Broad, flat beams of sunlight laser through the slight divisions between the thick curtains covering the large windows, affording Amy enough light to see where she is going. She also picks up details of the opulent room decorated in a contemporary motif, now ransacked to shambles. In the darkest corner, within a dried pool of smeared blood that looks as dark as crude oil, is a cluster of bodies that are stripped of clothing and flesh.

With the mansion being poorly lit or completely dark, Amy loses her bearings as Eli leads her down a hallway and makes a number of turns along the way. His final turn puts them in a passageway lit up by bright sunlight shining through a glass wall at the end of it. Amy makes out small trees, various flowering plants, white benches and a mound of dirt on the other side. She assumes they are going outside until she is close enough to notice a huge skylight in the ceiling.

Eli comes to a dead stop at the threshold of the atrium, as if he ran into an invisible force field. Shock registering on his face as he stares into the room. Amy steps beside him to get a look at what has him so disturbed. She gasps when notices a dark colored, emaciated, naked corpse lying upside down on a dirt mound located almost in the middle of the room..

Amy follows Eli into the indoor garden and remains silent as he settles down on one knee at the edge of the mound to inspect the corpse.

The word "Mummy" initially pops into Amy's head, until she realizes that the corpse's dirty skin doesn't really look like parchment. The carcasses' wrinkly skin makes it look like a giant prune with limbs and a head with a pronounced brow ridge. Its grimace, frozen by death, displays a set of fangs prominently standing out among the teeth framed by thin lips. But the most shocking thing is how the cranium of the odd-looking skull is broken open like a poached egg, with a flap of hairy scalp hanging like an open lid.

"This has gone from fucked up," Eli grouses, lowering his glasses as he rises to his feet again, "to all fucked up!"

"This is a senex, isn't it?" Amy asks, hoping that her assumption doesn't leave her looking like an idiot.

Eli nods his head as he studies the hand and footprints on the mound of dirt.

"But," Amy says, confused, "what's it doing here? Did you guys bury it?"

"No. This one's been here since the day he buried himself. From the features of his skull, we knew that he was a Neanderthal vampire, maybe first generation to The Primus, who somehow ended up here tens of thousands of years ago and chose this place to sleep."

"Don't take this the wrong way, Eli, but there's no way you can tell me that this safe house being built around a Senex's resting place is a coincidence."

"It's not," Eli says, lifting his sunglasses as he turns to Amy and stares directly into her eyes. "Amy, I need you to swear to me on your life that what you see here stays between us."

Amy raises her own shades and holds his gaze, then with all sincerity she says, "If you want me to keep something between us, then that's where it stays. I swear to you on my life about that."

Eli nods his head. "I found this senex about a decade after I found the one that was taken to The Civitas. Pelagius asked Lygia and me to keep it a secret, even from the Proconosul. He had this mansion built, and we've used it as an emergency safe house. Only a handful of vampires actually know about this place."

"Why would The Imperator keep the senex from the rest of The Synodus?"

"Because Pelagius knows that other vampires desire the stronger power that is in senex blood. That's the main reason why he put the senex who made him a vampire in a secure vault at The Civitas, and he decreed that all other senexs would be left to rest wherever they are."

Amy looks at the desecrated senex. "You think one of the vampires or humans who was protecting this place somehow discovered it?"

Eli sighs, shakes his head and glances at the shovel resting a few feet away from the mound. "Somebody knew exactly where to dig. Pelagius, Lygia and I are the only ones who knew about this senex. Pelagius is dead. I haven't sensed Lygia move this far east in over a year. And I just found out somebody dug him up and drained whatever blood was left in him, including whatever was in his brain. Most of those footprints seem to be made by chompers who wandered in and out of here, and I can't distinguish which was made by whoever dug him up, or how many there were."

"The dead paramilitary guys out front, you think they could have something to do with this, or it's a coincidence that they were trying to take this place for their own?"

Eli halfheartedly shrugs his shoulders, and says, "Right now, your guess is as good as mine. But if they came here, knowing what to look for...."

Amy sees Eli's dilemma. If the men who came in the Suburbans had knowledge of the senex, that would mean that either Pelagius or Lygia leaked the information about its location and now there is a vampire, or maybe even a rogue, running around who was made exponentially stronger from senex blood.

"We'll figure this out," Amy says. "And when it's time to go after whoever did this, I got your back."

Eli relinquishes a moderate smile. He is still overtly tense, but Amy's words appear to be something that he needed to hear, and they mean a lot to him.

"Spoken like a true regulare," Eli says, then he sighs. "Amy, you have no idea how much I wish I knew for sure you'll be able to handle my bloodline without going rogue."

"I'm going to be able to handle it, Eli. I know I am. Why are you even bringin' that up?"

"Because I still got business with Calavius and I'm probably going to have to hunt down a rogue hopped up on senex blood. I'm used to working alone, but I like having you as my partner."

"I like you being my partner, too," Amy says with a smile.

Eli remains straight-faced. "I promised I'll turn you when the time comes if that's still what you really want. But it's gonna kill me if things go wrong and I end up losing you."

Amy wraps her arms around him, and says, "That means a lot to me, Eli. But I need you to have faith in me. I'm not going to go rogue. My desire to make you proud of me by itself is all the motivation I need to make sure that doesn't happen."

Eli nods his head. "When I get the green light, I will make you my legare. But as of now, I want you to consider yourself my partner, not just my fountain. And I'm happy I found you, Amy. It's been more than a pleasure havin' you ride with me."

"I'm happy you found me, too. And for the record, I'm pretty sure you're gonna get laid a whole lot now that I'm ridin' with you..., partner."

Eli laughs and seals the deal with a quick kiss, then he goes back into regulare mode. He leaves Amy in the atrium with the senex, returning minutes later with a pair of pliers and one of the gas canisters from the Bronco. He uses the pliers to remove the senex's fangs and places them in his pocket. Another quick trip away and he returns with some of the mansion's thick curtains, which he wraps the ancient body in.

Once the senex is enshrouded, Eli makes more trips in and out of the atrium, chucking heaps of broken up furniture into the hole. Then as respectfully as possible, he drops the senex back into what is now its final resting place. After covering the body with more shattered wood, Eli empties the entire canister of gasoline into the hole and ignites the blaze with an emergency road flare.

"We're done here," Eli says as heat and thick black smoke bellow from the depths of the pit.

Amy nods her head and gladly takes his hand for him to escort her out to the fresh air. By the time the fire dies, the senex is sure to be as close to ash as it can get. The amount of wood Eli tossed into the hole, plus the gasoline-soaked curtain that the ancient vampire is wrapped in, all but guarantees a long, intense burn.

Eli maintains a steady pace down the hallway, but after a few steps into the greeting room he abruptly stops and cocks his head to the side, as if he hears something that doesn't sit right with him.

"More chompers?" Amy asks, drawing her gun.

"No," Eli responds. "I heard a small plane flying high close by, and now I'm hearing these weird humming sounds. It's kinda like the hums I hear in things like cell phones and laptops, but these are much different. More intense. And they're gettin' closer."

"But it's not another one of those missiles, right?"

"No, they're not moving really fast but-" Eli drops the gas canister and hoists Amy up over his shoulder, "-they're coming from above us!"

Before Amy could take another breath, she gets a firsthand glimpse of Eli's incredible vampire speed. The few seconds that she is carried out to the foyer makes her feel like she is riding a bolt of lightning.

Eli comes to a crisp stop at the threshold of the front door and remains motionless for a moment, then he lowers Amy to back to her feet.

Amy turns around to see what made Eli stop in his tracks and her heart detonates like a grenade when she sees six figures rapidly descending to the lawn on parachutes. She looks at Eli and finds his expression asking: "Are you seeing the same thing I'm seeing?" Amy nods her head.

Kwesi's crazy story about seeing a black Iron Man fighting chompers in Houston becomes completely credible as Amy and Eli watch the men wearing some sort of specialized armor get closer to the ground. All of them have the words MACE TEAM 1 printed vertically down the right side of their chest plates in bold white letters. The one closest to touching down to the ground first has lieutenant chevrons on his arms and LT. T. GRANGER printed horizontally across his left chest plate above two sets of numerals separated by hyphens.

Without hesitation, Amy trains her 9mm on the dark visor covering the face of the first soldier as his feet hit the ground and his parachute automatically breaks away from his armor. Her heart pounds in her chest as the other five soldiers land and rapidly form a semicircle in front of the house. She quickly scans the names on their chest plates as they get into formation.

Roberts, Sutherland, and Diggs don't appear to be carrying weapons, but they have their right arms extended towards the mansion. Camacho and Bradley, who are standing on the ends of the semicircle, are aiming what look like rocket launchers. And Granger, who is within the semicircle, is standing stiffly at attention. No one says a word, but all of the soldiers are posturing like they are waiting for an order to attack.

Amy is only a hair's breadth away from pulling the trigger herself. Even if these soldiers aren't here for her and Eli, the military usually identifies all civilians, whether they want to be taken to a safe zone or left alone to fend for themselves. She doesn't know about Eli, but if her fingerprints are scanned she might as well be a rabid chomper with a "Please Shoot Me" sign hung around her neck. The military does not waste the resources necessary to detain a fugitive of her status. A fair trial and incarceration are out of the question. As soon as they discover who she is, they will want to execute her on the spot.

As badly as Amy wants to squeeze the trigger and strike first, she takes into account that she is at a major disadvantage. The armor that the soldiers have on look like they're made of fiberglass, but most likely bulletproofed polymer. Eli can take a barrage of bullets, as long as he doesn't get shot in the head. But she doesn't stand a chance of surviving if slugs start flying. Her best bet is to wait for Eli to make a move and do whatever he says to do.

Eli protectively positions himself in front of Amy, and in his tight-lipped way of speaking, he says, "You boys a little early for Halloween, but come back later, and I'll have lots of candy for you."

With his voice sounding like it is coming through a speaker, the soldier with LT. GRANGER printed on his armor says, "We're here for Sigodur Vasa, where is he?!"

Eli's brow wrinkles and he says, "Don't know any Sigodur Vasa. Don't know you, either, as a matter of fact."

"My name is Lieutenant Trent Granger. I am an Army Ranger operating within the U.S. Joint Strike Force. I know you're lying about not knowing Sigodur. I'll give you one more chance to tell me what you know, or I can get it out of you the hard way."

Amy, suspicious why all of the soldiers aren't brandishing weapons, focuses on the arms extended towards her and Eli. Her eyes open wide when she notices holes that look remarkably like the bores of large caliber guns built into their suit, just above their wrists. She glances at Eli. Only able to see the side of his face, she can't tell if he knows about the concealed weapons since he is keeping a tight grin on his face.

"The hard way sounds like a plan, Ranger Granger," Eli growls. "And when you're crying for mommy cuz you can't take it no more, I'm gonna need you to tell me how you know Sig."

Granger nods then shifts his head.

Amy feels Granger's eyes now centered on her, invoking an unsettling feeling as if she just discovered a webcam in her bathroom. She slinks further behind Eli's back but keeps her eyes and her gun on the Granger.

"Amelia Angelica Goo-yen!" Granger says. "Lower your weapon and step away from the vampire!"

Eli glances at Amy but quickly returns his attention to Granger.

"If you tell me what you know about Sigodur Vasa," Granger continues, "I'll pretend I don't know you're a murderer and let you walk away from here. Or you can stand with that bloodsucker and die with him, too!"

Amy feels her whole body go numb, and she has no idea how she is managing to stay on her feet. In her peripheral she sees Eli clench his jaw tight, but he doesn't look at her. She figures he must want the answers to the same questions swirling around in her head.

Immediately, she regrets not opening up to him about her dark past when she had so many chances to. She worries about what he's going to think about her now that he knows she is a killer. Far worse than that, she has no explanation as to how Granger knows her name or what Eli is. As badly as she wants to say something to him, anything at all, not one word can seem to get past her throat. She can't see Eli's eyes but she feels them on her soul, and all she can do is shake her head, hoping that he doesn't think that she has betrayed him.

CHAPTER SIXTEEN

"So what's it going to be, Amy?" Granger says. "Live another day or stand with the bloodsucker and die?!"

Amy turns to look at Eli and declares loud and clear, "I'm with him! I'll always be with him! So, you can pretty much go fuck yourself!"

Eli turns to her and smiles, then he turns back to Granger, and says, "This is between you and me. Leave her out of it. Besides, real men don't threaten little girls. Understand me?"

"That 'little girl' is wanted for five murders, assaulting a deputy sheriff, and escaping custody. As far as I'm concerned, she's as much of a monster as you are."

"You gotta be mistaking her for somebody else."

"I don't think so. My facial recognition software IDed her, and I'm looking at her criminal history on my heads-up display as we speak. And save the innocent until proven guilty crap. If she was innocent, she wouldn't have run."

Amy glances at Eli at the same time that he looks back at her with one eyebrow raised. Hoping that he is willing to wait for her side of the story before passing judgment, she slowly tilts her head to one side as she shrugs her shoulders and lets her expression say that Granger is telling the truth, but there is more to it than that.

"Facial recognition software, huh?" Eli says, turning back to Granger. "That explains her, but how'd you know what I am?"

"Just one of the tricks my MACE can do," Granger responds. "You're burning at a steady hundred-and-eight degrees, and you show up as red as Rudolph's nose on my HUD."

"MACE?"

"Mechanized Armored Combat Exoskeleton. They're perfect for taking you bloodsuckers down. Just one flaw with them, though. And I'm sure you already know what that is."

Sarcastically Eli says, "Why, whatever do you mean?"

"You can't smell us. You can't hear us breathing or even our hearts beating. We were supposed to be completely stealthy, but your kind can hear the subsonic hum from our power cores. We were made aware of it by the vampire who's working with us."

Eli's demeanor instantly turns tense. His fists tighten, and the muscles in his forearms bulge, as he growls, "And exactly who is this helpful little shit you're working with?"

Granger shakes his head. "That's none of your business and this is isn't *An Interview With A Vampire*! Now, no more wasting time. Tell me where Sig is, or we can get down to business."

Eli uses his body to scoot Amy back into the doorway, then he says to her, "Take cover and wait until I'm done out here."

Before Amy can protest, Eli leaps from the front step and quickly soars the fifty feet between the house and the Bronco. His boots thump on the roof of the truck and he springs off of it with a high front flip, drawing both guns from his holsters. While still in the air he opens fire. Three rounds ping off the face shield and chest plates of Granger's armor, leaving behind only scuff marks where the bullets struck.

Eli lands among some of the fresh chomper corpses and looks at his smoking guns. He smirks, then shrugs as if their ineffectiveness is of no consequence to him. The Desert Eagles are returned to their holsters with grandiose twirls, then Eli beckons Granger forward with his index finger.

Granger raises his left arm and a small harpoon extends past his wrist. At the same time, bursts of fire spit from the holes that Amy suspected were muzzles in the armor of Roberts, Sutherland, and Diggs while streams of empty shells fly out from a slot under their elbows.

In the spilt second that Eli should be cut down by the barrage of bullets, he drops to the ground and the first volley of slugs strike the side of the Bronco. Then chunks of grass kick up from the ground as Eli rolls out of the bullets' trajectories, just in the nick of time.

Amy is relieved that Eli is fast enough to avoid being turned into a sieve, but she doesn't know how her champion gunfighter is going to beat Granger and his team if he can't use his weapons. She watches him closely as smoke creeps into the greeting room, and she smells the fumes from the senex's pyre.

Eli pushes off from the ground with his hands and flips into the air as bullets whiz past him. Amy badly wants to help him, but she and her Beretta are useless against these soldiers. All she can do is watch with baited breath as Eli lands on his feet and the soldier's cease-fire.

A bright cluster of strobe lights on all of the soldier's shoulders turn on and beam directly in Eli's face. Eli raises his hand and turns his head to avoid the lights as Camacho fires the rocket launcher-looking weapon he is holding. Eli immediately kicks the body of the chomper laying next to his foot as a net hurls towards him. The net wraps around the chomper carcass, crackling with electricity as Eli moves out of the way for the frying body to fly past him.

Moving in synchronized steps, Roberts, Sutherland, and Diggs open fire again as all the soldiers rapidly close the circle around Eli. Amy notices that their bullets are being aimed at the ground around Eli's feet. As she wonders why are they toying with Eli, Granger launches the harpoon tethered to his arm.

Eli swivels his body and catches the harpoon in the air. Then he turns his back to Granger, raises his arms above his head and yanks the cord connected to the harpoon. Granger appears to stumble forward from the sudden torque. But when Eli turns back around and rushes towards Granger like he was shot of out a cannon, Granger charges forward, too, with his arms set to wrap Eli up in a bear hug.

Amy hears a crash, like two cars in a head-on collision. Granger staggers backwards, with a spider web crack in his visor, while Eli stands shaking his hand. It happened so fast, Amy isn't sure if she saw the lightning punch that Eli threw.

The other soldiers must be questioning it as well because they are looking at each other as if they are surprised and don't know what to do. Taking full advantage of his speed and the soldier's indeterminate lull, Eli charges Granger again. He locks his right arm around Granger's neck and draws one of his Desert Eagles with his left hand.

Sutherland raises his weapon to shoot, but Eli fires first. Amy hears a sound that reminds her of a firecracker exploding in a metal bucket, and she sees Sutherland wildly shaking his right arm like it's on fire. Grayish smoke blows out of a vent above his elbow. Amy smiles when she realizes that Eli's shot must've hit the muzzle of Sutherland's weapon and caused a backfire, disabling his gun.

Roberts opens fire and Eli uses Granger's body to shield himself from the high caliber rounds.

Bradley and Camacho fire their net launchers.

Eli drops onto his back and flips Granger through the air, with the harpoon trailing behind him.

The net from Bradley's weapon encloses around Granger before he crashes into Bradley and bowls him over. The one from Camacho's weapon almost traps Eli, but he manages to roll out of the way before it can touch him.

Amy pumps her fist in celebration but stops when she sees Diggs look at Granger and nod his head. Diggs immediately takes off in a sprint towards her. Instead of running, Amy aims her 9mm at Diggs and quickly squeezes off rounds until her clip is empty.

As expected, the bullets do nothing to slow Diggs down. But he doesn't see Eli coming up behind him. Eli tackles Diggs at the front steps and begins twisting his arm behind his back. It looks as if Eli is having to use all of his might to overcome the resistance that Diggs is putting up, but he looks determined to tear Diggs' arm out of the socket.

When Amy sees a vent open on the shoulder of Diggs' armor and smoke bellow out of it like steam escaping a pressure cooker, she begins to believe that Eli might walk away with a souvenir—if they can get out of this.

Amy glances at the rest of the soldiers helping their commander out of the net, and she quickly reloads her weapon. By the time she has a new magazine in the Beretta, Granger is out from under the net and rising to his feet. She aims at his cracked visor and yells a warning for Eli to be aware that the rest of soldiers are coming, so he can either finish breaking Diggs' arm or give up on it and get ready for round two with the rest of them.

Eli heeds her warning and releases Diggs' arm. Then he lifts Diggs above his head as he rises to his feet. The acrid scent of burning electronics gives the air a distasteful texture as Eli cocks his arms back to catapult Diggs towards the rest of his team.

Just as Eli is about to follow through with the toss, a woman's voice blares from the speaker in Granger armor. "Elias, stop this at once!"

Amy can't see Eli's face, but his stillness reveals that he recognizes the voice and is second-guessing what to do. After a few seconds, in a voice fraught with dubiety, he says, "Rosa?"

"Yes, it's me, Dr. Rosa Contaldi. Now put that man down. You have caused enough damage already.

Eli shakes his head. "Nah, this can't be?"

As shocked as she is, Amy can only imagine how much more Eli must be to hear his magister, Lygia's, voice using her alias, coming from an intercom on an Army Ranger's anti-vampire combat armor.

"Yes, it's me, Elias. I know this must be a surprise to you, but I'll explain everything soon."

Eli continues to shake his head.

"Elias," the woman's voice says, "I am your keeper, and you are mine. We made that promise to each other when we were in the lost city of Coba. And if that's not enough for you, then, maybe you recall that I almost stabbed you the day after Kristin's twentieth birthday when I found out that you allowed her to have Jello-shots when you took her out?"

Eli carelessly lowers Diggs to his feet and shoves him away. "Where are you?"

"In the Gulf of Mexico. There are already choppers on the way to pick you up. You'll be safe here. You have my word on it."

Eli scoffs, "Safe?! These jackasses wanted to kill me, and they're looking for Sig. I'm trying to trust you, but you're not making it easy."

"Elias!" Lygia responds, "this isn't the place or time to explain everything to you. But I will when you get here. We have a problem on our hands and I need your abilities to help me solve it. So stop being stubborn and do what Lieutenant Granger tells you."

Eli turns to Amy, with an expression on his face like his arm is now being twisted, then he looks back at Granger and says, "What about Amy?"

"Who is this Amy?" Lygia asks. "Your fountain? What happened to Natasha?"

"Amy's my partner, and we're a package deal. I'm not going anywhere without her, and if anybody touches one hair on her head, these boys will be in pieces by the time the choppers get here!"

There is silence for a moment, then a man's voice comes through Granger's speaker. "This is General Alvin Limbeck, Mr. Kincade. Your partner is a level-one fugitive. The only way I can allow her on a military vessel is if the Commander In Chief is willing to pardon her, himself."

Eli shrugs, and says, "Well, I suggest you'll be giving him a call. Hopefully, he hasn't been turned into chomper chow by now."

The speaker goes silent. Amy hurries down the steps to stand by Eli's side. Granger appears to remain staring at them as his soldiers tend to the damage that Eli did to their power armor. Amy can feel a set of eyes burning into her skin, but they belong to Granger. She knows in her soul that Lygia is glaring at her and Amy consciously makes an effort to stand confidently, refusing to show any fear or anxiety in front of Eli's magister.

After a few minutes, General Limbeck's voice comes over the speaker again, saying, "You have the President's word that Miss Gouyen will not be taken into custody as long as you help Doctor Contaldi with our situation. If you cooperate with us, and Miss Gouyen admits to her crimes, her record will be cleared of all offenses. But she has to keep her nose clean. Do we have an agreement?"

Eli looks over at Amy. "Are you good with that?"

Amy nods her head. She doesn't trust General Limbeck, but she can tell from Eli's eyes that he wants to get to Lygia and find out what all this is about, and he might even go regulare on her ass if he doesn't like what he hears. Taking General Limbeck's deal is the only option that she has. She doesn't want Eli to go off with the soldiers alone. He held his own against them, but she feels that he would be better off with her watching his back. Besides, if she were to separate from him now the safest place that she knows of is Preacher's compound, and because of Calavius, she doesn't feel that is a good idea.

"All right," Eli says. "We have a deal, General."

"Roger that," General Limbeck says, then he addresses Granger. "Lieutenant, your ride is closing in on your position. I'm putting Lieutenant Shaffer in charge of outpost Bravo-Seven. You and your team escort Mister Kincade and Miss Gouyen back this fleet. They are to be regarded as friendlies and treated as such. That's an order."

The speaker cuts off, but Amy suspects that Granger and the General are still talking privately. When Granger finally turns around to go inspect his troops, Amy slightly lowers her guard to wrap her arms around Eli.

"You really are a badass," Amy says, putting her head on his chest.

"What, you didn't believe me?" Eli says, then he whispers into her ear. "That was tougher than I thought it was going to be, though. Those exoskeletons they got on are harder than anything I know of. I might've broken my hand when I tried to knock Granger's head off."

Amy immediately glances at Eli's right hand to inspect it for damage. The cuts on his knuckles have already begun to heal. She can't tell if he has any broken bones, but his hand is a little bit swollen.

"Do you need to feed?" Amy asks.

"No, I should be all right within an hour."

"But if you were to have some of my blood it will help you heal faster, right?"

"Yeah, but-"

"-But, nothing! You need to be a hundred percent around these pricks. I don't trust them, and I know you don't either. I'm here for you, Eli, and I need to do my part to help you."

Eli nods his head. "I'm going to leave my truck 'round back in the garage. We'll do it there. Plus I need a minute away from these guys so I can to think straight, again. Trying to figure out all the crap that's happenin' today is giving me a headache."

Seeing how frustrated Eli looks and feeling how tense he is, Amy wish she could do more to help. But she is as much at a loss as he is. Neither of them thought that the day would get worse after Calavius showed up at the compound. Now there is the matter of the unearthed senex. On top of that, they find out that the military is looking for Sig. As if things weren't complicated enough, Lygia is somehow working with the military. Trying to make heads or tails of any one of those things is baffling enough for her, and she can only imagine the chaos inside of Eli's head since he has a personal stake in this. Still, she feels as if she has to do something to at least help Eli decompress and get his mind right.

Granger twists the helmet on his head and air hisses like a can of soda being open. "Hey vampire!" he says, removing the helmet. "What's burning inside of the house?"

"An old friend," Eli responds. "Wanna join him?"

"Sig?!" Granger exclaims and signals Bradley to go check it out, then he glares at Eli. "If you're burning your buddy in there I need to know, now!"

"It's not Sig, dumbass. Why you got such a hard-on for him, anyway? If I didn't know any better, I'd swear he must've knocked up your momma or something."

"My interest in Sigodur is a matter of national security."

"National security, my ass. I know *personal* when I see it."

Granger grits his teeth in silence for a moment, then says, "I know you think you won that little skirmish just now, but the battle was far from over with. You had some unexpected moves, and you're faster than I expected, but we still had the upper hand."

"Whatever you say," Eli says and begins to lead Amy to the Bronco.

Granger smirks as he steps out of Eli and Amy's way. "I'm serious, bloodsucker. You have a weakness, and I promise if we ever go at it again I will use it against you."

"Go for it," Eli says. "I'm taking my truck to the garage, and we'd appreciate a little privacy until the choppers get here. Unless you're as much of a pervert as you are an asshole."

Amy looks back at Granger and gets a bad feeling from the way his unpleasant grin is now focused on her. Eli, being as cocky as he is, looks like he is dismissing Granger's threat but it seriously concerns her. She senses a deep seeded disdain within Granger towards vampires, and there is no doubt in her mind that he harbors the same sentiments towards her since she is loyal to a 'bloodsucker'. Keeping an eye on him is going to be one of her top priorities.

CHAPTER SEVENTEEN

Amy never thought that her first time flying would be in a Black Hawk helicopter. As thrilling as it is to zip through the airspace over the Gulf of Mexico, being in the chopper makes her think of Aaron and she misses him terribly. She imagines him sitting in one of the seats, eye closed, cradling his rifle as he gets his head ready for a mission. The image makes her proud of her brother.

She glances at Eli. He is sitting with his eyes closed and arms crossed while Granger watches him like a hungry raptor. Amy wonders what Aaron would think about his kid sister falling for a vampire. Aaron and Eli probably would've gotten along well with each other. They're both rugged kind of guys, a similar sense of humor, honorable, and both protective of her even though she can clearly take care of herself. And, like Aaron used to, Eli has a way of making her feel important to him.

One of the pilots turns around and holds his hand up with all five fingers splayed.

"E-T-A five minutes," Bradley says.

Granger nods his head and picks his helmet up off the floor, between his feet.

Amy gazes out the open door of the Black Hawk, searching for their destination somewhere in the vast, blue expanse of water. The helo gently banks left while the other Black Hawk that was behind them continues straight on.

She continues to look outside as the bow of a battleship comes into view. Not long after that, Amy discovers that the big grey ship, with his huge grey guns, is only one vessel in a small fleet. There are four battleships in total, as well as two smaller warships, an aircraft carrier, a massive cruise ship, a cluster of cargo ships, and a bright-white hospital ship with a big red cross painted on its sides.

The chopper transporting Amy and Eli comes to a stop and hovers close to the hospital ship as the one carrying Diggs, Sutherland, and Roberts approaches its helipad.

The sight of all the ships together in one place is awe-inspiring, but Amy is captivated by what is on the deck of one of the battleships. Standing at a 45-degree angle on its deck is a battery of missiles. There are ten on each side of the launching block, each missile forty feet long and resembling a bobsled with wings.

"I know, cool, right?" Camacho, still encased in his armor, says to Amy. "We call 'em HOGs because they smite like they're the Hand Of God."

"They do look cool," Amy responds, "but aren't they kinda small to be smiting anything?"

"Not these babies. They're super-lightweight, and their next-gen propulsion system tops out at Mach-one, so they come in fast and deliver a payload that packs a punch that's as close to nuclear as it gets."

"Camacho!" Granger snarls.

"Sorry, sir," Camacho responds, then starts to fiddle with an imaginary problem on the net launcher resting on his lap.

Bradley shakes his head and strokes his own net launcher like he's showing affection to a loving pet.

Eli opens his eyes. It's the first time that he has come out of his meditative state since the chopper took off from Outpost Bravo after they refueled. Amy knows that he hadn't checked out on her. Since they had to relinquish their weapons to Granger, he was most likely utilizing his heightened senses to be ready in case they were being set up. She also suspects that he appreciates the information that just came out of Camacho's mouth. Chances are that the HOGs are the missiles that shook the earth beneath them the night they were under the Bronco with a scorpion. The HOGs could also be responsible for the destruction of The Civitas.

Eli adjusts his cowboy hat while Amy turns back to observe the hospital ship.

The other Black Hawk has landed and the rest of Granger's team are disembarking. A small group of people—some in military uniforms, others in scrubs – are attending to the soldiers. Sutherland is indicating something wrong with his right arm, while Diggs points out whatever damage Eli did to his shoulder. The way everyone looks up at the hovering Black Hawk makes Amy think that they can't believe a vampire has compromised such special armor—and that vampire is here.

Amy grabs the straps of her backpack and picks it up from the floor. She would feel better if she had one of her guns, although they would do her no good against the entire army she and Eli are going to be in the midst of.

The chopper on the helipad lifts off and begins to make its way over to the aircraft carrier, then the one that was left to hover starts to descend. Granger slips his helmet back on and locks it back in place.

Amy notices Eli tilt his head and listens to things that she can't possibly hear over the dominating helicopter engine. She breathes a little easier knowing that he is on guard, but her anxiety won't rest since she is moments away from coming face to face with Lygia. Amy doesn't expect a warm reception from Eli's magister. The thing she fears is that she will see the passion Eli and Lygia once shared is still there. If it is, then that would mean the fire that's been raging between her and Eli over the past couple days is just lust running amuck and doomed to failure.

The Black Hawk touches down. Camacho hops out first, followed by Bradley. Granger scoops up the green canvas duffel bag containing Amy and Eli's handguns, ammo, and his katars. Eli's upper lip quivers and he snarls, reminding Granger of the warning he gave about what would happen in anything happens to his guns or his blades while in Granger's custody.

Granger hops out of the chopper and then motions for Eli and Amy to follow. Eli slips on his own backpack, then he slides closer to the door. Camacho and Bradley poorly disguise their efforts to cover him with their weapons, hoping that if something happens they might have a chance at snaring him in one of their nets. Eli's wry smile tell them, "Good luck with that."

Eli jumps out of the Black Hawk with one hand on top of his head to make sure his hat doesn't fly off. As soon as his feet hit the ground, he extends his arm to help Amy down. The heat of the day and the wind from the rotating blades make Amy feel like there is an invisible dragon breathing down on her until Eli considerately hunches over her and reassuringly snakes an arm around her waist.

There is an increasing whine of the chopper's engine. It lifts off to join the others on the aircraft carrier while Amy and Eli follow Granger towards the group of people waiting at the edge of the helipad.

Amy scans the faces of the people they are approaching. The older man with short grey hair on his head, clean-shaven face, thin lips, and a square jaw is obviously General Limbeck. His Army uniform is a dead giveaway. The other men and women dressed in Air Force, Marines, and Navy uniforms are of no interest to Amy. Her attention settles on the two redheaded women wearing sunglasses and dressed in blue scrubs. They look like they could sisters, both in their mid-twenties. The taller of the two has her hair pulled into a ponytail, bound by a blue scrunchy. Her broad, bright smile conveys how much she is bristling with excitement. The shorter, curvy woman, on the other hand, remains with her eyes glued to her iPad. She doesn't even seem the least bit concerned as her deep red, shoulder length hair whips wildly from the wind.

Granger, Camacho, and Bradley salute the General. After he reciprocates, Granger holds up the canvass bag and confirms that the "friendlies" are unarmed. General Limbeck inspects the damage done to the visor on Granger's helmet, then he orders his soldiers to join the rest of the team and wait to be debriefed. Granger protests, but when Limbeck reiterates his order, Granger loathingly marches off.

"Son, I'm not one who is easily impressed," Limbeck says, approaching Eli. "But from what I've seen, I'd say you're all balls."

"Better than small balls," Eli retorts in a bland tone.

"Absolutely right! And as long as you always fight with the same determination you fought my elite squad with, you'll most definitely be an asset to our alliance."

Eli focuses his gaze on the redhead with the curvy figure. "Alliance?"

"Yes," Limback responds. "Doctor Contaldi will brief you on our situation, but she assures me that you're one of your kind's best warriors. And she thinks you're probably our best chance of tracking down Sigodur Vasa."

Eli's hands tighten to fists as his face screws into a scowl. "I'm looking forward to hearing all that Doctor Contaldi has to tell me about what's going on."

Lygia looks up from her Ipad. Her expression is more of impatience than anything else as she maintains eye contact with Eli.

Lygia's skin is like flawless porcelain. She has high cheekbones, plump lips, and her deep red hair has a sheen that makes it look like silk. The vampire princess also has luscious full breasts, and the flare of her hips blend perfectly with the tantalizing curves of her thighs. Amy despises herself for feeling like a child trying to compete with a woman.

"I'll turn you over to Doctor Contaldi in a moment," says Limbeck, rebounding his eyes after a glance at Lygia. "But there are two things before I let you go. The first is to you, Elias. You've done significant damage to three of my MACEs. At least a couple million dollars worth, from what I've seen. Shall we discuss a payment plan?"

Eli shrugs and flexes his right hand. "You're gonna have to get it from your boys. Consider it tuition payment, since they didn't have any manners and I had to teach them some."

Limbeck appears fascinated as he stares at Eli's knuckles. "My MACEs are overlaid in a special carbon nano-tube fiber mesh that's strong enough to withstand a strike from a Stinger missile. Makes me wonder what you are made of."

Eli shrugs again. "Balls, remember?"

Limbeck bellows a hearty laugh and slaps Eli on his back. "Good one. Now tell me, that shot up the barrel of Sutherland's gun that caused the backfire in his armor, was that intentional?"

"All I can tell you is that the bullet went where I hoped it would go."

Limbeck laughs again and places his hand on Eli's shoulder. "I like you son, and I'm glad you're on my side. But from now on, I'm going to need you to play nice with my boys. We're not enemies." He switches his attention to Amy, and with more sternness in his voice, he says, "Hard to believe that a delicate thing like you killed five men all by yourself, young lady. I don't know what made you go on your rampage, and personally, I don't care. As far as I'm concerned, we have bigger problems on our hands than you. In a day or two, you'll confess your crimes to a tribunal and the President will sign your clemency papers. After that, Miss Gouyen, you should keep your nose clean. There will be no second chances."

Amy bites her tongue to keep from telling Limbeck what she thinks of him, as well as suggesting numerous ways he can violate himself. Instead, she nods her head and manages to say, "Thank you, sir."

Limbeck points to Lygia and the two soldiers standing behind her. He states that she will explain to Eli and Amy the rules that they absolutely have to follow while on board his vessel. One of the rules is that they are not permitted to go anywhere outside of their quarters without an escort. Maxwell, a tall, dark skin, muscular soldier is assigned to Eli. And shadowing Amy will be a blonde woman with a short haircut and a thick build, whose name tag identifies her as Sergeant Gould.

Eli and Amy offer no protest, and Limbeck nods his approval.

"Alright, Doctor Contaldi," Limbeck says as he turns to walk away. "They're all yours now."

The taller of the two redheads takes off like a shot, sprinting as quickly as her pink and white Sketchers can take her to Eli. She jumps the last few steps towards him and he catches her in a big hug.

"Hey, kiddo," Eli says, spinning the woman around. "I missed you so much!"

As Amy suspected, the taller redhead is Kristin, Lygia and Eli's adopted daughter.

"I missed you, too," Kristin says. "I was so happy when mom told me that you'll be here in a day or two, but here you are already!"

"Yeah, funny how that worked out," Eli says, lowering Kristin back down to her feet. "But now that I'm here somebody's got some explaining to do."

Kristin giggles. She looks over at Amy, then back at Eli. "Natasha didn't make it?"

Eli shakes his head. "No. This is my new partner, Amy," he says then looks at Amy, "and Amy, this is my daughter, Kristin."

Amy offers her hand and Kristin shakes it with a warm smile.

"I really need to get back to my lab," Lygia says, in her sultry voice.

"You're kidding me, right?" Eli says in disbelief.

"No, I'm not," Lygia replies, stopping in front of Eli. She leans in close like she is about to kiss him on the cheek, but she sniffs the side of his face on down to his neck. Then she turns towards Amy and subtly takes a long whiff of the air.

Because the sun is to Lygia's back Amy can see her eyes through the lenses of her sunglasses. Lygia looks her over from head to toe, then they settle on the fresh puncture wounds in Amy's neck. The way Lygia's brow furrows, Amy imagines that she is considering punching through her rib cage and ripping out her still-beating heart.

"Rosa," Eli growls, visibly agitated, "you gotta tell me right now what you're doing here and why is Kristin with you?"

Lygia appears offended by Eli's questions, but she answers. "The CDC contacted me at my lab, requesting my help with the Puissance virus. I agreed. However, I didn't know at the time that they had the technology to identify vampires. I was taken into custody. My reputation and the work I've done in genetics speak for themselves, so there was no question that I am not a threat. So, after some negotiating, an alliance was formed between the humans and us. Since then, Kristin and I have been here working."

"And why wasn't I told about this before?"

"Because my father knew that you would've taken matters into your own hands and started a war that neither side needed to fight," Lygia says, then turns to walk away. "We'll talk more about that and other things, Elias. But right now I need to get down to my lab."

"Lygia!" Eli says, reaching for her but stopping short of grabbing her by the shoulder. "Pelagius. I know that you already know about him."

"Yes," Lygia says, looking back. "When I stopped feeling my father's presence I asked General Limbeck to contact the nearest military base to help me find out what's going on at The Civitas. That's when I found out that the base was infiltrated and whoever did it specifically targeted The Civitas before turning the base over to the infected."

"What? Do they know who did it?"

"Their names, no. But they were vampires. Acolytes, to be specific."

Eli exhales hard like he was about to deflate. He closes his eyes and sorrowfully shakes his head, apparently blaming himself for the news that he just heard.

Amy feels the need to comfort Eli, but Lygia moves first, turning and lovingly placing a hand on his cheek.

"It's not your fault, Elias," Lygia says. "There are many more acolytes than The Synodus suspected were around. We'll deal with whoever's leading them this time, but we have other problems to take care of first. Right now I'm trying to get a handle on the Puissance virus and maintain our alliance between us and the humans at the same time. Considering the position both of us are in, it's best for all of our survival. So please cooperate with them, especially in the matter of finding Sig. I didn't want you to have to do it, but you're the best shot we have right at tracking him down."

"Why is everybody so interested in Sig all of a sudden?"

Lygia sighs and turns to walk away again. "We need to find Sig because he might be the key to stopping the Puissance virus, since he is patient zero.

CHAPTER EIGHTEEN

Amy hears the unmistakable crisp sound of a slap.

Initially, it seems like she blinked. But she knows that she didn't. Eli and Lygia's's amazing speed is responsible for the sudden change, like there was a film scene skip in reality.

Apparently, Eli grabbed Lygia by the wrist again to keep her from walking away, and Lygia physically demonstrated her displeasure. But it happened so fast, Amy didn't actually see either vampire move to the positions that they are in now. However, the sound of skin-on-skin contact did not escape her senses.

Lygia's plump pink lips are on the threshold of a smile, but she holds her composure. The wind continues to whip her red hair as she glances down at the hand clamped around her wrist. "Have you forgotten your manners, Elias," she says looking back up at Eli, "or do I have to reminded of who I am?"

Lygia's tone is every bit that of a monarch. The question was directed at Eli, but it reminded Amy that Lygia is the rightful successor to her father's position as the Imperator. Eli didn't instruct her to pay Lygia formal obeisance like what was required for Calavius. However Lygia is the new vampire overlord. Amy has to keep that in mind at all times. In order to be in Eli's world, she will have to submit to being one of Lygia's subordinates, too. And without Lygia's permission, Eli will never be able to make her a vampire. Swallowing her pride leaves a bad taste in Amy's mouth, but she has to accept it to get what she wants.

Eli releases Lygia's wrist and offers a contrite bow of his head. "I apologize," he says, "but you can't tell me that Sig is 'patient zero' and then just walk away."

"I never said you couldn't follow me," Lygia replies, turning around again. "And as you can clearly see, I still possess the ability to walk and talk at the same time. So, try to keep up. Okay?"

Eli grits his teeth as Lygia gracefully strides towards an open doorway of the big, shed-shaped structure at the edge of the helipad.

Kristin slides her shades up to her forehead and shakes her head as she stares at Eli with eyes like blueberries. "C'mon, you know you walked right into that one, right?"

Eli shakes his head, too. "Yeah, I shoulda seen it comin', but there's so much goin' through my head right now."

"Pshh! You don't know the half of it. Mom's going through it, too. On top of everything that's happened, she's trying to do the impossible. She won't admit it, but she's tired and frustrated. Until just now, she's been all serious, all the time. That's the closest I've seen her come to smiling in months, so play nice with her. She needs it."

"So what, I'm supposed to keep sweet-talking her?"

"Hey, you know what they say about flies and honey, right?"

"Yeah, but the thing is, I've seen way more flies on shit than I've ever seen on honey?"

Kristin giggles and moves to catch up to her mother. "You're not a piece of shit, dad. So play nice!"

Eli turns to Amy and sarcastically says, "Welcome to my world."

Knowing that Lygia would hear if she said exactly what was on her mind, Amy smiles and shrugs her shoulders.

Eli shakes his head and continues after Lygia and Kristin. His pace is brisk, but Amy matches his stride. The two soldiers, Maxwell and Gould, bring up the rear, maintaining their escort duties.

They enter a short hallway that is as bright-white as the hull of the hospital ship. Even with the sea air rushing in, Amy can pick up a strong antiseptic scent wafting from the walls and floor. She also hears footsteps clunking dully and reverberating metal. There are four grey doors, two on each side, each marked by the letter H and designated 1 through 4. And at the end of the hallway are two wide, stainless steel elevator doors, but instead of continuing on to the elevator, Eli makes the immediate left to follow Lygia and Kristin down a stairwell of steel grate steps.

Taking at least three steps at a time, Amy hustles behind Eli to catch up to Kristin and Lygia. Maxwell and Gould gallop behind her. One and a half flights down, they are all together again and Lygia begins to talk without looking back at anyone.

"I suppose the best place to start is to tell you that either Sig or Kelly, most likely both of them, went rogue," Lygia says.

Eli scoffs. "So I've heard, but I refuse to believe that!"

"I felt the same way until I saw proof of it, myself."

Lygia updates Eli with some of the information that the military shared with her.

A month before the first incident with the Puissance virus, a new thermometry satellite was being tested over Lousiana. The sensors on the satellite were designed to highlight all humans in a targeted area with body temperatures of 99 degrees or higher. The program was developed to gather data for the CDC in the event of an epidemic, as well as track the infection rate of viral outbreaks that threatened national security.

Since vampires run hotter than humans, Sig and Kelly showed up on the orbital sensors like flares burning on an onyx floor. The human that they were hunting also showed up in a warm and friendly shade of blue, running for his life. He was trying to make it off of the grounds of the safe house while their menacing red heat signatures moved like cheetahs, toying and taunting until they moved in for the kill. The DOD was immediately notified. And from that moment the satellite was parked there in orbit, keeping Sig, Kelly, and everybody else on property under constant surveillance.

After meticulous planning, a group of mercenaries were used to attack the safe house, engaging the security guards and drawing Sig, Kelly, and the two other vampires outside. While the vampires were occupied with eliminating the mercenaries, Lt. Granger and a platoon equipped with MACEs and high voltage net cannons dropped in from above. They were able to snare Kelly in a net first, then got the better of Sig when he tried to rescue her. The other two vampires weren't much trouble after that.

"And why am I just learning about this now?" asks Eli.

The group is now on the lowest levels below deck, and are walking down another hallway that is a little narrow but could pass for one found in any hospital. Most of the doors are closed. The ones that are open reveal rooms with desks, computers, examination tables and medical charts on the walls. One open room has a workstation with the computer monitors displaying a star dazzled screen saver. Behind the workstation is a window, showing part of an MRI machine in the next room. Another room is packed with boxy machines that appear to be various kinds of research equipment.

Amy glances at a diagram on the hallway wall. It's an overview cross-section of the hospital ship with numbers and letters that correspond with those marked on the doors on this level. In the middle of the diagram is a dark red block much bigger than the rest of the rooms represented in the diagram, with the words RESTRICTED printed in bold black letters. Judging from the designations on the doors they are passing, right now Lygia is leading them straight to the restricted area.

"We didn't find out about it until after the CDC contacted me to collaborate with them to find a vaccine or a cure for the Puissance virus," Lygia says. "But you weren't told because you were too close to discovering the identity of the acolytes' true leader. That was a higher priority. Besides, Trajanus was the logical choice to go after Sig since he could follow his link to his legare." Lygia takes a small pause, appearing to renew the moisture in her mouth. "Sig killed Trajanus and the other regulare whom was with him. Only Trajanus' fountain was left alive. Sig sent her back with a message for my father."

Amy feels like she could walk across the intensity in Lygia and Eli's gaze, like a tightrope, and she would rather know what was just communicated between them without a single word being uttered.

"The virus started getting out of control at that time," Lygia continues, turning back around. "The Synodus knew it was more important to make sure we were all organized and kept safe from the contagion."

"Speaking of contagion," Eli says, "you still haven't told me why you said Sig is 'patient zero'? How is that even possible? Every vampire I know who was infected died, and they didn't go peacefully."

Lygia sighs, then she taps the screen of her iPad and hands it to Eli with visible reluctance. "I had this downloaded for you while you were on your way here. This is the missing piece of your puzzle."

Eli takes the tablet from Lygia. Amy watches as a video starts playing. There is a muscular man on the screen, bound by huge clamps to a shiny metallic chair that resembles a Chaise lounge with armrests. An oval strip of metal is screwed into his face to cover his mouth. The top of his skull had been removed to expose a portion of the brain. It is Sig. His eyes are dull with exhaustion and the haunting look of despair.

The video plays out like a scene from a bad Sci-Fi movie. A metallic ring, the size of a car tire, is lowered by a thick telescoping pole until it is a few inches above Sig's head. Six skinny spikes arranged in a circle, all pointing inward at a 45-degree angle, slowly protrude from the center of the ring, extending down until they are less than an inch away from Sig's brain tissue. Beams of light erratically burst from the tips of the spikes, accompanied by a horrid buzzing that is similar to that of an X-ray machine. Sig's brow furrows as he appears to fight the pain.

Bluish arcs of electricity begin to dance around the metallic surface of the ring then they shoot down to the opening in Sig's skull. The undulating electric arcs resemble bony, ghostly fingers massaging his scalp. He continues to resist, but it isn't long before he releases a dreadful howl of agony and he passes out.

The screen freezes and Amy is thankful Sig didn't have to endure more of that torture, at least no more at that moment captured on the video.

As they approach a set of metal doors that look as if they are made to be blast-proof, Lygia explains that the machine above Sig's head in the video is called the Genesis Halo. It was created by the top geneticist working for Gen-Ascend, Dr. Andrew De Reske. Gen-Ascend was a private sector company like hers, but they did contract work for the DOD. The Halo was calibrated to dispense varying amounts of radiation at precise focal points. This was part of a process that Dr. De Reske developed in collaboration with Dr. Ivana Gianacola to bio-fabricate a living organism by assembling biomaterial around pre-programmed primordial cells. Initially, he used this process to develop smart enzymes which followed instructions to only attack cancer cells in a person with a specific genetic profile, but he also engineered organisms for other applications.

"Biological warfare?" Eli growls as the heavy metal doors slide open, revealing a short, dark red hallway with another set of doors at the end.

Eli's voice causes two older women dressed in scrubs to paste themselves against the wall. Maxwell and Gould put their hands on the handles of their sidearms. Amy positions herself between them and Eli while barking his name to warn him. But Lygia takes control of the situation by gesturing with her hand for the soldiers to stand down.

Eli raises his hands, indicating there isn't a problem. Maxwell and Gould nod at each other, and they ease their hands away from their weapons. Then Lygia gestures for the two women to continue their exit of the red area. They do so with haste, neither of them taking their eyes off of Eli.

"Yes," Lygia calmly says, walking to the other door. "That footage was taken in Gen-Ascend's secret, maximum security underground facility in the Bowery section of Manhattan. De Reske had already created an arbovirus that could carry out instructions to attack an organism with a specific genotype; from one single person to, say, only people with blue eyes, or even an entire race. De Reske created an evolved version of his arbovirus in Sig's brain, with the intent to have a weapon that would only work on vampires, but it ended up mutating into what we now call the Puissance virus."

Lygia pauses when she comes to the door and she removes her glasses.

Amy is stunned to discover that Lygia's eyes are hazel, just like hers.

Lygia stares at a panel of black glass that is on the side of the door. T hin, red beams of light shoot through the dark glass and dart from side to side on her face, traveling the length from top to bottom. The panel blinks red and Lygia steps to the side as it returns to a solid black again.

Kristin positions herse lf in the same place where Lygia stood and explains to Eli and Amy that everyone has to submit to the biometric scanner in order to get past this checkpoint. When they are all scanned, including Maxwell and Gould, the door finally opens up to reveal a longer red hallway with white floors and black doors.

Eli, looking as if his face will crack if anger makes it tighten any more, says, "So Sig has the virus, and it hasn't killed him. That's why everybody's so eager to find him?"

"Yes," Lygia replies. "There's still a major complication to overcome, but finding Sig might be my best chance of making a viable vaccine."

"Complication?"

Lygia sighs. "One thing at a time, Elias. Finding Sig and whoever's with him is the first obstacle to overcome."

Eli growls and shakes his head. "You mean Kelly and the safe house guards?"

Lygia lowers her head as she begins to walk again. "Kelly is dead, along with Raphael and Simon. Doctor De Reske succeeded at making a vampire-specific virus when he tested it on Kelly and it killed her, but not the chimpanzee that was infected at the same time as she was. Then he repeated his experiment in the others to confirm his success. That was before the virus mutated in Sig. It still kills us by destroying our brain functions due to a hyper onset of encephalitis, but in any host that isn't already a vampire, halfway through the brain degradation they are endowed with the force that makes us virtually invincible, leaving them perpetually stuck in the condition that everyone attributes to a zombie. In reality, those who are infected by the Puissance virus are simply brain damaged vampires."

The muscles in Eli's jaw tense up. "So why are you working with the people who made Sig a living petri dish; used Kelly, Rapha, and Simon as guinea pigs; killed who knows how many more of us, and pretty much fucked the world with the virus they were making to wipe us out?"

Lygia sighs, and says, "We are in an alliance with the U.S. Government, Elias. It's what Pelagius wanted. Mistakes were made on both sides, and now we have to work together if we want to save what's left of life on this planet."

Kristin timidly clears her throat, and looking at Lygia, she says, "You might as well tell him the rest of it now."

Eli's eyes jump from Lygia to Kristin, then back at Lygia again. "She's right. Don't give me a shovel full of shit when you can just dump the whole truck."

Lygia takes Kristin's advice and complies with Eli's request. The shit that she dumps on him is probably heavier than he expected. Sig was aided in his escape from the facility in Manhattan by Dr. Gianacola, the woman who helped Dr. De Reske develop the Puissance virus. This was after Dr. Gianacola got a tip that the CIA had found out she sold information and sensitive material to a fraction of the Chinese government. Among the sensitive material were samples of Sig's blood—with and without the virus—kept in specialized containers that steadily provided an electrical current to keep them viable.

With Dr. Gianacola's help, Sig got out of the doomed lab before the Anti-contamination Contingency Protocol vaporized everything in it. He killed the two soldiers who would've been watching him at the time, if Dr. Gianacola hadn't provided a distraction. Then he slaughtered twenty-eight Gen-Ascend employees as the two of them made their way out the facility. There was one person unfortunate enough to encounter Sig and be left alive in his wake. Dr. Andrew De Reske's back was broken by his Subject 1, Sigodur Vasa, then intentionally infected by the very virus that he created.

Sig was responsible for the first wave of chompers that emerged from the tunnels in Manhattan, but it can't be said that the worldwide pandemic is his fault. Evidence suggests that the Chinese operatives used the samples of the virus provided by Dr. Gianacola to infect people in strategic places all across the United States. They and their allies had sealed their own borders in an attempt to keep the virus out, but the virus still infiltrated them, too.

Now China has its own chomper infestation, but that's not their only problem. Someone made the decision to use Sig's untainted vampire blood to make super soldiers. They had no idea what could happen when a vampire goes rogue, but it wasn't long before they found out. So while the legitimate government is doing its best to exterminate chompers and keep its citizens safe, they are also embroiled in a civil war.

There is now an army of rogue vampires that will turn their attention back on the U.S. once they have conquered their homeland, and they must be stopped. That is what General Limbeck hopes Eli and the other regulares will help with.

Lygia stops in front of the black door at the very end of the hallway. Another round of face and iris scans are taken, then the door opens to a room full of lab equipment and two soldiers encased in MACEs. Kristin tells Amy she'll see her after work, then she excuses herself and slips past Lygia, heading straight for one of the two desks with computer workstations on them.

"I know it's a lot to absorb all at once," Lygia says, then she compassionately caresses Eli's cheek. "Take a minute to get your head back on straight. My experiment isn't going to take long. You can watch from the observation window if you want to. And when I'm done, we'll finish talking. Okay?"

Eli nods his head. Lygia smiles and makes her way into the lab, barely acknowledging Amy's existence. It has Amy seething inside, but she refuses to show Lygia that she has affected her in any way. Instead, she smiles and puts her arms around Eli, letting him know with a gentle squeeze that she knows what he's going through and she's here for him. And she feels a burst of happiness when he returns her embrace.

The things that she has learned from listening to Lygia are shocking, and she is still trying to wrap her head around some of it. She can only imagine the whirlwind raging in Eli's head, especially with his personal connection to some of what he has just learned. Then there is the issue of Calavius and everyone at the compound. Amy hasn't forgotten them, and she knows that Eli hasn't either.

CHAPTER NINETEEN

Looking down from the observation window in Lygia's lab, Amy thinks about Sig, and she wishes he could see what she is looking at. It's justice. Justice that she understands. Justice that she likes. Justice in the form of Dr. Andrew De Reske clamped to a stainless steel table with a hole cut out of his cranium. His eyes dying of hunger as he lives on as a chomper. She thinks Sig would appreciate it, just as she appreciates knowing that Aaron's killers got what they deserved.

Lygia's lab is divided into three sections. The first section is office space shared by Lygia and Kristin. One of their desks is achingly neat with files, papers, keyboard, monitors, pens, stapler, paper clip container, all laid out like a civil engineer's planned project. The other desk contains many of the same items, conveniently unorganized and peppered with objects like a spiky pink Kush ball, neon colored flash drives, a Lego version of Albert Einstein with a small Michigan University flag taped to his hand, and multicolored scrunchies slung over a corner of one of the monitors.

The other two sections are on a lower tier, divided by the same type of transparent material the observation window is made of. It's as clear as glass but appears to be some kind of polymer, about six inches thick. No one can get from one side of the lower tier to the other without first being enclosed in a semicircle-shape chamber. There they are showered by a white mist, then allowed to pass through a sliding door into the other half of the circle on the opposite side.

One side of the lower tier is a lab stocked with equipment like electron microscopes, spectrometers, and a lot of refrigeration units. The shelves and tables brim with jars, beakers, test tubes, petri dishes and other things of the sort. On the other side of the wall is a room that seems to be intended for autopsies, because of the stainless steel table and some of the medical equipment in it. But there are also other devices that are unusual, including something resembling a smaller version of Gen-Ascend's infamous Genisis

Halo.

Lygia, Kristin, and a man with a neatly trimmed brown beard are on the lower level. Each of them are wearing white biohazard protection suits, equipped with re-breathers. Lygia is alone in the section with the De Reske chomper. She is holding something that looks like a thick syringe as she stands behind him, staring at his exposed portion of the brain. De Reske's head is held to the table by a metal strip over his forehead, and another covering his mouth like the one that was on Sig in Gen-Ascend's Manhattan facility. He can't move his head, but his eyes have followed Lygia's every move. At the moment his pupils have rolled up into his head, leaving eerie white orbs in his eye sockets. There is no way possible for him to see Lygia that way, but he's giving it a good try.

"All right, Doctor Contaldi," Kristin's voice sounds over the speaker monitoring the communication between the biohazard suits. "G-72 is ready when you're ready."

Amy looks over and sees the bearded man hand Kristin an object just like the syringe Lygia is holding.

"Okay, Kristin," Lygia replies. "The modulator is primed and I'm going to do the extraction now. Our clock is running."

"Keeping track," Kristin says, heading towards the semicircle on that side of the room.

Kristin steps into the chamber. A door slides closed behind her and she is bathed in jetting streams of what looks like heavy steam. She raises her arms straight out to the side and slowly twirls around, allowing the mist to get her everywhere.

"Mmm," moans the soldier with the name Bader printed on the chest plate of his MACE. "I'd love to get in a real shower with that one. Get her nice and wet, then lather her up reeeal gooood."

"Yeah, I know what you mean," the other soldier, Mariano, responds.

Amy turns to glare at them, wishing their faces weren't hidden so she would know exactly who they are if she sees them again without their armor on.

Eli has already turned and closed the distance between him and them. He raps hard on the side of Bader's helmet with his knuckles, and says in his grittiest voice, "Keep it up and I'ma rip your arm off and beat your ass until you're nothing but a busted sack of jelly. Got it!"

"Fuck's your problem, bloodsucker?!" Bader says, turning to square up with Eli.

"Not the time, gentlemen!" Gould barks, quickly slipping her arm in the space between Eli and Bader. "And it's definitely not the place! Keep in mind that if there's so much as a crack in that window, this whole lab could be sealed off and ejected from the bottom of the ship. The air is going to be flooded with an accelerant and ignited, burning our bodies to a crisp by the time we hit the bottom of the sea."

"C'mon!" Mariano knocks on his left chest plate. "That window's treated with the same stuff as this. I've seen it take a point-blank shot from a fifty-cal. rifle without so much as a smudge. Cracking it, much less breaking it, is impossible."

"Listen, I just saw Granger and Diggs come back with damage to their power armor that this guy did with his bare hands. So I'm not counting on the impossible remaining impossible. Not today. Especially with you talking disrespectfully about his daughter right in front of him."

"His daughter?" Bader's head whips back and forth between Eli and Kristin.

"Yeah, my daughter!" Eli growls and bares his fangs in a menacing grin.

"He's the one the General's been waiting for," Maxwell says. "So, until those scientists clear out from down there, I suggest you boys shut your mouths and keep your eyes only on that chomper strapped to the table. Got it?"

Bader and Mariano don't say another word, at least none that can be heard outside of their private communication system. After a moment of staring at Eli, both armored soldiers simultaneously turn to keep watch of De Reske.

Amy looks back down at the lower level and finds Lygia staring up at them, annoyed. She assumes that Lygia heard the confrontation transmitted over the intercom because the heat of her gaze is focused on the two soldiers Eli was ready to mix it up with.

Eli tips his hat and gives her a nod.

Lygia nods back, then she proceeds to sink half the length of the needle into De Reske's brain and presses one of the buttons where a plunger on a normal syringe would be. Kristin, now in the same room with Lygia, pushes a button on a piece of equipment that looks like a copy machine. A tray slides open in the middle of it and Kristin retrieves a circular glass disk with her left hand.

"Four minutes," Kristin says, holding the tip of her syringe poised over the glass disk.

"Plenty of time," Lygia responds, approaching with her own syringe. "Apply G-72 to the slide, please."

"Right away." Kristin pushes a button and a cloudy, viscid fluid oozes out from the tip of the syringe, forming a neat puddle in the middle of the disk. Lygia joins her and releases the blood from her syringe over the fluid Kristin put on the disk. Kristin quickly places another circular disk over the one with the bloody concoction on it and returns it to that tray of the machine she got it from. Before the tray closes, Lygia is already on her way to the computer in the lab. Kristin eagerly joins her mother, keeping her eyes glued to the monitor.

The monitor changes from a blue screen with the CDC logo to a bustling microscopic world. The red and white blood cells are easy to identify among the particles floating like debris in space, including objects that look like Y's in an alphabet soup. What stands out the most is the vast number of organisms that look like worms with their bodies tightly coiled on one side. Some of them are a greyish color, but the majority of them are a strange shade of light-green.

Lygia's fingers dance over the keyboard and the machine that is magnifying the samples bellow a heavy hum. Four minutes go by with Lygia and Kristin staring at the monitor, hoping to see a change. But with every minute that dwindles down, their melting expressions convey obvious disappointment with the results.

"Time," Kristin says with a sigh. "I thought we might break through with this one. We have to be getting closer."

"Maybe," Lygia replies. "We'll keep trying. It has to snap if we stretch it far enough."

"What do you want to do now?"

"Archive this sample and let's call it a day," Lygia says, as she looks up at the observation window. "Tomorrow we'll try Generation 73, but we might have better results if we had a sample from patient zero."

Thirty minutes later, Lygia and Kristin's office is blanketed in the aroma of hot cheese and pepperoni. The personal pizzas that Kristin brought back from one of the mess halls aren't as good as one freshly made in a pizzeria, but still a delicacy in the apocalypse.

Lygia has cleared her office of all military personnel. Bader and Mariano were dismissed by her when the scientist with the beard left the lab. The De Reske chomper is by himself down there. Already paralyzed by Sig, and still clamped to the table as a precaution, there is no danger of him getting loose like Sig when he made his escape from Gen-Ascend's facility. So there is no more need for the special guard detail. Lygia was more polite to Maxwell and Gould when she asked them to wait outside the door. Lygia also tried to get rid of Amy, but Eli insisted that she stay.

"These are a seventy-second generation of the Puissance virus," Lygia says, talking about the green worm-shaped organisms displayed on one of her computer monitors. "We infected a genetically enhanced mouse with De Reske's blood, and we've been passing it down from one mouse to another ever since. What you saw Kristin apply to the slide was the virus harvested from the seventy-second mouse. Because of a spliced gene in the mice, we have green versions of the virus to differentiate them from the ones already present in De Reske's blood.

"I was hoping that the antibodies from De Reske's blood, these here," Lygia points to the Y-shaped particles, "would attack the weaker virus from the mouse, but so far they continue to exist in harmony with each other. I still want to keep going. Since every time we pass our blood on to make another vampire it loses strength, I figure that eventually I'll get a sample so weak, we'll have an idea of the generational limit of a bloodline."

Kristin swallows the bite that she's been chewing, then says, "We're also trying to see if we can use a modulator to disrupt whatever the energy is that give vampiric cells their special quality. The energy doesn't operate on a principle of physics that we understand yet, but I'm hoping a fluctuating wave of radiation before the vampire energy naturally deteriorates would at least give up a starting point to undo vampirism, returning a vampire to human."

"Why would you want to do that?" asks Eli.

"Because that's the complication I didn't want to mention earlier," Lygia says. "Developing a vaccine is one thing, but under the present circumstances there will be a side effect. Any human who takes it will become a vampire, and we can't have that."

"Excuse me?" Amy politely says. "I have a question."

Lygia cuts her eyes towards Amy, who is sitting in a chair at Kristin's desk, but she nods her head. "Yes, what is it?"

"I still don't understand why a bite from a chomper kills vampires, but..., according to what you've said, humans basically become brain damaged vampires when they're bitten by a chomper."

Lygia explains that the energy in vampiric cells absorb the energy, or life force, from other cells introduced into its network, except for when it encounters a stronger vampiric energy. In the latter case, the stronger cell does the absorbing and multiplies until it completely dominates, which is how weaker vampires acquire the power of stronger vampires by drinking their blood.

The life force energy in pathogens invading a vampires' network are normally absorbed by the vampiric cells within their immune system. But Lygia believes that when Dr. De Reske created a living organism in Sig's brain, some of the vampiric energy within Sig invaded the primordial cells during the radiation sequence of the process.

"So the virus became vampiric within Sig, and that's why his immune system didn't attack it?" Amy asks.

Lygia nods. "A distinguishing marker of vampire DNA is the unusually long length of our telomere. That's the section of DNA at the ends of a chromosome; in a way, it resembles a tail. The length of the telomere in the Puissance virus, as well as the victims infected by it, are the same as a vampire's. So, yes, the Puissance virus is vampiric. The only fortunate thing is that the vampiric energy passed along when the virus is transmitted is only a fraction of Sig's power. Infected humans are endowed with our immortality, but not nearly as powerful as our weakest vampire."

Lygia continues to reveal other troublesome things about the vampiric virus. Because its vampiric energy is weaker, it should be eradicated when introduced into a vampire's cellular network. However, it manages to appear equal in energy or somehow friendly to the host's vampiric cells. She believes it's a combination of the genetic programming that Dr. De Reske put into his new arbovirus and the vampiric energy that came from Sig somehow mutating when the virus did. Whatever the reason, the Puissance virus can move freely through a vampire's body and quickly multiply as it attacks the brain.

Normally the cells within a vampire's body will absorb the life force of any new cells introduced into it's network. But the cells of the Puissance virus are unsusceptible to this natural order, even though they are the weaker force. The virus is left free to rapidly replicate and destroy a vampire's brain. However, when a human is infected, the virus' attack is much slower and only last until the transition to 'chomper' is complete. During that time, the transformation process doesn't appear to be as traumatic and disorienting as it is when a human becomes a vampire. And an important note is that the virus will not attack if it is introduced to another organism with the same infection.

Lygia takes a sip from her bottle of water, then she continues talking. "Another indicator supporting my theory of Sig's vampiric force somehow mutating is the way an infected human goes through the transformation with virtually none of the side effects which they would have experience if they were turned by one of us. And there's the fact that the vampiric energy in the infected is transmitted through all biological fluids, no longer limited to only blood. Now, are there any other questions that you would like to ask, Amy?"

"Actually, yes," Amy says. "Why do chompers eat flesh if they're technically vampires?"

"Because they don't know any better," Kristin answers, lending herself as a buffer between Lygia and Amy. "With their limited cognition, all they know is that they feel hungry and they want to eat something that's alive and doesn't smell the same way they do. When they bite into living flesh, they get a mouth full of blood, which sates their appetite. So they eat the flesh of the living instead of drinking blood because they don't know any better."

"Thank you."

"No problem. I'll fill you in on anything you want to know about this stuff. I'll try not to geek it up too much for you, though."

Eli smiles at Amy, then he turns to Lygia. "With Trajanus gone, how do you expect me to find Sig?"

"You know the answer to that." Lygia crosses her arms and stares at Eli with eyes that invite him to challenge her.

Eli laughs mockingly, and says, "Not that crap again. I already have a headache, and I'm not in the mood."

"It's not crap, Elias. You were born with a form of ESP that makes you so good at finding people and things that nobody else can find." Lygia employs a much sweeter tone. "We know that The Primus and the first generation of vampires that he made were able to do things that we've lost through the passing down of our bloodlines. Vampires like you and I who are close enough to the original blood still have a hyper-tactile sense that borders on precognition. Vampires made from a more weaker blood barely have this ability, and it won't be long before the generations behind them don't have it at all. Just like the mouse, we took our G-72 sample from wasn't as strong as the one we used in the G-1 tests."

"Still, that's got nothing to do with me being good at finding things."

"Dad, seriously?" Kristin says. "You've always been able to find things I lost, even after I looked everywhere. Remember that summer I was at your ranch and the stray dog ran off with Mister Fuzzy Butt? You found my bear three miles away, in a ditch. No one would've thought to look there. There is something special about you."

"I'm gonna tell you guys this for the last time. I can find people and things because I use whatever information I have, and I follow my gut instinct. Anybody with a brain can do it."

"No, they can't," Lygia says. "My father knew you had a gift, too. That's why he sent us to search for The Primus. True, we didn't find him, but everything else that you found proves me right. Think about it. What led you to discover that hidden chamber in the temple at Coba'? How did you find those senexes when nobody, not even I, had a clue where to begin looking?"

"That reminds me," Eli says, disregarding Lygia's questions as he digs into his pocket. "You think we got problems from what you know. Well, that ain't even half of it."

Eli drops three fangs on a clear space on Lygia's desk. They click and clack, bouncing until they clink against a ceramic coffee mug and rebound to a stop.

One of Lygia's eyebrows arch higher than the other. "Whose are those?"

"The yellow one I took out of a chomper yesterday. Thought it might help with your research, and I wanted to know why it was in a chomper's mouth, to begin with. I just found out the answer to that. As for the darker ones, I got 'em from the senex at the safe house in Louisiana. Somebody dug him up and drained him."

"Did you tell anybody that he was there?"

Eli's brow wrinkles. "You know better than to ask me that!"

Lygia reveals that the safe house has been under surveillance since Sig's escape from the Gen-Ascend facility. When Eli and Amy showed up there, his high heat signature was assumed to be Sig's, that's why Lt. Granger and his team were scrambled from a nearby outpost. Other than today, the only other high temperatures around the house has been hordes of chompers or some humans making the mistake of scavenging the wrong place. It would've been impossible for a vampire to have gotten in and out of there without blending in with the chompers or being picked up by the satellite. satellite. So in addition to "Who?" it is also a matter of "How?"

"Don't forget," Eli says. "That senex was a Neanderthal, older than the one who turned your father or the one we found in Coba."

Lygia looks as if she just remembered there's a bomb in her hand and there is only one second left on the timer. "A first generation vampire."

"Yep. We probably got a rogue out there who is stronger than anything we prepared for. So, I got my work cut out for me."

Amy empathizes with the worried expression on Lygia's face. A rogue with the power of a first generation vampire will be extremely powerful. And vastly more dangerous than anything she and Eli ever faced as regulares. For the first time since meeting him, Amy begins to truly fear that Eli might end up losing a fight, or possibly even losing his life.

"And that brings me to something else I have to tell you," Eli says. "Calavius is still alive."

"What?!" Lygia responds in disbelief.

Eli recounts for Lygia the events that led him to Preacher's compound and everything that happened while they were there, right up to that morning when Calavius showed up with Nicholi, Aleksi and Kimiko. He doesn't bite his tongue when it comes to his suspicion about Calavius conveniently not being at The Civitas when it was struck by missiles.

"He wants me to bring you back to the compound, but that's not going to happen," Eli says. "I wanted to take his head off the moment he said that he was not the Imperator, but given the circumstances, he technically has the authority. I can't touch him without yours or Titus' permission. We don't need anyone questioning your legitimacy when you claim your place."

"You did the right thing. Sig is our top priority, but I think your hunch is right and we will have to do something about Calavius. I think we might have a way to find out if there is any truth to his story. And if he's lying, I'm sure you're thinking the same thing that I am."

As Eli and Lygia stare at each other, Amy thinks she sees something reconnect between them. She tries to analyze what it is and comes to the conclusion that since Lygia has stopped acting like a scientist and has gone back to behaving like the regulare she once was, Eli is more in tune with her. This is what she had expected to see when Eli and Lygia first reunited, but now that it's happening in front of her she can't help but feel jealous. It's as if she is watching the Eli that she has come to have feelings for slip away from her, right back to the place where he probably belongs.

CHAPTER TWENTY

It's late afternoon, and the sun seems to be stuck high in the sky above the Gulf, radiating vibes that say the day is far from done. Amy takes in the fresh air as she dangles her feet off the edge of the helipad, her mind wandering over everything that has happened since waking up this morning.

Maxwell and Gould are hanging back by the entrance to the ship, allowing Amy and Eli private space. It feels good to be alone with him again. She has felt like a third wheel for most of the day since coming on board the ship.

After Eli and Lygia came to a consensus about Calavius, the conversation turned more like a family reunion. Fond memories of Pelagius was shared, some of Lygia's going all the way back to his and her days when they were humans and citizens of the Roman Empire. Eli kept Amy engaged in the conversation, and Kristin was the glue that held them all together, but Amy still couldn't help feeling like an interloper.

Without talk about viruses, chompers, rogues, Sig, the turmoil within the vampire nation and all of the other things bulking up the mountain they must climb, Lygia loosened up a lot, and Eli also appeared relieved to have his mind distracted from his call of duty.

Lygia eventually became more cordial with Amy. Amy appreciated it, although her intuition was certain Lygia's nice behavior was to keep Eli in a good mood. Kristin's friendliness, however, felt completely genuine. Amy likes her, and she's looking forward to getting to know her better. The only problem is, Amy doesn't know if Kristin is aware that she is more than a fountain to Eli. It's obvious how much Kristin loves the vampires she calls mom and dad, and Amy can't help but feel like a home-wrecker with a conscience.

"You know," Eli says, nudging Amy's thigh with his own, "except for when you're sleeping, I think this is the longest you've gone without saying a word. It's freaking me out."

Amy laughs. "Don't worry, I'm good."

"What's on your mind?"

"Kristin. I like her a lot. But I gotta tell ya, it's funny to see her call you dad when you look like you're barely old enough to buy beer and she might be your big sister."

"Yeah, I know. She's already five years older than I was when Lygia's blood made me a vampire."

"So she's..., twenty-four? Wow, listening to her talk, especially when she slips into scientist mode, you'd think she was older than that. I mean, she sounds smarter than a college professor."

Eli's smile grows wider with pride. "Yeah, she's a smart cookie. She graduated from high school when she was fifteen, and she got her doctorate in molecular biology by the time she was twenty-two. She loves what she does, and I'm proud of my little girl."

"Dude, I gotta tell you, your 'little girl' is not a little girl."

"I beg to differ. It doesn't matter how old she gets, as a human or a vampire—if she chooses to become one—she's always going to be my little girl."

Amy nudges him with her shoulder. "Figures you'd be that kind of dad. I suppose she's always going to be an angel in your eyes, too, huh?"

Eli's eyes light up. "Yeah, and speaking of angels..., Angelica?"

Amy lowers her head and shakes it. Guilt feels like a wet blanket on her. She knows that Eli wants more than an explanation about the name Angelica. He must also want answers to the bombshell Granger dropped on him in front of the mansion.

"My mom told me that my dad started calling me his little angel when I was still in her womb, and since she loved *The Rug Rats* cartoon, Angelica was a no-brainer. I guess I'm lucky mom had already decided to name me Amelia, after my great grandma, by then or it would've been my first name. I'm still not stoked about it, though."

"Well, Amelia Angelica Gouyen, I think it's cute."

Amy sighs and looks back into Eli's eyes. "I'm so sorry," she says, earnestly. "I should've told you that I was a fugitive, and why I was on the run. I swear I was going to. I was just waiting for the right time."

"The men you killed," Eli says. "They were the ones who murdered Aaron?"

Amy nods her head.

Eli's smile brightens. "Good girl. I'm proud of you. Now, tell me what happened. And while you're at it, how the hell did you get out of jail?"

Amy first tells Eli the real reason why she gunned down Aaron's killers. She recounts what happened in the house that night, just as she told the story to Lark. She also confesses how good it made her feel to know that she got the people responsible for Aaron's death. Eli shows no sign of judgment, and she feels comfortable enough to go past the murders and tell him how she bloodied Sheriff Wade Mathis' nose with a headbutt after he handcuffed her and crossed the line from a frisk to copping a feel. Her second assault on a Sheriff's officer charge came when Wade made a disparaging comment about Aaron during one of her pretrial hearings. She managed to land a punch to his head before the other officers tackled her.

Amy hated Wade Mathis' guts. He had a sloped forehead that made him look like a rodent, and the wispy moustache he tried to cultivate didn't help his cause. But Amy has him to thank for her escape. It was a sunny Monday morning. The streets were busy with people going to work, school, or wherever else they needed to be. Amy had to be in court to hear the results of a psychiatric evaluation, and possibly file another pretrial motion, depending on the results.

That morning she came face-to-face with her first chomper. The prostitute in the cell next to hers was at the point of transformation where she was still able to think and talk, but she was already feeling the hunger of a chomper. If not for the bars between them, Amy might've been bitten that day. It took over a dozen sheriff officers to violently subdue the woman, who seemed impervious to pepper spray and tasers after she attacked one of them. Most of them ended up with bites, which they expected to get them a few days off from work. They got more than they bargained for.

The chatter coming over the sheriffs' radios escalated from pockets of disturbances to a city spiraling into chaos. The first reports were that crazed people, possibly under the influence of psychotropic drugs, were randomly attacking people in their own homes, on the streets, in stores, schools, offices, anywhere there was a place for people to be. Men, women, and children were all victims. And adding to the confusion, men, women, and children also fit the description of the attackers. There was no way of distinguishing the two until it was almost too late.

No one knew at the time that mosquitoes carrying infected blood had been spreading the virus that created the first wave of chompers in New Mexico where Amy lived.

All of the Sheriffs were needed to back up the police officers on the streets. So a decision was made to send all the county jail and state prison inmates back to their facilities and lockdown the courthouse. Because of her high profile case and her sociopathic behavior, Amy earned a "High Risk" tag, entitling her to a private ride in a Sheriff's cruiser instead of one of the vans with the other prisoners. With the limited number of officers available, Wade and his partner ended up with the duty to take her back. Amy had noticed that Wade wasn't looking well, but back then she didn't know anything about the Puissance virus, other than the wild and inaccurate rumors that spread from one jail cell to another.

Halfway to the county jail, Wade started eyeing his partner and Amy strangely. She thought it was the same malignant stare that she saw in the prostitute before she tried to bite her, and she mentally prepared to defend herself if she had to. When Wade looked over at his partner and leaned in, Amy knew that he wasn't going to kiss him. It didn't surprise her at all when Wade bit a chunk out of his partner's cheek.

Blood spurted on the plexiglass partition separating the front of the cruiser from the back, forming a crimson starting line for streaking drops to race down from.

A vicious struggle ensued in the front seats. The cruiser swerved left and right. Horns blared from passing vehicles. Wade growled. His partner screamed. Deafening, rapid pops of gunfire slammed through the cabin of the cruiser. The vehicle took a sharp left turn, straight into the path of a box truck skidding to a stop.

Amy was showered by fragments of glass and strips of plastic before slamming into the mangled door on the T-boned side of the cruiser. Before she knew what was happening, she was tossed back over to the driver's side of the car, then she found herself slamming into the ceiling, and she continued to ping-pong around the back of the cruiser as it rolled down an embankment until it came to a stop upside down in a ditch.

She never lost consciousness, but it took her a moment to gather her senses. Various parts of her body hurt like she just took a beating. Nothing felt broken, though. Her vision was clear, but she felt drunk. And what she saw when she looked through the bloodstained plexiglass didn't seem real.

The dead eyes of Wade's partner were staring at her. There was a huge gash in his right cheek, enough skin and flesh missing for molars drenched in fresh blood to be clearly seen. Wade had his partner's lower lip trapped between his teeth, stretching it as he hauled his head back with his eyes closed. Even with all the blood on his face, he looked like he was in ecstasy.

Amy was shocked and horrified, but she retained the presence of mind to know that she had a rare opportunity and she couldn't afford to let it slip away. She crawled out of the window that had shattered upon impact with the truck. Once out of the car, Amy swept her head back and forth to figure out the best direction to flee in. Something caught her eye. It was risky, but her best option.

Just as she was about to rise to her feet, she glanced at the front of the cruiser and saw Wade's eyes focused on her. He was lit up like a fiend spotting his favorite vice.

"And where do you think you're going?" Wade said with a devilish grin.

Instead of answerin g, Amy scrambled to her feet. She wanted to run, but with her legs shackled all she could do was hop in the direction of the culvert she just spotted.

Wade's hand reached for her ankle, but missed.

Amy hopped faster.

The front passenge r window was shattered in the crash, too, allowing Wade to get out ast easily as it was for her. So she didn't have time to waste.

A voice drew Amy's attention up to the road. She spotted the box truck driver climbing over a part of the guardrail that wasn't damaged when the cruiser slammed into it and flipped over. He was spitting commands for her to stop, and she wished he would slip and break his neck since he wanted to thwart her escape.

An agonizing howl made her glance back to see Wade crumple to the ground after trying to stand up. The jagged-tipped spike of bone sticking out from his thigh showed her that the universe had cut her a break. With at least one of his legs broken and the possibility that Wade's bulletproof vest didn't stop all the slugs his partner tried to put in him, Amy felt she had a chance of a fair race with her arch nemesis.

"You bitch!" Wade bawled. "This is your fault! Wait till I get my hands on you!"

Amy hopped as fast and as far as she could with each bound. She was making progress, but Wade moved freakishly fast in a combination skitter/slither. It was like having some kind of rabid, mutant lizard closing in on her heels.

She dropped down at the entrance to the drain, crawling on her knees and forearms, hurrying towards the darkness. Wade's fingertips brushed her canvas, jail-issued sneakers, unable to get a grip on them. He grunted from pain and growled from frustration or hunger, but didn't give up his pursuit.

Amy refused to look back. The only thing that mattered was moving ahead.

The diameter of the tunnel quickly started tightening after about twenty feet in. Amy felt the concrete start to brush her shoulders, head, and butt with every move she made. Dust and cobwebs clung to her. Soon she would have to drop down and try to outrun Wade on her belly. It wasn't a comforting thought, and that wasn't because of the residue coating the tunnel floor which smelled like a combination of mildew, compost and an exaggerated scent of concrete.

Wade's fingers found the toe box of Amy's sneaker and took hold. "Gotcha!"

Instinctively, she kicked, not thinking about the leg irons. She wasn't able to summon the desired force, and only ended up flat on the rough, clammy floor of the tunnel.

Wade pulled, hauling her back. Every inch closer to him is accented by the static from the metal handcuffs and leg irons chain scraping the concrete floor. The tight confines of the tunnel kept Wade from being able to bring her to his eager mouth. But if he kept dragging her backwards, they would soon be in a part of the tunnel where he would have more than enough wiggle room.

"A-A-Amy," Wade taunted. "I never realized it before, but you smell so fuckin' yummy! Do you taste like you smell? I'll find out real soon. And guess where I've decided to start eating you first...? That's right, and I'm not going to stop there."

Amy felt her heart pumping so hard, she thought it was trying to burst out of her chest to run to safety, leaving her behind to deal with the crazed sheriff.

She remembered the face of Wade's partner. Then she couldn't stop the image of what Wade threatened to do to her from pasting itself in her head.

"Hello! Officer?" an echoing voice pierced the thunder of Amy's heart.

It was the truck driver coming to assist the sheriff in apprehending an escaping fugitive. His voice didn't only surprise Amy. It also caused Wade to freeze, a half a second that was long enough for Amy to kick her foot down, slamming Wade's knuckles on the tunnel floor.

Wade yowled, loosening his grip enough for Amy to pull free. And like a madwoman tweaking hard, she inch-wormed herself back deeper into the tunnel faster than before.

Wade renewed the pursuit. "Get back here!"

Amy crawled for her life. "Yeah, right! Fuck you!"

Fingers hit the soles of her sneakers, but she refused to let Wade get a grip again.

The truck driver continued to call out, asking what he could do to help.

Wade kept coming.

Amy realized that it was getting harder to crawl. The tunnel was tightening more. She was now being limited to only being able to shimmy her way through. It slowed her down, but her desperate prayers were answered. Wade was no longer pawing at her feet. He couldn't. Not unless he could shed his medium build body for that of a svelte schoolgirl.

It took Amy a moment to realize that Wade could no longer squeeze through the tunnel like she could. Still, she put more distance between them before she stopped to catch her breath. She let the dank air quell the fire in her lungs while listening to the voice of the truck driver and Wade's furious cussing.

"I'll get you, Amy!" Wade yelled when his lexicon of bad words were exhausted. "One way or another, I'll get you!"

"Again, fuck you!" Amy yelled back. "And if I ever see you again, I promise I'll put a hole in your skull."

"I can't get through to nine-one-one," the truck driver said. "Should I try to flag somebody down from the road?"

"No, back up. I'm coming out," Wade responds.

"Okay."

"No, dumbass!" Amy hollered. "You better run! He's gonna try to eat you!"

The truck driver didn't listen. It wasn't long before his horrific screams were flooding the tunnel.

Amy crawled away. She made it to the sewers and shuffled her way around down there until she could rely on the dark of night to make her way through the streets again. After breaking into an auto body shop, she used a power grinder the cut the chains of her cuffs and leg irons. Then she ditch the orange jailhouse jumpsuit for a grimy coverall and scurried off to the place where Aaron taught her how to shoot. Late the next morning, she made her way home just in time to see the soldiers throw her mother in a pile of bodies and light them on fire.

After the soldiers left to take the people in her neighborhood to a safe zone, Amy took a moment to say goodbye to her mother. Then she gathered food, supplies, some personal items, as well as Aaron's thirty-thirty rifle and she hit the road, with no idea exactly where she wanted to go.

"You did good," Eli says, putting his arms around her. "And I'm glad you got away and ended up where I found you."

"I'm glad you found me, too," Amy says, with a smile. "And again, I'm sorry I didn't tell you all that before you found out. Honestly, there's a part of me that's scared you're going to tell me that you can't make me a vampire because of what I did."

Eli laughs. "It's supposed to count against you, but it would be hypocritical of me to do that. I went on a little rampage of my own after my father was killed. And there hasn't been a day gone by since that I regretted it."

Amy nuzzles the side of her face against Eli's, knowing that this moment will stay in her memory forever as the moment that she knew for sure she had a kindred spirit in this world.

"So," Amy says, leaning back to look at Eli, "it makes me happy to know that you still want to make me your legare, but how is Lygia going to feel about it?"

"She's not going to like it," Eli says, bluntly. "But I'll go to bat for you. I keep my promises, remember?"

Amy smiles, but it only lasts a few seconds before she sees Eli's expression quickly change and he turns to look back in the direction of the ship's entrance on the helipad. She turns as well and sees one of the elevator doors open, revealing the passenger inside. Lt. Granger, dressed in a black jumpsuit with his name and rank embroidered in silver letters on his chest. He steps onto the deck and aggressively marches straight towards Eli and Amy.

Eli is first to his feet, his stance telegraphing that he's ready to go for round two if that's what Granger wants.

"Hey, Bloodsucker!" Granger barks. "You're coming with me."

"Coming with you where?" Eli responds.

"Conference room. General Limbeck wants to see you and Doctor Contaldi A-S-A-P. She's already on her way. I've been sent to get you."

"What's this about?"

"Your buddy, Sigodur. He damn near killed a whole patrol, just to leave a message for you and her. Time for you to prove what side you're on."

CHAPTER TWENTY-ONE

Granger leads Eli and Amy into one of the conference rooms on Level 3. The first thing that draws Amy's attention is the wall on the left side of the room. It is covered in monitors, like high-tech tiles. All but one of the monitors displaying an aerial view of the landscape being flown over in remarkable high definition. The monitor in the middle—the largest one—is frozen on the smile of a baby-faced soldier.

General Limbeck's stone mug is in drastic contrast to the young soldier on the screen he is standing in front of. As jovial as he was earlier, he now looks like there is molten anger seething under his skin.

Lygia is already in the conference room, standing next to the General. She has ditched her scrubs for a black skirt that hangs to her knees and a white blouse, unbuttoned enough to still appear conservative while sneaking a peek at the top of her bust line.

Lygia's glare and the twitch in her eyebrows tell Amy that she wants to ask why is she here with Eli, but she doesn't want to make a scene.

The only other person who was already in the conference room is a young soldier, a fair-skin woman with short brown hair, wearing black frame cat eyes glasses. She is sitting at a dark brown wooden table in the middle of the room, facing the wall of monitors. On the table in front of her is what looks like a bulky briefcase, laying flat with the lid standing open at a 90-degree angle.

At first glance, the briefcase appears to be a gaudy laptop. But along with a keyboard and a monitor, there are also arrays of illuminated buttons and switches, plus a pistol-grip joystick that looks like it belongs in the cockpit of a fighter jet.

The brown-haired girl at the table is zoned out like a zombie, staring at the screen with her fingers coiled around the joystick. The lenses of her glasses are aglow with rectangular reflections from the monitor in front of her.

"Mister Kincade," General Limbeck says to Eli, "this is Specialist Melissa Skipworth. I expected to introduce her to you sometime tomorrow, but there's no time like the present."

"Skipworth...," Eli says, with his eyes glancing from the screen on Skipworth's device to the monitors on the wall. "Drone pilot, huh?"

"Yes, sir," Skipworth responds, eyes still on the screen. "But I'm well inclined in anything tech."

"I count footage from at least twelve drones up there, including what's on that screen in front of you."

"You're right. I'm running a search pattern with some other pilots over a sixty-mile radius from where our target was last sighted. I'm flying one over Lexington, Virginia right now but I can gain control of any bird within our system."

Studying Eli's face, General Limbeck, "Skipworth here is going to give you eyes in the sky to help you find your brother Sigodur. She'll be able to show you anywhere you want to see within the lower forty-eight with nonessential drones or satellite footage."

"Not really my method," Eli responds. "I prefer to be out there, feeling what I feel and goin' with my gut."

"But, you're willing to give this a try," says Lygia, her tone conveying to Eli that her statement is nonnegotiable.

"I guess I'm giving it a try."

"Good," Limbeck says, then he touches the screen with the baby-faced soldier on it. "This was taken from the body-cam of Sergeant Calib Masterson, three hours ago."

"I'm talkin' you, man," the baby-faced soldier says, in a southern drawl when the video begins to play. "Her hair smells like strawberry shortcake, and her lips taste like pumpkin pie. It drives me crazy every time I'm with her. I could just eat her up. Know what I mean?"

The footage they are looking at was shot from a camera mounted on Masterson's protective eyewear. He is walking alongside the soldier with the baby face, wearing the same type of glasses. There are others with them, four walking ahead and two more behind, patrolling what looks like it was an affluent neighborhood.

The once well-manicured lawns are now overgrown and littered with random household items, as well as the personal belongings of the homes' former occupants. Some of the houses on the street have been burned down. The ones still standing have broken down doors and shattered windows, their opulent facades now tagged with graffiti damning the rich to death in whatever special safe-zone they were taken to. All of the posh homes have been violated and robbed of the upstanding pride they once boasted. Even all of the luxury vehicles left behind have been damaged, vandalized, and picked clean of anything that could be scavenged for survival.

"C'mon man, pumpkin pie?!" says a soldier with tribal tattoos flourishing on his nearly sunburned neck. "Alex, lemme give you the real, bro. Yo girl, she like ninety-five pounds, lookin' like a runway chick with legs fo' days, right?"

Alex shrugs his shoulders.

The tattooed soldier continues. "You ain't never see her eatin' nuffin' but salad and appetizers and shit, right? Like, y'all go out to dinner and she nibblin' on the parsley, leavin' all the meat and potatoes and shit all on the plate, right?"

Alex shrugs again.

"Check it. The reason why yo chick be smellin' and tastin' like food all the time is 'cause she be hidin' that shit and sneakin' bites when you ain't lookin', dawg. That's what's up, brah! When you get wit' her again, frisk her ass. I bet you find some snacks hidden in them big, fake titties of hers."

"Carson!" the brown-skinned soldier walking next to him says. "Would you please shut your corny, counterfeit Riff-Raff, wannabe ass up! You're just mad because your girl smells like three-day-old fish and she tastes like meth and Jack Daniels."

Carson glares, then emphatically says, "Yo, McAllister, I knew you was the fool I done stole that ratchetty bitch from! That's how you know her so good, brah?"

The street explodes with laughter. Fingers point. Fists bump. Happy faces display bright teeth through big smiles. Camaraderie is high among the young soldiers.

The laughter comes to an abrupt stop when a voice from behind yells out, "Chomper, six o'clock!"

The camera view swooshes around and settles on the chomper. It's a girl no more than 10-years-old. Thanks to obesity before she became a chomper, she's at least twice as wide as a healthy girl her age. Large blots of her matted, blonde hair are now dyed brown by old blood. Twigs and dead leaves have become snared by her unruly locks. Her white dress would make her look like she was on her way to Sunday school if it didn't look like it had been dragged down a country road with her still in it. Her face is dirty, and there is no mistaking what has stained her mouth down to her chin.

The fat little chomper glowers at the soldiers. However, it defies its nature and doesn't attack. Since chompers live to eat, it's extremely odd that she isn't trying to satisfy her unquenchable appetite.

"Weird," baby-face Alex says.

"Lil Butter Ball kinda cute, yo," Carson jokes. "Lookin' like she 'bout to go hunt fo' rotten Easta eggs then eat the bunny and shit."

"Somebody put it out of its misery," Masterson says.

"Carson or the chomper?" McAllister asks.

A round of laughter flows.

"I got it, Sarge," volunteers the taller of the two soldiers at the back of the pack; the one who initially spotted the chomper and sounded the warning.

The soldier raises his M-16 and takes aim at the Butter Ball chomper, slowly advancing towards it. The chomper stands its ground. The other soldiers within frame casually wait for their team member to dispose of the nuisance. He stops about fifteen feet from the chomper and the moment comes when he should pull the trigger. Everyone waits for a report from the M-16 and chomper brains to blow out the back of the little girl's head.

A whoosh sound slices through the silent neighborhood.

The soldier starts to turn left, the same direction of the sound. Something in a blur comes in fast, collides with his face, and blows away everything above his jawline. Blood, brain, and bone disperse in a burst, like a firework. A bowling ball slams into an oak tree on the right side of the street, bouncing off as fragments of bark and splintered wood splash violently.

The almost-headless body of the tall soldier drops to his knees and topples over. The bloody bowling ball bounces past.

The camera swiftly pans left as Masterson whips his head in the direction the bowling ball came from.

A figure emerges from the side of a white house. It's Sig, dressed in black jeans, boots, and a long length black shirt that is opened to expose his chest and abs. His flaxen hair has grown back a couple inches, and the hole that was cut out of his cranium seems to have completely regenerated.

In Sig's hand, he holds a samurai sword, angled slightly out to his side. He strolls forward with flashes of the morning sun exploding off the intimidating katana's lustrous curved blade, while the tip brushes over the peak of the wild grass.

Masterson trains his weapon on Sig, the camera view running the length of his M-16. "Drop your weapon!" he barks.

The order is echoed by other soldiers, along with, "Face down on the ground, now!"

"Face down?" Sig says, striding forward. "You mean, like your friend over there? Oh, that's right, he doesn't have much of a face left, does he?"

"Sarge, please lemme smoke this geek?" Carson pleads.

The camera whips from side to side as Masterson shakes his head. "Hold on. Something's not right."

"Damn right, somethin' ain't right! He gotta go!"

The camera quickly jumps from Sig to the body of the fallen soldier, over to the bloody bowling ball, over to the little girl chomper, then back at Sig. "What the hell's going on here?"

"We'll figure it out later," Carson says and opens fire.

Carson's rifle rattles and star-shaped fire blazes around the muzzle. Sig darts to his left, keeping ahead of the rounds being blasted in his direction. Carson tries to keep up with him, adjusting his aim as he continues to fire. Sig unexpectedly stops and drops to the ground while Carson's line of fire sweeps over the top of him.

Carson tries to reacquire his target, but Sig doesn't give him a chance. In an unbelievable burst of speed, Sig closes the thirty feet separating them, then there is something that looks like a scene skip in the video. One moment Sig is in front of Carson, then like magic, he's standing behind him.

Carson stops firing. He moves to turn his body around, and in an instant, he becomes a foot and a half shorter. His legs, cut from just above his knees, are laying on the ground as if they were prosthetics. Unbalanced on his severed limbs, Carson starts to topple over as his arms separate, forearms falling away from his elbows.

Amy sees Eli and Lygia quickly dart a glance at each other.

A couple of seconds drag by. In those brief, excruciatingly surreal ticks of time, the soldiers can't seem to process how Sig could possibly have severed Carson's arms and legs without them seeing it done. It doesn't seem real.

The lull crashes and all hell breaks loose in an eruption of gunfire, accompanied by the pinging of spent shells falling to the asphalt.

The video takes on the appearance of a first-person shooter game. The muzzle of Masterson's rifle tries to keep up with Sig. The task is more difficult than it should be. Sig moves so fast, it's impossible to tell what direction he's going or where he will appear. When he does come into sight, he's within striking distance of a soldier who just ran out of bullets.

No one fires, in fear of hitting their own man. But a couple of them take advantage of the time to rapidly swap-out their depleted magazines for fully loaded ones.

Sig has more than enough time to arc his katana and bring it down viciously on the soldier's right shoulder. The blade glides through him like he's made of butter and it exits under the left side of his rib cage. Then Sig is on the move again, easily outrunning the volley of bullets that riddle the soldier's severed body as it slides apart.

Sig bounces to the next closest soldier, Martin, according to his tag. He is futilely shooting at a zig-zagging blur.

Sig blows past Martin.

Martin stops shooting.

Sig does a 360 spin in front of the next closest soldier, a tall and stout man. Then Sig spins again in the opposite direction, ending up behind the man with his left arm locked around the soldier's neck.

Martin's knees buckle and they hit the ground hard. His head pops off and gushes of arterial spray pump from his freshly cut neck, like a distasteful fountain.

Before Martin's body falls flat to the ground, a crimson smile soaks through the uniform of the stout soldier that Sig has in a choke hold. The cut across his belly widens and belches out a lurid deluge of intestines that wetly slap the street and spill over on itself.

The eviscerated soldier blows a panicky scream that sounds like an old air raid siren. His hand's paw at his guts in a desperate attempt to shove them back in.

Alex and McAllister move quickly to flank Sig while the sergeant moves ahead. Each of them alter tri-burst shots as they tighten the space between them and their target. The eviscerated soldier's body is sprinkled with bullet holes.

The obese chomper, lost in the chaos and carnage, growls and takes off. She charges at McAllister like she has been slingshotted towards him.

McAllister turns around to shoot, but the chomper is on him before he has a chance to get her in his line of fire. Her weight and speed hit with enough force to knock McAllister onto his back. The best he can do to defend himself is to grab her by her throat to keep her from getting her mouth close enough to bite him.

Sergeant Masterson quickly switches his aim from Sig to the chomper.

Sig flings the eviscerated soldier at Alex, bowling him over, then Sig flicks his wrist.

A jerky movement of the camera signifies Masterson's body experiencing a jolt, just as he takes a shot. He stumbles backwards.

The camera pans down and shows the handle of Sig's Katana pressed against Masterson's chest. The blade penetrated all the way through his body, up to the hilt.

Masterson's shot was thrown off his mark. McAllister is still holding the chomper by her plump neck and is now reaching for his sidearm. By the time he has it, Sig is already there.

Sig clutches McAllister's forearm and steps on his shoulder. The sidearm pops off shots into the sky. Sig pulls and twists McAllister's arm, yanking it out of the socket and wrenching it completely around.

McAllister bawls in pain. His Beretta clunks on the ground. He uses all of his strength to hold off the chomper, which is much stronger than she would be if she were still a human girl.

Masterson drops to his knees. He tries to raise his assault rifle, but he can't bring it level or keep it steady.

Sig scoops up McAllister's Beretta and flings it over the white house on the property that he emerged from. Then he unclips the strap on McAllister's M-16 and tosses the rifle far away, too. Next, he affectionately musses the chomper's hair and turns around, setting his sight on Alex.

Alex looks like he's barely regained his wind. And now with Sig bearing down on him, he is visibly scared to death. He raises his rifle, but Sig snatches the muzzle and bends it with only his thumb. Sig then yanks Alex up and relieves him of his useless M-16, as well as the semiautomatic handgun in the holster at his side.

Masterson continues to force himself to get a bead on Sig. But the more he tries to raise his rifle, the heavier it looks in his hands. Still, he tries as he watches Sig drag Alex over to McAllister and the chomper.

McAllister has rolled over and is now on top of the chomper, looking like he is laying on top of a large pillow as he keeps her head pressed to the asphalt. It's all he can do with only one good arm.

Sig grips Alex by the back of the neck and forces him down, bringing his face mere inches away from the chomper's chomping teeth. Alex wriggles his body in a mad spastic way, shrieking as he tries to get away. McAllister shakes his head and pleads with Sig for him not to do it.

Alex's baby face is shoved flush against the Butter Ball chomper's face. She takes half of his nose in the first bite, then like a piranha she fills her mouth with chunk after chunk of skin and flesh. McAllister's hand around her neck must be making it hard for her to swallow but she still frantically works her jaw as blood rains down on her.

A single shot cracks the caterwauling and a slug slaps into Alex's temple, silencing him when it rips through the other side of his head.

Sig looks at Masterson and chuckles with amusement.

The camera looks down, then the ground rushes up and the image quakes upon impact with flashes of static. When the video stabilizes, it is a sideways view from the level of the street. Carson and his limbs are in the shot, laying in a large pool of his blood.

Moments later, Sig's boots walk into frame. The image on the screen rumbles again and now shows the ground pulling away. Once Sig has hauled Masterson up by the collar, he uses his left hand to grip the sergeant's jaw. Sig lifts Masterton's head, manipulating the dead man's face to look directly at his.

"All right," Sig says and smiles, proudly showing off his fangs for the camera. "I don't have much time before a drone has me in range, so I'll make this quick. I'm sure Lieutenant Trent Granger of MACE Team One will eventually see this. I haven't forgotten you, Granger, you prick. We'll meet again soon. And when we do, what I did to your brother is going to be nothing compared to what I'm going to do to you."

Amy and Eli both glance at Granger and see the rage washing over him.

"Next," Sig continues. "Elias, my brother, and... Rosa, my sister, I know you're back together again. And I'm sure your new allies are going to let you watch this... unless they want more of their kid soldiers to die. I want you to find me, Elias. Playtime's over. Our God is restless, and we need you to find him before he rises. I need you to use your gift. Bring Rosa with you, too. I have answers that she's been looking for, and I want to make things right. Plus, we have business to take care of. I know how things look, but I need you to trust me. I was in a bad way before, but I'm better now..., as much as I can be."

Masterson's head slumps when Sig releases his jaw. Then time seems to stretch like taffy while Sig slowly withdraws the full length of his sword from Masterson's chest. Once it is free, Sig lets Masterson drop to the ground; the camera capturing the clear, blue sky above.

Sig lays his sword over his shoulder and starts to walk away, but he abruptly stops and turns around with a sly smile on his face. He bends down and pulls the goggles from Masterson's face, then he casually walks over to McAllister, who is still stuck in the precarious position of holding down the chomper or letting it go and try to fend it off with one arm and no weapon.

"Keep it up," Sig encourages McAllister as he gets down on one knee. "Your base should be sending help. If my little princess here doesn't wear you out before they arrive, you might just live to tell about this."

Sig then slips the goggles onto the Butter Ball chomper's bloody face, leaving it there, so the camera has a close-up shot of McAllister grimacing as he burns energy to hold her down.

"Clock's ticking, Eli," Sig says, in an upside-down view of the camera. "Hope you're ready for the fight of your life. And don't forget, Playtime's over."

The video freezes on Sig's nefarious grin.

"Well," General Limbeck says, "any thoughts?"

"We're sorry about what happened to those men," Lygia says. "We'll make sure Sig pays for his crimes."

"I'm sure McAllister would like to see that."

"He made it?" Amy asks.

General Limbeck nods his head, then he focuses on Eli. "Is there anything you'd like to share with us?"

"Like what?" Eli asks, defensively.

"For one," Granger says, "how did Sigodur know you and Doctor Contaldi are back together? Did you send a message to him somehow?"

"That's a stupid question!" Amy snaps.

Lygia narrows her eyes, looking displeased with Amy's outburst but she doesn't say anything.

"What I mean," Amy says, more calmly, "is that we've been under constant surveillance ever since the soldiers surprised us at the mansion in Louisiana. There's no way we could've-"

"What about when you were in the garage?" Granger interrupts and crosses his arms over his chest.

Amy taps the bruise and new puncture wounds on her neck. "We were busy. But you already know that. You were outside the whole time, and you inspected the garage yourself before we left."

"She's right," Eli says. "And I don't appreciate us being accused like this. Hell of a way to maintain an alliance if you ask me."

Granger scowls.

"We had to ask," General Limbeck says. "I personally would like to know what Sigodur meant by your restless God rising again, as well as why you need to find him first. Not to mention this 'business to take care of' that he spoke about."

"General," Lygia says, "everything that Sig said in his message is tantamount to the ranting of a lunatic. There is a faction of our kind who believe God had something to do with our existence, but as far as we know, Sig never subscribed to that theology. As for the 'business to take care of', we'd only be guessing if we tried to figure out what he meant."

"Tell you what, General," Eli says, pulling up a chair next to Skipworth and her drone control console. "We're going to find Sig. And when we do, you'll have all the answers to all the questions you want to ask."

CHAPTER TWENTY-TWO

As exhausted as Amy feels, her brain just won't shut off. It's only 6:30 in the morning. She has been laying on the bottom berth in a small stateroom, at the edge of sleep but unable to cross the border into dreamland. All she can do is lay with her eyes closed, watching memories of the past few days play like a movie being projected on the back of her eyelids.

The small room reminds Amy of the jail cell that she once was held in. The size is about the same. The fixtures are strangely similar, as well: something to sleep on and a desk with a stool by the opposing wall. The only thing missing is a stainless steel toilet/sink combo. There is one perk in the stateroom that would be a plus in any jail cell: a private bathroom. The one in the stateroom has a shower the size of an old phone booth, and barely room for the sink and toilet that fills up the rest of the space, but Amy is grateful for it. And a bonus is the clean, flowing, hot water.

The pseudo cell doesn't really bother Amy. Out of everything that she's been thinking about for the past hours, Eli has been on her mind the most. If he had come to bed with her, it may have been easier to drift off in the security of his arms. But he ended up spending the night in the conference room with Skipworth after insisting Amy went to bed when he caught her nodding.

None of the drones in Skipworth's network were able to pick up on Sig's trail after he killed all the soldiers that McAllister was on patrol with. There was no shortage of chompers roaming about, but the rogue vampire was nowhere to be found. Even a satellite with thermal imaging—like the one that first spotted him and Kelly—couldn't pick him up again.

Not being able to find Sig motivated Eli to find him even more than before. Determination blazed in his eyes like he had something to prove. He even tried to get Skipworth to turn over control of a drone to him so he could feel more like he is out there searching. He burned with frustration when she absolutely refused. Considering the millions of dollars each of Skipworth's toys cost, and Eli not being a qualified pilot, Amy understood her resistance.

After a quick break, mainly for Skipworth and Amy to get something to eat, a new tactic was employed. Instead of trying to pick up on a cold trail, Eli got Skipworth to access archived drone and satellite footage of places that he thinks Sig might have been. They also moved drones and satellites to those same places to see if something would stand out or give a clue about where Sig is or what he's doing.

Eli wants Sig bad, but a part of Amy wishes he doesn't find him. Not a word was uttered about it, but the silent communication between Eli and Lygia during the video footage of Sig and the soldiers told Amy that Sig has become more than he was before. It's even possible that he was the person who dug up the senex and drank its ancient, powerful blood. If true, then most likely, Eli will be no match for him.

Sig's weird message about their God being restless bothers Amy, too. And she hasn't forgotten how Sig told Eli to be ready for the fight of his life. Twice Sig specifically told Eli that "Playtime's over". She doesn't know what it means, but she is convinced that it can't be anything good.

A knock at the door makes Amy open her eyes. She wonders if Kristin has come back to check on her since she didn't feel like eating breakfast. It's been a little over an hour since Kristin said she was going to the lab and she would come back around lunchtime. So, most likely, it's not her. And since Eli is sharing the stateroom with her, he wouldn't knock unless maybe he wants to give her a heads-up in case she's in a state of undress.

"Just a minute," Amy says, swinging her legs off the berth, then she quickly slips on a pair of jeans.

Amy opens the door and is surprised to find Lygia standing there with a covered, insulated tray in her hands. On top of the tray is a slender, blue mug. Amy involuntarily remains frozen after being caught off guard by the unexpected visit. Lygia has acted as if Amy doesn't exist. And when she does acknowledge her, Lygia makes her feel like a bothersome gnat. So a visit is the last thing that Amy expected. And being alone with Lygia makes her feel like she is naked in a spotlight.

Lygia doesn't wait to be invited in. She steps forward, causing Amy to step back and out of the way.

Before Lygia shuts the door, Amy catches a glimpse of Gould, now back on guard duty, giving her a nod.

When the door closes, Amy places a fist over her heart, lowers her head, and says, "Imperator."

"Call me Lygia when we have privacy, or Doctor Contaldi when among outsiders," Lygia says, wearing a stoic expression. "I haven't officially accepted my father's place yet, so you don't have to pay homage to me. But you should respect me."

"I do," Amy says, hoping that her heart doesn't change its beat and betray her.

"Good. Now, I'm here because I asked Kristin how was breakfast with you and she told me that you weren't hungry this morning. Are you feeling ill? Is there a health issue I should know about?"

Amy shakes her head. "No, nothing like that. Thank you for your concern, though. I'm just not hungry."

"You are at least fifteen pounds underweight."

"Just one of the side effects of the apocalypse," Amy jokes.

Unamused, Lygia places the tray and mug on the table. "We can sense when our legare aren't feeding enough, and I know that Elias needs more nourishment than he's been getting. Now, more than ever, it's imperative that he be in the best shape of his life. And to bring that to fruition, he's going to need a steady supply of blood. It is not safe for you to keep feeding him at your current weight. Not like he needs to be fed."

"Eli can have as much of my blood as he needs," Amy says. "It's always available to him whenever he wants it."

"That being said, I want you to take in a minimum of twenty-five hundred calories per day, at least until you are back to a healthy weight. And try to eat foods rich in iron and potassium. Elias likes the taste of blood that is high in those minerals. I am looking into finding him another source of blood, but he'll still be feeding on you as well. Oh, and from now on, would you two please use a siphon? Your neck is unsightly."

"We will," Amy replies, rubbing her fang scars and the bruise around it. "And I apologize for that."

Amy bites her bottom lip to keep from saying what else is on her mind. She promised to be Eli's fountain, but Lygia is speaking as if that is all she ever will be.

"You should know," Lygia says, "I just brought Elias some of those power bars that he enjoys so much, and I was able to spend some time alone with him. There were things that we needed to discuss privately. And at the end of our talk, he asked my permission to make you his legare."

Amy's breath catches in her throat.

"Elias has never asked me for anything," Lygia says, "and I would give him the world if he wanted it. But..., I don't know what he is thinking with that request. As much as I like to make him happy, allowing you to drink his blood is something that I cannot condone."

Confounded, Amy finds herself speechless. She believed that Eli would eventually talk to Lygia about making her his legare, but she hadn't expected it so soon. And hearing that Eli and Lygia have very recently spent private time together is like a brier digging in on her brain.

"Please," Amy says, her voice cracking. "Give me a chance to prove that..., I'm worthy of your bloodline."

Lygia laughs. "Do you understand that you will most likely die if you drink his blood? Even if you are strong enough to survive the transformation, it will be a constant struggle to keep the power from taking control. And when you lose control, either Elias or I will have to decapitate you."

"I'm willing to take that risk."

"And why should I risk you becoming another rogue or even an acolyte? The fact that you tried to rob him after he saved your life is enough for me to say no. And yes, he told me that he made you shoot him, but it still doesn't sit well with me. The fact is, I don't trust you."

Amy feels her heart turn to stone and sink down to her bowels. She knows that Eli had to tell Lygia about her, but she wishes that he kept the mistake she made a secret between them. And she can't help but wonder what else Lygia knows. Until she finds out from Eli himself, she'll have to walk on eggshells.

"I was desperate, and I made a mistake," Amy says. "I didn't try to rob Eli until I discovered he was lying to me. And I really wouldn't have tried it if..., the world wasn't what it is now. And please believe me when I say I am not a risk. I would never betray Eli. And I will never betray you."

Lygia arches an eyebrow, and says, "But I gather you would betray me before you betray Elias since you put his name before mine?"

"No, that's not what I meant!" Amy says shaking her head. "Eli is important to me, and I'm thankful to be a part of his life. You are also a part of my life because you are an important part of his world. And I wouldn't ever betray either if you."

Lygia stares at Amy for a moment, then she tells Amy that there are things that she must know if she plans to be a part of Eli's life. Number one on the list is that, even thoug h she and Eli aren't in the committed relationship they once shared, there is no doubt that he will always belong to her. Then she informs Amy that she is not the first stray cat that Eli has picked up and thought he had feelings for, and she won't be the last. And Lygia stakes her claim that Eli's heart has been hers for over a century, and he will be hers for as long as they both live.

"Elias is like the mustangs that live on his ranch," Lygia says. "You can corral them and give them all the love in the world. You can even ride them for as long as you want. But they aren't truly happy unless they're running free. I allow Elias to run free, but his heart will always belong to the one who broke his wild spirit. And that one is me."

Amy remains silent. The muscles in her jaw feel like burning knots from how hard she is gritting her teeth.

"You are obviously brimming with rage," Lygia says. "Tell me what you want to say."

"I really shouldn't," Amy growls.

"You have my permission to speak frankly. If there is something you want to tell me, this is the time to get it off of your chest. Or, you can remain silent and cowardly."

"Okay, you asked for it," Amy smugly says, happy to take the gloves off.

"Here's something I think you should know. It's pathetic how you think you can keep your claws in a guy like Eli. You think I don't know he likes to be free? He's a real man. They don't make 'em like him anymore. And I like him a lot, but I'm not delusional, like you! We get along really well because we do what we do and just call it a day. No strings, no nothing. You think you can own him without really owning him. That's the dumbest thing I've ever heard in my life! No wonder he only bangs your brains out every now and then, and he's probably out the door before you even get out of bed to wipe his com-"

Amy sentence is caught in her throat. Before she realizes what is happening she becomes weightless and the back of her head hits the wall while Lygia constricts her throat as she holds her up with one hand.

Amy tries to pry Lygia's fingers from her neck. She glares at Lygia, expecting to see her eyes inflamed with rage. But what she finds instead is that Lygia is as cool as morning dew.

Amy continues to struggle. She even considers calling for help. But even if she could swallow her pride any more and scream bloody murder, no sound can escape her throat at the moment. The best she can do is try to fight, which she does. But there's no chance of overpowering a vampire, and she ends up burning precious energy that isn't being replenished by a steady air supply.

When Lygia finally releases her, Amy falls to the ground and crumples like her legs have become boneless.

Amy's hands quickly go to her own throat, hoping for soothing relief as she madly takes in big gulps of air to fill her burning lungs.

"Don't misunderstand," Lygia says, towering over Amy. "That wasn't about Elias. I honestly don't care what you have to say about you and him or him and I. But there is a difference between being frank and being disrespectful. Women know the difference between the two. Little girls must be taught which is which."

Amy glowers, entertaining thoughts of finding some way to kill Lygia as she listens to her speak.

Lygia extends her hand to help Amy to her feet. "Elias has told me what he believes are your strengths, as well as your flaws. He believes your strengths are stronger, but I beg to differ. I believe you are too impetuous to ever be a vampire."

"But," Amy mumbles as she is pulled up to her feet, "you don't even know me. No disrespect, Lygia, but I don't think you should judge me only on a mistake I made when I met Eli and just the things that have happened since we've met yesterday."

"Elias knows you barely much longer than I do. Should he not judge you by what's happened in that scant amount of time, too? Or is it different with him since his opinion of you is so favorable?"

Amy sighs. "I just want you to give me a chance."

Lygia's gaze focuses like a laser. "Has Elias told you about how dangerous his blood is? Or why?"

"Yes. I know he's powerful because he was turned by you, and you were turned by Pelagius, so his bloodline has a shorter connection to the senexes and The Primus."

Lygia smiles. "If I ever decide to give you permission to become one of us, you will be much better off if let someone like Antonio or one of his legares turn you. If Elias gives you his blood, you will regret it. And he will be taught a hard lesson."

"What do you mean?" Amy says, bristling, more to defend Eli than herself. "You wouldn't harm, Eli. And if you tried to, I won't let you."

Lygia laughs as if that is the funniest thing that she has ever heard in her life. Then, while regaining her composure, she tells Amy that Eli bears the curse of being the most honorable man that she has ever met. Even though he was the scourge of the Wild West when she met and hired him to track down Hadrianus, she saw what was in his heart before he showed it by coming to her rescue and saving her life. Pelagius also saw how honorable Eli is and there is no question why he considered Eli his most trusted regulare. Eli will always do the right thing. And because of that, Lygia would rather Eli not have to live with the guilt of what he will be forced to do if Amy ever drinks his blood.

"Elias will always do what is required of him," Lygia says. "He efficiently carries out his duty like a cold machine, but unfortunately he's not. He has a heart, and if his duty requires him to drive a dagger through it, he will do so without question. I want you to think about that. And while you're at it, consider this: Elias and I have already agreed that when Kristin decides to become a vampire, it's too much of a risk for her to be turned by either of us. As much as I love my daughter, and as much as I would love to feel connected to her at all times like I feel with her father, Elias, don't you think there must be a good reason why I don't want to turn her?"

Amy sighs, feeling that speaking about Kristin would be talking about family business, in a family that she is not a part of. So she remains silent.

"And," Lygia says, "you should also give some thought as to how much Elias really cares about you if he's willing to give you blood that he wouldn't dare give to his daughter."

Lygia's dig makes Amy want to snap, but she catches the impulse before any insults leap from her tongue. Lygia's passive aggressiveness gets under Amy's skin far more than if Lygia were to outright attack her. And it burns her up, even more, to admit that she doesn't have to swallow her pride and kowtow to Lygia. If she wanted to, she could follow her natural instinct to give Lygia a long list of objects, accompanied by a short list of places where she can shove them. But then she wouldn't have what she really wants. Amy can even let Lygia think that she has won this battle by just saying that she accepts being turned by Lark or Preacher or some other vampire. But now more than ever she wants Eli's blood, just as she only wants Eli.

"I have a long day ahead of me," Lygia says, moving the mug to the table, then lifting the lid from on top of the tray. "You eat, get yourself together, and think about all that we've discussed. You have to get permission from General Limbeck if you want to go back to the conference room. If you want to go down to my lab, Gould has already been instructed to escort you whenever you're ready. Or she can give you a tour of the parts of the ship that are not restricted. Either way, there are plenty of things to keep you occupied during the day."

Amy glances at the food Lygia has brought her. There is oatmeal, blueberry pancakes, a heap of scrambled eggs, four sausages and two bananas. She picks up the mug and finds it surprisingly heavy.

"It's a smoothie," Lygia says, following Amy's gaze. "It's full of vitamins and antioxidants. And there's some protein powder added for good measure."

"Thank you," Amy says, and in her mind, she makes the plastic mug with Lygia's smoothie in it number one on the list of things that Lygia can shove up a specific orifice.

CHAPTER TWENTY-THREE

Opuses of angst, performed by Linkin Park, blast in Amy's ears as she sits cross-legged on the berth. She continues to inhale deeply and exhale as slowly as possible while doing mental combat with the eidolon of Lygia that refuses to leave her head. Nothing she has done was effective at wiping away the residue from her confrontation with Eli's magister.

Although Amy wasn't hungry after Lygia left she wolfed down the big breakfast for Eli's sake. She wants to be able to nourish him when he wants to feed again. After eating, she knew that sitting in the room all day was going to drive her insane, so she asked Gould if she could run around the deck of the massive hospital ship. The request was denied. But Gould—who was thoughtful enough to bring Amy an iPod to listen to music on—managed to secure an hour in one of the gyms for Amy's use.

Amy tried to take out her frustrations on one of the heavy bags in the gym. Her arms and legs felt like they were made of lead by the time she gave up punching and kicking the Lygia surrogate that was swinging by a chain. Though tired, her blood was still boiling so Amy used up the rest of the hour on one of the treadmills.

After the workout Amy tarried in the shower much longer than necessary, thinking about ways to alleviate the pent-up energy still in her system. One solution, in particular, is most appealing, especially considering that a wish she had made the night before had been granted and there's nothing left to hold her back.

Amy shifts her weight over to one side and plucks at the wedgie forming in the seat of the black Lycra shorts that Lark gave to her. She settles back down as the current song begins its fade to silence. Amy opens her eyes to scan through the other albums on the iPod and is surprised to find Eli in the stateroom with her. He is standing with his arms crossed, his back and one foot pressed against the door.

"Oh shit!" Amy says, popping the white buds from her ears as she stands up. "Tell me you didn't see that?"

"I just came in," Eli's says as his eyes roam over the subtle curves, nicely accented by the skin-hugging shorts and stylish sports bra Amy has on. "But I did see that."

"Hey, eyes up here, buddy," Amy jokes, although pleased with Eli's reaction.

"If you insist," Eli says, slowly moving his gaze up from Amy's cleavage. Halfway up he pauses, focused on her throat. He swiftly closes the gap between them and brushes Amy's hair aside, studying the redness on her neck, on the opposite side that he's been feeding from. "Who the fuck put their hands on you?"

"Nobody," Amy says, lowering her head. "That's nothing."

"The hell it's nothing! Tell me whose neck I'm gonna break!"

Amy shakes her head. "Stay out of it, Eli. It's chick shit. I can deal with it. If some dude did something to me, I'd let you do your thing if there was anything left of him when I was done. But this is something I gotta do on my own."

Eli ponders for a moment, and asks, "Lygia?"

Amy nods her head. "That's why I need you to back off. She's never gonna respect me if I let you fight my battles. This was nothing. We just introduced ourselves and set some boundaries. I got this. I just need you to promise me one thing, though?"

Eli sighs with a growl. "What is it?"

Staring into his eyes, Amy intensifies her gaze so that there is no question of how serious she is. "Don't ever come to me after you've slept with her. I don't take anybody's sloppy seconds, and I'm damn sure not taking that bitch's."

Shaking his head, Eli says, "Amy, I'd never do that to you."

"Good, because if you do, I swear I'll chop off your cock. You'll probably grow it back, but you'll get my point."

Eli responds with a laugh.

Amy already feels better, just from being back together with Eli. As much as he has cheered her up, she wants something more. She puts her arms around him and initiates a soulful kiss.

Eli returns her embrace and matches her intensity. His kisses are different from what she has experienced with other guys. Even when he is aggressive with passion, his kisses are filled with adoration instead of a rushed step to get into her pants. And now she desperately wants to get into his.

Amy's hands go from caressing Eli's body to raising the hem of his shirt. He breaks their embrace, only for a moment to allow her to pull the garment over his head. Then he removes her sports bra with ease. She doesn't know if Eli has already sensed that she is no longer menstruating, but she intends for him to find out.

Eli's lips speckle her shoulder and chest with tender kisses. When he moves down to her breasts, her stiff, brown nipples transmit the voltage of pleasure received from his hot mouth and fondling swipes of his tongue. He takes his time, prolonging her moans as she twirls the curls in his hair with her finger. His lips seem to reluctantly leave her sensitive nipples, only to patiently trek in search of a more sensitive place to play.

His hands squeeze and caress her backside as he alternates between kissing and nibbling his way down her belly. She feels his fingers creep under the waistband of her shorts and slowly peel them down from her hips. Then he slides the tight material down her thighs until they fall to her ankles.

His lips tease her inner thighs, sending a teasing message to his main target before his fingers gently begin to slide her panties off. Amy is ferried deeper into a new realm of pleasure with every kiss of his lips, every artful touch of his tongue, and the firm suction of his mouth attending to the most responsive parts of her anatomy.

Eli's tongue plays the key role in conducting a symphony of sensations within her. Its balmy caress hits all the right spots, slow and steady at first, then gradually increasing in intensity and quickness until Amy discovers that there is no limit to where Eli can apply his vampire speed.

Her knees buckle, but Eli's grip on her hips keep her on her feet. With the flutter of a hummingbird's wing, Eli's tongue stimulates Amy to the point where modesty no longer has a meaning. She pants hard and fast, squealing in enjoyment as a forceful orgasm rapidly gathers in the pit of her stomach. Never in her wildest dreams did she think that pleasure could be so good. It scares her. She clutches a handful of his hair and enthusiastically encourages Eli to keep doing what he is doing, not giving a damn if Gould and Maxwell hear her outside of the door. The same goes for Lygia, who may be within earshot for the ranger of a vampire.

The enhanced grace of Eli's tongue quickly pushes Amy over the edge, and an explosion of pulsing waves of pleasure makes her feel as if her slick vagina is clapping. With a firm hold of Eli's head, she presses her crotch against his face and thrashes uncontrollably. Eli continues the sweetest torture with lashes and swirls of his tongue. When her orgasm finally dies down, she expects Eli to stop. He does, only long enough to lay her on the berth. Then he goes back to work, leading her from one rapture after another.

After the third orgasm quakes her body, taking her to heights of ecstasy she has never reached before, Eli releases her from a pleasure that is becoming too much to bear. One last kiss of his lips on her pink button incites a torrent of aftershocks, then Eli grins as he rises to his feet to take his pants off.

Amy sits up on the berth as Eli frees his engorged member from its confinements. As soon as Eli is done kicking off his boots and removing his pants, she catches him by surprise when she takes him in her hand and pulls him closer.

A smile stretches across his face when she begins to stroke his erection. It's not long before she leans in and tightens her lips around him, applying the pressure of suction. Eli hisses like a punctured tire, then he rocks his head back and moans as Amy reciprocates the pleasure that he has just given her.

Amy uses his reactions to guide her performance. She dwells on the temperature of his appendage, wondering if it feels as hot as it does because of all that vampire blood rushing to the one place, or if the sensitive nerves in her mouth are just making her think that it is. Regardless of why, his heat refuels her arousal and she finds herself eager to feel his burning erection somewhere else.

When she feels Eli's hand on top of her head, she looks up to find him staring down at her. His mouth is partially gaped, and his eyes clearly convey how good she is making him feel. Knowing that she is succeeding in pleasing him boosts her confidence and she tenaciously puts her all into sucking him, hoping she will give him something he will always remember.

As her tight jaw muscles begin to burn, Amy hears Eli tell her how badly he needs to make love to her. Initially, she thinks she might be doing something wrong, but the desperation in his eyes show that he really wants to connect with her in the most intimate way. It is what she wants as well, and since her jaw feels like it might fall off if she doesn't stop now, she happily complies.

With her nerves now buzzing, she lays back on the mattress and receives him with open arms. His torrid body presses down on her, and their passionate kissing resumes. The unobstructed contact of his manhood on her pubic mound makes her canal flood. She spreads her legs, eager with anticipation. Eli glance down at Amy's carnal invitation and groans in delight. He positions himself to enter her while looking into her eyes to question one last time if she is sure that she wants him to completely cross the line. She acknowledges her desire with a nod of her head. Eli interlaces his fingers with hers. Then with his eyes locking their souls together, he gently pushes into her. Amy bites her lip and groans from the pleasure of him spreading her insides with his hot, hardness.

Eli's tender strokes generate the pleasure that she has been wanting to feel ever since the first time she felt herself get wet for him. She wraps her legs around him and completely lets go of all thought but the joy of sex with the only person that she wants to be with. Her fingers dig into his back, and her tongue resumes the familiar intimacy that it has with his mouth.

The passion and ecstasy continue within the cramped space in the berth. The verity of positions they get into are confined to the basics, but the duration of speed and aggressiveness in Eli's thrusts allow Amy to ride wave after wave of natural delight, cresting at the pinnacle of pleasure when each of her orgasms rocks her body in epic proportions. She loses all track of time. All she knows is that she has been engaged with Eli longer than she has ever had sex with anyone before him, and if it never stops she will know that she has somehow died and ended up in her heaven.

Every time Amy looks into Eli's eyes, she senses his selfless desire to please her more than he cares about his own physical gratification. Lygia's words about her being just one of many stray cats in Eli's life floats into her thoughts, but it lives a short life once her heart tells her that she is more than that to Eli, just as he is more than that to her.

When Eli's wincing face betrays that he is losing control and won't be able to hold out much longer, she persuades him to let her get back on top. She pushes herself to ride Eli harder than they've gone throughout the entire encounter. Her plan to push Eli past the point of no return does work, but her vigorous thrusts, increased speed, and grinding hips trip her own switch and hustles the swell of another orgasm. She stares into Eli's eyes, communicating an eternal bond that is as emotional as it is physical, and they bring each other to rapture expressed in grunts and groans until they end up laying in a sweaty pile—with Eli still strongly occupying space inside of her. She tries to catch her breath as she feels his simmering fluid coating her walls, and she forms a conclusion as to why Lygia is so possessive of Eli. Over a hundred years of sex that good would leave any woman whipped.

Eli begins to chuckle.

Amy raises up and stares at him. "What's so funny?"

"I came down here to make sure you're okay and see if you needed anything," Eli replies. "I had no idea I was going to end up getting something I needed really, really bad."

"So, does that mean you enjoyed the ride, cowboy?"

"Does this answer your question?" Eli makes his still erect penis throb inside of her, triggering another round of aftershocks that send Amy into convulsions.

"Oh, I'm gonna get you for that one," Amy playfully says and settles her head on Eli's chest. "Hey, how's the search going?"

Eli's words drip with disappointment when he tells Amy that his night was a colossal waste of time. Skipworth set drone after drone in search patterns over places that Eli thought Sig might choose to hide out. Nothing stood out in the unordinary world that the United States has become.

It frustrated Eli to try track Sig down from a remote location instead of being out in the elements like he preferred to be. He also realized that he was looking for the Sig that he knew, not the Sig who was on the video. They were not the same person. So he had Skipworth play the video of Sig massacring the soldiers on a loop while they expanded the search. He tried his best to convince Skipworth to turn over the controls so he could fly a drone for himself and feel closer to the place showing up on camera, but she continued to absolutely deny him.

After a long night together, Skipworth needed a break to relieve, refuel and refresh herself. Before they left the conference room, Skipworth requisitioned a satellite, at Eli's request, and commanded it to move over Waco. Then he came back to the stateroom to check on Amy.

"I really want to get my hands on that drone controller," Eli says. "If I can just get something to make me feel like I'm more out there, I might be able to trigger whatever it is that makes my gut know I'm onto somebody's trail."

"You really think it will help?" Amy asks.

"Can't hurt. Watching that video of him helped, but I'm not feeling that... spark."

"Well, get me in that conference room with you and maybe we can double team her so you can get some-" Amy mocks a hip-hop dialect as she says, "-playtime, bay-bee!"

Eli raises up, causing Amy to raise up, too. "Why did you just say that like that?"

"What?" Amy asks confused, "playtime, baby? You never see those commercials for the video games and social media platforms developed by Playtime Media? That's their catchphrase. The little rapping thumbs always say it at the end of the commercials, 'It's playtime, bay-bee!'

Eli holds Amy's face in his hands and plants a big kiss on her lips. "You are fuckin' incredible! Get dressed, we gotta go."

CHAPTER TWENTY-FOUR

Skipworth guzzles the rest of her energy drink. Without taking her eyes off of her monitor, she sends the can arcing through the air. It clanks on the rim of a metal wastepaper basket in the corner off to her right and drops with a clunk at the bottom. She celebrates her score with a slight smile and a subtle fist pump.

Amy can't figure out if Skipworth senses the tension that has the conference room feeling like an aquarium, or if she is oblivious to it because she is so excited about being in control of one of the Air Force's top of the line war machines: the Specter. It's a drone that looks like a miniaturized version of the F-35 stealth fighter, armed with a 35mm cannon and an assortment of missiles, plus it has the capability to hover.

Gould and Maxwell, posted in the back of the room by the door, appear uncomfortable. That's a noticeable difference from Maxwell's sheepish smile and Gould avoiding eyes contact while her cheeks turned red when Eli opened the stateroom door. It was obvious they heard the erotic ruckus Amy and Eli made while being intimate with each other. If something was going to be said about it, Eli didn't give them much time before he insisted that one of them contact Skipworth and tell her that he needed to see her back in the conference room immediately.

General Limbeck, standing behind Skipworth with his arms crossed over his chest, looks as if he is going to spontaneously combust if the footage from the drone flying over Pittsburgh doesn't yield anything more than a waste of time. Eli told him that it was just a hunch, and there was no guarantee, but Sig's message has sowed a seed of distrust that has already started to germinate.

Granger didn't need Sig's help. His distrust of Eli, vampires, and anybody associated with them is already as big and strong as a redwood. Granger is standing on the right of Skipworth, Eli on her right, and it feels to Amy like there are electrified lines of barbed wire crisscrossed between them.

Amy has her own metaphysical grudge match going on with Lygia, who has placed herself between Amy and Eli. In this round, however, Amy feels that she is ahead on the scorecard. She knows that Lygia can smell Eli and Amy all over each other, as well as their recent sex. Lygia earns points for maintaining her composure, but Amy knows the real reason why Lygia's jaw muscles are tight, and there is an artery the size of an earthworm bulging on her temple.

"We'll be in camera range within two minutes," Skipworth says and glances up at Eli. "I still can't believe you want to see Playtime's campus. I'm getting butterflies just imagining what it must look like now."

Eli breaks his side-eye joust with Granger and returns a smile to Skipworth. "Think you still remember your way around and what's what?"

"It's been five years since I did my summer workshop, but yeah, it was a simple layout. Got the administrations building, visitor's center, library slash D-I-Y lounge, lecture theatre, 2 gymnasiums, 4 cafes, the gamer dome, the crash pads, the powerhouse where energy collected from the photovoltaics and wind farm is stored and distributed. Then there's the crown jewel dead center of the campus: The Sapphire. That's where the massive server farm is located, as well as the A.I. computer they were working on."

Eli nods his head.

Amy is eager to see the campus. If not for Playtime Media's ambitious project to develop an artificial intelligence computer beyond the capabilities of any that already exist, right now Eli and Skipworth would probably still be flying blind. He had heard Playtime's catchphrase before, but it didn't click until Amy recited it. That brought back a memory of a day he was visiting with Sig and Kelly. While drinking beers in the living room after dinner, they caught a segment on 60 Minutes about the leap that Playtime Media made since they expanded from the gaming world into the realm of artificial intelligence. Eli joked that they were on the verge of giving birth to Skynet, referring to the Terminator movies. Sig joined in, stating that the campus itself would be the AI's first target, "And when it does, Playtime's Over."

Amy finds herself torn. On one hand, she wants Eli's hunch to be right, so he'll prove to Limbeck and Granger that he is everything and more that Lygia said he was. But the flip side is that if he is right and he finds Sig, then he will go after him. The scary thing about that is Sig wants Eli to come after him. She can't figure out why Sig would give Eli a clue to his location when there is no foreseeable gain in it for him.

"Okay, here we go." Skipworth types in a command to release the drone from autopilot, then she wraps her fingers around the joystick. "I'm going to keep the drone high enough for it not to be detected, but the camera is strong enough for us to look around like we're right above the buildings."

Amy squints as she watches the main monitor. The drone is flying over what seems to be an unattended wheat field and it's coming up on the edge of a forest. She can't see much of the ground beneath the lush canopy of the trees as the Specter zooms over the forest. She glances at a countdown clock on the corner of Skipworth's screen. In thirty seconds when the clock hits all zeros, the foliage suddenly breaks, giving way to a grassy field with a large array of solar panels reflecting the dazzling sun.

Using her left hand to mash buttons on her keyboard, Skipworth slows down the speed on the drone and manipulates the camera view so that it covers more ground.

Playtime's campus appears to be a virtual ghost town, at least on the outskirts. The grass is tall, weeds reign wherever they are fated to grow, and litter has the freedom to blow wherever the wind takes it.

"Shall I circle the perimeter first?" Skipworth asks, glancing at the reflection of General Limbeck in her monitor. "Or shall I take us in for a run through?"

"Take us in," Limbeck says.

"I agree," Granger says, and looks at Eli. "Unless there's more to that secret message that you're not sharing with us."

Eli sucks his teeth and says. "If there was anything else, you'd already know about it. Now stop buzzing in my ear, I'm looking to see if something jumps out at me."

Lygia nods in agreement. "If there was more to tell, you'd already know about it. Now, let him do one of the things he does best."

Amy's bites her lip to keep from smiling, as well as to restrain herself from taking a dig at Lygia about other things that she knows Eli does best.

Skipworth sets the camera in a slow sweep back and forth as she moves the drone forward. In moments they move past the field and cover a parking lot. The few cars remaining seemed to have been disabled after their collisions with other cars or light poles, while others sit with their doors or hoods open. Next to a T-boned Honda Accord is evidence of carnage: the bones and torn clothes left behind of an unfortunate victim.

More remnants of chaos appear as they move further into the compound. Skipworth follows the broadest of the connected concrete paths that spiderweb the campus. Some of the bikes that were once ridden daily along them now laying rusting where they fell. Chompers come into frame, wandering among the dead who died alongside their precious electronic devices and bags full of books, papers, and various personal effects. Judging from the age and appearance of the chompers and the items left behind by the dead, it would seem that Playtime Media was the site of extreme Geek on Geek violence. Victory belonging to the chomper Geeks.

"That's The Crash Pads," Skipworth says, as the camera pans across a four-story brownstone. "It's more like a college dorm on the inside. It was a great place to eat and sleep for the employees who wanted to stay on the campus for the night."

The majority of the ground floor windows are missing glass or left with pointy shards still stuck in the frame. Some of them were obviously broken from the inside out, evidenced by the shattered pieces scattered on the ground.

However, a lot more of them appear to be broken in. Most of the windows on the higher floors are still intact, though, some of them are wide open. There appears to be no sign of live humans or vampires inside, just the occasional chomper looking for anything to be found alive.

Skipworth maneuvers the drone further in. Amy is impressed by how vast Playtime Media's property actually is. Instead of a few acres containing a cluster of buildings, the campus spans a few miles from one side to the other. Besides the walkways and bike paths that spread between the grounds of each building site, there are life-size statues of video game characters speckled all over the place. And it seems that the Playtime employees weren't just relegated to the gymnasiums for the recreational needs. As the drone moves from one building to the next, Amy notices courts for basketball and volleyball, a baseball diamond, even a duck pond dotted with rowboats.

The Crash Pad, library, lecture hall and one of the gyms yield zero results. Skipworth announces that since they are close to the center of campus, The Sapphire should be the next structure they see. Sure enough, she is right.

An oval-shaped building that looks like it is constructed purely from large sheets of blue glass comes into view. They also find a high concentration of chompers milling about around it. There are more chompers that look like they were young IT professionals before they turned, but this horde is also comprised of men, women, and children spanning the age range of mortality. Speckled among them are chompers dressed in the uniforms of police, firemen, medical workers, fast food staff, and a lot of soldiers.

The inside of The Sapphire remains unseen because the one-way glass offers only a reflection from the outside. The roof, on the other hand, does yield a buzz of activity. Amy estimates at least sixty chompers standing around on top of it. She imagines that they were occupants of the building who sought refuge up there and got stuck as the virus took them over. She begins to feel sorry for them when a small light glows brightly in front of a figure lying across the top of one of the massive air conditioning units, then it slightly looses some of its luminance.

Skipworth and Eli look at each other at the same time.

"I'll zoom in on it," Skipworth says.

"Appreciate it," Eli replies.

Skipworth types commands into her console, setting the drone to hover in its current position. Then she taps the mouse pad to highlight a box around the figure on the screen. The monitor blinks and the image in the squared off area takes over the full size of the screen, showing a young man with bright red hair, smoking a cigarette.

"What the...?" Granger grumbles.

Amy glances at Eli and sees his face grim with anger.

"Do you know this man?" General Limbeck asks.

Eli remains silent.

"Yes," Lygia answers in Eli's place. "He calls himself Phoenix. He's part of that rebel group of vampires that I told you about."

Eli's eyes burn the question, "What are you doing?" to Lygia.

"As far as we can tell," Lygia continues, "Phoenix is one of the highest ranking members of these rogue vampires. We suspect that there is only one, maybe two vampires above him, but we haven't been able to identify them yet. Elias almost had him in Seattle, but the virus stared spreading and things only got chaotic from there."

Granger chuckles. "You couldn't even catch a punk kid, huh?"

Eli clenches his fist but manages to ignore Granger as he studies the figures on the roof. "Is this camera equipped with the thermal imaging that you told me about?" he asks Skipworth.

"What you need that for? You already know he's a vampire, and his heat signature is gonna look the same as a chomper."

"It's a hunch," Eli replies.

With General's Limbeck's blessing, Skipworth types another set of commands and the figures on the screen suddenly morph into glowing, figure-shaped blobs. Phoenix and most of the figures around him appear bright red, but one standing off to his right is an icy blue.

"What the fuck?" Granger says.

"Are the calibrations correct?" Limbeck asks.

Skipworth's fingers dance over the keyboard and a series of number overlays the image on the screen. "Yes, Sir. The trip point is ninety-nine degrees Fahrenheit. The blue is a confirmed human." She pulls the camera back to get a full view of the roof and discovers five other humans, each positioned at the edge of the roof like centuries on lookout duty.

Amy glances at Lygia and Eli. Both of them look as confused as she is. Humans and vampires in the midst of a swarm of chompers without the slightest sign of aggression from them is unheard of. There was only one other time anyone in the conference room has seen a docile chomper, the Butter Ball that was with Sig less than twenty-four hours ago.

"Can you do me a favor?" Eli asks. "Go back to the regular picture and give me a close up on the faces of the humans and whoever is around them?"

Skipworth doesn't even wait for permission from the General or Granger. She immediately does as Eli requests. The first human she targets is a woman with purple hair standing close to Phoenix, with an assault rifle in her hand. Eli identifies her as Karma, Phoenix's fountain. The other humans are unknown to him, as well as the vampires standing close to them.

"So what do you think, Mr. Kincade?" General Limbeck asks. "Is Sigodur Vassa is that building?"

Eli shakes his head. "I can't say that he's in there right now, but he might be, or eventually he will be. Either way, I'm sure this is the place I can nab him."

"Nah, bloodsucker," Granger growls, "Sigodur is mine."

Eli glances at Granger and shakes his head. "You know what, you're right. You take on Sig, and when he's done with you, I'll take it from there."

"Hey, I took your boy down once. Believe me, I'ma to do it again. And if you get in my way, I got something for you, too."

General Limbeck clears his throat to put a wedge between Eli and Granger's sparing. Then he instructs Skipworth to maintain surveillance on The Sapphire with the drone. She is to also move the nearest DOD

satellite into a geosynchronous orbit over the Playtime Media campus and keep watch for anyone entering or leaving, especially

Sig. In the mean time, General Limbeck was going to video conference with the Joint Chiefs of Staff and the President. By the time the repairs are completed on the MACEs Eli damaged, they should be decided on the best strategy for the operation..

Amy can tell from the grim look on Eli's face that he is ready to go to Playtime's campus now but is aggravated because he is stuck on the hospital ship until General Limbeck gets him a ride back to land. Lygia, on the other hand, is much to calm and collected. Lygia's openness with General Limbeck causes Amy concern, and she can imagine how Eli must be busting his brain trying to figure out why she is spilling secrets that have been kept for so long.

"Hey," Skipworth says to Eli, after the General and Granger exit the room, "that other satellite's in place if you still want to take a look."

"Absolutely," Eli responds.

The words were barely out of Eli's mouth before Skipworth was typing in commands. The screen above the one showing the drone footage blinks and a wide angle view, looking like picture shot from the edge of the atmosphere comes on. It's too far up to make out any details, other than irregular blocks of land in various earth tone shades of green, brown, even yellow assembled like a rushed patchwork quilt..

"Okay," Skipworth says, "I'm dropping in on the coordinates of that compound the ATF raided you told me about."

The camera view rapidly zooms in on the top right corner of the screen. The close up happens so fast, Amy wonders for a moment if the satellite suddenly fell out of orbit.

Details begin to evolve in the vast expanse of landscape. The irregular grids come into focus and reveal streets making up the blocks of cities and towns. Neater squares and circles identify farmland. The topographical texture of hills and valleys add more dimension. A small rectangular shape in a clearing behind some hills gets larger as the focus of the camera centers on it. Shrubs and bushes speckling the dusty landscape surrounding the compound can be made out almost as clearly as the structures within its rectangular walls.

The camera stops zooming in. If she didn't already know that the image was being transmitted from a satellite, Amy would swear that Skipworth had one of her drones hovering about a hundred feet above the center of Preacher's compound. The resolution of the image is so detailed, Amy can count the rows in Lark's braided hair. It's a surprise to see Lark wearing jeans and a baggy shirt instead of the outfits that has earned her the name Hot Pants.

"Son of a bitch!" Eli growls.

Amy knows exactly what made Eli's rage spike. The compound is not the peaceful community with everybody going about their day like it was when they were there. It's barely eight o'clock in the morning and Calavious has everyone gathered in the center of the compound. He is flanked by his guards, Nicholi and, Aleksi. Kneeling on the ground in front of him are Preacher and Kwesi, obviously against their will. There is something wrapped around their torsos and wrists. it takes Amy a moment to realize that it's not rope, it's rebar bent into service as restraints.

Most of the compound's residents are gathered in a crowd, standing behind Preacher and Kwesi. Amy recognizes most of their faces. There are other faces, though, that she doesn't recall but feels like she should. She finds it odd that those unfamiliar ones are the only men brandishing long guns, while the people she knows are unarmed. She focuses on one of those faces, a bearded man with a pot belly, wearing a bandana over his head. The very second his identity clicks, Amy gasps.

"Those are the militiamen Preacher was holding prisoner," Amy says, turning to Eli. "I remember that guy from when Lark showed me the detention building. He made a nasty comment to me."

"You did tell Antonio and Kwesi not to do anything until you returned or sent word, right?" Lygia asks.

"They understood I wanted them to stand down," Eli responds.

"Any idea what's going on, then?"

Eli shakes his head. "No, but I have a bad feeling." He puts his hand on Skipworth's shoulder and says, "Got thermal imaging on this one, too, right?"

Skipworth nods her head and switches over to the function that Eli requested. As Calavious appears to give a haughty speech, his form turns ruby red, along with every vampire within camera view, including the armed militiamen.

Eli turns to Lygia and says, "You need to get me back to shore so I can take care of this before we go after Sig."

Lygia bites her lip, then responds, "I'll talk to the General, but it might take a day to get clearance. It's a fuel conservation issue. We have to understand that."

Eli tightens his fists. "Look, just get me my blades from Fuck Face Granger. I'll swim back if I have to."

"Try to be patient, Elias. Even if I could get you on a chopper right now, you still won't make it back in time to stop this."

"If I get permission, I could get a drone there within twenty minutes,"

Skipworth says, switching back to the high definition camera view. "But in a tight group like that, I won't be able to guarantee no collateral damage."

"Hell no!" Amy says. "That'll put too many of our people at risk. Even if you just target with machine guns, the panic will have everybody running in every direction, including the line of fire."

Lygia initially looks upon Amy with scorn, but her glare quickly softens. "She's right."

Amy is taken aback, left wondering if she just hallucinated what Lygia just said. But her shock doesn't have a chance to linger. Her full attention is drawn back to the screen when Kwesi suddenly springs forward, lurching at Calavius.

The militiamen aim their guns, unnecessarily. In a blink, Aleksi is in front of Calavius with his double swords drawn and set to defend. Nicholi, on the other hand, had flung the chain that is attached to the handle of his sickle weapon and managed to get it wrapped around Kwesi's neck. Kwesi's neck. Amy sees Lark start to make a move, but Stretch wraps her in a bear hug and keeps her in place.

Kwesi writhes on the ground, choking from the torque Nicholi pulls the chain with as he stands with one foot on his chest.

Preacher appears to be pleading a case to quell any more violence.

Calavius moves Aleksi aside and approaches Preacher. He grabs a handful of Preacher's hair, then drops a bombing punch down on the side of Preacher's face. Calavius spouts a few more words, then he unleashes a barrage of punches to Preacher's face and head.

When he is satisfi ed that Preacher has had enough, Calavius releases Preacher's hair. Preacher falls over, landing on his side then rolling face down. Leaving Preacher bleeding on the dusty ground, Calavius turns his attention to Kwesi. He issues a set of orders, prompting Aleksi to take action.

While Nicholi continues to strangle Kwesi with the chain, Aleksi mercilessly rains down a barrage of kicks and stomps on his head and body. Kwesi does his best to defend himself, but the few that he does manage to block doesn't measure up to the many more that land. Eventually, Kwesi appears drained as he lays virtually lifeless on the ground taking blows.

Calavius spouts more orders. Aleksi squats down and grabs Kwesi's right leg, bending it at the knee and propping it up and a forty-five-degree angle. Calavius then steps up, raises his foot high, and brings it down hard on Kwesi's shin. No sound is necessary to know that Kwesi's tibia and fibula both received devastating fractures.

One leg is not enough to satisfy Calavius. With Aleksi's assistance, he proceeds to break Kwesi's other leg and then both of his arms as well.

The rage of the crowd witnessing Calavius' brutality shows in their tense postures, but they remain compliant. Most likely fulfilling a previous request from Preacher.

Calavius barks more orders and two of the militiamen vampires move in on

Kwesi. Each grab him by one of his feet and begin to drag him towards the back of the compound. Amy starts to wonder where they might possibly be taking him and she mentally runs through the buildings in that area of the compound until a horrifying thought pops into her head.

"The well," Amy whispers and turns to Eli.

Eli lowers his head and nods it.

"Is that where the infected militiaman is being kept?" Lygia asks.

"Yeah," Amy responds. "With his arms and legs broken and hands bound like that, Kwesi won't be able to climb out of there. He's not even going to be able to defend himself."

"Don't count him out just yet," Eli says in a dreary monotone. "The chomper has never fed, so it's weak. And it still has those little arms. As long as Kwesi is conscious when he hits the bottom of that well, he should be able to hold his own, even in the bad shape he's in."

Amy doesn't know if Eli truly believes what he just said or if his intent was to instill hope, but she clings to it rather than reside in the sorrow of Kwesi being the weird chomper's first meal. She grits her teeth and focuses on the image of Calavius, and says, "I'm gonna kill that guy."

"No," Eli growls. "I am."

Lygia takes Eli's hand and squeezes it. "I'll meet with the General as soon as he is available," she says. "And I want you to meet me in my quarters in an hour. Come alone."

Lygia's request to see Eli alone gets under Amy's skin, but she doesn't react. The fact that, for the first time, Eli didn't insist that Amy come along with him does sting, but she doesn't let that get to her. Instead, she watches Becca and Jodie lead the way as Stretch and Bear drag Lark towards the back of the crowd as discretely as possible. Amy is thankful that there are vampires there who has Lark's back and know to get her away from the epicenter of Calavius' tyranny before she encounters his wrath as well.

Lark is safe for the moment, but she fears Preacher's fate as she watches two militiamen on the roof of his cottage rig a length of rope to an overhanging beam. There can only be one purpose for it, and she dreads the high probability that she is right.

CHAPTER TWENTY-FIVE

Amy's body is stuck in the stateroom, but her mind is wandering all over Preacher's compound. Being left alone by Eli, and the fact that he's been with Lygia for over an hour has taken a back seat to the concern she has for her new friends. It doesn't matter to her that she had only met the vampires and humans at the compound only the day before. They made her feel like family, and she regards them as such.

She worries about Lark but finds some solace in knowing that Stretch and the rest of Lark's boys have her back. Kwesi and Preacher, however, are left to endure hellish ordeals all on their own. Eli said that Kwesi might have found a way to keep the chomper at bay and give his limbs time to heal. It encouraged her some when Eli reminded her that the chomper hadn't fed on anything since the other militiamen threw him down the well, and its arms are dwarfed. Even hobbled, Kwesi has the upper hand.

As for Preacher, he has essentially been turned into a cat toy for Calavius to paw at whenever he feels like it. At Calavius' request, the new militiamen vampires put a noose around Preacher's neck and slowly hauled him up from the ground. With her emotions already running wild, Amy couldn't stop tears, hot with anger and sorrow, from streaming down her cheek. She watched Preacher wriggling wildly as he hung from the rope, unable to die from asphyxiation. The agony that Preacher appeared to be going through made Amy wish he was still mortal so he could be put out of his misery.

While Preacher was writhing at the end of the rope, Amy heard Eli whisper, "C'mon, Antonio. Focus. Take control. Use that frickin' faith of yours if you have to." When Preacher appeared to stop resisting, she had to wonder if Eli's words have traveled on the wind to his ear. Preacher slowly took control of his body and ended up swinging in a Zen-like state. There was no way of hearing what Calavius told everyone at the compound, but Amy could imagine the stern warning of what would happen if anyone tried to cut Preacher down.

The handle on the stateroom door slowly turns, drawing Amy's attention.

The door opens and Eli enters the room. The stoic expression on his face offers no clue as to what the private meeting with Lygia was about, but she expects that he remembers the warning she gave him the day before about coming to her after having sex with Lygia.

Eli closes the door behind him and walks to the middle of the room where Amy is sitting crossed leg on the floor. He helps her up and takes her into his arms.

"You okay?" Amy asks, returning his embrace.

"Yeah," Eli says. "Things just moving kinda fast and I don't know how the next couple days are gonna turn out."

"What do you mean?"

"My gut is telling me that Sig is there at Playtime. I expect to find him at The Sapphire when I go in with Limbeck's toy soldiers. Granger thinks he and his team can take Sig, but he has no idea what they're really going up against. Most of them..., hell, probably all of 'em, won't be coming back from this mission. Good chance none of us will."

Amy pulls back and stares into his eyes with concern. "What are you talking about?"

"The Sig we saw on that video footage, he's much faster and stronger than the Sig I know. I don't know how, but I'm sure he's our senex-fueled rogue. And I don't know what else is going on with him. Can't assume that the weird shit with chompers acting so docile around him is the only surprise we got coming."

Amy holds Eli's face in her hands. "That doesn't matter! You can take Sig, Eli. I believe in you. And I'm coming with you!"

Eli smiles, and says, "I expected you to say that. But I can't ask you to follow me to your death, Amy. You all but got your clemency. You're free now. You can stay here with the fleet or go back to shore and do whatever you want. You don't have to follow me."

"I told you, I'm in this with you, Eli. And that means all the way to the end."

"I don't suppose I can talk you out of that?"

"Damn right you can't! And you better not try to leave me, either. I'll never forgive you if you do that to me."

"I know you wouldn't." Eli resumes his serious demeanor. "Before I go after Sig, I'm going back to the compound. Limbeck promised to fly me back to my truck tomorrow morning."

"Good!" Amy growls. "The sooner we get back, the better."

Eli pauses for a moment, his blue eyes penetrating her more deeply than ever before. "You know, Lygia has a right to be concerned about me turning you, right?" he says. "It's more dangerous than you think and you'll be much safer if you let Preacher or Hot Pants turn you."

Amy scowls, and says, "I only want you to turn me, nobody else but you."

"If that's what you really want, Lygia just gave me permission to turn you. We can do it whenever you're ready."

Eli's words stun her like a concussion grenade. She processes what he said over and over until she is sure she heard him right. Then she explodes with excitement and hugs Eli with all her might. "I want to do it now!"

Laughing, Eli says. "I knew you were going to say that, too."

"What a minute. Lygia just told me this morning that she wasn't going to give permission for you to turn me. Why did she suddenly change her mind?

Eli sighs, and says, "Because I promised to give her something she wants. If we make it out of the shit storm coming over the next few days, I'm going to be her Proconsul, along with Titus. And, to be honest with you, she wants to see if you really can handle my blood. If it kills you, or it makes me have to kill you, she loses nothing. If you handle it as well I told her I expect you to, it will help her determine if she can follow her heart and turn Kristin, herself, one day."

Amy shakes her head. "You'll be giving up your freedom for me. You need to be out, running free. Not cooped up in some vampire headquarters with Lygia, dealing with politics. I can't let you do that. I'd never feel right about it."

"I have no intention of being couped up anywhere. Lygia understands that I'm by her side, but I'm not taking an office job. Now, the only thing I need is for you to be the confident ass-kicker that I know you are. Anything less than that, and you're not going to survive this."

Amy nods her head, fully accepting the challenge, regardless of the consequences.

"When we do this," Eli says, "you're going to have to listen to everything I tell you, and fight hard to do what I say."

Amy enthusiastically agrees to listen to Eli and do all that he tells her. She knows full well that there is a chance she will end up dying because of her decision, but nothing is going to change her mind. And if she survives becoming a vampire, as well as keep herself from being killed if she goes rogue, she knows that her infinite life expectancy might be cut short if she goes into battle against Sig with Eli. But her mind is made up, and nothing is going to change it, leaving only one thing left to deal with before she accepts Eli's gift.

Eli leans in and kisses Amy. She returns his kiss and wraps her legs around him. She feels herself being carried over to the berth as she falls deeper into their passion. Feeling like she is in a dream, she and Eli continue to kiss and caress, stripping each other's clothing off before he lays her on the mattress.

Amy relishes the heat and weight of Eli's body on hers, and as she spreads her legs to accommodate him, it sinks into her that this could be something more than her last time having sex as a human. It could possibly be the last time before she dies. It doesn't matter. She is happy to know that her last time, as a human or forever, is with somebody that she has genuine feelings for. She wishes he could've been her first, but she's good with knowing that he could be her last.

The ascending bliss makes Amy feel like closing her eyes and enjoying the ride, but she keeps her gaze entangled with Eli's. She moans unrestrictedly when he pushes into her, slowly filling her with his fiery manhood. He makes love to her tenderly, only breaking eye contact to kiss her neck and breasts, and to suck her nipples. The only things that rivals the intense pleasure he pumps into her body is the intense warmth gushing in her heart.

Amy compares the first time that they were together. It was like delicious Cherry Coke escaping a bottle that was all shook up. It was perfect for the moment. This time, being with him is like hot, melted chocolate slowly pouring into her open mouth, even when the intensity of their passion increases. She takes in every touch, every emotion, every ounce of pleasure from one orgasm to the next. The pinnacle of her experience is when she recognizes that Eli is on the verge of climax and she gives him her all until she feels his hot streams ejaculated into her.

After Eli's orgasm, he remains on top of Amy, as well as inside of her. She is glad that he does so, not wanting to separate from him, now or ever.

"Amy," Eli whispers softly into her ear.

"Yeah," Amy whispers back.

"You know how I feel about you, don't you?"

"Mmmhm. You know I feel the same way, right?"

"I was hoping so." Eli engages her in another passionate kiss, and says, "No matter how things turn out when you wake up, don't ever doubt my feelings for you, okay?"

"Okay. But what do you mean, when I wake up?"

"Even if my blood doesn't kill you, you're still going to pass out after you drink it. I wanted to make sure you knew how I felt before I turned you. Now you know, and the only question left is..., are you ready?"

Amy stares into Eli's eyes. As nice as it would be to cuddle with him a while longer, then maybe make love at least one more time, she is ready to take the next step. "Yeah. I'm ready."

"Alright." Eli plants his arms beside Amy's shoulders and raises his upper body. "I'm going to give you enough of my blood for you to turn as soon as possible. It's a harsh taste so you might have to force yourself to swallow it."

"That's not going to be a problem."

Eli smiles and nods his head. "For you, I'm sure it's not. Okay, let's do this!"

Amy pays attention to his mouth as his lips form a tight seal. He winces as his jaw moves like he has bit down on something. Her eyes remain locked with his as he lowers his face down to hers. When their lips come together, Amy parts hers to allow in his tongue, and she receives a gush of liquid that wants to scorch her mouth but isn't quite hot enough.

The blood coming out of the puncture that Eli's fangs put in his own tongue has that familiar coppery flavor, but it is mingled with a harsh bitterness that she could never have imagined.

Eli slowly grinds her, the erection that never went away providing more pleasure as she forces herself to get past the horrid taste and suck more of his blood. After a few large quaffs, Eli begins to clot, and he resumes kissing her as his tongue heals. Now that she has been given the gift that will make her a vampire, she devotes herself to every one of his tender strokes.

The passion in Eli's lovemaking evolves quickly, his emotion embedded in his actions, leaving Amy with the comforting thought that if she dies from his blood, she would know that her killer did truly love her. She embraces her feelings for him as she tries her hardest to hold off the orgasm that he is inducing, but it is only a matter of time before her fingers are raking across his back as the most violent form of satisfaction is delivered. When her orgasm subsides, Eli slows his pace until he completely stops. She wants to question why he doesn't continue, but his mouth and his tongue keep hers too engaged to speak.

With her mind and body completely under his control, she basks in the incessant bliss of the afterglow—until a warm sensation takes seed in her stomach. In a matter of seconds, the warmth becomes a burning as if she swallowed a smoldering lump of coal. Her eyes open wide and she groans, worried that something has gone wrong.

Eli stops kissing and stares into her eyes. "That's just the beginning. I'm sorry to tell ya, it's gonna to get worse."

Amy clutches the sides of her belly. Even with the fear that the pain she already feels will get worse, she groans, "Don't worry, I can take it."

Eli crawls off of her and kneels on the floor next to the berth. "It's going to get to the point where you feel like your whole body is on fire, and that's when you're going to pass out. Don't worry. We all pass out. And the sooner it happens, the better. If you start screaming, I'll cover your mouth, but don't think I'm trying to hurt you. I'm here for you, and I'll be here when you wake up. Okay?"

Amy nods her head as the burning starts to feel like there is an acid coated steel brush scouring her guts.

Eli gently strokes Amy's cheek, and says, "When you wake up you're going to hear a lot of loud noises in your head. Listen for my voice and focus on it. Can you do that for me?"

Amy nods her head, and grunts, "I will."

Eli smiles, and says, "Do you remember when you told me you didn't know why you bothered, but you keep fighting every day, and you survive?"

Amy nods again.

"You keep fighting and surviving because of you have an indomitable spirit. It's one of the first things that I saw in you, and it's one of the reasons why I like you as much as I do. So don't you dare think about dying on me, Amy!

You got what it takes to survive the transformation, and you're going to have to tap into the indomitable spirit to control what you're going to experience when you wake up. I believe in you, and I know that you can do it."

"I won't die," Amy says, now curling into a fetal position. "I'll hold on, for myself and for you. I promise."

"I know you will," Eli says and kisses her on the forehead.

Amy closes her eyes and the pain that she thought couldn't get any worse actually does. She finds it ironic that minutes ago she was experiencing the greatest pleasure known to a human being, now she finds herself at the extreme opposite side of the spectrum. But she accepts what she has to go through because all good things come with a price, and right now she is paying for something that will be priceless.

Slowly and steadily the burning agony begins to radiate outward, and not long after that, it begins to feel like magma has seeped into her entire circulatory system. Her natural instinct forces her to tense every muscle that she feels in control of. The pain in her stomach is still intense, but her heart is now giving it competition. As anguishing as the burning in those two organs feels, Amy wills herself to not scream. But she doesn't fare so well when her brain undergoes the same torturous effect. She holds out for as long as she can, but when she can't take it anymore, she opens her mouth. Eli's hand covers her lips to trap the shrill that was going to blast from her core. She ends up biting into the palm of his hand as she screams for her life.

Through tearful eyes, she sees the concern on Eli's face as he reassures her that she is going to be okay. She wants to keep up the good fight and make it through the process, but a part of her wonders if she has made a big mistake. The hell she is going through has her thinking it might be better if she just died right now. It's only a matter of moments before her whole body feels like she has been submerged in boiling oil, and when she begins to feel lightheaded from her body going into shock, she doesn't try to fight it.

She gazes at Eli, hoping that this isn't the last time that she sees his face, at least in this lifetime. Soon everything turns black, and she is in merciful unconscious.

CHAPTER TWENTY-SIX

Amy is jolted awake by a disturbing deluge of erratic noise randomly alternating in volume.

The light in the room is much brighter than it was before and it seems to be blinking at least a thousand times per second. Confused and disoriented, she closes her eyes to lessen the assault on her senses.

The sound of her own respiration blares in her ears then yields to the chatter of multiple conversations. The rumble of a machine reverberating through metal takes over. A door slams shut, followed by a sharp metronomic tick like the second hand moving on a wrist watch. There are many more sounds that are harder to distinguish among the undying din, including multiple rhythmic thumps, one of which so prominent, she could swear that her heart has been transplanted into her brain.

Panic hastens hysteria. Amy throws her hands up to cover her ears. Eli appears over her, catching her wrists and pinning her arms against her chest. She scowls, ready to curse him out.

Eli's lips move, but his words are indistinguishable among the chaos. The concern in his eyes helps to free up one coherent thought in Amy's head, and she recollects what happened before she passed out.

The noise is only the tip of the assault on her senses. Her core feels like a furnace, and her skin is as hot as it would be if she had spent hours laying in the sun. The feverish burning is uncomfortable, but nothing compared to the three separate, but equally powerful sensations which overwhelm everything else that she feels within her body.

One of those powerful sensations is the unbearable pang of hunger. It is so intense, she feels as if her empty stomach has started to digest itself. To satisfy the craving she would be willing to gorge on a platter of vermin if one was placed in front of her, and she would keep stuffing her mouth even after it was overflowing from her gullet.

The second sensation Amy feels is the presence of power, a force unlike any other. It is so palpable, it can only be described as a living entity within her that is energizing every inch of her body. She remembers Lark telling her that being a vampire made her feel alive, and like something is alive inside of her. Amy fully understands that now, and she can also see why Lark believes in the Sons of God theory. This sensation of power makes her feel like a supreme being ready to burst out of her mortal shell and conquer the whole world.

The last dominant sensation is that of an incredible pull. She feels it throughout her entire being, from the surface of her skin deep down to the marrow in her bones. The most intense of it is like the gravity of a black hole concentrated in the place where she feels butterflies in her belly when her emotions are running wild. The pull is interfused with the ominous sixth sense kind of perception that alerts her when she is being watched. Instinct tells her that the pull is tethered to a specific source and it explicitly makes her think of Eli. It is the link to him that she will feel for as long as they both live, his signature on her soul.

The noise and the inner-sensations aren't all that Amy experiences. There is also a torrent of scents and odors that seem to hit her as randomly as the sounds that she is hearing. She smells salt, paint, detergent, disinfectants, deodorant, plastic, and other chemicals. There is also a familiar oaky scent mixed with sweat and now infused with something that effects her like a strong aphrodisiac. The alluring scent makes her wet. The arousal, coupled with the connection she feels with Eli causes her to focus on him.

When Eli moves his mouth again, she makes out his voice among the racket.

"Eli?!" she says and winces from the bombing of her own voice in her head.

"Focus, Amy," Eli says. "You can control how loud or how low everything you hear is. You just have to rewire your brain to process everything like a vampire. Now, imagine there's an equalizer in your head, and you can turn up or turn down any sound you choose. Try it. Tune down everything but me."

Amy imagines that there is a lever assigned to each individual sound rattling in her head and she tries to tune them down one at a time, starting with the bass drum beat of her heart. After failing to accomplish any changes, she begins to worry that the non-stop clamor will soon fracture her sanity.

Afraid of what will happen if she doesn't succeed, she puts all of her mental energy into isolating Eli's voice, and she tries to make everything else fade away. It doesn't happen as automatically as she would like but with Eli's constant encouragement, the more she forces her will on something that she shouldn't be able to control, the easier it gets to disregard what she doesn't want to hear and tune it down to background noise.

Eli's voice becomes clearer as she gains enough control of her hearing to make the noise in her head more tolerable. But her mind isn't set free. The hunger and the awareness of power within her becomes savage without the noise to rage against it. The desire to satisfy her hunger steers her eyes to Eli's neck. She feels the urge to lurch and sink her teeth into him, regardless of not having fangs to punch neat little holes into his artery. That thought makes her fear she is heading straight for the worse case scenario. If she can't control her impulses, she might go rogue right here in front of a regulare who does not neglect his duties. And if for some reason he can't bring himself to do it, Lygia will be more than happy to step in and finish her off.

Thinking about going rogue—and dying soon after—causes Amy to lose control of the sounds in her head again. But instead of trying to regain it, she imagines a small box in the center of her body and pictures herself forcing the unruly energy into it.

"Did you hear me?" Eli asks.

"No," Amy responds, now trying to multitask forcing the energy in the box and willing all the sounds but his voice to become background noise.

"I asked how you're making out with the noise," Eli says as he helps her sit up.

"The volume is still going up and down," Amy responds, discovering that Eli has redressed her in her tank top and panties, "but I think I almost got the hang of it."

"Don't worry, it's like learning how to ride a bike. Once you get the hang of it, it becomes automatic."

"Why's the fucking light blinking like that? It's annoying the hell out of me."

"Florescent lights always blink that way. Your brain wasn't able to process it before, but now it can. And much more. Now, I need you to tell me how you're feeling?"

Amy takes a moment to think of the best answer. "Famished."

"I know. Kristin will be here in a little while to feed you." Eli unscrews a bottle of water and hands it to Amy.

The plastic bottle crinkles and collapses under Amy's grip, sending a spout of water to splash on Eli's face. His response is to chuckle as he shakes his head.

"Sorry about that," Amy says, with a giggle. She guzzles the remaining liquid from the bottle, noting that it's no longer tasteless now that she can detect the minerals, a hint of chlorine and whatever else was used to treat the water.

"Don't worry about it. You're gonna have to get used to your new strength, too. Now, I need you to honestly tell me how else you feel."

"I feel...," knowing that the answer could possibly kill her, Amy says, "like God."

"That's about right. Remember, you control that power you feel inside of you. It doesn't control you. Right now you probably want to tear into me and then take on the world, but entertaining that lust is like straying over to the dark side. So don't do it!"

"I got it. I'm trying to focus on the feeling of power, and I'm trying to put it in an imaginary box."

"Good girl. I wish there were more time to get you better prepared. But we have to settle on a crash course and learning on the fly, just like I had to learn. Lesson one: you are a vampire now, and you must always protect your head and your heart. If your heart gets damaged, you will be slower and weaker until it repairs itself. But your brain is the most important thing. Protect it at all times. If you're decapitated, or you catch a bullet that does serious damage to your brain tissue, you will die." Eli quickly sets the bottle cap on top of his thumb and uses his middle finger to flick it at Amy.

With the speed of a bullet, the bottle cap pings Amy on the forehead and ricochets away. "What the fuck, man!" she says, and punches him on the arm.

Eli smiles, and says, "Your powers are almost as strong as mine, so I know you felt that coming before it hit you. Your skin can pick up vibrations in the air around you, and if something feels dangerous, you'll know it. Pay attention to that feeling and react to it, especially when your head is in danger."

Amy realizes that Eli is right. Before the cap hit her, she felt something on the exact spot where it impacted on her forehead. The sensation was like a soft poke from a finger that sent ripples over the surrounding area like a rock disturbing the calm waters of a pond.

"You should also know that high voltage is dangerous. It won't kill you, but it can incapacitate or knock you out. That's why Granger and his boys were trying to get me with those nets."

"Got it."

"Now, wanna see something really cool?"

"Hell yeah."

Eli ever so gently strokes Amy's arm with his fingers, causing the butterflies in her stomach to feel like sharks in a feeding frenzy. "Close your eyes and concentrate on the surface of your skin."

Amy does as she is told. When Eli stops stroking her, she focuses on the sensation of his touch lingering on her skin. She begins to wonder what it is that he wants her to see, then she hears him snap his finger. In a flash, the image of the room around her pops in and out of her mind, like a vi vid memory of where everything is, except the image was completely without color.

"Whao!" Amy exclaims.

"It's like a form of echolocation," Eli says and snaps his finger again for her to catch another flash of the image. "You can utilize it anytime you concentrate on it, and it'll get easier to do it over time.

A sudden knock on the door sounds like thunder, spurring Amy slaps her hands over her ears. The door swings open and her nose picks up a new batch of scents: perfumes, soaps, more chemicals, sweat, musky odors—male and mostly female. The range of her hearing is also extended with the door open, enough for her to clearly pick up on the details of conversations going on throughout the corridors and inside the rooms.

"I hope you aren't in here neglecting your duties, Elias," Lygia says, entering the room with Kristin following behind her.

Amy finds herself thankful that Eli put some of her clothes back on, especially with Maxwell peeking from his post in front of the door with Gould.

"She's making good progress, considering what she's going through," Eli says. "She's won't go rogue on us."

"We'll see. She's obviously struggling with the craving. Whether you want to admit it or not, she still has a long way to go and plenty of time to lose control."

"Nah, she'll die fighting before she lets it take her over. Trust me, she'll be right as rain by morning. Just wait and see."

Lygia examines Amy's eyes with skepticism. Next, she presses the back of her hand to Amy's forehead and then her neck, gauging her temperature. Then she turns her head to the side and appears to focus her hearing on the sound of Amy's thundering heart.

Amy accesses Lygia's scent, and she finds it appealing. She also finds it annoying that there is something in Lygia that she also smells in Eli, meaning that they share more than she even imagined before. As far as she knows it could simply a be sign of their shared bloodline, but it still annoys her because it's a reminder of the bond he has with his magister.

"Humph!" Lygia says, turning towards Eli. "I'll be impressed if she lasts more than an hour."

Amy feels her anger shoot straight past the boiling point, quicker than ever before. The vampiric force inside of her flairs like a demon drawing power from her rage. As badly as she wants to initiate round two with Lygia, the faint voice of reason inside of her head needles through the brewing malevolence and reminds her that she needs to remain in control or she will prove Lygia right. Instead of letting the rage sink its claws in any deeper, she uses Lygia's words as inspiration to try harder to stay in control—just to prove her wrong.

Amy looks directly into Lygia's eyes and shoots a complacent smile, then she continues to practice restraint. The potency of the attraction in her link to Eli makes Amy wonder how he must feel now that he is tethered to both her and Lygia. If he feels the pull as strongly as she does with him, then Eli must feel like the taut rope in a vicious tug of war. With that in mind, she can't begin to fathom how Preacher must feel with his brood back at the compound.

"Thank you for this," Amy says. "I couldn't believe it when Eli told me that he has your permission to turn me."

"No need to thank me," Lygia says, removing what looks like a thick pen from a pocket of her lab coat. "I meant what I said to you earlier. And I didn't do this for you. I did it for him..., and for her."

Amy glances at Eli, then and Kristin. Keeping in mind that Lygia sees her as a guinea pig in her consideration of making Kristin her daughter forever,

Amy holds back the words, "And for yourself," from escaping her lips.

Without warning, Lygia presses the tip of the device in her hand against Amy's upper arm and depresses the plunger on top of it. Amy feels a slight shock, then the pinch of a needle piercing her and ejaculating a warm liquid into her muscle.

"-The fuuuck!" Amy exclaims, realizing that what she thought was a pen is actually an auto-injector.

"It's fine," Eli says in a stern voice as he places his hand on Amy's shoulder to calm her. "That's to help you."

Amy picks up on his virtual warning for her not to protest. Trusting him with her life, she doesn't, even though the injection site feels as if Lygia has just put out a cigarette on her skin.

"Alright," Kristin says, retrieving a black leather case from the pocket of her lab coat, "we should really hurry up and give her first feeding."

"Fine, go ahead," Lygia says, turning around. "And Elias, remember if your little pet loses control let me know if you don't have the heart to put her down. I'm here for you. I'm always here for you."

Kristin removes packets of alcohol swabs from another of her pockets and a long strip of rubber.

"I appreciate you doing this," Eli says.

"I don't mind," Kristin responds. "She needs blood, and I can spare three pints to help her get a grip on the hunger. We should do this at the table, though. I think it will be easier for her if we're both sitting down."

"Right," Eli says, and extends his hand to help Amy up.

Amy nods her head and gets up from the berth to take a seat at the table as Kristin sits on one of the stools.

Eli opens the case and begins to assemble the pieces inside. "All right, Amy, the reservoir on this siphon holds a quarter pint of blood. Wait until it is full before you draw it through the tube. There are safety valves built into the siphon to keep you from sucking blood directly from Kristin or blowing an air bubble into her vein, but you still have to be careful. There's always a chance that the blowback valve might malfunction and we don't want an accident."

"Ahh..., okay," Amy responds.

"It'll be fine," Kristin says to Amy. "Just listen to my dad and do exactly what he tells you."

"I will," Amy says. "And thank you."

Kristin smiles, then she looks at Eli. "You know, she does look like she's struggling to maintain control."

Amy loses control of her hearing again, but this time she recovers quickly. Lygia saying that she looks like she is struggling is one thing, but hearing Kristin say it, too, is a revelation as to how obvious it must be to everyone.

The battle to control the hunger and power is becoming harder. Kristin's heart beating in her chest might as well be a dinner bell ringing in Amy's ear.

Amy can also smell every appetizing scent that the redhead is emitting, making her taste buds explode from the imaginary flavor of Kristin's salty skin and warm blood. Amy pushes herself harder to keep it together and hopes that the craving becomes easier to stomach after her first nourishment of blood.

Eli smiles at Amy and says, "It's natural for her to have a hard time right now. She's contending with blood that's way stronger than what was in any of the other vampires you've seen turn before. Having been there, myself, I'd say she's doing a helluva job."

Kristin smiles at Amy. "There must be something very special about you for him to have so much faith in someone he hardly knows."

Amy looks at Eli and can't hold back an adoring smile for her knight in shining armor. She discovers that her emotions cause most of her senses to focus on him. She hears his heartbeat quicken as he gazes into her eyes. All other smells fade as his testosterone-charged scent dominate her olfactory. The magnetic pull of her soul rises above the hunger and the sense of omnipotence. She remains focused on him and uses that as a crutch to help keep everything else in check.

"I just ask that you don't take my mom's hostility personal," Kristin continues. These two have been close for a long time, and you can understand that they share something special, too."

"I'm not trying to get in between what they have," Amy responds. "I respect your mother, and I'm just trying to fit in where I am now."

"I get that. I just want you to know that mom isn't the bitch she appears to be sometimes. And while we're at it, I like you, and you're cool with me as long as you're cool with them."

"So we're all cool," Eli says, tightening a tourniquet around Kristin's arm.

Amy stares at Kristin, trying to appreciate her not taking a negative stance against her, considering Amy's position in the love triangle with her mom and dad. When Eli swabs the area of Kristin's skin where he has chosen a vein to tap into, Amy can't resist fixating on the juicy network of blood vessels.

Handing Amy the open-ended hose of the siphon, Eli reminds her again to wait until the reservoir is full then gently suck until he tells her to stop.

Amy nods and watches with rampant anticipation as Eli pierces Kristin's skin with the tip of the needle and tap into the targeted vein. A gush of dark blood rushes into the body of the syringe. Amy has to swallow the saliva inundating her mouth before it drools from the corners of her lips. Eli pumps Kristin's blood into the reservoir and Amy ends up averting her eyes before the sight of what she craves the most causes her to willingly release the reins and take what she desires straight from the source.

Eli gives her the okay, and she seals her lips around the hose. She has to force herself to gingerly pull on it like she is giving a soft kiss instead of sucking it down like a Slurpee on a hot day.

Kristin's blood works its way up the hose, and the moment the first warm splash coats Amy's tongue she feels bliss set in as she savors the luscious flavor mingled with the taste of salt and iron. The first swallow goes down with pure delight. Its effect on her appetite is like a sprinkle on a bonfire, but each one that follows plays a part in soothing the savage beast. Amy continues practicing restraint as she drinks, feeling more in control every time she drains the reservoir. By the time she ingests three pints of blood, the hunger is more bearable; the difference between starving and peckish.

The agony is gone and the beast is content with its meager rations. But it will gladly feast until her stomach bursts if Amy ever lets it. She knows better than to entertain that thought, so she expresses her gratitude to Kristin and puts more focus on showing the raging force inside of her who is boss.

Kristin gives Amy a hug and promises to make arrangements for her to have another feeding in the morning, as well as Eli. Then Kristin kisses Eli on the cheek and says goodbye to them. After Eli closes the door, Amy rushes to him. She wraps her arms around him and initiates a kiss that arouses her more than she anticipated. A dirty thought pops into her head, but before she moves her hands from Eli's back to undo his pants, he pulls back and looks into her eyes.

"Still hungry?" Eli asks.

"Yeah, a little," Amy responds, "but I can focus more on everything else now that the pain is gone."

"Good. Remember, you'll never satisfy that hunger, no matter how much blood you drink. And if you ever do try to fill that void, it'll only be a matter of time before you lose all control and a lust for more than just blood will take over."

"Gotcha. But right now I'm lusting for something else."

Eli lets go of her and shakes his head as he takes a step back. "No. Not yet."

"Why?!"

"You need to only focus on one thing right now, and that's maintaining control of your senses and the energy inside of you."

"But I got it under control."

"Yes, but you're still forcing yourself to keep that control. Trust me, I know it's not easy, but we have to work on that before we do anything else. Sorry, but that's a consequence of having my blood in you instead of Lark's or Preacher's."

Amy sighs, and nodding her head she says, "All right. You are my magister, and I'm your legare. You know what's best, and I promised to listen to you."

Eli takes Amy's hand in his. "You are more than my legare, Amy. And as soon as I'm sure you got the hang of being a vampire, I'm going to show you just how much you mean to me."

"Yeah?" Amy smiles. "You better bring it, too, cowboy."

"Baby, I'ma bring it, screw it in, bolt it down, and stamp my name where you'll never forget what's mine."

Amy giggles. "Can I ask you something personal?"

"Go ahead."

"What made you fall out of love with Lygia?"

Eli growls and rolls his eyes, appearing to admonish himself for walking into that one. "People change over the course of a lifetime, Amy. When you love someone, you can compromise. But when your lifetime is an eternity, there's no limit to change, and you can only compromise but so much. After about a century, Lygia and I became two different people, and it was better for both of us to be apart more than we were together. And in case you're wondering, I don't know what this thing between us will evolve into. I can't promise you that we'll be together until the sun burns out. But I can promise that I'll always give you my best until one of us says, 'when.' If the day comes when you need to go your own way, I won't hold you back, and you'll always have a special place in my heart."

Amy rushes in and envelopes Eli in her arms again. This time, however, she uses her vampire strength to lift him off his feet with the greatest of ease, and she squeezes him hard. Eli responds with a protesting rant about not being the chick in their relationship, and she laughs as she puts him back down. Then, after another kiss, she fully commits to doing everything that he says to gain full control of her senses and power.

CHAPTER TWENTY-SEVEN

Watching the sunrise for the first time through the eyes of a vampire makes Amy feels like an alien discovering a new planet. She marvels at the vibrancy of colors within the daily event that she never would have known was there, including a hazy shade of green.

She takes a deep breath of the rich, salty air and smiles as she embraces the bitter/sweet taste of destiny. All that she has lost cannot be measured against what has been gained, but the heartache and pain and fear and fighting for survival has led her to find a bright side here in the midst of the apocalypse. Against all the odds, she has found happiness, and a noble purpose, neither of which she felt were in the cards for her.

The same Puissance virus that has brought mankind to its knees had put Amy on a path to witness the beautiful scene before her. If not for the virus, she probably would have ended up behind prison bars, overflowing with bitterness and rage until the day she died. But her date with the Reaper has not been canceled. In fact, the appointment may have been moved up to a day in the very near future. If Death does claim her, she'll die with her head held high because she proved that she has what it takes to leave this world as something better than what she came into it. And at least she will go down alongside the vampire that she is falling in love with.

The sunlight grows stronger as the fiery sphere continues its ascent over the watery horizon, bringing with it one of the adversities of being a vampire. She defies the torturous UV rays hurled at her by the nuisance at the center of the galaxy, resisting pain that evolves from the sensation of pins piercing her eyeballs to railroad spikes being twisted in her sockets. The increasing light not only intensifies the agony in her eyes, but it also brings the blindness of a whiteout. It takes her a moment to regain the outline of the aircraft carrier anchored near the hospital ship. But the details of the huge vessel is lost to her.

Knowing that it is going to take some time to adapt to properly discerning things in the daylight, Amy lowers her sunglasses over her eyes and acknowledges the feeling of power living inside of her. The impelling vampiric energy did not submit as easily as she thought it would. It took hours to develop the discipline necessary to fully impose her will over the urges and the cravings. She still feels like a deity among men and a small measure of resistance is necessary to keep the beast in check, opposed to the strenuous thought required before.

Her senses of sound and smell are now responding to her commands with the slightest of whim, now that her brain has adapted to process the input more efficiently. And after the three pints of blood provided by one of the donors that Kristin brought to the room, the hunger is more endurable.

It was a pleasant surprise to discover that the flavor of her donor's O-positive blood seemed to have a better taste than the A negative that flows in Kristin's vein—which, at the time was the best thing she ever had in her mouth. Amy found herself wondering what the blood type and taste of Eli's donor was, but she thought it best to keep that kind of thinking to herself.

It will be some time before Amy can say that being a vampire is second nature to her but she believes that she can maintain enough control to keep from going rogue, now and in the future. The one thing that she has no rule over is her link to Eli and the emotions connected to it. Her feelings for him, intertwined with feeling his presence is now the dominant force within her. She is more than happy with that. Sensing his existence makes her own feel worthwhile, and feeling his presence is almost as good as feeling him inside of her. That notion rings especially true after the quality of intimacy that they shared during the early hours of the morning. Things got so hot and heavy in the room, the guards who relieved Gould and Maxwell couldn't look Amy or Eli in the eyes when Kristin showed up with the donor this morning.

The first time that she had sex with Eli was a magnificent experience. She was a human, experiencing pleasure enhanced by supernatural means. The second was extraordinary because it marked the pleasure and pain of her rebirth. Her third time with him was nothing short of absolutely phenomenal. She still feels high from the last orgasm she experienced about an hour ago. As a vampire, her heightened senses, both physical and emotional, increases the pleasure that Eli makes her feel. And she is endowed with the power to give it back to him as good as she is getting it, which only ends up increasing her own gratification. Being with him falls under the shadow of addiction, and she desires more of him, as much as possible. Their days may be numbered, so she intends to continue exploring her sexuality with him every chance that she gets.

Amy feels Eli's presence moving behind her. She hasn't been separated from him much since she woke up a vampire, but she can tell that he isn't far. Instead of turning around she tunes up her hearing to clearly eavesdrop on the conversation that he is having with General Limbeck and Skipworth.

"It's not too late for me to make arrangements for the chopper to take you and Ms. Gouyen back to that compound in Waco," says General Limbeck.

"Thanks, but no thanks," Eli replies. "I've got some business to take care of, and flying in on a Black Hawk is just going to complicate things for my people on the inside."

"I assume you mean, 'regulare' business?"

"It's a loose end that I need to snip before I can focus on Sig and that Chinese vampire army that you're worried about."

"Well, good luck, Mr. Kincade. Lieutenant Granger will return your weapons when you're back on the mainland. And when you hit the road, you won't be stopped for questioning since I put out a description of your vehicle and your names to all the patrols between Louisiana and Texas. Oh, and Miss Gouyen's warrants have been cleared from the database. I'll hand over her clemency papers when the mission is complete, and she confesses before the tribunal, but as of now, she won't have any problems. If you do run into one, just give me a call on the sat-phone Specialist Skipworth has for you, and I'll have it cleared up immediately."

"I appreciate the help, General."

"No problem. Have a good flight, and I'll see you at Fort Dix in two days—unless a situation arises and we need to move on Playtime Media's campus immediately."

Amy taps into the echolocation imaging ability that Eli taught her and she sees General Limbeck shake Eli's hand and then turn to walk away.

"I'll keep eyes on you guys," Skipworth says, handing a new satellite phone to Eli. "In case I can't communicate with you directly, I'll bring in a drone and buzz you if there's danger or rock my wings if it's all good."

"Thanks. I'd appreciate it."

Amy hears herself growl before she realizes she's doing it. She manages to catch herself before she physically moves to issue a warning to Skipworth. Amy knows that Skipworth isn't a threat to her relationship with Eli, but her vampiric nature is infused with a primal instinct to claim and defend possession of her mate.

Eli and Skipworth give each other a fist bump, then she heads off in the direction of the entrance to the ship.

"Hey, vampire!" Granger says as he and Skipworth pass each other. "I need a word with you before we leave."

"Make it quick," Eli responds. "I've got things to do out there in the real world."

"Look, I just want to get something straight between us. I don't trust your kind, and I definitely don't trust you. But the General insists that we have to work together on the mission, and I always follow orders. What I need you to understand is when we're out in the field, I'm the one in charge."

Eli smirks. "Those dead mercs on the mansion's front lawn, you were in charge of them, too, right?"

"Those mercenaries were hired to take care of the guards, lure my targets out, then get the hell out of my way. The same applies to you. And here's a word of advice: leave your little girlfriend at the compound you're going to. When I got your boy, Sigodur, we were having a hard time pinning him down. But when he heard his bitch scream, he gave me the one second I needed to grab hold of him so he couldn't dodge another shot from a net-cannon. If you're going to back me up, I'm going to need you to keep your head in the game instead of worrying about Pocahontas over there."

Amy turns around and glares at Granger. It was clear that he didn't like her because of the company that she kept, but his disdain has grown worse since he found out that she has become a vampire, herself.

"Let me tell you something," Eli says, squaring up with Granger to emphasizes his point. "If you disrespect my woman again, I'll tear out your tongue and put it back in your mouth by way of shoving it up your candy-ass! And don't tell me what to do with her, either. Oh, one more thing: if you ever call Kelly a bitch again, especially after what you and your people did to her, I'll break your fuckin' jaw. Do we understand each other? If not, we can get back to our unfinished business."

Granger smirks, and says, "One day we'll get the chance to get back to that business. Right now we have a common enemy to fight, so you go ahead and do whatever you have to do to be ready to help me capture Sigodur. We can get personal after that."

"It's a date."

"Yeah, it is," Granger says, and turns to walk away. "Get ready, we're lifting off in five."

Amy calms her anger and strolls over to Eli. "That guy's is such a prick!"

"That's giving pricks a bad name. Forget him. How are you feeling?"

Amy smirks, and says, "I'm good. I just wish we didn't have to stop what we were doing before Kristin showed up with breakfast."

Eli grins. "Me, too. I got a feeling that we're not going to get much sleep in that little cottage back at Preacher's compound when we turn it tonight."

"Shouldn't your mind be on something other than sex right now?!" Lygia says as she steps onto the helipad with Kristin walking beside her.

Eli grits his teeth and sighs in frustration.

The animalistic energy surges inside of Amy. She bristles as she bares her teeth—sans fangs, but she reels in the urge go berserk on Lygia and pretends to be indifferent.

"Not the time for this, Lygia," Eli says, turning around.

Lygia puts on a smile as she approaches. "I only want you to be focused on what you're getting into."

"I'll be focused, just like I always am when I go after somebody."

"Elias..., I still think I should be going with you."

Eli shakes his head. "When Amy and I show up without you, Calavius will think he has the upper hand. I'm going to use that to my advantage. Besides, I can take Nicholi and Aleksi. As for Calavius, he might be a little faster and stronger, but I can handle him.”

“All right, I suppose I’ll have to trust you on this one. But I swear, if anything happens to you-”

“Lygia, this is what I do. I got this. Then I’ll handle Sig and get things back to normal.”

Lygia nods her head and extends her arm to hand Eli a tablet. “Give my regards to Calavius.”

“Will do.”

When Eli takes the tablet from Lygia, she closes in and kisses him on the lips. Amy’s growls with her mouth gaped in a rictus of rage and jealousy. Her fists tighten and she wishes more than ever to even the score with Lygia. Knowing that this isn’t the time or the place for a vampire catfight doesn’t help her disposition, but she does her best to not react to Lygia’s provocation.

“Mmm,” Lygia says when she pulls away. “Go get him, my champion regulare. And keep an eye on your puppy. She looks like she’s losing control.”

CHAPTER TWENTY-EIGHT

The Bronco slows to a stop on the peak of the hill overlooking Preacher's compound. Eli remains silent and focused on the walls of the fortress.

Amy has never seen anyone as primed to face danger headlong as Eli is. She understands it, though. His blood has her feeling like a living war machine, and she is ready to demolish anyone considered an enemy. But as confident as she is, she knows that there's no guarantee either one of them will live long enough to see high noon.

The only thing she regrets is that once she gets out of the truck, her skin will no longer be blessed by mollifying breeze from the air conditioner. Her elevated core temperature doesn't make her feel as miserable as she used to when the mercury shot past 100 degrees, but now she gets why Lark likes to run around looking like she makes a living giving lap-dances. She considered wearing a pair of jeans for the fight ahead but settled on some cutoffs and a tank top.

"Okay," Eli says, turning to face Amy. "Don't try to go up against Nicholi, Aleksi, or Calavius—matter what! You're stronger and faster than them, but you're no match for their skill and experience. You can handle the militia guys, but you have to listen to your body and react without giving it a second thought. Trust what you feel but stay in control. Got it?"

Amy nods her head, disregarding the surge of vampiric energy that disagrees with the limited role Eli wants her to play. She got a taste of what she is capable of when Eli stopped the Bronco for her to see what she can do with a machete, and she ended up cutting down a swarm of chompers like a weed whacker on a rampage. It was exhilarating to find out exactly how fast and strong she has become and she can't wait to put her powers to use again. However, she knows that dismembering and decapitating regulares like Nicholi and Aleksi cannot be easily done as it was with the chompers. And her gun will be practically useless against them unless she gets a chance to shoot at point-blank range.

Another step that Eli took to prepare Amy for what is to come was to squeeze off shots at her, each meant to graze. The first one bit into her thigh, but she learned a valuable lesson from the experience. Just like with the bottle cap, she felt where the bullet would strike. Once she knew what the warning sensation was like and the sliver of time that she had to react, she was better prepared to evade all the others. Eli was proud of her. Any bullets fired at her inside the compound with the intent to kill, she thinks she will be able to avoid them, just the same.

Well aware that the Bronco has already been spotted by the guards manning the posts, Eli grabs two bottles of water from the back and passes one to Amy. After chugging half of his, he caresses the fading scar on Amy's thigh.

"Ready to do this?" Eli asks.

"Fuck yeah! Let's go!"

Eli leans over and kisses her passionately. Then, without saying another word, he slips the Bronco into neutral and lets it roll down the hill. Amy smiles, knowing that what just happened wasn't a kiss goodbye, nor was it a good luck kiss. It was a direct message from his heart to hers. A message well received.

Eli steps on the accelerator, sending the Bronco rocketing down the hill.

Amy realizes that she doesn't feel an ounce of the fear that she always respected when entering into a potentially dangerous situation. Instead of her nerves being on edge, she finds herself eager for conflict. The vampiric energy within her is like a tiger pacing in a cage, impatiently waiting for the slightest opening that it can take advantage of to break loose and finally be what nature intended it to be.

Eli speeds towards the compound, not knowing if the doors are going to swing open or not.

Amy takes a deep breath and consciously makes an effort to remain in control of the beast now lurking in her Apache blood.

Close enough to make out the guards on the ramparts, they see a bearded man aim his rifle at the Bronco. Stretch pops up behind him—as if he bounced up on a trampoline—and a hole pops open on the bearded man's forehead.

Stretch turns his handgun on the other guard and exchanges shots with him while the bearded man's body flops over the rail. When the second guard falls dead, Stretch crosses his arms over his chest in the shape of an X, signaling that the compound is in distress and violence is the only option.

Amy and Eli glance at each other. Stretch has taken on the part that Kwesi was to play if things had gone bad by the time she and Eli returned. The plan is already set in motion and there will be no turning back now.

After witnessing the exchange between Stretch and the militiamen guarding the wall, Amy feels even more encouraged. Stretch being able to shoot two of them meant, either, they haven't been trained to sense and respond to approaching bullets or their vampiric powers isn't nearly as acute as hers. Taking them on shouldn't be much of a problem.

Gunfire erupts behind the walls of the compound, making it sound like a war zone. The gate swings open in time for Eli to not have to choose whether to brake or sacrifice his truck. He barrels into the courtyard and the crowd gathering there quickly clear space for him.

The Bronco skids to a stop. Amy hops out with the machete in hand, and her Beretta tucked in her waistband. Eli exits the other side and draws both of his katars.

"Amy!" Lark says, gripping a .32 caliber revolver in her hand as she rushes over with her arms wide open.

"Lark?" Amy responds, acknowledging the odd feeling of seeing Lark dressed in loose fitting jeans, a long shirt, and a baseball cap.

"I'm so glad you guys are back," Lark says, wrapping her arms around Amy. She gasps and pulls back to look at Amy's face. "You're one of us now!?"

The moment she made contact with Lark, Amy felt a link similar to the connection she constantly feels with Eli, but not nearly as strong. She smiles at Lark and nods her head, acknowledging the obvious.

More gunshots crackle from deeper in the compound as Eli comes around the Bronco, and says, "What's the story, Hot Pants?"

Lark lets go of Amy and hurries to throw her arms around Eli as if she thought she would never see him again. "Ninety degrees, man. Ninety, fuckin', degrees."

Amy looks around at the faces that she recognizes and sees only two expressions. Some of Preacher's people look relieved that Eli is back in the compound, while the other seem worried to death.

"I'ma need a little more from you than that," Eli says, looking around.

"We got control of the front. Bear and his crew are working their way towards us. Half our guns got taken. Calavius had his goons turn the militiamen into vamps, but that doesn't make a difference. We can still do this."

"Where's Three Feathers?"

Lark sighs. "Some bad shit went down after you left, so we're gonna have to do this without him and Kwesi."

"I already know what happened to Kwesi and Preach. What happened to Three Feathers?"

Lark appears puzzled as to how Eli already knows about Kwesi and Preacher, then she shakes her head and says, "Feathers is dead, man. Calavius had him killed when he stood up to one of the militia bastards who got aggressive with one of our girls."

"What?!"

Lark quickly explains that almost immediately after Eli and Amy left things got crazy at the compound. Calavius called everyone together in the square and gave a crazy speech about the world being a different place now, and they have to be prepared to seize the moment when the time comes. He also told Preacher's legares that they are spared from death for being illegitimately turned, but they would still have to earn the right to be vampires, starting with a pledge of loyalty to him. Later that day, Calavius freed all of the militiamen prisoners after making a deal to turn them into vampires, in exchange for their undying loyalty, too.

Less than twenty-four hours ago the compound had its darkest day after Calavius set a list of new rules for everyone to follow or face execution. Then he ordered everyone to turn their weapons over to the militiamen vampires. Lark and the others hid what they could but had to give up some to appear to be in compliance. During the weapons roundup, one of the militiamen felt the need to frisk one of the young human girls. The moment he put his hands on her, it was clear that he wasn't looking for weapons. Three Feathers saw what was happening. He stepped in and broke the militiaman's neck, which would have killed him if he was still human.

Calavius deemed Three Feathers a traitor and had Aleksi behead him where he stood. Then he had Preacher and Kwesi seized. What happened after that, Amy and Eli saw for themselves through the same satellite looking down at them at this very moment.

"Young lady!" Calavious' voice booms, "For someone who's been so quiet all this time, you suddenly have a lot to say."

Amy turns and sees Calavius approaching, twirling his cane in his hand. Nicholi and Aleksi are positioned at his sides, both brandishing their weapons and looking ready for a fight. Behind them are five militiamen vampires, including one with a neck brace, protecting Calavius and his henchmen from a rear attack. The militiamen aren't armed with bladed weapons and seem very comfortable with their assortment of machine guns and assault rifles.

"She's not your problem," Eli growls at Calavius. "I am."

"Where is Lygia?" Calavius asks, glancing at the body of a militiaman vampire close to where Jodie and Becca are standing. "I expected you to bring her back here?"

"She wanted to come, but I told her it wasn't necessary. It's my pleasure to take care of this for her."

Calavius laughs, and says, "And just what are you here to take care of, Elias?"

Eli clinks his katar blades together and points the tip of the one in his right hand at Calavius. "A rogue vampire, and the leader of the acolytes! Now, any final words before I chop off your ass so you can kiss it goodbye?"

Nicholi steps forward, holding the sickle part of his weapon by the wood handle, with the chain looped around his wrist. He looks eager to take on Eli but is halted when Calavius waves for him to stand down.

Calavius lets out a hearty laugh and says, "Pelagius' lap dog is once again barking up the wrong tree. Will you ever get tired of it, Elias?"

"Wrong tree, huh? So you tellin' me not to believe my lying eyes?"

"I admit that in recent years I've come to see the truth in Hadrianus' revolution, but I am not the leader of the acolytes. I'm not the reason you always come up short whenever you get close to identifying the leaders of the dissenters. Think about it, Elias. Who has been pulling your strings since the day he assigned you the task of finding this new mysterious proxy of Hadrianus.

Eli laughs. "Really, Calavius? That's your best attempt at a mind game? There's no way you can prove that Pelagius was the same person that he had me looking for. I know for a fact that he didn't believe we should rise up and take control of the human race. He wanted us to exist alongside them, without them knowing it."

"True," Calavius responds, "but Hadrianus' words were his tool to weed out vampires who would one day question his rule. The core of Hadrianus' teachings, after all, is that we are oppressing ourselves by following the Imperator's rules to live in the shadow of an inferior species."

Eli shakes his head. "You're lying. Just like you lied about where you were when The Civitas was bombed. I got time-lapse satellite footage showing that your yacht's been run aground in Canada for weeks. I'm willin' to be you found out it was stolen after you fled The Civitas and was probably on your way to see if there was anything salvageable from the outpost when you ran into Bushy-browss Barney."

More of Preachers vampires arrive, led by Bear and Cruz. They take up position behind Calavius and his men to cut off their path of retreat and stand ready with the few guns they have, as well as an assortment of tools to be used as weapons.

"This so-called satellite footage, courtesy of Lygia, I suppose?"

"Of course."

"Lygia, who revealed what we are to the government of the United States of America? Hypocritical of Pelagius to allow her to do that, don't you think?"

Eli shakes his head. "If you're trying to use that smoke screen to make a case for me to leave you alive, you're wasting your breath. We were exposed by rogues, and the virus forced us into a truce. But that doesn't matter. After what you've done here, I doubt anyone will care when I split your skull in half. As a matter of fact," Eli looks at Lark, and asks, "Hey Hot Pants, you or your people have a problem with that?"

Lark shakes her head, and says, "Nope. He's a dick!"

The rest of Preacher's people nod their heads in agreement.

Eli looks at Amy and winks at her. She finds his level of confidence scary, and she has no idea how he plans to take on Calavius and two other regulares all by himself.

Eli looks back at Calavius and grins. "I'd be lying if I said that this wasn't something I've been lookin' forward to. Pelagius knew that either you or Titus would betray him one day. I'm glad it's you. I liked Titus."

Calavius shakes his head, and says, "Elias, you're wrong about Pelagius. I found the original copy of Hadrianus' manifesto hidden in his office. But that doesn't matter right now. Before you get yourself and the rest of these insurrectionists killed, you should know that Sigodur wants you alive. I would like to deliver you that way to him, but I won't lose any sleep if I don't."

Eli glares, and says, "Sig, huh? Did he tell you that when he warned you to get out of The Civitas?"

Calavius laughs, offering no answer to Eli's question.

"That's alright," Eli says. "I'll see Sig soon enough. I hope that whatever you gave him in exchange for saving your miserable life was worth it, cuz you're about to die."

"I tire of this!" Calavius grouses, then he grips both ends of his cane. He pulls it apart, revealing the slender, double-edged blade that had been concealed in the shaft of the cane. "Now submit to my orders or face me and die!"

Eli laughs. "You want to go one-on-one with me?"

"I wouldn't have it any other way, Devil Badger."

Eli holds his hand up to signal Amy and the vampires on his side to not get involved unless someone on Calavius' side does first. Calavius does the same with his vampires, then he and Eli start moving to the open space in the center of the crowd.

Calavius' confidence gives Amy a bad feeling. Even though he is a generation of vampire that is stronger and faster than Eli, he should know Eli's reputation better than anyone else here in the compound. Yet still, he is more than willing to match swords with a regulare of Eli's caliber. She tightens her grip on the machete and feels the wood crack in the palm of her hand, causing her to remember that she has to remain conscious of her new strength.

With a nod of their heads, Eli and Calavius raise their weapons and charge each other. Metal on metal clink as Eli blocks a strike from Calavius' sword with the H-shape handle of the weapon in his left hand, while Calavius simultaneously uses his scabbard to block a strike from the blade in Eli's right hand. They explode into a dance of strikes and parries, both moving at incredible speed.

Now that Amy's brain is able to process things better than it could when she was human, she can follow vampire speed as clearly as if it were normal. She anxiously follows the duel as Eli doggedly attacks and Calavius effortlessly blocks or evades the blur of katar blades. Calavius has the advantage of distance because of the length of his sword, compared to Eli's short katars. That doesn't deter Eli, though. He adamantly continues his attack, throwing jabs with his blades and blocking strikes while closing the gap between him and Calavius a little at a time.

Calavius spins around and lowers his sword to chop Eli's legs off, but Eli jumps up and arcs his right arm to bring a blade down on Calavius' skull.

For a microsecond, it looks as if Eli is going to end the fight by splitting Calavius straight down the middle, but Calavius raises his blade to avoid the deathblow and he counterattacks with a quick kick that lands flush on Eli's chest.

Amy's breath gets caught in her throat when she sees Eli shoot through the air like he was shot out of a cannon. He flies backwards and comes to a sudden stop when his back slams into the Bronco, leaving behind a huge dent in the front quarter panel.

CHAPTER TWENTY-NINE

Calavius' guards and vampire militiamen laugh in amusement as Amy rushes to Eli's aid.

Kneeling at his side, she holds the machete defensively in case Calavius moves in to finish Eli off. "You okay?"

"I'm okay, Amy," Eli says, fixing his crooked sunglasses back over his eyes. "Just don't forget what I told you."

"But-"

"-No buts!" Eli rises to his feet. "Trust me, I got this." He rolls his head around his shoulders, brushes the shoe print from his shirt, then he points a blade at Calavius and begins to laugh like a lunatic on nitrous oxide.

"I have always suspected you were a bit of a psychopath," Calavius says. "Obviously, you are."

Eli rubs his chest, and says, "You know, I think you cracked one of my ribs. The Calavius I know is supposed to be stronger than I am, but not strong enough to do that."

"But I am now, aren't I?"

"The senex. You got to it, too, huh?"

Calavius releases a villainous chuckle, and says, "Well, since Anaximenes wasn't going to wake up any time soon, it seemed like a shame to let all the power in that ancient blood go to waste. So yes, I got into Pelagius' vault and gave myself an upgrade."

Eli's brow furrows, and he tilts his head, appearing surprised and confused by Calavius' answer. He regains his composure, then says, "I can't tell you how happy I am to hear you say that. Now, let's do this without holding anything back."

Amy looks at Eli with the same confused expression as Calavius. Unless Calavius' kick has knocked a screw loose in Eli's head, there is no reason she can think of why he should be happy to hear that his opponent is running on senex blood. And when Eli winks at her, she doesn't know if she should try to slap some sense into him or let him do whatever insane thing he has planned in his head.

Calavius readies his sword and scabbard again. "Have it your way. But remember, you brought this upon yourself."

Eli responds by charging in, swinging his katars like a madman. Calavius once again deflects the strikes from both blades and sidesteps enough for Eli to end up behind him. Then Calavius goes on the attack.

Amy fears for Eli as the slim blade rains down on him with a vengeance, causing him to take up the role of defense. He is forced to use both of his weapons to block Calavius' scabbard from lashing him and sword from splitting him in half, all while being pushed back towards Clavius' goons.

Amy considers reaching for the Beretta. It's of no use against Nicholi and Aleksi; only a slim chance of possibly slowing them down a bit if they try anything against Eli. But Eli warned her about getting into it with the regulares, and she knows that he will be pissed if she provokes one of them.

When Eli is backed up to within arms distance of Nicholi and Aleksi, Calavius stops swinging his blade and arrogantly invites Eli to attack him again.

Eli smirks and raises his right arm almost straight up. With his weapon in hand, he looks like he is doing an impression of the Statue of Liberty standing proud.

Amy notices the heel of Eli's right foot rise up so that only the tip of his boot is on the ground. Then, in a burst of speed and fury, he executes an about-face maneuver and makes his move in one perfectly executed sneak attack.

Even with her enhanced perception, Amy almost doesn't see Eli swing his blade to strike Aleksi's head above his ear. The katar cuts a clean line over Aleksi's eyebrows and comes out the other side of his head before he knows what hits him. Eli's knife almost gets to taste Nicholi's skull as well, but Nicholi managed to stop it with the inner curve of his sickle before it cut into him.

Aleksi's swords drop to the ground, then he falls to his knees and topples over. His cranium off pops off with the sound of a wet, sticky kiss and wobbles like a furry bowl full of frozen vanilla pudding.

Nicholi's right arm trembles against the force Eli uses to push the outer curve of the sickle against his face. The sharpened edge of the sickle threatens to split open his skin. Nicholi's left hand is also struggling as he desperately holds Eli's second katar from sinking into his belly.

Calavius charges in with a roaring war cry while swinging his sword. Eli drops to the ground and rolls to his left. Nicholi rocks his head back, narrowly avoiding getting slashed by Calavius' blade.

Eli pops back up to his feet and sets himself to defend against another attack.

With a flick of his wrist, Nicholi uncoils his chain and swings the sickle over his head like a helicopter blade before he flings it towards Eli's legs.

Eli jumps before the chain wraps around him. He does a front flip in the air and comes down on Calavius with both katars aimed to impale. Calavius is quick enough to knock one blade off course while twisting his body to evade the other. Then he goes on the attack, impressively making Eli defend himself with both of his weapons again.

Nicholi comes up behind Eli, now swinging the chain and sickle in a criss-cross pattern in front of him. Amy's impulse is to charge in and even the numbers in the fight, but she holds back—even when the tip of Nicholi's sickle slashes a diagonal line into Eli's back before he slips away to avoid further injury.

Eli disregards the long cut on his back and alternates between vicious attacks on one opponent and turning to fend off lethal blows from the other. But as impressively as Eli is holding his own, he is not left unscathed. Nicholi is able to land another superficial laceration across Eli's back, and Calavius' blade leaves a slash on his shoulder that would have taken Eli's arm off if he had not twisted his body enough to avoid the worst of the damage that could have been inflicted.

Amy tightens her grip on the machete a gain and makes up her mind to join the fight if Eli takes another hit, regardless of how mad he will be or what happens to her.

Calavius and Nicholi continue to double team, Eli. Despite their best efforts, they cannot get him in a position to finish him off. Frustrated, Nicholi lets out a guttural roar as he flings the sickle towards Eli's neck. Eli responds by quickly flicking one of his katars at Calavius, then he ducks the sickle and closes the gap between himself and Nicholi.

Calavius deflects the blade that Eli threw at him and Nicholi launches the sickle at Eli again.

Eli swings his remaining katar so that the handle extended over his forearm hits the chain in mid-flight. The chain wraps around his wrist, and Eli snatches the sickle by the handle. He then wastes no time driving the tip of the sickle into the underside of Nicholi's jaw. The curved blade emerges through Nicholi's nose, and Eli swings him around as Calavius moves in for the kill. The death blow that was intended to decapitate Eli ends up slicing through Nicholi's neck instead. Nicholi's body falls to the ground, rhythmically spurting arterial blood while his head swings on the sickle like a weird deep sea fish caught on a hook.

"What is the meaning of this, Elias!" Calavius says, pointing his sword at Eli. "You have always been fast, but never that fast. Unless...."

"That's ri-i-i-ght." Eli releases the sickle, allowing Nicholi's dripping head to join his fallen bo dy, then he smirks and says, "Senex

blood. It does a body good."

Amy's jaw drops as things begin to fall in place. She now knows why Eli had been so wary about turning her with his blood and why Lygia was so against it. The ancient blood in his veins is as dangerous as he warned, and that must explain why she feels so powerful.

"But, how?" Calavius asks.

"Anaximenes wasn't the first, or the only, senex that I found. The artifacts recording the vampire the Maya called Fire Skin wasn't all that Lygia and I brought back from the Yucatan. But, unlike you, we had Pelagius' blessing to sacrifice him. We are Pelagius' insurance policy to keep an asshole like you from taking control in the event something happened to him. I didn't think that this day would actually come, but here we are. And it's going to be my pleasure to finally end you!"

"That changes nothing!" Calavius says, attempting to maintain an air of sovereignty. "I can still slaughter you and everyone else here! Now end this before I end you all!"

Calavius appears to be confident about enforcing his threat, but Amy knows differently. She can hear his heart rapidly pumping fear. Eli's heart rate is elevated as well, but his is beating in a stronger, steady rhythm. She glances at the other vampires and notices that they don't seem worried about reprisal, either. She assumes they sense the same thing that she does.

"We'll see about that. By the way, Lygia wanted me to give you her regards. You might want to look up. I'm pretty sure she's watching right now, just waiting for me to finish you off."

Calavius glances up at the sky for a brief second, then he looks at the militiamen vampires, and he yells, "Kill them all!"

Instantly, all hell breaks loose. The militiamen open fire. Preacher's legares return fire with the weapons they have and rush their attackers like an unorganized band of marauders.

Amy sets her sights on a skinhead aiming an MK-5 at her and Lark, while his skinny partner covers his back. The MK-5 rattles off shots and Amy feels invisible fingers poke her chest and neck as ripples flutter over her skin. She heeds the warning and moves out of the bullets trajectories, pushing Lark clear as well.

The clang of Eli and Calavius' weapons ring out as they resume combat.

Two of Preacher's legares fall from headshots they couldn't avoid.

Jodie and Becca lead the rest of the vampires to converge on the militiamen. The enraged mob takes some critical hits but end up overwhelming Calavius' men, cruelly bludgeon most of their skulls. The militiaman vampire with the neck brace is beaten down most severely. He writhes on the ground while being kicked and stomped. Some of the legares manage to grab hold of his limbs and savagely twist them from their sockets. Only then do they crush his skull, finalizing retribution for Gregory Three Feathers.

The skinhead and the skinny vampire militiamen are forced to turn their guns on some of Preacher's legares to keep from getting their brains beaten in. The legares evade the barrage of bullets by scattering in different directions. Lark and Amy see it as an opening and immediately bear down upon them with a vengeance.

Amy swings the machete with a purpose. The sharp edge of the blade finds its mark, slicing through the skinhead's wrist with little resistance. The severed hand tumbles away from the handle of the MK-5 and arterial blood spurts onto Amy's face and chest.

Now that Amy is a vampire, the taste of vampiric blood is immensely more bitter than when she drank Eli's. But blood is blood, nonetheless, and it sparks a frenzy.

The skinhead turns to run for his life but Amy's clutches his stubbly skull with her palm over his forehead, and two of her fingers dig into his eye sockets. She feels something rubbery that squishes as she gets a sure grip. The militiaman screams in agony. Bloody fluid spurts from his eyeballs as they rupture under Amy's fingertips.

Holding his head like a bowling ball, she raises her machete high and starts hacking at his neck like she is cutting a path through a tangle of jungle vines. A pulsing, bright-red geyser erupts from the fischer opening in the skinhead's neck. He gurgles a blood-curdling scream.

The scent of blood rolls through the air like an invisible fog, palpable on Amy's tongue as she breathes it in; the beast within begs to consume the precious fluid being spilled and wasted. She continues to intentionally bury the machete only deep enough to slightly increase the damage with each fall of the blade instead of lobbing his head off with one merciful blow.

More and more blood spatter finds its way into Amy's mouth. The beast within relishes the acerbic treat. Amy fights the urge to lean in to place her mouth over the gash to drink the rest of the skinhead's blood like she is shotgunning a can of beer. The only thing that stops her is one coherent thought: Eli. Disappointing him is the last thing she wants to do, and she knows that is what will happen if she breaks a rule that he explicitly warned her about.

Amy regains her senses and looks past the beads of blood on the lenses of her glasses. She aims the machete blade at the center of the wedge carved through flesh and bone. Utilizing her vampire strength, she cleaves the skinhead's skull from his body. Then she turns an finds Lark staring at her as she straddles the skinny militiaman's back, the revolver in her hand still smoking from pumping bullets into his brain.

Seeing the questions in Lark's eyes, Amy shakes her head and says with her eyes, "Trust me."

Lark nods her head.

The both of them turn towards the sound of clashing blades. Immediately, Amy tosses the severed head over her shoulder like unwanted litter. She wipes her face with her tank top while hurrying over to the circle formed around the blade fight.

Calavius appears to be flustered, and his strikes are being delivered with more desperation than skill. Eli's grin taunts him as he easily blocks the clumsy attacks.

Eli glances at Amy and smiles as if he had been waiting to see her again. Then he advances on Calavius, steadily increasing his speed with each swing that he takes. Calavius backs up and starts moving in a circle around the improvised ring as Eli stubbornly stalks him. Much to everyone's astonishment, Eli explodes into a fast, fluid, agile flare of gleaming metal and fury.

Calavius does his best to block the incoming katar blade. He is thoroughly overwhelmed and has no defense when Eli does a spin move that ends with him launching a jab that plunges his blade deep into Calavius' chest.

Calavius pauses, in shock and in pain. Eli withdraws his blade and executes a sweep kick that takes Calavius' feet from under him. As soon as Calavius' back hits the ground, Eli drives his katar through the center of Calavius' torso, burying the blade down to the hit.

Amy notices Calavius' legs go limp and she realizes that Eli has severed his spine.

Still in control of his arms, Calavius attempts to swing his blade at Eli's head. Eli avoids the strike and catches Calavius' arm, then he twists it around and around until it is completely dislocated. Calavius' other hand reaches for the katar handle in a desperate attempt to yank the blade out of him, but Eli thwarts his plan and dislocates that arm as well.

Sensing the tyrant's imminent demise, Preacher's legares break into a cheer. Amy pumps her fist and gazes at Eli with adoring eyes. Eli, seemingly oblivious to the celebration around him, pins Calavius shoulders to the ground and yanks the chain and medallion away from his neck.

"You don't deserve to die with this around your neck," Eli says, then stuffs the sign of The Synodus into his pocket.

Calavius shakes his head. "Release me, Elias! You don't have the right to do this!"

"I can make this easy for you, but you have to tell me who besides Sig is working with you. And I want to know exactly how Pelagius died."

With a laugh full of disdain, Calavius says, "Like I would give you the satisfaction, you dog! You are a child compared to me. I'd rather die knowing that you're still lost and confused than lower myself into submission to you."

"Figured you'd say something like that." Eli and yanks his katar out of Calavius' chest and raises it high above his head. "But you're forgetting that I don't need you to talk. There's someone else here I can get everything I need from."

Calavius' eyes widen to the size of ping-pong balls. His mouth falls open, but the last words he is to speak are absent of sound.

Eli smiles big enough to expose his fangs, then he drops the blade down on Calavius' head. The dull thud of a melon busting open sounds as the katar splits Calavius' skull straight down the middle. His head opens like a book, revealing the gory anatomy in full detail.

"Hey, Hot Pants," Eli says. "Let the humans know it's safe to come out and get some of your guys together to build a pyre to burn this asshole's body and the rest of his people. I'm going to get Preach and Kwesi."

"Gotcha," Lark responds. "But my boys already went to cut Preacher down and get Kwesi out the well. They should be on the way to the infirmary by now."

"Okay. Good job."

"Thanks, dude." Lark pulls her shirt over her head and immediately looks more comfortable in her sports bra. "Hey, can I have Nicholi's sickle-chain thingy? It's kinda cool, and he's not gonna need it anymore."

Eli smiles and nods his head. "Go ahead. It's all yours. You damn sure earned it." Then he looks at Amy and raises an eyebrow at the amount of sticky blood on her and the machete blade. "You know the only thing you're missing right now is a hockey mask, right?"

"Aw, shut up," Amy says, then she drops the machete and rushes to him.

"You listened to me today. I'm proud of you."

Amy stares at the wound on his shoulder and is glad to see that it is already healing. "It wasn't easy. For a minute there I thought you might be in trouble. I'm just glad you're okay."

"I told you I had it. But it looks like I done lost another one of my T-shirts."

"Hey, I had nothing to do with that one."

CHAPTER THIRTY

The craving never goes away. The closest it comes to satisfaction is a level of contentment after feeding. Managing it had not been much of an issue for Amy after swallowing three pints of blood from her donor before leaving the hospital ship. She had been aware of the hunger since then. It registered more like background noise. But since the skinhead's blood sprayed on her while she slaughtered him, the craving within her has grown. And now, with the tantalizing scent of O-Positive blood in the air, she has to actively keep herself in check.

"I'm so glad you guys are okay," Amy says, holding Preacher's hand as she sits at the edge of his bed in the infirmary.

"I admit it looked bleak there for a little while," Preacher rasps. "But I knew God would get us through from the moment I heard his voice telling me to calm myself."

The scent of blood is still fresh on Preacher's breath. Amy resists the impulse to lean in and kiss him, then lick his mouth clean. Instead, she dips a rag into a bowl of warm water and says, "That's funny, Eli whispered something like that when we watched them hang you. Don't tell me you actually heard him from miles away."

Preacher shakes his head. "No. It was the same voice I hear when I'm in prayer. Nice to know you and Eli were supporting me at the time, though."

Amy smiles and gently cleans the bruise encircling Preacher's neck. Her fingertips can sense the ridges of the rope impression dug into Preacher's skin. She doesn't dare to imagine what it must have been like to hang by the neck for over twenty-four hours, lungs burning for air and no hope of dying. Preacher hung in there, though. And he will be fully recovered within a few hours.

As for Kwesi, he survived the pit. He was conscious when he hit the ground, and had the presence of mind to roll into the approaching chomper and knock it over. After that, he was able to bide time by laying on top of the comper's torso, safely out of reach of its tiny arms and hungry mouth. He said the pain was excruciating as he held his limbs as straight as possible to give them a chance to mend, but he endured.

Hours crept along until Kwesi was healed enough to have sufficient use of his limbs. He eliminated the immediate threat by stomping on the chomper's skull to crush it but was still stuck since he didn't have the strength to break free of the rebar wrapped around his torso and wrists. He also didn't have the strength necessary to jump high enough to escape the depth of the well. He said he wasn't worried much, though, since he had faith that Eli wasn't going to let Calavius have his run of the compound for too long.

Amy glances at the cot next to Preacher's. Lark and Kwesi are sitting side by side on the edge of it, their arms and thighs touching. The events of the past few days have uncovered something between them, evidenced in the warmth that radiates between them when they gaze at each other.

Jodie and Becca are sitting on the other side of Kwesi's cot, re-glazing their lips with a shared stick of lip gloss. Now that she knows firsthand the possessive nature of vampires regarding their mates, Amy is astounded that Jodie seems indifferent about Lark and Kwesi's new closeness. It could be that Jodie doesn't care, or it could be that she is intimidated by Lark's dominance. Whatever the reason, Jodie seems to prefer foregoing a confrontation. At the moment, Jodie and her sister appear to be more interested in Amy than anything else.

Kwesi looks over and says, "Vampire Amy, I can't believe Eli turned you already. How does it feel to be on our side of the fence?"

"It's more incredible than anything I ever imagined," Amy says.

"Know what's weird?" Jodie says. "There's something different about Eli's scent, and you... got it, too."

"Fuck's that supposed to mean?"

"It's nothing bad," Becca responds. "We just never ran across a magister and legare that shared something like that. Maybe there's more of a part of him in you since he's got that special blood."

Amy isn't sure what to make of Jodie and Becca's observation. She can identify everyone that she's come across, just by their natural smell. Eli has only smelled one way to her since she's been a vampire. It's specific to him, just like everybody else's. But, there was something similar between him and Lygia. It was faint, but there. She assumed that it had to be something to do with the bloodline that they shared.

"You know," Lark says, with a smile. "She's right. Since he turned you, there's something different in him, and you have it in you, too. Maybe that's how vamp blood works when the bloodline is so close to The Primus?"

Kwesi and Preacher both look confused. They weren't present when Eli revealed his secret to Calavius, so it's news to them.

Eli enters the infirmary, holding onto the satellite phone that Skipworth gave him. He walks straight over to where everyone is, and Kwesi rises up to engage him in one of their bro hugs.

"Good to see you again, brother," Kwesi says.

"Good to see you, too, brother," Eli responds. "I'm just sorry I couldn't get back here sooner."

Kwesi shakes his head. "What happened with Three Feathers isn't on you, man. And trust me, nobody wants to die, but he was at peace with losing his life for protecting someone else."

Eli nods his head.

Amy wipes the sweat from Preacher's brow as she recalls the brief time she spent with Gregory Three Feathers. Then her thoughts get sidetracked when she hears multiple footsteps and the voice of a woman demanding to be released. She tunes her hearing to focus on the heartbeats and her brain separates four different pulses.

All eyes turn to the door and wait for it to open. When it does, Stretch comes in first. Bear and Cruz follow, firmly holding Kimiko — Calavius' wife, and fountain — by her upper arms as the escort her inside.

Upon first sight of Eli, Kimiko tries to back out the door but ends up with her feet skidding over the floor as Bear and Cruz move her forward.

Kimiko makes her body rigid and holds her head high as she says, "I don't know anything, Elias! Now tell these people to let me go!"

"I don't have a lot of time, so we'll make this quick, Kimi," Eli says. "Lie to me once, and I'm going to drain you to within an inch of your life. Then I'm going to have you turned into a vampire. When you wake up, you'll be chained to a picnic table with a cage around your head to protect your brain from the swarm of chompers I'm going to let loose on your ass to eat you alive, and you're going to feel every bit of it. Understand me?"

"How dare you threaten me?!"

Eli zips over to Kimiko and clutches her throat, then in a low growl, he says, "Drop the attitude, bitch! The only thing I want to hear from you is what Calavius and Sig talked about, and what Sig wanted from him."

Kimiko scowls and pugnaciously stares at Eli.

Eli shrugs. "Okay, you don't want to talk? No problem. I'll just ask Sig myself when I see him." He grabs Kimiko's hair and yanks her head to one side. He bares his fangs and wastes no time using them to puncture Kimiko's neck.

Kimiko shrieks as Eli audibly sucks and slurps the blood from her carotid artery. His aggressiveness is nothing short of brutal, and it gives everyone pause, wondering if he has crossed into rogue territory. Kimiko cries for help, and when she realizes that no one is going to dare to stop Eli, she screams, "Sigodur wanted the Saudi Scroll! He wanted the Saudi Scroll!"

Eli continues to feed from Kimiko for a moment until he appears to force himself to pull back.

The scent of Kimiko's blood kicks Amy's craving up another notch. The sight of it dripping down Kimiko's neck like cherry infused maple syrup makes her mouth water. She uses the control that she's learned to tune up the scent of Kimiko's blood instead of turning it down and she savors how she can practically taste it through the air.

Eli licks the nectar from his lips, and says, "The Saudi Scroll? What does he want with that?"

Keeping the pressure on her neck, Kimiko shakes her head. "I don't know. We never met Sig in person. I only know that Sigodur wanted the scroll because Aleksi asked Calavius what was Sigodur going to do with it?"

"So, Sig was at The Civitas?"

Kimiko shakes her head. "I don't think so. When they were talking about the scroll, Calavius spoke of somebody taking it to Sigodur. No name was mentioned, though, just 'He will take it to Sigodur, himself.'"

"Anything else?"

"I don't know how important this is, but Calavius told me that Sigodur might have lost his min d because he was preaching something about god being mad at him, and he needed you to help him find god.. So nobody was supposed to harm you if they crossed paths with you."

Amy and Eli exchange glances, then return their attention to Kimiko.

"Why would Sig want me to help him find god?" Eli asks. "That's Preacher's department, not mine."

Kimiko shakes her head. "I don't know about that. But there is something else that you might want to know."

"Yeah, what's that?"

Kimiko swallows the saliva gathering in her mouth, and says, "Someone knows how to control the chomper things. A swarm really was attacking The Civitas before we slipped out but we walked right past them, and they didn't do anything to us."

"Elias," Preacher says, "you think what she's saying is possible? Sig knows something about God and he, or somebody else, has been bestowed dominion over chompers?"

"Two days ago I would've said this bitch is crazy, but after what we saw yesterday, I know that she's at least telling half the truth."

"No, it's the whole truth!" Kimiko pleads.

Preacher sits up as if he just received an adrenaline shot. "What did you see yesterday?"

Eli quickly recaps what happened from the time he and Amy showed up at the safe house to this morning before the got on the Black Hawk to be flown back to Louisiana. Preacher and his legares are left spee chless after discovering that Sig and Kelly were behaving like rogues when they were spotted by a satellite, which led to them being targeted by the military. Anger blossoms on their faces when they learn exactly how the Puissance virus was created. That expression gives way to disbelief when Eli tells them about the video of Sig and the Butter Ball chomper taken from Masterson's body cam. And Eli wraps up by telling them about what he and Amy saw on the roof of The Sapphire on Playtime Media's campus.

Eli lets everyone absorb what they just learned, and he turns his attention back to Kimiko. "How did Pelagius die?"

Kimiko lowers her head, and says, "I don't know. I was in my suite when Calavius went to a daily briefing. After a while, the alarm sounded when the chompers attacked. Calavius came back to the suite and told me that we had to leave, then we met Nicholi and Aleksi at one of the escape tunnels. It wasn't until we were away from The Citivas that I learned that Pelagius was dead and I learned what was going on."

"Even with Anaximenes blood, Calavius couldn't kill Pelagius on his own. Who helped him?"

"I swear I don't know. Maybe Nicholi and Aleksi, maybe they had more help, but I don't know. I swear that's the truth."

Eli growls, then he looks at Preacher and says, "I'm done with her. I suppose you're gonna welcome her to your flock now?"

Preacher nods his head. "If she wants to stay with us she's welcome. She didn't know what was happening until it was too late, and there was nothing that she could do to stop Calavius."

"Your house, your rules," Eli says. "But if she so much as swats a fly while she's here, she's chomper food. No if, ands, or buts about it!"

"Ahm," Lark says. "When you guys go after Sig, I'm going with you."

"I'm in, too," says Stretch.

"That's three of us," Bear adds.

Cruz shrugs and says, "What? You think y'all rolling without me?"

Jodie and Becca look at each other, nod their heads, and both enthusiastically say, "Yeah, we're down!"

"Look," Eli says, "I really don't know what I'm gonna be walking into, and I don't know if I'm gonna to be able to walk out. I don't even want Amy coming with me, but she's hardheaded, and she's not gonna to take no for an answer. I can protect her, but I won't be able to protect all of you."

"Dude, you won't have to protect us," Lark says. "We can hold our own, and you're going to need more than Amy to watch your back. We might not be regulares, but we're vampires. This is our business, and we need to take care of it. Matter of fact, I'm willing to bet every vampire in this compound will want to roll with you when they find out what's going on. You need a vampire army on your side, and you got one!"

"If I wanted an army I'd be out rounding up more regulars right now. Besides, do I have to remind you that two of you got killed by some punk-ass militiaman puppies today? You really think it's gonna be easier going up against Sig and the acolytes on his side?"

"Don't matter. We gotta fight. Clavius called us illegitimate vampires and said that we would never truly be accepted because we did nothing to deserve The Primus' gift. So we want our chance to do our part and earn our respect."

Eli glances at Preacher, and says, "Please talk some sense into your puppies."

"I don't think they need to prove themselves to anybody," Preacher says, "but they are right about you needing more help. That's why I'll be joining with you, too. And judging from the look in Kwesi's eyes, he's in, as well."

"Damn right!" Kwesi says.

Eli shakes his head and looks to Amy for support.

"Sorry, baby," Amy says. "I'm with them on this one. You're a total badass, Eli, but can't do everything by yourself. And I don't trust Granger and his boys to have your back like we will. Besides, I know I'm the new kid on the block, but between my link to you and the presence I feel of every vampire in this compound when we touch each other, it's like we're all family. And family takes care of its own, even if we all die fighting together."

Every vampire in of the cottage nod their heads in agreement and stare down Eli with steely eyes, boldly stating that they are not taking no for an answer.

Eli puts his hands to his head and circles his thumbs on his temples. After a moment, he says, "I'm the regulare here, and I'm callin' the shots. You puppies are stayin' behind. You're not ready for what's out there."

"How do you know?!" Lark snaps. "You don't know what any of us been through before Preacher turned us, or what's happened since then. You can't tell us 'no' just because. We're vampires, just like you. And we have the right to fight for what's best for all of us. You can't just shut us down without at least giving us a chance to prove ourselves."

Eli turns to Kwesi. "I suppose ain't no talking to you, either, huh?"

Kwesi crosses his arms over his chest. "You know me better than that."

"Okay," Eli says. "Y'all wanna jump in the fire, fine. Let's see how you deal with the heat in the frying pan first. Then you can get back to me on what's best for all of us."

"What's that supposed to mean?" Lark asks.

"Killin' militiamen and chompers is easy. Takin' on other vampires is tougher, though, do-able. But goin' up against a rogue like Sig is like signing your own death warrant, and I'ma show you exactly what I mean. I'm gonna put you puppies through hell over the next couple a days, so you'll know what it's gonna be like. If you still want in by the time we're done, I won't fight you no more on this. Deal?"

Stretch scoffs, and says, "You ain't saying nuthin', man."

"We'll see," Eli responds, then he looks at Preacher. "As for you, old friend, you're needed you here. Your people are gonna need you to lead them, and this is where you should be."

Preacher tries to plead his case, but Eli refuses to listen to a word. Eventually, even Preacher's own legars agree that he is needed more at the compound than on a suicide mission, and he reluctantly drops the argument.

"First thing's first," Eli says. "I gotta call General Limbeck and see if he's willing to let you guys back me up."

"Well," Amy says, "he wants you more than you need him. I'm pretty sure you can persuade him."

"We'll see," Eli says, staring into Amy's eyes. "By the way, you do know that you're gonna be training with them, right?"

Amy shrugs. "I'm cool with that."

Eli smirks, and Amy gets the feeling that she is going to regret those words. But as far as she is concerned, it doesn't matter what Eli throws at her. She belongs to the vampire nation now, and she feels a kinship with Preacher's legares. She is used to fighting for survival, but it feels better to fight for something that she knows is right, like protecting family and the one that she loves. If she dies doing that, then she can truly say that she has done something worthwhile while she was living.

CHAPTER THIRTY-ONE

Battered and exhausted, Amy and Lark sit shoulder to shoulder stuffing protein bars into their mouths and guzzle cold bottles of water.

Eli has turned a back corner of the compound into a gladiator training school. The loud pinging of rebar poles striking each other reverberates off the walls as Stretch, Bear and Cruz do their best to defend themselves from Eli's attack. The rattle of an AK-47 adds to the calamity. The boys successfully evade the barrage of bullets, and Eli rewards them for their accomplishment by brutally beating them with swift strikes of merciless rebar. With all three of his opponents down and showing no desire to get back up, Eli complements them on the improvements that they have made, then he points out the things that they are still doing wrong.

Eli stayed true to his word, and for the past two days he has put Lark, Stretch, Bear, Cruz, Jodie and Becca through a special kind of hell. To their credit, they have been able to hang through the worst of what Eli has thrown at them so far. There were times when Jodie and Bacca couldn't possibly go on any further, but they earned everyone's respect when they refused to give up.

Amy was not exempted from the beatings and shootings that he is passing off as training. As badly as she has had her ass kicked, she is proud to have earned her fangs the true regulare way: her magister knocked the teeth out of her mouth during a training session.

Being Eli's legare comes with blessings and a curse. As far as the blessings go, Amy is much faster and stronger than the other vampires. She can sense the path of a bullet better than they can to avoid getting shot—most of the time. The curses, on the other hand, involve Eli being more harder on her than anyone else. Another is that sleep will never again be the peaceful obliviousness that she once used to enjoy. When she goes into the trance that vampires call sleep, Amy is still aware of everything that is happening around her because her brain never shuts off. It's like sleeping without being completely unconscious. Her mind and body does get the recharge that they need when she is in a trance, but sleep will never again be what it once was.

Amy and Lark watch as Stretch and the others go limping off towards the mess hall in search of nourishing blood and a high protein, high calorie bite to eat. Between the beatings and the bullets, Lark, her boys, Jodie and Becca have proven their determination to do their part in the upcoming mission. Otherwise, they would have quit after the first day. But they stuck it out and the grueling hours of training have fostered a noticeable improvement in everyone—including Amy.

Kwesi jumps down from his sniper's perch on the roof of one of the buildings. He lays Eli's AK-47 on the ground and picks up one of the rebar poles that are being used in substitution of swords. Eli grins and nods his head, eager to fight someone who is more of a challenge than one of the younger vampires. The mega-alpha male comes out the most when he is fighting. Amy can clearly see the eye of the tiger in him, and it turns her on.

Kwesi and Eli square off and begin stalking each other. The blood staining the sandy ground teases the vampiric energy in Amy as much as it did when it was initially spilled. She has the hunger in check but keeping it under control is still almost a full-time job. Whenever she feeds from Stephen—the fountain that she has chosen to nourish her with human blood while she is here at the compound—she fantasizes about sinking her teeth into his neck and draining him, instead of consuming a measured amount through the hose of a siphon. She has thought about asking Eli if she should be concerned about the slow progress that she is making in that department but decided to fight it out on her own. She doesn't know what it feels like to go rogue, but if she thinks she is closing in on the edge of something, she intends to tell him.

Kwesi glances at Lark and winks as if he knows he can take his opponent. Then he returns his attention to Eli and continues to slowly move in a circle, intimidatingly twirling the rebar in their hands.

Amy is glad to see Kwesi looking as good as he did the first time she met him. His legs are completely healed, and all of his strength has returned. The only scars on him are the ones that were already there before he became a vampire.

The puffy scar tissue latticed over Kwesi's back makes Amy sad, but Kwesi wears them like a symbol of his defiant spirit. As long as he lives, he will resist oppression and readily fight it in whatever form it presents itself.

Amy and Lark glance at each other. The scent of testosterone is strong in the air, overpowering the blood and sweat on Eli's battlefield. Amy is keyed in on Eli's scent as Kwesi charges at him, swinging the rebar maliciously. The clanking of the poles shatters the silence again, accompanied by the trash talk between Eli and Kwesi as they spar.

"Know what's thirty degrees?" Lark says as she rubs the splotchy area on her upper arm where a huge, black bruise is in the process of healing.

"It sure ain't the frickin' weather," Amy says, carefully enunciating her words to avoid lisping since she isn't acclimated to the fangs in her mouth yet.

"No. I'm talkin' about how Eli and Kwesi are, like, the bad boys that we always fall for but they aren't the assholes that the bad boys always turn out to be."

"Yeah, I like that about them, too. Eli's a badass, and he knows it, but it's like almost everything that his parents taught him about respecting women is hardwired in his brain."

Lark giggles. "Yeah, you're right about the almost part, unless they taught him how to kick a bitch's ass. I don't know how, but I'm gonna get him back for the whooping that he's been putting on me. Kwesi, too. I swear this morning I shitted out one of the bullets he put in my ass yesterday."

"Way too much information! Besides, you can't take it personal. They're only being tough on us because they want us to know what it's going to be like if we take on Sig and the vampires he's got working for him."

"Easy to say when you got Eli kissing your boo-boo's, among other things, at night to make it up to you."

"Psssh! I was so frickin' tired last night when we call it quits, all I wanted to do was sleep. And I can't even really do that anymore."

Lark turns and looks at her with accusing eyes. "C'mon! You trying to tell me y'all ain't do the nasty last night. Yeah, right. Slut!"

"Who you callin' slut? Skank!"

"Who you callin' skank? Whore!"

"Who you callin' whore? ...Strumpet!"

Amy and Lark glare at each other for a moment, then they both break out in laughter.

"I just made up my mind about something," Lark says.

"Yeah, what's that?"

"Kwesi. I'ma hit that tonight."

Kwesi glances at Lark.

Eli takes advantage of Kwesi's lapse in concentration and sweeps the rebar pole down low, whacking the back of Kwesi's knees.

Kwesi's legs fly up in the air. He flips over and lands face-first on the ground. In a flash, Eli drives the tip of his rebar into the ground just inches from Kwesi's skull.

Lark gasps and covers her mouth. It isn't until Kwesi starts chuckling that she starts to look relieved. Amy breathes a sigh of relief as well, and she recalls Granger's warning to Eli on the morning they left the hospital ship. All it will take is a microsecond for Eli to take his mind off of Sig to worry about her and the results could be disastrous. The last thing that she wants to be is a liability, but she believes with all her heart that she has to go along to help him, even though he has demonstrated that he doesn't need anyone's help.

"Thanks for making me look bad in front of the chicks, man," Kwesi says, as Eli helps him to his feet.

"Hey, don't blame me for that one," Eli says. "P-u-s-s-y, bro, it'll getcha every time."

"Yeah." Kwesi glances at Lark again. "Whadda you say we take a break until the puppies heal up a little bit."

"A break, huh? I see Hot Pants got you wide open like a greedy kid's mouth with a slice of pie in front of it."

"Funny you should mention the words pie and mouth in the same sentence. I swear I smell some-," Kwesi pretends to sniff the air, "-'pie' on your breath. Apache pie if I'm not mistaken."

Eli grins like the canary who ate the cat.

Kwesi laughs, and says, "So I guess it's true what they say, you know, you are what you eat?"

"Don't know, but if you spend the night with Hot Pants and somebody calls you an asshole tomorrow morning, you'll have your answer."

"Hey!" Amy says. "You idiots know we can hear you, right?"

Eli and Kwesi erupt into laughter, then they start making their way over to the wall where Amy and Lark have futilely sought refuge in the shade. When Eli is within a foot of Amy, he swings his pole to strike her in the arm, and she catches it before it hits her.

"Very good," Eli says, nodding his head approvingly. "Your reflexes are getting much better."

Lark glares at Kwesi, and warns, "Don't even think about it! I'm still fuckin' sore from him beating the crap out of me and you shooting me in my ass all day yesterday."

"Well, it's such a cute ass," Kwesi says, resuming the flirting that he has been doing since Lark kept him company as he healed, "I just couldn't take my crosshairs off of it."

Eli shakes his head, and says, "At least you and your friends are better at dodging hot lead now. I arranged for you guys to have Kevlar helmets and jackets, but you still want to get shot as less as possible."

"You got us body armor, but you still got Kwesi taking shots at us? What the hell, man?!"

"You guys can't sense bullets until it's almost too late, so I have to get you to react to it a lot quicker," Eli says, and sits on the ground next to Amy. "If I had a couple months, then we would've been able to start off easy. But this is going down tomorrow, so it's gotta be the hard way."

Lark sulks, knowing that more live-fire exercises are on the way and she might get shot again by the end of the day. Kwesi doesn't pass on the opportunity to nuzzle his shoulder against Lark's and spout words to encourage her.

"Thirsty?" Amy says as she offers Eli her bottle of water.

"Thanks," Eli says and takes a big gulp. Then he examines the fading contusions on Amy's arms and legs, and he lifts the front of her shirt to make sure he didn't hurt her too badly when he struck her in the stomach.

"Inspecting your handiwork?"

"I'm sorry I have to put you through this, but we can't do a montage and turn all you guys into ninjas in two minutes. I gotta bring the pain and hope you learn as we go. Or, you guys can give up on the idea of coming with me."

"That's not gonna happen!"

Kwesi looks over and says, "I gotta hand it to you girls, you're tougher than I thought. And as long as y'all hang in there, none of the guys are going to quit."

"As much as I've had the crap beaten out of me," Amy says, "there's no way I'm quitting now."

"Well, it's almost over," Eli says, "When the boys come back we're gonna spar using real blades instead of rebar. We'll knock off around ten tonight because I want everybody to get some rest, so we're all a hundred percent when the choppers pick us up."

"Sounds good" Lark says.

Eli smiles, then he takes Amy's hand. "You know, we've never been on a date. Whaddaya say we have a candlelight picnic or something later."

Amy nods her head and smiles. "I'd like that a lot."

"Is that a private thing," Kwesi says, "or you want to make it a double date?"

From the expression on Eli's face, Amy knows the answer that Eli is about to give, but she gives the answer that she wants before he can say a word. "That'll be cool. Us and you guys hanging out, picnicking, shooting any chompers that might crash the party. It's all good."

Lark smiles to thank Amy. Both girls know that Lark and Kwesi can go have a picnic on their own, but they want to be together while sharing private time with the guys. It is the closest thing that they can have to the way the world used to be, and it will be something precious to experience since there is a chance that on the day after they might die.

Eli shrugs, accepting that his alone time with Amy will be less than he originally planned, but Amy already knows that she is going to make it up to him by separating from Lark and Kwesi while they are out to do it in the great outdoors.

Amy smiles at Eli and kisses his lips. What she wouldn't give to have Sig surrender to Eli if they do find him at the Playtime's campus, but this is still her life, and things like that just don't happen. For now, she doesn't want to think about tomorrow. It's best to just endure the pain and enjoy the pleasure that she has to look forward to until fate revels if it is going to be kind or cruel.

CHAPTER THIRTY-TWO

The beast within Amy claws at the lid of her imaginary box. It's as if it understands blood will soon be shed, and that inevitability has excited it.

Less than ten minutes to go before she jumps out of a helicopter to battle chompers and hostile vampires. Amy finds herself missing the tension that she used to feel in her gut when she was mortal. Respecting fear's warnings kept her from getting careless. And now, with The Grim Reaper mere miles away, awaiting a bountiful harvest, she's as cool as if she's riding to the water park for a day of play. Amy reminds herself that she can't let her sense of omnipotence cause her to be one of the souls that the Reaper lays claim to on this day.

In the history of time, no day and night has ever passed as quickly as the past twenty-four hours. The bladed weapons training was brutal but beneficial. Eli's students learned precious lessons with every cut and every stab that had them bleeding well into the evening. After gorging on donor blood to heal wounds and hasten recovery, they were given a good luck feast by Preacher and the compound's residents. Then Amy, Eli, Lark, and Kwesi left the compound for a date night in the apocalypse.

Lark had led them to a lake where they swam in their underwear. Then the couples split up for alone time, although they were within earshot of each other. A night under the stars, making love to Eli, was the best way Amy could imagine spending her possibly last night on earth. She even had to smirk when she stared up at the sky and wondered if Lygia's eyes were staring down at them through the DOD's satellite.

"Life is fleeting," Amy thinks to herself, and she wonders if the person quoted had realized that death was in the immediate future.

Amy opens her eyes and looks at the serious faces around her. She and Lark trade smiles, both of them still finding humor in the seating arrangement of the Black Hawk that they are flying in. Lark might as well be a piece of candy sitting between Kwesi and Stretch, who used to be her friend with benefits. On Amy's side of the chopper, Eli sits as a buffer between her and Lygia. Everybody appears to be focused on the mission, but their body language tells all.

Lygia being at Fort Dix was no surprise. Seeing her dressed in tactical gear, ready to join the mission was. Eli tried to talk her out of it, but Lygia's reasons for joining the party is the same as Preacher's legares. She doesn't want to just inherit the title Imperator, she wants to earn it. She hasn't used a sword in decades, but she is still a regulare. It is her duty, and she is the most qualified to help Eli capture a rogue of Sig's caliber.

As for Lygia's attitude towards Amy, nothing has changed, but Amy is getting better at blowing it off. The only thing that sticks in Amy's craw is the fact that she has to put her fist over her heart and bow her head to show respect to Lygia now that she has officially taken her father's place as Imperator. Amy now has to follow Lygia's orders, and she can forget about evening the score between them. Laying one finger on the Imperator is tantamount to treason and Lygia will be able to justifiably order her death. And knowing Lygia, she will order Eli to do it, just to test where his true loyalty lies.

Amy hears the voice of the lead Black Hawk pilot say, "Apaches breaking formation. ETA, five minutes to drop point."

"Copy that, Captain," Granger's voice responds. "All right, everybody strap up, lock and load, and wait for my command. And don't forget what we discussed in the briefing this morning."

Amy rolls her eyes and slaps a fully loaded magazine into one of the M-4 Carbine compact assault rifles that General Limbeck provided for the vampires going on the mission who wanted them. It's nice to have the M-4 and her Beretta at her disposal, but today's weapon of choice is Calavius' sword. Bullets will eventually run out but a blade stronger than titanium will last forever. Eli promised to have a regulare bladed weapon—one of her choice—made for Amy if they survive the day. She looks forward to finding a design that fits her, but Calavius' sword will do nicely until that day comes.

Everybody slides balaclavas over their heads and secure gold tinted goggles over their eyes. Amy bends down and tightens the laces of her bloodstained hiking boots. She could have worn the combat boots that came with the tactical gear she has on, but she found them uncomfortable. Besides, if she dies today, she wants to go with Aaron's dog tags around her wrist and the most comfortable boots on her feet. She wouldn't have it any other way.

"All right, puppies," Eli says into the mic on his headset, "don't forget what you've learned, and don't any of you try to be a hero. And most importantly, if Rosa, Kwesi, or I give you an order, you obey it! Understood?"

Lark and Stretch nod their heads. Bear, Jodie, Becca, and Cruz's voices respond, "Yes, sir," through the headsets.

Eli looks over to Amy and waits for her response.

Amy covers her mic and glares at Eli, as she mouths the word, "Puppies?"

Eli tilts his head to the side and releases a soft sigh that tells her to lighten up.

"I don't need to remind any of you," Lygia says, gripping one of Aleksi's short swords, confiscated from Cruz by Eli for her, "but I will. Only Elias and I or Lieutenant Granger and his team are to engage Sigodur. And under no circumstance is he to be killed. If he dies, any chance of finding a vaccine for the virus dies with him. I truly appreciate this brave thing that you are doing, but I don't want to lose any of you today. So please take care of yourselves and watch each other's backs. All right?"

"Yes, Imperator," all vampires—including Amy—respond.

"Two minutes to drop zone," the pilot warns.

Kwesi turns to Lark and fixes the strap under her chin to keep her helmet in place, then he air kisses her. Stretch growls and racks his M-4, still not accepting the fact that the few times he had been with Lark was just sex, not a relationship. Kwesi appears to ignore him.

Amy knows that the mega-alpha instinct that comes with vampire blood is urging him to defend his position as Lark's current mate. However, everyone knows that personal issues will have to be put on the back burner until today's mission is over. Whoever is left standing after that can deal with their crap, then.

Eli checks to make sure Amy's balaclava is secure over nose and mouth, then he adjusts the elastic strap of her goggles, so it isn't too tight around her head. When he picks up her helmet to put it on her, she shakes her head, refusing it. He smiles at her, knowing that she doesn't need it as much as Lark and the others. He nods, showing that he is confident that she won't get shot in the head.

Once Eli is satisfied that Amy's gear is on properly he turns and makes sure that Lygia's is secure as well. The gesture makes Lygia's day. Amy is indifferent to it. Eli's heart always beats normally when he is with Lygia, and Amy doesn't care if Lygia wants to delude herself. She is more concerned with making her brain tune down the smell of neoprene and whatever chemicals were used to ensure the hooded mask is totally liquid proof. It is an asset that she wished she had on the days her breath was bad and she wore her respirator to go looting.

"Sixty seconds to drop zone, Lieutenant Granger. Executing pattern Delta six on Arrowhead's mark."

"Copy that. All right people... and vampires. Hit 'em hard when we hit the roof. Camacho, make sure you Sutherland have that roof clear of hostiles when we come back up."

"Copy that, Lieutenant."

"Dr. Contaldi, make sure your people stay out of our way. If we need assistance, I'll ask for it."

"All right, Lieutenant Granger."

Eli gets up and slings his own AK-47 across his back, then he adjusts the

Desert Eagles in his shoulder holster. Once done, he stands at one of the open doors and surveys the campus that they are flying over.

Amy stands next to him and looks ahead of the five Black Hawks flying in a tight V-formation. Skipworth's Specter drone is shadowing them from above; there for observation and emergency air support, if necessary.

The two Apache helicopters that flew ahead flank the blue building known as The Sapphire. The roof is big enough to easily accommodate the hundreds of chompers gathered on the roof, staring at the choppers with their mouths gaping. The amount of chompers surrounding the building have increased as well. Amy figures that at least a thousand of them are insulating The Sapphire from anyone attempting to come in on the ground floor.

The Gatling guns mounted on the front of the attack choppers spit fire as their barrels rotate. Strings of bullets rip through multiple chomper bodies, sending heads and limbs flying in different directions before the slugs dig into the rooftop.

The six vampires on the roof, including the elusive Phoenix, return fire with their M-240 machine guns and draw the attention of the Gatling guns. Unlike the chompers, the vampires are anything but easy targets. They manage to dodge the zig-zagging lines of bullets coming at them, while the clueless chompers in the way are cut down.

The Apaches continue shooting as they move to evade the bullets being fired back at them. No one expects them to hit a vampire, just harass them as much as possible as the Black Hawks maneuver into position above the building.

"Go! Go! Go!" Granger commands.

Amy kisses Aaron's dog tags as Eli jumps out of the chopper, slipping his katars from their scabbards as he falls through the air. Amy immediately follows behind him. Plummeting the thirty feet between the helicopter and the roof, she sees the other vampires and the twelve soldiers in special armor raining out of the other Black Hawks.

Eli lands on both feet and quickly decapitates a chomper in a basketball jersey. Amy lands behind him, feeling less of an impact from the fall than she would feel from jumping off a chair. She immediately raises her sword and slashes a bearded chomper's skull in half. The other vampires land and immediately put their swords and machetes to work. Granger and his soldiers opt to open fire from the guns in the right arms of their MACEs. The net cannons slung across their backs are being saved for Sig—if they find him.

The roof is covered in bloody bodies—some dead, some only mangled from the Gatling guns. Eli sets his sights on Phoenix and begins to slash a path over to him. Amy swings her sword with killer precision, making sure she doesn't place her feet near a chomper's decapitated head as she follows behind. The roof is covered in bloody bodies—some dead, some only mangled from the Gatling guns.

Phoenix notices that Eli and two of Granger's soldiers are closing in on him. He smiles, then he whistles to the vampire closest to the door and twists his body out of the way of a barrage of bullets.

The Apaches continue to provide support from above, making more of a mess than anything. Amy feels a warning ripple across her back and she ducks out the way of a volley of bullets. She turns her head and sees a vampire with short, blonde dreadlocks charging at her, squeezing off more shots from his M-240. The beast within breaks out of the box Amy had stuffed it in, and it fills her with savage fury.

Amy roars as she breaks away from Eli and Lygia. She raises her blade and rushes towards the vampire who made the mistake of drawing her attention by shooting at her.

The M-240 rattles off more shots. She follows her instinct to evade the bullets, then she takes a page from Eli's playbook. Knowing that her response time significantly lessens as she gets closer to a gun, and the thick Kevlar vest that she has on is keeping her senses from being as keen as they would be otherwise, she kicks a chomper with no legs at the dreadlocks vampire and puts on a burst of maximum speed.

The vampire ducks to avoid being bowled over by the chomper turned projectile, and he visibly appears surprised by how fast Amy is upon him. He raises his machine gun to block the slim, double-edged blade from being buried in his skull but doesn't anticipate Amy twisting her body and changing the path of her swing in midair. Instead of coming straight down, she sets the sword on a course arcing off to her right and carries the momentum into an upswing. The blade glides through skin and muscle, moving from his left hip up to his right pec.

Amy adds another burst of speed to the motion already carrying her body into a spin. She turns completely around in a fraction of a heartbeat and lands her sword on his left pec and cuts another diagonal gash down to his right hip. The middle of the X that Amy carved into the dreadlocked vampire's body bulges, then separates like flaps and gives birth to a rush of viscera.

The vampire drops his weapon to clutch the glistening organs pouring out of him. Amy spins another 360 degrees, ending with her sword completely passing through the vampire's neck. Then she plows the tip of the blade into the head of a chomper that is crawling towards the tantalizing entrails in front of it.

Proud of herself, Amy smiles and takes a brief second to savor the scent of the warm vampire blood pooling at her feet. She listens to Lark and the others communicating with each other through their headsets. When she looks up, she sees Lark use Nicholi's sickle to finish off a chomper that just had its torso shredded.

Granger and his squad have broken into three groups and managed to corral three of Sig's minions. With a four-on-one advantage, the soldiers seem to have control of the vampires. Amy quickly draws her Beretta and empties half of the clip into the disabled chompers dragging their mangled bodies towards her, then she turns her attention back to Eli.

Eli and Lygia are moving closer to the door where the vampire that Phoenix whistled to is shooting at them. As for Phoenix, he is giving Granger and the three soldiers with him a much harder time than Granger expected.

Amy shoves the Beretta back into her new holster and moves to rejoin Eli and Lygia, but she pauses when she sees them stop and look at each other. The door suddenly bursts open and Amy doesn't believe her eyes when she sees two black panthers pounce onto the roof from the narrow stairway.

Her olfactory senses focus on the pungent scent of the panthers, mingled with what smells like a combination of baking soda, cheddar cheese, and chicken livers. Everyone knew the dangers involved, but chomper panthers never made the list of things to watch out for.

The first panther releases a bellowing roar and heads straight for Eli and Lygia. The other locks its eyes on Lark like it found something about her scent undeniable.

Amy thrusts the tip of her sword into the rooftop and raises her M-4. Her first instinct is to save Eli, but that proves to be unnecessary since the panther ends up running into a living buzz saw. Before severed sections of panther succumb to the pull of gravity, Amy smiles and trains the M-4 on the panther rushing past her to get to Lark.

Kwesi steps in front of Lark with Aleksi's other short sword ready to do some slicing and dicing of his own.

Amy opens fire and peppers the panther's torso with hot slugs. The panther jumps high in the air, twisting and twitching its body in the way felines do when startled. When it lands on all fours, it glares at her with rage and hunger in its eyes.

The bullet-ridden panther opens its jaws wide and growls at Amy. Amy growls back, forgetting that the balaclava is concealing her own fangs. It's just as well because the panther's fangs might as well be rhino horns compared to hers.

She fixes her aim at the big cat's head as it scampers towards her. The beast within makes Amy think about dropping the gun and taking the panther with her bare hands, but chances of catching a chomper panther by the toe and making it holler for her to let it go are slim, so she remains focused and squeezes the trigger when the panther gets within a dangerous ten feet. Bullets punch through the panther's head, sending blood spurting and chunks of flesh, brain, and patches of black fur flying.

Kwesi nods to say "Good job." Amy nods back, then she turns and sees Phoenix up-nod in Eli and Lygia's direction, signaling one of his comrades to run interference for him as he makes a break for the stairway.

Amy aims her rifle to block Phoenix's path before he gets to the door but

Lygia in advertently steps in her line of fire as she is about to squeeze the trigger.

Phoenix ducks into the doorway. Lygia starts to follow him with her short sword ready to strike him down, but she stops after a few steps and switches from attack to a defensive stance.

Amy hears the wailing and groaning of more chompers coming from the stairway. Seconds later a fresh horde pours out onto the roof, pushing and shoving each other out of the way.

CHAPTER THIRTY-THREE

Eli savagely wields his katars, dismembering and decapitating the vampire whom Phoenix wanted to slow him and Lygia down. Then he glances back at Amy. She can't see his eyes, and he doesn't say anything, but she knows that he is telling her to be careful. She nods her head as she moves closer, and the three of them commence to slaughtering. Bodies begin to pile up at their feet as they swing away at the swarm threatening to overwhelm them.

Amy has killed quite a few chompers at close range, but never has she been splattered and sprayed by so much of their tainted blood. She should be drenched, but the chemical that her gear is treated with turns the hot liquid into beads that roll off like crimson balls of mercury. Her boots, on the other hand, are soaked. She imagines how crimson her white socks must be at the moment.

Granger and the majority of his soldiers join Amy, Eli, and Lygia. The vampires slash chompers with swift strikes of their blades and the soldiers help decimate the horde by shooting bullets or punching holes through their skulls with the harpoon tips extended over their left wrists. Soon after, Kwesi, Lark and the others join the fight. Together they mow down the chompers until that section of the roof is thickly carpeted with bodies laying in a shallow lake of blood.

Granger and nine of his soldiers take the lead and enter the building, pulverizing the few chompers that trickle out along the way. Amy stays behind Eli as they make their way down the stairs. Her ability to see in the dark help her feel comfortable about advancing through the unlit stairway. She likes being able to look out for more panthers — lions, and tigers, and bears, too, if Sig has a sense of humor. But all she ends up seeing is a burst of muzzle flashes from Phoenix laying ambush fire on Granger and his men when they make the turn at the halfway point on the stairs between the roof and the tenth floor.

The soldiers return fire, continuing to proceed down the steps. Phoenix quickly retreats. Amy hears his footsteps moving at vampire speed away from the doorway.

Granger stops at the doorway to the tenth floor and sweeps his gun hand back and forth to make sure their entry is clear of attackers.

"Sig's not up here," Eli says as he moves past the soldiers.

"Hold it, bloodsucker!" Granger barks. "We sweep this place from the top down, that's the plan. There's a lot of ground to cover, and we get it done quicker by sticking together!"

"Elias," Lygia says, "how do you know Sig isn't on this floor?"

"My gut's tellin' me Sig is here, and he's somewhere further down," Eli says. "Not all the way down to the ground floor, maybe halfway there. I say we forget about Phoenix and go further down."

Lygia turns to Granger. "Lieutenant, if Elias says Sig's downstairs somewhere, he probably is. He has a gift for this kind of thing."

Granger shakes his head. "We're going top down to trap Sigodur or flush him out. If he's further down and he makes a break for it before we get to him, the Apaches will alert us, and then we'll change the plan. For now, we do it this way. And if this Phoenix is a big a part of Sig's operation as you think he is, we'll get him to spill intel or terminate him like the other bloodsuckers on the roof."

Eli growls and goes to move on to the next floor, but Lygia grabs his shoulder and says, "Granger is in command of this operation, Elias. We agreed to do this his way. If Sig's downstairs, we'll get to him. Right now I need you to follow the plan that has already been set until we have a reason not to."

Eli grits his teeth and growls again, but he submits to the words of the Imperator.

Amy would rather follow Eli's uncanny instinct. She is sure Lygia really wants to, herself. The only conclusion Amy can draw is that Lygia must be concerned about causing friction within the human/vampire alliance on the first joint mission between the two species.

"All right," Granger says. "We split when we hit this hallway. Diggs, make sure you stay in contact with me. And if you run into our primary target, keep him in check but do not try to capture him until we link back up."

"Copy that," Diggs replies.

The soldiers pour into the hallway first. Five go right, led by Diggs. The other five go left, with Granger bringing up the rare. Eli, Lygia, Amy, Lark, and Kwesi follow Granger and his men. Stretch, Bear, Cruz, Jodie, and Becca go the other way.

Amy's vision of the end of the hallway is obstructed by the soldiers, but her nose picks up the sickening odor of chompers. She also smells the strong scent of paint, as if it had recently been applied to the walls. The thing that puzzles her are the humming sounds she hears. They're not the high pitch annoyance that are emitted from the soldier's MACEs. Something about these hums reminds her of a refrigerator.

"Stop!" Eli yells, throwing his arms out to stop the vampires from advancing any further.

More chompers turn the corner at the end of the hallway and head straight for the soldiers. Granger and his men open fire on the chompers. Amy hears gunfire erupt behind her as well.

"Granger, fall back!" Eli says.

"Damn it, Kincade!" Granger says, turning around as his men continue to walk forward and shoot. "What now!"

Before Eli can explain what's on his mind, Phoenix appears from around the corner with his machine gun blazing. Granger's men return fire. Phoenix dips back around the corner, and the bullets end up devouring sheetrock where they strike.

The gunfire ceases, and everyone hears Phoenix laughing.

Granger and his men begin to move in on him.

Three explosions send balls of fire and flying debris into the hallway. Then thick, hissing jets of a whitish gas rapidly fill the corridor like an angry thunderhead intent on swallowing everything in its path.

Eli pushes Amy and Lygia with just enough force to make them move backwards without knocking them over.

Amy hears the panicked tones of Granger's men talking all at once in her headset and a bloodcurdling male's scream. Her back slams into Kwesi's solid physique and the whole group moves out of reach of the prowling mist. They end up all the way back at the stairway door where they bump into Cruz and the other vampires.

Granger shuffles backwards as well, slightly shrouded by the edge of the cloud until he escapes the limit of its reach. When he stops moving Amy notices a layer of frost on his MACE, with vapor mystically wafting from it like a popsicle on a hot summer's day.

Reports of malfunctioning MACEs flood the speaker in Amy's headset.

"It's a super coolant," Lygia says to Granger. "Something colder than liquid nitrogen. Maybe liquid carbon? Playtime had a department in this building dedicated to developing an efficient way to process gases into a liquid that was better at keeping the processors in their supercomputer from overheating. Whatever it is, it's cold enough to compromise the integrity of the carbon nanofiber mesh on your exoskeletons."

"That's gotta be why Sig chose this -" Eli cuts his sentence short and yells, "Everybody down!"

Gunfire erupts from both ends of the hallway.

Amy feels ripples on her head and chest.

Two hands land on Amy's shoulders—one Eli's, the other, Lygia's. They both push her down to the floor as whizzing swarms of heavy caliber bullets criss-cross the air above them, some ricochet off of Granger's MACE as he fires back at the unseen shooters.

Amy closes her eyes and focuses on the colorless image projecting in her mind from the sound waves colliding into her body. She sees Granger's men standing like statues, frozen in place by the super coolant. Bullet strikes knock pieces of their protective armor away, like the eggs shells being chipped off of eggs. With the armor compromised, the soldiers inside are exposed to the deadly mist creeping into their units. More bloodcurdling screams express the cruel agony they experience from beginning to flash-freeze.

Granger's men are spared further torture when Phoenix and his vampires fire grenades from the grenade launcher mounted under the muzzles of their M-240s. The semi-frozen soldiers blown apart in the blasts don't get a second thought from Amy. But she acknowledges the pang in her heart and is saddened to see that Bear did not escape the initial blast of super coolant. He was frozen solid by the time the bullets shattered him into icy chunks of meat and bones.

The gunfire stops and everybody springs back up to their feet. The heavy mist has begun settling on the floor, revealing massive holes blown through the walls and the remnants of eight long, metallic cylinders that once contained the super coolant, as well as what is left of the devices that were being used to keep it in its liquid state.

Granger begins to update Camacho and Sutherland on what just happened.

Amy looks at Jodie and sees that some of the hair sticking out from under the back of her balaclava has been crystallized by the cloud. Death's icy fingers had grazed Jodie but she, Becca, Stretch, and Cruz are all right. Amy notices Eli glance at Jodie's hair, too, then he looks down the hall where Bear was killed. His jaw muscles tighten. Amy can imagine how much he is blaming himself for losing one of Preacher's legares on his watch.

"Hey, Devil Badger!" Phoenix says from around the corner. "So, how does it feel to finally be soooo close to me, yet still so far?"

Eli sheathes one of his katars, freeing his right hand to draw one of the Desert Eagles in his shoulder holster. "I don't know. Why don't you stop running and ask me that to my face?"

Phoenix laughs. "Yeah, right! I'm having too much fun playing cat and mouse with you."

Eli sets his feet like he is about to attempt a leap over the mist undulating on the floor, but Lygia grabs his shoulder and shakes her head.

"Phoenix, you have my word that you will not be hurt," Lygia says. "Now step out from behind that corner and talk to us."

"Ahhh, yes, Pelagius' daughter. Lygia, right? Sorry, baby, no real vampire is gonna follow your orders. You and your pops don't even want us to have our fangs. It's our right to be what we are, and our fangs are a symbol of our power and freedom. Besides, you chose to hold hands with the enemy, even after you learned that those parasites used Sig to make a super virus meant to kill every one of us. So, as far as I'm concerned, there's nothing to talk about. Lucky for you, I'm not the boss."

Amy hears footsteps approaching from the stairway. They don't cause her concern because of the high pitch hum accompanying the footfalls. The number of heartbeats around both corners does warrant her attention. Phoenix has four people with him, all most likely vampires, and there are five other heartbeats on the other side of the hall.

"Screw this!" Granger says, using the tip of his armored foot to test the evaporating pool of coolant. "Get out here now, bloodsucker! If I come over there to get you, I'm tearing your ass to pieces, then I'm going to make what's left of you take me to your boss!"

"Aww, please tell me that's Lieutenant Trent, Fuck Face, Granger," Phoenix says. "I heard a lot about you. By the way, how's the family?"

Granger raises his right arm like he wants to fire, but he maintains enough control to keep from wasting his bullets.

Camacho finishes making his way down the stairs. Eli signals to him that there are hostiles at either end of the hallway, as well as a dangerous substance on the floor.

"If you guys are done having fun with our pet chompers," Phoenix says, "Sig's downstairs in the fifth-floor lounge waiting for y'all to join him. You got a clear path from those stairs down to where he is. Nobody's going to make a move on you, as long as you guys don't make a move on any of us. So, play nice, and I'll see you there."

Amy hears Phoenix and the others begin to walk away. She turns to Eli to see what he wants to do.

Eli roves his gaze from Lark to Kwesi and on to the other vampires, then he settles on Amy. "I've already lost one of you, and I don't want to lose anymore. I shouldn't have brought you guys along in the first place. Get back up to the roof. Lygia and I will take it from here."

"No fuckin way!" Amy says. "We knew what we were gettin' into when we signed up for this, and there's no way in hell I'm taking a seat now. Bear would tell you the same thing, and you know it! We're vampires, and we stand together, even if we all fall. We came here together, and we stay together 'til the end. That's the way it is!"

All of the other vampires nod in agreement.

"Are you guys sure?" Lygia asks. "No one expected this trap that Sig set up, and we don't know what else he has up his sleeves."

"Hey, we didn't expect frickin' chomper panthers either, but we took care of that," Amy says.

"Right," Kwesi says. "And not knowing what Sig has up his sleeves is all the more reason why you need us. It's like Amy basically said: All for one and one for all."

"Are you bloodsuckers kidding me!" Granger grouses.

"Stay out of this!" Lygia snarls. "My first responsibility is to protect my people. The one that I failed is one too many, and I cannot ask them to put themselves in further danger."

"I don't care if they go or not. We need to figure out what's Sigodur's game. Unless you're going to tell me that you're planning to just waltz down to the fifth floor, hoping he's there and you don't end up in another trap."

"I don't waltz," Eli says. "But yeah, I'm heading straight down there, like I shoulda done in the first place when my gut told me to."

"And what are you going to do when you get yourself into something that you can't get yourself out of?"

"I don't think we have to worry about that, at least not yet. Sig knew your game plan, and he had those canisters put in the walls for you guys, not us. And if his flunky says he's down there waiting for us, then he is. You and your boys go about this however you want. We, 'bloodsuckers,' got this."

"All right." Lygia admiringly places a hand on each of her vampire's shoulder one at a time, including Amy. She puts her hand on Eli's shoulder last, then nods her head and says, "We stand together, and we're all leaving together. So let's do what we came here to do."

The vampires file out into the stairway, led by Eli and Lygia.

Granger looks at Camacho and shakes his head, but he reluctantly follows behind.

CHAPTER THIRTY-FOUR

After eviscerating and decapitating an acolyte, taking on an infected panther and butchering chomper after chomper, Amy feels strange walking down four flights of stairs without coming across so much as a cockroach to crush underfoot. The entity lurking within her had been content with the carnage of the battle on the roof, and now it is eager to get back in the thick of it.

The path from the tenth floor on down is clear, just as Phoenix said it would be. Amy and the other vampires do detect the scent of recently painted walls in the other hallways above, as well as more chompers and vampires. Chances are, Sig had all the entrances above the fifth-floor booby trapped, probably the ones below, as well.

On the fifth floor, Amy follows Eli and Lygia down the hallways leading to the lounge from the stairwell—according to the signs posted. The walls and doors of the offices they go past are all made of clear glass, some tainted by grime or crusted blood. The office spaces inside are vast, with areas reserved for banks of workstation computers, conference tables, and huge monitors to display presentations. Most of the space, however, seems dedicated to activities like yoga, Karaoke, and Virtual Reality gameplay.

A right turn takes them to another hallway leading to a room at the end with 5 LOUNGE written on the door in multicolored letters. The door and walls of the lounge are made of glass, too, but it has a frosted finish to it that denies any view of the inside.

Amy's enhanced hearing picks up a plethora of sounds. There is a lot of video game gunfire, reminiscent of the real battle that just took place above. She also hears a the bop of paddles hitting a ping-pong ball and the hollow rap of it bouncing across a table. Throughout all of it, there is the flutter of multiple voices engaged in different conversations.

There are too many heartbeats for Amy to count or keep track of. The aroma of hot electronics, a bit like the scent of cinnamon, is thick to her sense of smell. She tunes it down and skims over the scents identifying male and female by odors, body sprays or perfumes, and hair products. She also picks up the strong presence of potato chips, nachos, candy and other forms of junk food that she misses greatly. And she can't ignore the smell of cheddar cheese, baking soda, and chicken livers.

There is also a musky odor. It's not as overpowering as what she smelled from the panthers, but she expects to find some kind of infected animal inside the lounge.

Amy keys in on the footsteps approaching the door from the other side. Eli and the others do, too, and they all raise their weapons.

The door slowly opens. A svelte young girl with clumpy bangs, dark eye makeup and piercings through her eyebrows smiles and says, "Man, you guys are really uptight."

"You think!" Eli says and snatches her wrist. "You're human?"

"Duh! I'm not old enough to be a vampire yet, and Sig says I'm too cute to become a chomper."

"And where is Sig?"

"Chillin' by the window. C'mon in, he's been waiting for y'all." The girl turns around and flaps her fingers for everyone to follow her.

The lounge is a huge open space. Off to the left, the wall is lined with 20 large monitors displaying different virtual realities; some set in space, some medieval Earth, others underwater, while some depict the world the way it used to be before it became chomper paradise. In front of each monitor is a person wearing a VIVE virtual reality headset, holding the controllers used to manipulate the avatars in the virtual world they are experiencing an adventure in. To the right are long tables with computers and monitors on them. Each table seems to be dedicated to the team of gamers sitting at them, respectively, talking trash to each other and their opponents. The wall behind them is top to bottom whiteboard, drenched in a hodgepodge of computer code, strange symbols with letters or words under them, and numbers that look like longitude and latitude, as well as GPS coordinates. Drawn directly in the middle of the board is a set of teeth with vampire fangs; the word FREEDOM written in graffiti above it.

Besides the gamers playing VR or teamed up at the tables, there are other humans and vampires speckled around the room in small groups. Some playing ping pong or air hockey, others chow down on junk food at a juice bar, while others lie reposed on beanbag chairs—including Phoenix's fountain, Karma, whom Amy remembers from the drone surveillance footage.

Amy estimates somewhere between seventy-five and a hundred of them in all, varying in age from mid-teens to late twenties. The majority of them look like the type of people that the pre-chomper society would have judged to be misfits and outcasts because of their tattoos, piercings and clothing style ranging from geek to punk to emo. Most surprising of all to her is that at least half of them are sporting fangs like hers, a direct violation of The Synodus' rules.

The far wall of the room, the one straight ahead, offers a clear view of the east side of Playtime's campus—the same direction Skipworth approached The Sapphire from three days before. The glass is fully transparent, unlike the opaque blue on the other side that obstructed the drone from seeing the activity in the lounge and other rooms in the building.

Phoenix is by the glass wall, holding two katanas in his hands as he stands next to a black leather La-Z-Boy. Amy can't see the person in the chair, but she's willing to bet her life she knows who he is. He is the main source of the Puissance virus' scent that she is smelling. Oddly enough, the musky animal scent is coming from the chair, too.

Everyone except for the gamers stop what they are doing. There are plenty of weapons within reach, but no one makes a move. The only thing that Amy takes as hostility is the way some of the male vampires sniffing the air as they leer at her and Lark.

Relying on her hyper-tactile sense to warn her of danger, Amy accompanies her magister and their Imperator into the room. The other vampires in their raiding party follow closely, with Granger and Camacho bringing up the rear. The path between the door and the window wall is wide enough for everyone to walk side by side if they wanted to, and still have plenty of room to spare. But they move no more than three wide, eyes set on their main targets while keeping guard of their flanks and behind.

The La-Z-Boy swivels around and Sig smiles as he pats the chimpanzee sitting on his lap. "It took you a little longer than I expected, but I knew I could count on you to find me, Elias."

Seeing Sig in the flesh renews a feeling that Amy had been missing. She knows all too well what he is capable of. He is a presence to be feared. That notion goes far beyond the creepy way he looks stroking the head of a chomper chimpanzee.

Granger and Camacho reach for their net cannons, prompting Sig's allies in the room to arm themselves in response.

The chimp bristles, but doesn't show more aggression.

Sig signals for his people to stand down, then he says, "Come now, Trent. The two of you against all of us? Think about that one."

"Nothing to think about, bloodsucker. You're coming with us. And when we got what we need from you, I'm going to make you pay for killing my brother!"

Sig echoes Granger's words in a mocking mumble. Then he smiles and aims his index finger at the chimp and says, "If it's any consolation to you, I named my friend here Little Mikey, after your brother, Michael."

"You know what," Granger lowers his net cannon, "why don't we just do this? Me and you, right here, right now."

Sig chuckles. "All in good time, Fuck Face. Right now I need to have a talk with my old friends."

Lygia turns around, and says, "I'm sorry about your brother, Lieutenant, but please pull it together. If Sig wants to talk, we'll talk. There are questions that I need answers to, and I'm not going to get them in the middle of a fight."

"We didn't come here for a Q-'n'-A!" Granger snarls. "You can do all the talking you want when we get him back to the lab."

Eli pulls the balaclava and goggles off of his head. Then he turns around and glares at Granger with fury storming in his spooky blue eyes. "Would you please shut up! Like she said, we got questions that need answers, and I'm not going to let you fuck this up more than it already is!"

Amy and the others remove their headgear, as well.

Camacho looks over to Granger, nods his head, then lowers his net launcher.

Knowing that the soldiers can communicate on a separate frequency, Amy wonders what Granger has just told Camacho, besides an order to comply. She trusts her intuition telling her that a plan was made between them and Sutherland, who is still up on the roof.

Sig slowly claps his hands, and says, "Well said, brother. Man, I've missed you. You, too, Lygia; Kwesi. Shame you guys killed my panthers but well done, Eli and..., Amy."

Amy's heart booms in her chest at the mention of her name.

Eli's eyes widen.

Lygia shoots a venomous look, accusing her of treason.

"How do you know her name?" Eli says.

"There are eyes and ears all around you, my friend."

Tension falls on the group like an anvil from the sky. Amy darts her eyes around and sees Lark, Stretch, Cruz, Jodie, Becca, even Kwesi exchange suspicious glances, but nobody says a word.

"Plus," Sig says, "I have a special connection with chompers since they're turned by the virus that was created in me."

"What do you mean?" Lygia asks.

Sig knocks the top of his head with his knuckles. "After Doctor De Reske opened up my skull he put more in here then he bargained for. I can see through them, hear through them, feel what they feel. And they follow whatever I desire for them to do. Well, the ones close by, at least. Takes more concentration when there's a lot of them, but as you saw outside, it's do-able."

"Telepathy?" Lygia says, talking to herself more than to anyone else. "The senex might be close enough to The Primus, or maybe the concentrated doses of radiation from the Genesis Halo on the frontal lobe? Could it have mutated or activated...? Tell me when you first felt it."

Sig tells Lygia that after a couple of hours under Dr. De Reske's machine he felt like he had died. He was no longer in his body. He felt like he was everywhere. Then he realized that he was within every vampire who had conscious thought.

Submerged in the ethos of every vampire, Sig saw everything they saw, heard everything they heard, and was privy to every thought that crossed their minds—including secrets. He knew which vampires were loyal to Pelagius, who conspired with acolytes and who were full-fledged disciples of Hadrianus. And having access to the Imperator, himself, Sig also discovered the things that Pelagius shared with very few or had kept completely to himself—including the fact that he allowed his daughter and the vampire he loved like a son to break a cardinal law of The Synods. Being a part of Eli and Lygia's being gave him confirmation of what he learned from Pelagius, as well as the location of a secret buried in the atrium of the safe house.

Sig's connection to all of the other vampires didn't last more than a few hours before Dr. De Reske's experiments changed him. After Dr. De Reske and Dr. Gianacola managed to create the Puissance virus in his brain, he felt as if he was no longer part of the vampire's world. His magister to legare link with Kelly, and his legare to magister link with Trajanus, was different. He knew the bloodline connection still existed between them, but he no longer felt it.

Sig remained in a state of isolation until the first primate was infected with the virus. It was then that he found a new connection with another living being, and a way of communicating with feeling and no words. The connection was the same with the other primates that were experimented on, as well as Kelly and the two other vampires who had been captured with Sig.

"That's how I got cool with little Mikey here," Sig says, rising from the chair. He sits the chimp back in the seat and continues talking. "It's also how I felt everything that Kelly felt when they infected her with the virus that they made in me. She was in so much pain, and she was so scared. And there was nothing that I could do for her, or even Raphael and Simon when they went through it, too."

"Wrong!" Eli growls, practically startling those who were hanging on Sig's words with fingers of sympathy. "What you were supposed to do was mercifully take care of Kelly the moment she went rogue. And if you went rogue first, then you knew it was only going to end badly, so you shoulda gotten away from her."

Sig nods his head. "You're right, Eli. I should've taken care of Kelly. But when you love somebody as much as I loved her, you stay with them and try your best to keep them from going too far over the edge. I pray that you never have to go through that. I know you think you can do it now, but if the day comes that you have to slay Lygia or Amy, it's not going to be that simple. Trust me, your knives will be the heaviest things in the world if you ever have to raise them against your magister or your legare."

A sense of guilt makes Amy focus on maintaining her heartbeat. The vampiric energy inside of her is lusting for violence and blood, and she doesn't know if that means she is close to going over the edge like Kelly did. She is willing to accept death from one of Elis's katars if she ever goes rogue and it comes to that, but she doesn't want to think about that now.

"Sig," Lygia says, and cautiously approaches him. "I know how much you loved Kelly, but you went too far."

Amy, Eli and the rest of the group move with Lygia in closing the gap between them and Sig.

"I know," Sig says. "I can't change what happened, but I wanted you guys here to make things right."

"Good," Lygia responds. "Then you can help me undo some of the damage. Since the virus was created in you, I should be able to come up with a vaccine with your help. Maybe I can even find a cure."

"Stop it, Lygia," Sig says, shaking his head. "As much as you want to believe you can save them, you know you can't. There's no cure for the infected. They're too far gone. And any vaccine you come up with will turn humans into vampires. We can't have that. Besides, we all have bigger problems. Our God is on the verge of rising up and devouring us all. He wants back every piece of him that's in all of us."

Lygia stops within a few feet from Sig. "Explain."

Being within striking distance has Amy anxious. She would never make a move without Eli or Lygia's order, but it's tempting with the advantage to pounce on Sig and subdue him before he can even reach for his sword.

Sig nods his head. "When I had that connection to every vampire alive I also felt something else. I didn't know it at first, but I realized that it was The Primus. I was in its consciousness, too."

Sig tries to put what he believes into words as best as he possibly can. He understands The Primus to be a creature made of living energy, not of our world. About two hundred thousand years ago a catastrophic event created a small rift in the barrier between our universe and the one that was home of The Primus. The rift was only open for a flash of a moment; enough time for The Primus to be sucked through and trapped here. Unable to survive in an environment that doesn't have an electric charge, The Primus sought refuge in the first thing that it found with electricity in it: a Neanderthal.

After the creature adapted the Neanderthal's body to accommodate its presence, The Primus learned that it could sustain its own life-force energy by devouring the life-force energy contained in the blood flowing through the bodies of the creatures in this world. The ancestors of modern humans were the most desirable. However, The Primus realized that humans and most other animals would soon face extinction if kept trying to satisfy its appetite while in it's conscious state. So it was left with one option: go into a form of stasis that his species is capable of.

Before going into stasis, T he Primus turned a few of the Neanderthals who worshipped it into the first generation of vampires by transferring a part of itself to them through the blood of it's host. The transfer established a link between them that did more than kept them connected. The link allowed The Primus to receive sustenance whenever his legares fed. Part of whatever life-force energy they took in was transmitted through the link; the foundation of why magisters sense if their legares aren't feeding enough. The connection between The Primus, his legares, and every vampire throughout the bloodlines makes them continually feel the hunger of their original creator as they explore the world, serving as its eyes and ears.

When Homo sapiens began to be the dominant species, The Primus made a Neanderthal pass on his bloodline to one of them: the senex now known as Anaximenes. He was given the set of rules that all vampires still follow today. A time came when the vampire Neanderthals had to bury themselves and sleep, too. Although hibernating, they still served as a conduit between the legares they created and The Primus. Every generation of the bloodline passes energy through their creator to sustain The Primus.

As humans evolved, The Primus had Anaximenes pass his bloodline to Pelagius, then made him and the other vampires who didn't look like modern humans go into hibernation. That is why vampires are what they are. The small part of The Primus within them grants powers and eternal life, and in turn, they give a part of their energy to sustain it.

Amy flashes back to the pizza party in Lygia and Kristin's lab on the hospital ship. Kristin mentioned using a modulator to disrupt whatever the energy is that give vampiric cells their special quality, and the energy doesn't operate on a principle of physics that she understood yet, but when they do, it would be a good start to return a vampire to human. If not for the looming danger in the room, Amy would've liked for Kristin to be present to learn that her theory was fairly accurate.

"Plausible theory," Lygia says, fascinated by Sig's story. "But what makes you think it's true?"

"Because I know it is," Sig says. "I lost the connection I had with The Primus, but since I took on the power of the senex you guys were hiding, I catch flashes of its consciousness from time to time. Besides, I haven't had to feed on many humans since those homeless people in the subway tunnel. Every one infected by the virus passes a little of their energy to me when they feed. I'm basically The Primus of the Chompers."

"Sig," Kwesi says, "that's crazy, man."

"No, old friend. It's true. And here's another truth: The Primus is tired of sleeping. It wants to rise from its slumber and take its life force back from all of us. Then it's going to feed on a few thousand humans, itself. When it's satisfied, it's going to start a new bloodline with just one, like it once did with the first Neanderthal it turned."

"Bullshit!" Eli grouses and moves forward aggressively, but is stopped by Lygia placing a hand on his chest.

"No, brother," Sig says, unconcerned by Eli's hostility. "It's true, and if we don't find The Primus and destroy it before it gains the strength it needs, we'll all be doomed."

Footsteps from the hallway cause Amy to turn her head towards the doors to the lounge. She focuses her hearing and picks up two heartbeats. She also manages to isolate their scents; one a man, the other a woman.

Eli and Lygia look back at the door, too. Then they turn and stare at each other.

"You smell him, too?" Eli asks.

With a confused expression, Lygia nods her head.

Amy loathes not knowing what Eli and Lygia are talking about. A stroke of envy runs through her as she thinks about how much Eli and Lygia are behaving more like partners than she and Eli are. She also knows that he and Lygia have been in situations like this throughout the decades that they were both regulares, so it is only natural that they are as in tune as they are. Still, it gets to her.

The lounge door opens and a middle-aged man with his hair pulled back into a short ponytail steps into the room. He is wearing black slacks and a white shirt with the top two buttons open. Around his neck is a necklace with a medallion on it, just like the one that Eli ripped from around Calavius' neck. And in his right hand, he loosely grips the handle of a gladius—the distinctive short sword of an ancient Roman soldier.

The man is accompanied by a woman with long blonde hair and blue-green eyes. The little black dress she has on makes her look like she is ready for a dinner party, although she appears nervous as she eyes Granger and Camacho.

"Pelagius' precious daughter and his most beloved dog have finally arrived," the man says, making his way into the room. "And accompanied by government soldiers. What has this world come to?"

Amy knows that the newcomer has to be a vampire, and she gets the answer to her question of who he is when she hears Kwesi whisper the name, "Titus."

CHAPTER THIRTY-FIVE

Eli turns and glances at Amy. From the expression on his face, he regrets bringing her along. The situation was already dangerous, now there is an unknown variable in the equation. Sig and the acolytes were going to be enough to keep his hands full. Now that Titus is in the mix, no one knows how things are going to play out.

"Doctor Gianacola?" Granger says, addressing the woman with Titus. His tone confused but laced with anger.

Dr. Gianacola shrinks behind Titus, then she nods her head and simply says, "Lieutenant."

"You're as much responsible for my brother's death as that monster over there!" Granger says, raising his gun hand. "You're a traitor to your country and a traitor to your species, as well, I see. I have every right to execute you on the spot!"

Titus completely shields Dr. Gianacola with his body and raises his Gladius. "Lieutenant, Granger, is it? I wouldn't do that if I were you. The only reason you're alive right now is that I'm allowing it. So don't provoke me. You have been warned."

Granger lowers his arm and remains oddly silent.

Titus smirks and begins to escort Dr. Gianacola around Amy and her group.

"You're here," Lygia says, tightening the grip on her short sword as her eyes follow Titus' every step. "How did you get out of Germany, much less travel all the way here with the borders locked down?"

"Fair question," Titus says. "The answer is, I was here before everything was sealed off. I had to come back when Elias got too close to my young protege over there."

Eli glances at Phoenix, then returns his attention to Titus. "You were in Seattle?"

"Yes. I almost had to cut you from the bloodline there, but lucky for you the Puissance virus came along and changed everything."

Amy understands the rage she sees brewing in Eli. What surprises her is the spaced-out look on Lygia's face. Whatever's going through her mind has her looking like she has checked out.

Eli lowers his head and shakes it. "It was you. It's always been you, either steering me in the wrong direction or giving the heads up to the ranking acolytes that I've been after. You're their new leader."

Titus greets Phoenix by placing a hand on his shoulder and nodding approvingly. Then he stands beside Sig and says, "Don't feel too bad, Elias. It took me a century to build a network of vampires I could trust to be patient enough to wait until our time came and to keep our secret, even if it meant self-sacrifice. I didn't even convert Calavius until a few years ago. Speaking of which, I stopped feeling my dear magister a few days ago. I assume you had something to do with that since you have a way of finding and executing a lot of my followers. Kudos to you on that."

Lygia's brow furrows, and she says, "You've hunted down acolytes, yourself. I've seen you interrogate and execute them. You were more brutal than any regulare ever was."

Phoenix smirks and says, "It's called commitment to the cause, baby. We're ready to die for what we believe in, if it comes to that. Can you say the same?"

Eli trains his glare on Sig. "You been with him all his time, too?"

"No," Sig responds. "I didn't find out about him until they did that experiment on me and I was in his head, too. I did contact him after I escaped because I was enraged about Kelly and I wanted revenge. But the things I've learned from my connection to The Primus changed my priorities. That's why I need you. You're going to help me find The Primus."

Eli laughs. "Even if I took you seriously, there's no finding The Primus. I tried that. Didn't work."

"But you didn't have the information in the Saudi scroll. Sig points to the gamer teams sitting at the long tables. "I gave them what little I understood from being in The Primus' thoughts, and they used the supercomputer in this place to decipher the language in the scroll. It was written by a first generation vampire, describing the place he would go to pay homage to his sleeping god. We've narrowed it down to an area close to the Saudi-Iraqi border, and I'm counting on you to pinpoint it from there."

"Listen to him, Elias," Titus says. "I wouldn't have gotten the scroll for him if I didn't believe we were all in danger. I know we have our differences to deal with, but that can wait until we've taken care of this most important matter."

"The scroll," Lygia whispers. "You're the one who gave it to Sig?"

Titus nods his head.

"It wasn't just Calavius...." Lygia's eyes ignite with fury. "It was you! You helped him to killed my father!"

Lygia moves forward, and Sig gently places a hand on her shoulder to stop her.

Eli edges closer, not in full attack mode, but ready to pounce is Sig makes a malicious move.

Sig notices Eli. Phoenix and Titus do, as well. Amy, Kwesi, Lark and the others ready their blades and keep a cautious eye on the young misfits keeping cautious eyes on them. Just one cagey move from either side is all it will take for a tsunami of violence to hit the lounge, but everyone remains balanced on the pinnacle of tension.

"Lygia," Titus says, "I loved Pelagius like he was my own brother. And just like him, I love every one of our kind like they are my own children. After what happened to Sig, we needed to make a change before the humans destroyed everything in this world, and us along with it. Even now, with more than half of them either dead or infected, they're still on the verge of war with the option of nuking everything left alive. As much as our blood makes us want to dominate everything, even if we go rogue, we would never go as far as to destroy everything, including ourselves."

Lygia points the tip of her sword at Titus. "You killed my father!"

"I tried to reason with him after Sig told me what happened to him and Kelly. He knew that we couldn't trust the humans, but he still wanted to keep the truce with them. I did my best to make him understand that we would never again have another opportunity like this. Right now the humans are corralled like the cattle they are, and the time is primed for us to strike. I truly am sorry about Pelagius and all of the other vampires loyal to him who died at The Civitas, but sacrifice is the lifeblood of a revolution. This is the dawn of our era, Lygia. We can do this together. You can be Imperator, and I will serve as your Proconsul, if only you agree to see it our way."

Lygia makes her move in a flash. She raises her short sword to strike Titus.

"Lygia, wait!" Sig says, snatching Lygia's wrist before she can bring her blade down on Titus.

One of Eli's katars slices through the air.

Sig releases Lygia and steps back before he loses his arm.

Phoenix tosses Sig his katana, which he catches and sets in position to defend himself.

In that instant, gunshots ring out as Granger and Camacho open fire on the acolytes charging at them.

Amy's warning system alerts her of danger by making her feel a thin line on her skin, stretching diagonally from one side of her neck down across her back. She hunches down and turns around, raising her sword to block the machete that was going to strike her and gasps when she sees that it's not one of Sig's people who just tried to kill her.

"What the hell, man?!" Amy grouses, as she pushes Cruz away from her.

"I tried to get you alone to bring you over to our side, but you're too loyal to the regulare," Cruz says, then continues his attack.

Amy feels a true appreciation for the hard training that Eli put her and the others through. Even though he had only a couple days to drill instructions into her head, the things that he thought her comes as automatically as her ability to shoot accurately under pressure.

Amy stays on the defense, altering her form every so often to avoid being struck by a bullet. Because of her hyper-tactile sense, she doesn't have to look around to see what's going on. Eli and Sig are fiercely going at each other, as Phoenix stalks Eli with his own blade poised to strike. Lygia is savagely attacking Titus to avenge her father. Lark, Kwesi, Stretch, Granger, and Camacho have their hands full with the acolytes converging on them with blades and guns—including Jodie and Becca, who have revealed whose side they are really on. And Dr. Gianacola is being whisked through the mob by the purple haired Karma, leading her to safety.

Cruz keeps up his aggressive attack. Amy remains focused on defending herself as she pretends that his strength and speed might be too much for her. In her peripheral, she sees Kwesi run his short sword through an acolyte's belly and slash all the way through the right side of his torso, then immediately turn around to chop another acolyte's arm off. She knows that Kwesi will be all right, but Lark is being doubled-teamed by Jodie and Becca.

Amy reluctantly takes her mind off of Lark and everything else going on around her as Cruz tries to bombard her with a series of high, chopping strikes. She lowers herself a little further each time she blocks his machete, then she springs up, swinging her blade hard at the oncoming machete.

With her full strength behind the force of her swing, Curz's machete is cut in half like it was made of plastic and the tip of Amy's blade gouges open Cruz's cheek. Cruz steps back and presses his hand against his bleeding wound, his eyes dart at his broken machete, then at Amy.

"This is a regulare blade, stupid!" Amy says and advances on Cruz with her sword held low to strike in an upward angle. "Now, get ready to taste it, bitch!"

Cruz tries to block with what is left of his machete, but Amy strikes with enough force for her sword to knock it out of his hand and continue on, cutting his head in half from the left side of his chin up to his right ear.

Before Cruz's body drops at her feet, Amy glances at Eli and sees him step out of the way of Sig's blade. Phoenix attacks from behind, swinging his own katana like a baseball bat—and Eli's head is the ball. Eli throws up an arm, and there is a clank when the handle of his katar extended over his wrist and forearm blocks Phoenix's strike.

Eli kicks Phoenix square in the groin, inciting a howl like a wounded dog as Phoenix flies backwards. Then he turns around in time to block a downward strike from Sig by throwing his katars up and together to form an X, like scissor blades.

"Stop this, Elias!" Sig growls, imposing his strength through his sword, attempting to force Eli's arms down. "I'm stronger and faster than you, and you're going to make me hurt you if you keep this up."

The slashes on the front and back of Eli's ta ctical jacket and the bleeding wounds in the center of them show Amy where Sig has already struck him with his blade. She begins to worry. Sig is quicker and more powerful than Calavius was, and it shows. She fears for Eli's safety, but doesn't lose hope in him.

"Doesn't matter," Eli replies. "I'm going to avenge Pelagius, even if I have to die trying!"

"Whoa. I wasn't on Pelagius' side, but I didn't know they were going to kill him or destroy The Civitas, either."

"The hell you didn't!"

"It's true. Titus told me he will get the scroll for me. He never said how. Part of the reason I brought you here-"

"Mutha-fuckaaaa!" Phoenix bellows as he comes in, swinging his sword in a clumsy, downward arc.

Eli gives in to Sig's pressure, allowing this arms to be forced down low enough for the katana's sharp edge to almost kiss his forehead. But to Sig's surprise, Eli erupts with a burst of power, pushing the katana up and away.

Sig stumbles back a few steps, giving Eli the opportunity to turn around and block Phoenix's sword with one of his katars and drive the other into Phoenix's head, starting under his chin until the top of the blade pops through his fiery red hair. He kicks Phoenix in the chest and rips the katar free out through the young acolyte's face. Then he spins back around in time to move his other katar in position to stop Sig from eviscerating him.

Amy's heart wants her to assist Eli, but her conscience knows that Lark needs her help more than he does. Her heart also tells her what Eli would want her to do, so she turns around and hisses, "Bitcheees!" loud enough for Jodie and Becca to hear, then she makes her move.

Jodie sees Amy coming, and she leaves Becca to handle Lark while she takes on Amy.

More acolytes, armed to the teeth, pour in from the hallway through the frame where the frosted glass door was before it was shattered to thousands of pieces by bullets. Amy estimates that the size of the mob is now double what it was before the melee began.

Riding a wave of rage, Amy allows the beast to come out and play, releasing full control of her sword to it.

Like Cruz, Jodie is only armed with a machete, and it doesn't have a prayer against the magnesium alloy making up Calavius' regulare blade. She tries to use it to block an arching high strike from Amy. Half the machete blade falls away and Amy's double-edged sword slams into Jodie's left shoulder, cutting through her rib cage and spine before it exits above her right hip.

Jodie's eyes open wide and her mouth gapes as the top section of her torso begins to slide down the slant. Amy finishes turning her into a carnal collage by wildly swinging her blade to slash another diagonal through the other side of Jodie's body, then she hacks off Jodie's arms and legs and wraps the brutality up with a clean beheading.

While Jodie literally falls to pieces, Amy has to twist and duck out of the way of a barrage of bullets. Then she sets her eyes on the acolyte in a Motor Head concert T-shirt trying to hit her with 9mm slugs from an old Israeli Uzi. She sets her feet to take on the metal-head but pauses when she realizes that she is hearing the rotors of the Apaches helicopters getting closer. Every vampire in the room seems to realize it, as well. The majority of them turn towards the window wall, granting the view of the campus and the scores of chompers waiting outside.

The Apaches come into sight, both float in sideways from opposite ends of the lounge's window walls. The Gatling guns mounted on the front of each begin to spin with a sickening whir.

Sig and Eli stop fighting at the same time, and together they turn and yell to everyone, "Watch out!"

CHAPTER THIRTY-SIX

The Gatling guns on the Apaches begin to blaze rapid fire.

Segments of the glass wall shatter one after another as the rotating barrels sweep back and forth.

Vampires duck, dodge and scatter to avoid the large caliber slugs streaming in at high velocity. Huge holes punch through Sig's La-Z-Boy spitting tufts of upholstery stuffing out the exit holes. The ping pong and air hockey tables fly apart, flinging debris in all directions. Bowls full of potato chips and candy, as well as cups and bottles containing sugary drinks explode when bullets tear through them. The bean bag chairs are pitch around the room like a soccer ball kicked by an invisible giant; tiny spheres of styrofoam spew from each one like baby spiders desperately bursting forth from their egg sacks.

The lack of training in Titus' acolytes is revealed when they start falling victim to the Gatling guns. Amy sees massive holes explode in the T-shirt of the metal-head, ejecting chunks of tissue and blobs of blood as it knocks him off of his feet and sends him flipping over what's left of the pool table. He is one of the lucky ones. Other Acolytes lose their heads or limbs right before her eyes. Almost half of them end up dead or severely injured within fifteen seconds.

A bullet grazes Lark's shoulder as she dives out of the line of fire from one of the guns. The Kevlar covering her skin is no match for the heavy caliber slugs spitting from the Gatling guns. It's just one of the close calls that she, Kwesi and Stretch experience.

Eli and Sig evade bullets much easier than the others. But that soon changes when one of the Apaches concentrates most of its fire on them.

Lygia and Titus are the only ones still fighting, manipulating their bodies or momentarily splitting apart to avoid the bullets that fly in their direction, then they resume combat. Lygia's rage is evident. Titus, on the other hand, seems calm and casual.

The chimpanzee, Little Mikey, is pinging around like he is made of super bouncy rubber. Amy isn't sure if the chimp can feel sensations on its skin like she can, or if instinct alone is guiding it to stay out of the way of the zigzagging lines of bullets.

The only people in the lounge who are not under threat of being cut down by the Gatling guns are Granger and Camacho, due to the impenetrable shells of their MACEs. They continue to punish the acolytes who dared to challenge them, mostly by way of puncturing their bodies and heads with the tip of their harpoons.

The Gatling guns continue swaying left and right, spraying entire room with lead. Amy devotes the majority of her attention to the sensations on her skin, focused on the ripples warning of a bullet strike. She keeps herself from acquiring any new holes as she makes her way closer to Lark. She hopes that her stronger perception will help the both of them. As she moves, she hears a familiar pulsing thunder.

When Amy glances in the direction of the noise she sees Eli popping off shots from one of his Desert Eagles at one of the Apaches. Sig has Eli's AK-47, adding more bullets to the barrage. Together, they turn the pilot and copilot into mangled, perforated corpses. The helicopter wobbles in the air. Then it starts to spin around. The tail and rear rotor bulldozes two empty window frames as it turns completely around, then it slowly drops out of sight.

The other Apache turns to train its gun on Eli and Sig, leaving it wide open for Kwesi, Lark and Stretch to open fire on it with their M-4s. Having no other choice, the gunner turns the Gatling back around to thwart Lark and the others before his chopper is also shot out of the sky.

A loud explosion shakes the building and a fireball races up to the sky. A puff of fire licks a section of the open wall, and toxic black smoke rushes in as Granger and Camacho run past Amy with their guns firing bullets at Eli and Sig.

Amy goes to run after them but pauses when she sees Titus block Lygia's sword with his gladius then hit her square on the bridge of her nose with the pommel on his sword's handle. Lygia's head rocks back from the impact and Titus lunges his blade into her heart.

Granger and Camacho collide with Eli and Sig, and the lines between friends, allies, and enemies become blurred.

With blood gushing from her nose, Lygia screams as Titus twists his bade inside of her.

Amy follows an impulse and charges at Titus as he yanks his gladius out of Lygia's chest and casts it high to behead her. Amy swings her sword to strike him down first, but Titus instantly turns around to deflect the blow.

"That sword doesn't belong to you, young lady," Titus says, pushing Amy away from him. "And you are fighting on the wrong side."

"The hell I am!" Amy responds.

In her earpiece, Amy hears Eli holler, "Amy, watch out!"

With all the bodies and bullets moving everywhere in the lounge, it had become almost impossible for Amy to keep track of everything going on around her. Her focus has been on detecting bullets aimed at her and keeping track of Eli and Lark. Everything else had faded to a form of background noise, including the blunt sensation on her right leg indicating something is approaching her.

Amy turns and sees Sig's chimpanzee take a leap at her. With no time at all to think, she instinctively straightens her arm. Her blade pierces Little Mikey through his chest and the force behind his momentum propels his little body to glide smoothly down the entire length of Amy's slender blade.

A sharp pain ignites in Amy's wrist when Little Mikey's mouth clamps down on it with incredible force. The sleeve of her tac-jacket has protected her from the brunt of the chimp's ravishing teeth, but the skin exposed under her cuff has been pierced.

Each heartbeat is equivalent to an eternity as Amy processes what just happened. An animal infected with the Puissance virus has just bit into her, sealing her fate. She can be grateful for the vampiric blood inside of her. It is going to grant her death instead of allowing her to turn her into a chomper. But she can't forgive Little Mikey for taking away her thready hope of a victory today and forever with Eli.

Like a jackhammer, Amy's pummels Little Mikey's head with her left hand until he releases her wrist. Then she clamps onto his neck, holding him firmly as she yanks her blade straight down for it to exit between his legs. Then she swings her sword and chops off the top of Little Mikey's head like a champagne bottle being opened by a saber.

A sound comes from outside like a car backfiring, and the Apache's engine begins to whine as if it knows that it is going to die and it's frightened.

Lygia reaches for her sword, but Titus steps on the blade, and says, "Amy is all but dead, Elias. Lygia will be dead in a moment. Then I'm coming to finally take care of you."

Hearing Titus threaten Eli snaps Amy out of contemplating her death sentence. Using her supernatural means of perception she finds Eli as she keeps her eyes on Titus. Eli is holding Camacho's right arm to keep the muzzle of the MACEs gun pointed away from him. Camacho fires the harpoon from his left arm, which Eli barely avoids by throwing his head to one side.

Sig and Granger are next to them, slugging it out toe-to-toe. Each blow retribution for the loved ones that they lost because of each other. Sig's face is cut and bruised from Granger's armored hand, and the visor on Granger's helmet is as spiderwebbed as it was when Eli had hit the last one with all his might.

Lygia rises to her feet, clutching her chest. The damage to her heart is not lethal, but she is weaker than she was before. "Get away from him, Amy!" she says. "He's too dangerous for you to go up against!"

"Doesn't matter," Amy says, keeping her eyes on Titus's shoulders like Eli taught her to do so she will know the very moment he moves to strike. "I'm not afraid of him."

"No! He also has Anaximenes' senex blood in him. As fast and as strong as you are, he's a better swordsman. You're no match for him!"

Amy recalls Eli's warning to her before they went back into Preacher's compound. He didn't want her going up against Calavius or his personal guard for the same reason Lygia is warning her of now. Calavius' respectable swordsmanship made him a force to be reckoned with. Titus appears to be even better, and he also has been upgraded by the blood of the senex who made Pelagius a vampire.

"It don't care!" Amy glances at the blood trickling from the holes in her wrist. "As long as I'm alive I standing with you and Eli and whoever y'all stand with. Even if I have to fall alone. We're vampires, and that's what we do, right?"

"How admirable," Titus says, then he kicks Lygia in her gut and slashes at Amy as he moves towards her. "Now, young lady, let's see if you are also stronger and faster than you really are supposed to be.

Amy blocks lethal blows as she backs up. With Eli's blood in her and the beast raging, she is equipped to take on Titus, but Lygia is right, she still is no match for his skill. Putting her more at a disadvantage, her wrist is functional but it hurts like hell, and she can't move it as fluidly as before. She doesn't know how long she can last up against a swordsman whose skill has been seasoned over the centuries, but she is determined to kill Titus or die trying.

Two M-4 Carbines rattle, and Titus pulls back to avoid the bullets that end up pocking the wall. Lark and Stretch are doing the shooting, as Kwesi charges in with his sword. Amy follows her instinct and goes on the attack, striking hard and fast. But Titus blocks all of her blows, as well as the ones that Kwesi tries to land.

Lygia retrieves her sword and joins them. Her help would have been more beneficial if she weren't injured, but she and the shots from the M-4s does help to keep Titus too busy to focus all his efforts on one opponent.

Eli roars. In her mind's eye, Amy sees him twist his body around while clutching Camacho's wrists. Then he thrusts his arms forward, flinging Camacho over his shoulder and sending him flying out the open wall.

Amy feels something glide over her ribs and leave a burning trail between her breasts. The deep cut across her chest is a consequence for the split second that she was distracted. Without full concentration, her reaction time slowed just enough for her to feel the sting of Titus' sword. Had he been aiming to kill her instead of just backing her up, she would be dead.

Kwesi also receives a slash that cuts across his shoulder and chest as he tries to swerve his body away from Titus' unrelenting gladius. And Lygia narrowly protects her neck in time to keep her head on her shoulders.

"Titus!" Eli grouses, charging in as he draws his katars from their sheaths.

Titus darts his eyes at Eli.

Amy swings her sword.

Titus leans back enough to keep from being decapitated, but the tip of her blade does catch his throat and superficially slit his skin. He retaliates by plowing his elbow into Amy's gut, knocking the wind out of her as it sends her crashing into the side wall.

In pain, Amy struggles to breathe again. Her vision narrows on the sharp edge of the gladius coming down at her head. With no time to react, she shuts her eyes and accepts peace, knowing that she will soon be with Aaron and her mother and the father that she never got a chance to know. Her only regret is that she will never find out if what she has with Eli would've evolved into the legendary kind of love that she hoped it would.

Amy hears the swipe of something sharp slicing the air, then a loud clank above her forehead. She opens her eyes and sees one of Eli's katars holding back the gleaming edge of the gladius that was about to split her head in half.

More gunfire breaks out and slugs whiz in front of her as Titus backs up to get out of their way.

Eli glances at Amy, rage burning in his eyes. Then he doggedly purses Titus with his intent crystal clear. Titus puts everything that he has into deflecting the rapid strikes from both katars but has to turn to stop Lygia from landing a death blow. Within that fraction of a second, The Devil Badger drops the katar in his left hand and revives the strategy that earned him the scar on his chest and back.

Titus spins back around and swings his sword downward, blocking the katar in Eli's right hand from cutting his legs off.

The Desert Eagle in Eli's left-hand booms and a .45 caliber slug blows Titus' left wrist apart, leaving it loosely dangling by a strip of skin and tendon.

Titus manages to keep an awkward grip on his sword with his right hand. However, his expression of pain and surprise reveal that Eli had caught him completely off guard.

Not wasting a single moment, Eli uses the butt of his gun to knock Titus' sword aside. Then he thrusts his katar in an upwards angle. The tip strikes under the edge of Titus' rib cage and sinks in deep to pierce his heart and lung.

Titus gasps.

Eli withdraws his katar and punches Titus in the jaw, spinning him around to look into Lygia's eyes as she moves in on him.

In one swift strike, Lygia's blade passes through Titus' neck with the ease and grace of a magic trick. He stands for a moment, staring at her. His mouth gapes. A thin line, like a crimson choker, bleeds around his neck. His legs tremble. His knees buckle. He collapses.

Titus' body hits the floor and jets of arterial blood spurt from his neck when his head pops off and wobbly rolls until it comes to an abrupt stop between Amy's legs.

Amy sees Titus' eyes turn in their sockets to stare up at her. His brow furrows as his face grimaces. Immediately, she pushes the head away from her crotch and pulls the Beretta from her holster. Holding the gun with both hands, she squeezes the trigger and empties all the bullets remaining in the clip into Titus' still-living brain.

Eli flashes a smile, but his whole expression changes when he hears Sig bawl, "Nooo!"

Everyone turns in time to see Sig pounding Granger's visor as he straddles him. The fractured face shield shatters in an eruption of black shards, and Sig continues his pile driving assault.

A dull, hollow thud resonates from inside of Granger's helmet when Sig's knuckles finally kiss sweet flesh and fragile bone. His hand and wrist become painted with blood and nuggets of brain matter. Each blow a squishy, splat-and-suck sound that grows louder, as if Sig's hand is plunging in and out of a thick puddle of mud.

Sig drops his hand into Granger's caved-in face one final time, leaving it there in the gory mush of brain and pulverized bone. Then he sighs and lowers his head, surely thinking about Kelly.

CHAPTER THIRTY-SEVEN

Eli takes Amy's hand and hauls her up to her feet. His eyes roam over the slash running between her exposed, bloody cleavage. It has already begun to heal and is nothing of a threat to her. He then darts his eyes down to the wound on her wrist where Little Mikey's teeth sank into her. A gooey matrix has already begun to form a scab across each hole in her skin and flesh. It will be as good as new within a couple hours if the virus that was transmitted to her doesn't claim her life by then.

To Amy's surprise, Eli shows no sign of horror or grief regarding her imminent demise. She wonders if the chimp being a chomper has gone over his head since he attention is drifting over to Sig now that he knows her wounds are regenerating.

After planting a quick kiss on her lips, Eli swiftly retrieves his discarded katar and points it at Sig.

"All right," Eli says. "We can pick up where we left off if you want, but you're still coming back with us."

"We can finish measuring our dicks another time," Sig says, scooping up his katana as he rises to his feet. "I brought you here so you and Lygia can learn the truth and decide if you want to avenge Pelagius. It would've been better if you took him alive and gave him a fair tribunal, but she is Imperator, so it's still legit."

"Damn right it's legit. Now, what kind of example are we going to make out of you?"

"We'll have to get back to that. Right now, we have to get out of here as soon as possible. I heard Granger called in a missile strike before I could get completely through his helmet. A couple HOGs are going to be coming this way. And if they're launched from the nearest battery we have, maybe five minutes, tops, before they hit."

"Are you serious?" Lygia asks.

Sig nods his head as he looks around and sees that all the vampires and humans on his side who were wounded by the Gatling guns have been taken to safety by the ones who weren't. "I have to make sure those kids get out safe. You guys shouldn't come with me, though. I can bring them back over to the right side, but I'll need some time, and they're not going to want to talk if they see you."

Eli raises his arms to a pugilistic pose, his blades poised for another round. "You don't really think we're letting you walk away, do you?"

"Let him go."Lygia, says.

"What?!"

"Those are confused and brainwashed kids, Elias. They deserve a second chance if they want it. Let him get them out of here. That's an order." She then looks at Sig, and says, "If what you told us about The Primus is true, then you know what you have to do if you want Eli's help to find him."

"You have my word that Hadrianus' insurrection is finally over and all the acolytes will either fall in line or face the consequences."

Lygia nods her head. "Meet us at Preacher's compound, and we'll figure this whole thing out. And bring Doctor Gianacola with you. I'm not giving up on creating a human-friendly vaccine. With you and her, I have a better chance to get it done. Agreed?"

Sig nods back, "Agreed. I'll see you in a few days."

"Just one more thing," Eli says when Sig turns to leave. "The Civitas. Did you really have nothing to do with it being destroyed?"

"Like I told you, Eli, I just wanted Titus to get me the scroll. I didn't know he and Calavius were going to kill Pelagius and desecrate his senex. And I damn sure didn't know about the missiles until I heard them hit. I know I'm not completely innocent in why things are so fucked up now, but we'll settle my sins after we take care of The Primus. Right now, we really have to go," Sig says, then he takes off towards the door frame.

Eli looks as if he wants to go after him, but his eyes settle on Amy, Lygia, and the other vampires. "C'mon, we're getting the hell out of here."

"Do you think we'll have enough time?" Amy asks.

"One way or another, we'll find out. You good to run?"

Amy considers staying behind and letting the missiles take her out before the Puissance virus does. But she decides to spend whatever life she has left with Eli. "Yeah, I'm good."

Eli nods, then he looks at Lygia and says, "You're not at full strength, so," he slings her over his shoulder and ignores her protest. "You guys stay on my tail. Hit the ground running and plow through or jump over anything in your way until we're either safe or dead. Got it?"

As soon as everyone nods, Eli takes off towards the opening where the windows once were. Amy follows right behind him and punches through the curtain of black smoke rising up from the wreckage of the first downed Apache.

Soaring through the air, she gets a good look at what she is leaping into. The thousands of chompers around The Sapphire don't have a clue that oblivion is racing towards them at Mach 1. Even if they weren't blinded by the sunlight, they wouldn't see the missiles coming.

Wherever Sig is, whatever he's doing apparently requires his complete attention because he is no longer exercising his influence over the chompers. Judging from the large huddle gorging on the limbs and organs of the pilots who were forced to land the second Apache at the edge of the parking lot, Sig hasn't been in control of them since some time before he left the battle arena that was once the lounge.

It hasn't been that long since Camacho was tossed out of the building, so Amy is surprised that she doesn't see him fighting his way through the massive swarm. None of the Black Hawks are in sight, but she hears them and Skipworth's Specter off in the distance, so chances are that Sutherland is no longer on the roof, either.

Eli's lands on a female chomper dressed in a paramedic's uniform. He rides her head down to the ground, crushing her skull under his boots. Amy flattens the paramedic chomper's rib cage when she lands on her, and she follows behind Eli as he carries Lygia like a heroic firefighter rescuing a victim from a burning building.

Leading with his free shoulder, Eli accelerates and bowls over every chomper in his path, clearing a trail for Amy and the others behind her. As hard as she is running, Amy feels like she isn't using her full potential to keep up with her magister. She realizes that he is holding back his top speed so she and Preacher's legares and Kwesi can keep up. Even moving at the fastest pace that Lark and Stretch can muster, the chompers in Eli's way don't realize what hits them until it's too late. The only thing that everyone behind him has to do is focus on running.

It takes about twenty seconds for them to break through the sea of chompers. More than twice that to make the straight shot over to photovoltaic array at the edge of Playtime's campus.

Eli blows past the solar panels and heads straight for the forest that Skipworth flew over during the first reconnaissance mission with the Specter. Amy stays on his heels as he weaves around the trees in his way. She recalls the wheat field on the other side of the woods. If her estimation is correct, then they should be almost two miles away from the campus by the time they emerge from the woods. If they were dealing with conventional missiles, then that would be a good thing. But that distance might not be enough to escape the devastating range of the Hand Of Gods rocketing towards them, especially if they strike in multiple positions to increase the range of maximum damage.

It takes the group about a full minute to clear the woods. Everyone keeps in stride as Eli mows a trail through the overgrown amber waves of grain. Sig crosses Amy's mind. She wonders if he and his band of misfits have also made it away from the campus. He probably had a contingency plan in place for such a scenario, but he, the vampires, and the humans with him would have had much less time to get as far as Amy and the others have gotten.

Amy hears something like a roar zip across the sky. She glances over her shoulder to see how Lark and the rest are doing. A bright light flashes off in the distance that they just came from. Two explosions like erupting volcanos roar over the land and the ground quakes under her feet.

The entire back of Amy's body vibrates a warning. Her heart thumps as she watches twin pillars of fire race up to the clouds back in the area where Playtime's campus is located.

The leaves on all of the trees in the forest, blow towards her. The tree trunks bend, then snap like pencils when a squall of debris rushes forth. Stretch, Kwesi and Lark bend backwards as they are lifted off their feet. Amy turns around just as Eli tackles her to the ground and covers her and Lygia with his body.

The ridiculously powerful high-amplitude compression wave slams into them, knocking Eli off of his legare and his magister and forcefully sweeps them all up in the wake of the explosion. Amy cartwheels through the air and loses sight of everyone in the thick dust, dirt, and debris flowing like water in a flash flood.

The only reason Amy knows that Eli is about ten feet off to her right is because of the link they share through his bloodline. As for her warning system, it is working just fine, hyperactively alerting her of which parts of her body are in the flight path of something hurling towards her. She listens to it as much as possible. However, not being in full control of how she can move, she ends up getting dinged by branches, shards of glass from the solar panels, pieces of concrete, metal and other forms of rubble birthed from the destruction.

Amy's forehead warns her of imminent impact. She rocks her head back as much as possible, just in time to see a stop sign whirl past her face. As she breathes a sigh of relief, her back slams into the ground and debris rains down on her as she carves a trench in the soil.

When Amy comes to a stop, the upper half of an uprooted evergreen lands hard on top of her chest, knocking the wind out of her. Her insides were already tender from the blast of the shock wave, and now she might have some broken ribs. Her breathing is severely compromised. She takes as many shallow breaths as she can and mentally pumps herself up to push the tree trunk off of her, but it begins to move on its own. When the needle-like leaves of the branches clear her face, she sees that Eli and Lygia are the ones responsible for the levitating lumber. They are both covered in dirt, cuts all over their faces and bodies, splinters of wood and glass embedded in their skin. But neither appear to be seriously injured as they toss the tree clear.

"How bad are you hurt?" Eli asks, showing full concern.

"Not too bad," Amy responds, and groans from the inner and outer pains that she feels as sits up.

"We all suffered internal injuries from that shock wave," Lygia says, putting a hand on Amy's shoulder. "Give your body time to start regenerating before you push it. We're safe for now."

"I'm just glad you guys are safe." Amy's gaze roams back and forth between Lygia and Eli. She does her best to hold back a tear. She doesn't have much time left with Eli, but Amy finds solace in knowing that Lygia does love him and will be there for him long after she is gone. "I don't mind dying," Amy says, "now that I know you two are going to be okay."

Eli shakes his head. "Unless those assholes drop another missile on us, none of us are dying right now."

Amy holds up her right hand and turns it so he can see the dirt-coated bite marks on her wrist. It's the only way she is strong enough to tell Eli that she won't be around much longer.

Eli chuckles and glances at Lygia.

Lygia smiles and gently caresses Amy's cheek. "Titus would have finished me if you hadn't come to my aid. I would owe you one, but I think we can call it even."

"Huh?" Amy says, confused.

Lygia turns to Eli and then caresses his face, too. "Good to know that I can trust my Proconsul to keep confidential matters confidential. Go ahead and tell her. I'm going to see about the others."

Eli nods his head. After Lygia walks off, he says, "Remember when you woke up after I turned you?"

"Yeah."

"Lygia injected you with a vaccine against the Puissance virus that morning. I got one, too. She broke Limbecks's rules and protocol by doing it, but she wanted us to be prepared for all possibilities, including the chance we somehow got infected. You're one hundred percent safe."

Amy feels stunned into a dream-like state. If Eli is telling the truth, then she has a second chance at eternal life. Not knowing what else to do, she throws her arms around him and celebrates her new lease on life by kissing him like they haven't seen each other in ages. She loses herself, enjoying his tight embrace and the touch of his lips, even with the taste of dirt coating them.

"Jeeze!" Lark says, "Why don't you guys just get a room already?"

Amy breaks the kiss and is glad to see that, even though her friend is as banged up as she is, Lark is just fine.

"You okay, Hot Pants?" Eli asks.

"Thirty degrees, man. Well, maybe about sixty. I feel like a giant just stomped on my ass, but I'm all right."

Eli laughs and sets his eyes on Kwesi as he approaches with Lygia and Stretch. "Good to see you guys still in one piece."

"Gonna take a little bit more than that to get rid of me," Kwesi says, then he and Eli clasp hands and squeeze tight.

Stretch grumbles, then he bends down and picks up Amy's lost sword. "I think this is yours," he says, as he approaches Amy with it.

"Thanks," Amy says, as she accepts her weapon. "Anybody see my gun?"

Everybody chuckles and end up sitting in a circle. The vampires help each other remove the assortment of foreign objects stuck in their skin as they give their grimy, battered and bloodied bodies time to regenerate before they figure out what their next move is going to be.

"I'm very proud of you all for what you did today," Lygia says. "No one will ever challenge your legitimacy as vampires. I'll personally see to that. And I'm so sorry about Bear. I'm afraid that the best I could do is honor him posthumously."

Stretch lowers himself down to one knee, places his fist over his heart, bows his head and says, "Thank you, Imperator."

Everyone else, including Amy and Eli, does the same.

Amy notices Lygia appear to be grateful by the display of respect and loyalty, and it makes her earnestly pledge allegiance to the vampire she still considers a rival for Eli's heart.

The moment of reverence is broken by the faint sound of helicopter blades and the roar of a jet engine off in the distance. Everyone gets back on their feet and readies whatever weapons they still have. Eli replaces the magazine in one of his Desert Eagles with a fresh one and hands it to Amy. Then sets up the other hand-cannon for himself. Lark, Kwesi, and Stretch still have their M-4s, and Lygia draws a Glock from the holster on her hip.

Running is no longer an option. As far as everyone is concerned, the military would have been better off dropping another bomb to disintegrate them instead of sending another chopper and Skipworth's attack drone to finish them off.

The drone is coming in fast from the north. First appearing as a black dot in the skyline, it enlargens and slowly reveals its shape as an aircraft. Quickly, details of its F-35 war machine design become clearer—including the two missiles mounted under each wing.

Everyone anxiously awaits the drone to shoot bullets or bombs so they can react appropriately. But the drones ease up to them slowly and hovers in the air by way of the fan in the center of its body, and the jet exhaust on its back end now pointed downward.

Eli steps forward, his Desert Eagle secured with both hands. He has it trained on the area that would be the cockpit of aircraft, right where he knows that at least one of its cameras is.

The drone rocks in the air, one wing subtly dipping low while the other rises up.

Eli then removes his left hand from his weapon and does a thumbs up. The drone rocks again.

"We're good," Eli says.

"Skipworth's 'all safe' signal?" Amy asks.

Eli nods his head. "Looks like, at least for right now, we have a cease-fire. But everyone still stays on point."

They all lower their weapons, but keep them in hand and wait for the Black Hawk approaching to get closer. Amy is thankful that vampires are able to adjust their hearing. Having to listen to the noise from the drone, as well as the chopper would have driven her cray.

The Black Hawk reaches the area of the wheat field that has been mowed and flattened by the torrent of debris. It touches down on a patch of land that isn't severely littered. Camacho exits with his hands in front of him, gesturing his peaceful intent. Then he twists off his helmet, and says, "Before you guys start shooting, we can fix what happened back there at the compound."

"And how do you plan on making that happen? Eli says.

"Look, Granger was in command back there. The gunships shooting up the building, that was his call. When you attacked us, it made the situation worse. General Limbeck had no choice but to retaliate when it was clear Lieutenant Granger was going to be murdered by Sigodur.""Granger brought that on himself."

"I admit that the situation could've been handled differently. We acknowledge that you probably wouldn't have turned your guns on the choppers if they didn't open fire first, but the parameters of the mission changed drastically from the moment our soldiers were caught in that trap."

Eli sucks his teeth, and says, "That's not on us. I tried to warn your boy, but he didn't want to listen."

"We know. And considering that we still have problems that would be better handled if we work together, the General hopes that we can salvage our alliance."

"Maybe we can salvage our alliance," Lygia says, stepping forward, "but there's going to be changes. Take us back to Fort Dix. I want to talk to the General in person, then get my daughter out of there."

"I can do that," Camacho says, then he gets back in the chopper and waits for everyone to get in.

Everyone remains silent as the Black Hawk takes to the sky again. Before they turn to make their way back to Fort Dix, Amy gets a look at the aftermath of the two HOGs striking Playtime Campus. All that remains is a deep oblong hole in the earth where The Sapphire and surrounding structures once stood. The blast ring radiates from both points of impact, overlapping in the middle while spreading outwards. Amy knows that she and the others were lucky to get as far away from ground zero as they did. What she experienced at the outer edge of the blast ring would have been many times worse if they hadn't at least cleared the forest.

As they fly on, Amy wonders what the future will bring. If Sig is right, then there will be no cure for the Puissance virus. Amy respects Lygia for wanting to try again with Sig's blood and Dr. Gianacola's input, but she's not optimistic about the chances of success. With no cure, there is only one way to get rid of the chompers, and that is to kill them all. The vaccine in her is only good for vampires. Lygia would never vaccinate the entire human race and risk what can happen on a planet of vampires.

Amy also considers the other things looming on the horizon. If war with China is imminent, it won't be restricted to human-on-human violence now that the enemy has illegitimate rogue vampires on their side. And to top it all off, there's Sig's claim that The Primus is on the verge of rising from his resting place to devour scores of humans and every vampire in the world.

But with all the adversities in the foreseeable future, Amy is certain of three things. One: she was destined to be what she has become. Two: the family that she lost has been replaced by a new, larger one. And three: the vampire whose arms she is in will be the love of her life for as long as she lives.

Amy takes Eli's hand and squeezes it, letting him know that no matter what happens she will be by his side, as he legare, his partner and his lover—always.

EPILOGUE

Amy and Lark move in perfect unison. Their fluid footwork and the subtle but sharp thrusts of their kendo sticks now a lovely choreography executed solely by muscle memory. The evening's training exercise on the rooftop of one of the dorm buildings in Preacher's compound is a stark contrast from the harsh sessions Eli put them through to train or dissuade them a few days before.

As she moves, Amy gazes at the dazzling array of colors painted over the horizon by the setting sun. She thinks about her mother, father, and brother. She still misses them, but now that the pain and rage she had been holding on to has finally been released she can't shake the feeling that she has allowed their souls to rest in peace.

Night creeps in and the colors of dusk fade away, yielding to the sky a multitude of tiny points of starlight. Amy and Lark complete the final sequence of the exercises Eli had instructed them to do, then they face each other and bow. After laying their sticks down next to their actual weapons, they sit side by side at the edge of the roof and drink from the bottles of water that were frozen solid hours earlier when they first began the evening training session.

Lark has no intention of becoming a regulare, like Amy is destined to be if fate allows her to complete her training. But she does want to improve her ability to fight for and protect her loved ones and their community. Training with Amy over the past couple of days has also given Lark something else to focus her mind on besides missing Kwesi.

It shouldn't take more than a week for Kwesi to return from Seattle with Tijeri, the regulare who delivered Pelagius' message to Eli to go to Lygia and protect her. But Amy knows that for Lark a week might as well be a month.

Messages have been sent to other regulares closest to Preacher's compound, reporting what has happened to the previous members of The Synodus, the destruction of The Civitas, and a proclamation that Lygia is now the Imperator and Eli the first member of her Proconsul. The regulares have been instructed to inform all of the vampires under their care of the news and for them to await further instruction. Five regulares in particular, including Tijeri, are summoned to Preacher's compound. The five are the ones that Lygia and Eli agree are best suited for leadership roles in the joint operation with the U.S. Military to destroy every rogue vampire made from Sig's stolen blood. There is another purpose behind Tijeri's summoning. Amy is the only one with knowledge of Eli and Lygia's agreement on Tijeri being named Proconsul if he wants the position. Amy is looking forward to meeting the centuries-old samurai who will make her regulare blade one day. And she can't wait to see the expression on his face when he finds out that he can be the third member of the new Synodus.

Lygia and General Limbeck came to an accord that repaired the fracture in their alliance. In order to mend fences, General Limbeck didn't put up too much of an argument when Lygia told him that she was going to continue her quest to develop a human-friendly vaccine in her own lab in Jacksonville, if-and-when Sig shows up at the compound with Dr. Gianacola, like he is supposed to.

An agreement was also made that vampires are to be treated as equals to humans and no longer be targeted by the military. In exchange, they will do their part to help to eliminate the chompers roaming around that have escaped the bombings. And in cases of rogues or vampires breaking the rules, regulares are to handle the situation. As for the impending campaign against the Chinese rogues, Lygia is going to ask the five regulare that she summoned to Preacher's compound to be her generals in her small army of vampires. And if they choose to accept the positions, then the first task will be gathering those who want to voluntarily serve as soldiers.

Lygia also made sure to secure Amy's clemency. Amy confessed to her crimes in front of a military tribunal at Fort Dix, and once she took responsibility for her actions, General Limbeck made good on his promise. So now her life has a complete restart.

Amy sights Preacher walking towards the cottage that Lygia and Kristin has been staying in. She expected Preacher's faith to have crumbled when he learned what Sig told them about the origin of The Primus and why vampires exist. But Preacher remained steadfast in his belief, saying that all scripture is not a literal account but parables that offer understanding. Regardless of where The Primus came from and its motives, it is also a child of God, and the power that it passed on through the bloodlines of vampires still makes them children of God. Amy doesn't agree, but she admires Preacher's conviction.

Three rapid tweets, whistles repeated in intervals two seconds apart, register in Amy's ear. Both she and Lark turn and look towards the front gate. One of the guards has spotted something that requires everyone to be at attention.

Preacher stops in his tracks. The door to Lygia's cottage opens and Eli emerges, slipping his cowboy hat over his head. Lygia comes out next, still giving instructions to Kristin to remain in the cottage until she gets back.

Amy and Lark reach for their weapons and immediately hop off the roof. Everyone greets each other with nods and quickly make their way out to the front gate.

"What's the situation?" Eli asks the guard standing on the wall, peering through high power binoculars.

"Got some kind of convoy heading our way," the guard answers. "I count fourteen sets of headlights. Not military, though. A bunch of different vehicles."

Eli and Lygia glance at each other, then he looks at Amy and ticks his head up towards the parapet where the guards are. He takes two long strides forward and leaps up to the top of the wall. Lygia follows. Amy, Lark, and Preacher do the same.

Amy catches sight of a string of headlights as soon as she is high enough to see over the wall. The vehicles have already made their way down to the valley floor and are coming straight towards the compound. The guard was right about the vehicles not being military. They appear to be an assortment of cars and SUVs, led by a classic Camaro with its high beams blazing.

There are only nine vampires left at the compound, including Amy, Eli, Lygia, Lark, and Preacher. All the others have gone on messenger missions for Lygia. The shortage shouldn't be much of a problem if all of the occupants in the vehicles are humans. If they are all vampires, it might be a bit more problematic but not a dire situation. Preacher and his five legare that have stayed behind can hold their own, and they have the three of the four most powerful vampires fighting alongside them. The most powerful of the four, however, could be in one of the vehicles. And if he is, it's not clear at the moment if he has come to fulfill his part of the deal he made with Lygia or if he has decided on a different path.

The vehicles slow down as they get closer to the compound, and begin to spread out from the single line formation they were in. They come to a stop about four hundred yards from the front wall and idle with their headlights illuminating the dusty valley ground.

"So, what do you think?" Lygia says to Eli. "Refugees or raiding party?"

"One way or another, we're about to find out," Eli says. "You stick to the plan while I take a walk with my protegee here."

Amy holds back her smile. When she sees Lygia take Eli's hand and squeeze it the beast within her wants her to growl at Lygia to remind her which one of them Eli belongs to, but she doesn't give in to its demand. She has more control over it now, and she remains unfazed by Lygia show of affection for Eli. Like any other vampire, there's a chance she might go rogue one day. But as long as Eli is her anchor, she is sure she won't.

Thinking it best to no longer keeping any secrets from Eli, Amy confessed that there are times that she struggles with the way her vampire blood makes her feel animalistic. He told her that it wasn't a big deal as long as she kept exercising her willpower to dominate the beast.

"Okay, let's go," Eli says and leaps off the wall.

Amy winks at Lark, then takes the leap herself.

Twirling her sword, sheathed in its silver tipped cane scabbard, Amy keeps her eyes peeled for suspicious movement from any of the shadowy figures inside the vehicles. "If this is Sig," she says, speaking low enough for their conversation to remain private as they walk, "does this mean we'll be going in search of The Primus soon?"

"Can't say for sure," Eli responds, "but Lygia doesn't want us to ignore it if there's a chance what he believes is real."

"Well, if The Primus is out there, you'll find him. With that special ability you have, you can find anything."

Eli turns and smiles at her. "I don't know if I can find anything, but I did find the best thing ever after I picked up on your trail and followed it to that farmhouse. Chalk it up to my ability, luck, fate, or whatever. All I know is, when I met you I finally found something I've always been looking for."

The driver's side door of the Camero eases open with a long creak. Eli remains calm, not reaching for his guns or his knives. Amy maintains a relaxed demeanor, as well, but stays on guard as she watches Sig emerge. And she doesn't consider his warm smile a reliable compass of his true intention.

"So you really showed up," Eli says, continuing to get closer to Sig's car. "I'll give you credit for that, at least."

"You should've known that I'd come," Sig responds. "Bet ya didn't expect me to bring an army with me, though."

The rays of the rising sun have yet to dissipate the chill that staked a claimed the desert overnight.

A Bedouin leader, atop his camel, overlooks his caravan with concern. The men, women, children, even the animals all look exhausted after trekking throughout the night. Normally, they would stop to make camp before sunset, but that hasn't been an option for the last twelve hours.

He turns to his left and raises his binoculars up to his eyes. A swarm of chompers can be clearly seen traversing the dunes a few miles away. He slowly swivels over to his right. More chompers, at least a hundred of them, walking at a steady pace. He turns around, as much as he can in his seat on his camel. Another swarm of hungry things that will be more than happy to eat everyone and every living thing within the group of nomads.

His group has encountered the crazed people before. They quickly learned that there was no talking or reasoning with the cannibals that were almost invincible. There was only one thing to be done when encountering them. But they never had to deal with more than a few at a time.

The four men, six women and eight children in the caravan aren't even a fraction of what is needed to take on the hundreds of chompers in either of the swarms. When they first spotted the chompers trailing them from behind, it was frightening. Terror within the group intensified after the swarm off to the right was spotted. Then the third swarm appeared over the horizon on the left, leaving the desperate Bedouins only one direction of safe travel. All through the night, everyone's thoughts centered on what might happen if a fourth swarm appears in front and boxes them in.

The leader's fears revolve around the exhaustion he sees in his people and their animals. He doesn't know how much longer they can go without rest and proper food. Something would have to be done sooner, rather than later.

The twelve camels suddenly stop and rear up, as if startled. The Bedouin desperately tries to get his beast under control. But like the other riders having the same issue, he has no such luck. The camel bucks hard, throwing the Bedouin from his saddle. He lands hard on his shoulder and manages to roll out the way of stomping hoofs just in the nick of time.

The caravan falls into total chaos. The animals seem to have gone mad. The nine camels that were able to break free from their masters are sprinting off ahead in a rebel pack, followed by the three dogs that belonged to the group. The six goats, however, have scattered in every direction, most heading straight for one of the dangerous hordes. Some of the men attempt to give chase to the wayward animals, while others try to calm the panic-stricken women and children. The men trying to run are struggling to stay on their feet, and even look to be having problems lifting their legs.

The Bedouin's mind races to find an explanation as to why all hell has broken loose. He realizes that the throbbing he feels is not just his body protesting the trauma from the hard fall. The ground is quaking. The pulsing has been subtle, but it's continually getting stronger and faster.

Struggling to find solid footing for his feet to settle on, the Bedouin sets his eyes on his wife and children. The intensity of the nightmare they are living is evident on their faces. He tries to hurry towards them, but his feet feel heavy, and all the more it feels like he is trying to move through a liquid thicker than water. Total terror overcomes him when he realizes why.

The ground is vibrating in a way that is making the solid surface more like quicksand. The desert floor at the center of the group has dropped, like a hungry sinkhole suddenly appearing to devour the travelers crossing over it. The people and whatever animals are left have no choice but to be carried down to the center of the pit by the flow of sand. At the center of the funnel, they are absorbed into the ground, regardless of how desperately they fight and claw to stay above it.

In a matter of moments, the Bedouin leader ends up in a bundle of bodies. The desperate fighting and flailing that everyone is doing does very little to help them stay above the sucking sand. Instead, they blindly beat and batter each other. Sand covers the Bedouin's face. He manages to take one last deep breath as he and his whole caravan sinks out of sight.

The loose sand starts to become more dense, feeling like it is tightening around the group. The pressure increases. Bones break. Muffled screams get lost in the crushing sand. The compression increases exponentially, squeezing all the bodies together like a bunch of grapes in the grip of a powerful fist.

When the ground finally stops quaking, the desert is once again at peace. The sun continues its daily work, heating the air and the sand.

The chompers that were following the caravan finally reach the area where the people and animals had been swallowed up. They continue walking. Beneath their feet, blood of the Bedouins and their beasts of burden provide The Primus sleeping underground a scarce but scrumptious treat.